MW01673378

The History of the Cotton Famine

SALZWASSER
VERLAG

R. Arthur Arnold

The History of the Cotton Famine

Reprint of the original, first published in 1865.

1st Edition 2022 | ISBN: 978-3-75259-020-3

Verlag (Publisher): Salzwasser Verlag GmbH, Zeilweg 44, 60439 Frankfurt, Deutschland
Vertretungsberechtigt (Authorized to represent): E. Roepke, Zeilweg 44, 60439 Frankfurt, Deutschland
Druck (Print): Books on Demand GmbH, In de Tarpen 42, 22848 Norderstedt, Deutschland

THE COTTON FAMINE.

THE HISTORY

OF

THE COTTON FAMINE

FROM THE FALL OF SUMTER TO
THE PASSING OF THE PUBLIC WORKS ACT.

WITH A POSTSCRIPT.

BY

R. ARTHUR ARNOLD

RESIDENT GOVERNMENT INSPECTOR OF PUBLIC WORKS.

NEW EDITION.

LONDON:

1865.

PREFACE

TO

THE ORIGINAL EDITION.

'THE HISTORY OF THE COTTON FAMINE' should be a welcome chapter in the annals of our country, for it records one of the greatest of our national triumphs.

The period to which I have carried the history in this volume, may be considered the termination of the 'Famine.' The succeeding winter and spring were marked by severe distress,—which indeed still prevails in certain localities, —but the improving condition of the markets, the great decrease of indigence as compared with that of the winter season of 1862, and the salutary influence of the Union Relief Aid and the Public Works Acts, suggest that the crisis had been passed at the close of the Session of 1863. Much that would be an iteration of the doings and sufferings of 1862 remains to be told. Yet it would not be an uninteresting progress to follow the revival of this great industry, from these times, so exceptional in all their circumstances, to the full re-establishment of the cotton manufacture upon a broader and surer foundation than it has ever yet occupied.

I am confident that the restoration of this manufacture is not far distant. Nor can I see any reason to suppose that the great increase of working power which has been added during the years of Famine, is larger than the world's demand will furnish with employment. That this extension is calculated to depreciate manufacturing profits, there can be little doubt; and I apprehend that no one, well acquainted with the district, has failed to perceive that unless invention makes rapid advance, the manufacture will be crippled for want of labour.

The Appendix to this volume includes copies of the Union Relief Aid and Public Works (Manufacturing Districts) Acts, together with the Manual of the Central Executive Committee, and a Report by Mr. Rawlinson, C.E., showing the purposes to which the loans borrowed under the provisions of the Public Works Act are now being applied. Of these public works—which engage my official labours—it is well known that great as are the benefits that have attended their progress, even these are very inferior to the advantages which will be permanently secured by their completion.

I cannot but be conscious of having failed to do justice to the charitable efforts of individuals both within and outside the district. A long-drawn record of their names and their good deeds might have made my pages more illustrious, but I have a strong conviction that such are not those who will censure the preference for matter more instructive and historical.

I am very much indebted to the distinguished gentlemen—the Special Commissioner and the Government Engineer—with whom I have the pleasure of being associated in Her Majesty's Service. To Mr. Maclure, the Honorary Secretary of the Central Relief Committee; to Mr. Gibbs, the Secretary of the Mansion House Committee, as well as to many other gentlemen, I owe the acknowledgment of valuable information.

R. ARTHUR ARNOLD.

MANCHESTER: *July* 1864.

THE HISTORY

OF

THE COTTON FAMINE.

CHAPTER I.

INTRODUCTORY.

LONG before Eve span,—long before Lancashire was dry land, or the Mersey a river,—the Manufacturing Districts were being prepared to become the home of a great industry. Geology is the parent of geography. When Dr. Buckland, in commencing his Bridgewater Treatise, started his three travellers upon three imaginary diagonals, drawn from the south-western to the north-eastern shores of the kingdom, the route of the second lay across the coal-fields from the Tamar to the Tyne. Rightly enough did he suppose that such a traveller would regard England as nothing else than a stupendous manufactory. It is not then mere chance which centres a particular industry in a particular locality; there are always favouring circumstances, if not indispensable conditions, sufficient to account for such a concentration. To roll back the history of our island to the time when the coal-measures, and all the carboniferous group of strata were deposited, is indeed a task impossible to man. The foot-prints on the sand-rocks, the leaf-prints in the coal-beds, hidden from all touch of life since the foundation of the world, these are our mute instructors—these proclaim to us that most certain limitation of our knowledge concerning the work of Creation.

The district with which this history is concerned, is also remarkable in its natural features, for its especial adaptability to the manufacture of an exotic raw material. If the primeval restlessness of this portion of the earth's crust had not upheaved some of the older and harder strata to the surface—if the chalk of Kent or the sand of Norfolk had here superimposed, the streams which fed the infant industry of Lancashire would never have existed. These streams owe their perennial supplies to the geological features, and the geographical position of the district. The elevation of most of the towns in this part of the kingdom is very considerable. Even Manchester is 120 feet above the sea-level; Bolton is 200 feet higher than the Cotton Metropolis, and superior elevation generally ensures increased rainfall. London is 50 feet above the level of the sea, and endures an average rainfall of 24·8 inches. Manchester prefers a damp atmosphere for her spinning-rooms and weaving-sheds, and rejoices in a rainfall of 37·3 inches; while Bolton, in consideration of standing so much higher in the world than either, is drenched with 49·5 inches per annum. Greater still is the rainfall upon the hills around Glossop, and still greater is the moisture in the mountainous region upon the Cumberland border. In the neighbourhood of Windermere, the rainfall in 1860 equalled 102·58 inches. Lying on the western coast, the cotton manufacturing districts are exposed to the aqueous vapours of the Northern Atlantic, where the union of the heated Gulf Stream with the Arctic waters envelopes Newfoundland in perpetual fog, and produces the rain-clouds which are so often an unwelcome sight upon our western horizon.

This unusually large supply of water-power was among the first causes of the pre-eminence of this district in the cotton manufacture. Its surface, very varied in altitude, is grooved by the hand of Nature in deep channels, worn in strata, generally impermeable, which collect the rain-water, and gather it into manageable streams. With what patient devotion these streams have given themselves to the prosperity of Lancashire! Merrily they rippled over their pebbly beds, when the mill-wheel was theirs, and theirs only. They threw themselves, or were led into reservoirs, and have continued to supply the district with pure water, so soft, that as compared with that of London, it is estimated to require one-half less soap, and one-third less tea, to produce equal results in the washing-tub, or in the more social tea-pot. They were not offended when Brindley said they were good for nothing but to feed canals. They suffered themselves to be led over hills and across valleys at the will of the engineer, and now, when they have fallen to baser uses, and are made to feed the boilers of their successful rival, and to act as the main sewers of the district, they still do their office to the best of their ability. But their day of greatness has passed away. In manufacturing progress, as in human civilisation, there are the barbarous, the picturesque and the prosaic epochs. In the history of the cotton manufacture, the hand-loom represents the first, and the water-mill the second; but the poetry of this manufacture departed when Watt perfected the all-subduing mechanism of which Newcomen had an imperfect vision, and the iron muscles of the steam-engine became the power of the cotton districts.

But Nature had beforehand provided Lancashire with an inexhaustible supply of food for this untiring helper. The superiority of steam over water power consists in the greater force, speed, and regularity of movement,—in the security which it affords against the accidents of floods and droughts. Had it not been for the extensive coal-field which underlies the larger part of Lancashire at no very great distance from the surface, this county could never have become the seat of a trade so enormous. All the larger cotton towns, with the single exception of Preston, are situated upon, or in close proximity to, the strata known as the coal-measures; and perhaps, from her less grimy throne on the new red sandstone, 'proud Preston' has had some reason to call her sister towns black. The coal-field of Lancashire is of very irregular form. Its northern boundary extends from Colne through Blackburn to Ormskirk. thence it stretches in a southerly direction, and venturing within the patrician purlieus of Knowsley, it runs across the Manchester and Liverpool Railway, and returns again towards St. Helens. Leigh is its southern boundary at one point and Broughton at another. From some miles north of Rochdale it extends southerly with an average width of six or eight miles, far into the heart of Cheshire. But on this narrow part of the coal-field are located some of the busiest towns in the cotton district. Oldham is there, famous for cotton and coals, for Cobbett and colliers. Ashton is there, renowned for the wealth of its manufacturers and the warmth of its polemics. Stalybridge is on the coal, where it is said that the spindles move more rapidly than in any other town, and where the Irish immigrants abound so thickly. Stockport looks out upon this narrow coal-field. It extends to and beyond Macclesfield, which has been associated during the Cotton Famine with the cotton towns, although it is engaged in the silk trade, and the main cause of its depression is in the whimsical changes of unstable fashion. On the southern and western sides of this coal, there extends a bed of new red sandstone, which originally overlaid the Lancastrian coal-fields, and was removed from it by denudation as the coal-measures rose to their present elevation. The merest school-boy in geology cannot doubt this, if, following the line of contact, he observes how the strata of the sandstone—evidently originally laid in horizontal planes by water—dip away from the uplifted coal-measures. What does not Lancashire owe to Nature! Had the upheaval of her surface continued during its submersion, the coal-fields might have shared the same fate as the red sandstone which once covered it; the hills between Lancashire and Yorkshire, between the cotton and the woollen trades, between the coal-fields of the two counties, might have been of obdurate granite instead of being composed of workable millstone grit, and the great hearts of Lancashire and Yorkshire, instead of producing clothing for millions upon millions of human beings, might have echoed with the crow of the grouse or with the tinkle from the bell-wether of the mountain flock.

It is not necessary now to do more than generalise the geological features of the district. A more minute inquiry would include a survey of the drift beds which overlie the coal, and which form the surface of a large part of Lancashire. Wishing to offend no one, it is still hardly dangerous to state broadly that the red sandstone district is that which is the most agreeable in the English dominions of King Cotton. Alderley Edge, the chosen seat of much of the textile aristocracy, is a bold bluff composed of this rock. Chorlton, Rusholme, Cheetham, and part of Broughton—all very eligible and pleasant suburbs of Manchester—are on the sandstone. The Mersey winds its way through this formation from Stockport to its mouth. The immemorial elms of Knowsley and Rufford Parks attack it with their roots. Cuerden Hall enjoys an equally good foundation. Preston and Garstang are upon the same footing. Of the soil of Lancashire lying to the west of this sandstone formation, the greater part is made up of alluvial deposit, where rich pastures, fat oxen, and good corn-fields abound. The north of the county about Lancaster is composed of millstone grit, which passes into upper limestone shale about Clitheroe. Of these formations, those in the north and east of the county—the limestones and millstones—are the oldest; that is to say, in the original stratification the coal-measures which occupy the middle of the county rested upon them, and the sandstone upon the coal. It was a fortunate move for Lancashire when they were lifted for her enrichment and service.

The geographical advantages possessed by this manufacturing district may be included in one word—Liverpool. Yet it must not be supposed that Liverpool made the cotton trade; the reverse is more nearly the truth. But no one can take credit for the construction of the Mersey. None but Nature's hand could have carved out that magnificent estuary lying in front of and above Liverpool. Whether the cotton trade could have adopted another port it is impossible to say; but it is quite certain that there is none possessing anchorage so wide, so deep, so sheltered, and yet so accessible. The shore at Liverpool afforded unusual facilities for the construction of docks, and the same wind which bore a vessel from the Mersey would waft her across the Atlantic to the rich Sea Islands, or to New Orleans, the great emporium of the Cotton States of America.

The natives of Lancashire are wont to boast the purity of their origin as true Anglo-Britons, and some carry this very pardonable pride so far as to assert the same of their dialect. There may be good grounds for this. All those invasions which form the chief events in the history of this country up to the commencement of the twelfth century were made upon the eastern and southern shores. The Picts had possessed themselves of Scotland. The Danes ravaged the eastern side of the country; while the south was the prize for which all who could get there fought. The Norman conquest must have tended to drive many of the Anglo-Saxon race northwards, and the moors of Lancashire may have become the home of these people. Or it may be, that this part of the kingdom, then uncared for, unreclaimed, and to a great extent inaccessible, preserved unmolested and free from admixture with foreign races its aboriginal population. It may be that Lancashire is entitled to this distinction, and that here the Ancient-Britons would feel most at ease, were they to revisit their old home. But how would they be astonished, if, with their woad-dyed faces and rude implements, they could now see their descendants tending the elaborate machinery of a power-loom, or dyeing, not themselves only, but also clothing for millions beyond the seas!

Pure Lancashire dialect,—such as may be heard in Ancoats, such as is talked at Bacup—is easily distinguishable from the merely broad talk of a Northumbrian. It is even musical; and the regard which the people of the county have for it is shown in their fondness for poems written in the local dialect, and still more by the way in which such verses affect them when the theme is homely and pathetic. Lancashire is, no doubt, a county of very ancient settlement; and among the poor as well as the rich there are many families which might date their location from the Heptarchy. But what America has been to Europe, Lancashire has been to England—the great drain for surplus population. For nearly a century she has been offering to the working classes such reward for their labour as it was impossible to obtain elsewhere. For years and years she has wanted 'hands' as she now wants cotton, and her demand was not made in vain. Nowhere else upon an equal space of God's earth has population obeyed the summons of capital to an equal extent, or with equal fecundity. From north, east, and south, numbers have flocked to share the profits of the cotton trade; and from the west, across St. George's Channel, crowds of Irish—fleeing from a poverty at home which would seem starvation to an Englishman—have swollen the army of cotton-workers.

The natural increase of the people has been no less remarkable. Sentiment is not necessarily destroyed by the acknowledgment of facts. The laws of population are inevitable. The doctrines of Malthus were received as the laws of political economy have generally been received by the multitude. But he did not condemn matrimony, nor suggest any unnatural restriction upon the increase of population. He did but show what was the unfailing consequence of the civilised state upon the laws of population, and how, as this state becomes more developed, prudential motives would affect the natural instinct. It is not debasing to human nature to acknowledge that an urgent demand for labour will increase the procreated supply. In a poor and unimprovable country, an increase of population diminishes the wealth of the community, while under contrary conditions such an increase tends directly to augment the common resources. This is merely an exposition of fact. It would be as false in the one case to recommend celibacy, as in the other unduly to encourage matrimony. But it is well known that surer than argument will be the stationary or retrograde condition of the population in the decaying country; while in the prosperous locality it will need no impulse to progression at a rate commensurate with the increasing wealth of the community.

The population of the cotton districts has had every encouragement to increase. And while thus referring to the 'cotton districts,' it will be well to make a momentary interpolation. In the course of this history, these districts will often be referred to under the common denominations of 'Lancashire,' the 'cotton districts,' and the 'manufacturing districts;' all to some extent fallacious, for there are other cotton districts, and other manufacturing districts, while Lancashire, in such a reference, includes portions of Cheshire, Yorkshire, and Derbyshire. It need hardly be said that there are sufficiently good precedents for this use.

In 1861, the population of Lancashire amounted to twelve per cent. of that of England and Wales. But the births in this county amounted to thirteen and a half per cent. of those of the English and Welsh populations. Such had been the effect of a superior demand for labour. In 1801 the population of the county of Lancaster amounted to 673,486. In 1861 it had grown to 2,429,440. In the same period the population of Manchester rose from 94,876 to 460,018. The population of Burnley had grown from 4,000 to nearly 30,000 in the same interval; and all the cotton towns would show a somewhat similar rate of extension. Taking the whole county, the population had increased 100 per cent. in little over thirty years—a rate faster than would seem possible unless aided by immigration. Thirty years ago, great efforts were made to induce agricultural labourers to migrate into Lancashire, and among the ablest, and possibly not the least effective, were those in the form of letters from Messrs. Henry and Edmund Ashworth to the Secretary of the Poor Law Commissioners, giving a full account of the improved condition of some families which had abandoned their pastoral life in Buckinghamshire, and had found in manufacture greater prosperity than they had experienced in agriculture.

It is often remarked that many of the features of American society are reproduced in Lancashire. And why is this? These features, which some think very ugly and others very much admire, are nothing more than manifestations of the supremacy of labour. Labour and capital rule in the manufacturing districts. A fish out of water is in a comfortable position compared with that of an idle man in a Lancashire town, where for the most part, master and man, millionnaire and the poorest of his hands, eat to live, and live to work, ten hours a day for five or six days of the week.

The extraordinary increase of the population in Lancashire is greatly due to continuous immigration, but also to a natural rate of increase by births unexampled in this country. Dr. Kay (now Sir James Kay-Shuttleworth) estimated in 1835, that from 1821 to 1831, 17,000 persons per annum had flocked into Lancashire from other parts of the United Kingdom, and that at that time the

Irish and their immediate descendants dwelling in Manchester and Liverpool numbered 110,000. During the last twenty years the annual rate of increase has been about 40,000, of which probably one-fourth only is due to immigration. That the population of Lancashire is far from being all native, is evidenced by the fact, that in 1851 as large a proportion as 27 per cent. was returned as having been born elsewhere. In 1861 this percentage had fallen to 26·4, showing that immigration was declining, but that even then more than one-fourth of the population of Lancashire was foreign. In 1861 there were 640,844 dwellers in Lancashire who were not born within the county. Of this number 217,320 could boast Hibernian nativity; 37,260 were emigrants from Scotland; 17,329 were born abroad; 374 drew their first breath at sea, and the remainder came from other counties of England and from Wales. Every county has its representatives in the manufacturing districts. Here are Londoners by thousands, hundreds of men and maids of Kent; nearly two thousand Somersetshire lasses, a large muster of Yorkshiremen, and a fair representation of the Principality. So that whatever it may once have been, the population of Lancashire is certainly now a conglomerate, the better perhaps for being thus compounded.

The purpose of this introduction will be completed when a survey has been taken of the chief industry of the county, including that fringe of the adjoining counties of York, Derby, and Chester, which together form the cotton districts. Long before the natural resources of the district were enlisted to assist in the cotton manufacture—long before the keel of the 'Mayflower' grounded on the New England shore—long before the streams and the coal-fields of Lancashire did suit and service to King Cotton, the spinning-wheel and the hand-loom were busy in the hovels of Bolton and Manchester. Lancashire was *the* manufacturing county when Elizabeth began her splendid reign, and whilst the Spanish Duke of Alva was ravaging the Low Countries, he drove to the shores of England and to the county of Lancaster many skilful artisans from the thriving towns of Belgium. Bolton became the home of a number of these refugees, who worked diligently as subjects of Queen Bess, and probably with more benefit to themselves than when they were liable to the continuous alarms endured by those who dwelt in the land which was the shambles of the mediæval wars of Europe.

But if it be sought to discover why Lancashire, at this early time and with no apparent advantage over other counties—save that of climate—became the home of the cotton manufacture, it may well be answered, that the circumstance arose from its comparative incapacity for agriculture, from the moisture of the temperature, and the ready supply of fuel. Lancashire in the time of Elizabeth was one wide expanse of desolate moor and unwholesome bog-land. Cultivation was only attempted here and there; land drainage, even in its rudest form, did not venture to operate upon a case so hopeless. The towns fixed themselves on the banks of the rivers and warmed the moist atmosphere with the peat which lay so ready to their hands. Clustering round some well-dowered abbey or dependent upon some grave monastery, the villages grew, their inhabitants plying the distaff and the shuttle as their only means of subsistence. And so it came to pass, that when the thrifty weavers of Ghent sought a new location, they found themselves at home in Bolton-le-Moors.

But while the cotton manufacture was thus giving feeble signs of life in this country, there was a land far across the globe, where it was already a most ancient and most honoured form of industry. While the handicraftsmen of Lancashire were fumbling over their coarse yarn, and turning out clumsy fabrics composed of cotton and wool, there were millions of deft workers in the empire of Aurungzebe, weaving such fabrics as can only be equalled by the finest machinery now within the giant mills of Manchester. What encouragement there is for commercial ambition in the fact that cotton, which has received within our own time at least kingly attributes, was then chiefly imported for the manufacture of candle wicks; while Lancashire did a lively trade in rushes for the same and less honourable purposes.

To India belongs the origin of the cotton manufacture. Shall not England henceforth remember this more truly? The debt she owes to Greece for value received in literature,—are not the defunct Bavarian dynasty and the dower of the present boy-king, some acknowledgment of it? She has well repaid Italy for her teaching in art. It will be a strange but a happy instance of retributive justice, if India, whose cotton manufactures first excited our envy and cupidity, should become a chief source of our supply of the raw material, and turning her lithe fingers from the wheel and the web to the cultivation of the cotton plant, should provide Lancashire with the raw material and receive clothing in repayment.

No Europeans have ever yet been able to vie with the Hindoos in the fineness of their hand manufactures. Those who are acquainted with the race, and know their frequent lubrications and their listless inactivity, will hardly be surprised at this. A Hindoo woman needs no clasp to her armlet any more than she would to her finger ring; it passes over her hand. And if time is money in the East, as it is said to be in the West, Her Majesty's subjects in Hindostan are the most prodigal people upon earth. The nomenclature of the cotton trade is to a large extent Eastern. 'Cop,' a term so familiar in every spinning-mill and on every exchange throughout the district, is simply an Anglicism of the Indian word for cotton. Far to the south of Bombay, near the western coast of India, lies the town of Calicut, to which belongs the honour of giving a name to all the calico ever produced. On the banks of the Tigris stands the city of Mosul, once the narrow home of the muslin manufacture, and from this city the name of the fabric is derived.

Towards the latter part of the eighteenth century, the English cotton manufacturers suffered so severely from competition with the goods brought over in the vessels chartered by the East India Company, that every artifice was used, and it is even said that in some places threats were resorted to, in order to induce the women of this country to wear the coarse textures of home manufacture in preference to the more beautiful fabrics of India. Nothing is more curious in the history of the cotton trade than the readiness it has displayed at all times to accept protection for itself, and to denounce the use of this defence by other trades. Not that this is by any means an unnatural feature of any industry. Need we, as an example of this, remember how, when it was proposed to abolish the duty on the importation of raw cotton, the flax spinners petitioned against this step on the ground that the wearing of cotton caused erotic sensations, and thereupon set themselves up as protectors of the morals of the people?

For nearly three thousand years India possessed a virtual monopoly of the cotton trade; and had it not been for the invention and improvement of our machinery, she would still have maintained supremacy. As it is, the manufacture is not progressing in India. Her hand-spinners are in the same position as our own hand-loom weavers, professors of an art which has long since been distanced by invention. Their occupation must go where those of the stage-coachmen and the Great Moguls have gone before. The irresistible logic of facts confirms their sentence. In 1815 there were but eight pounds of cotton yarn exported from England. Eight hundred thousand pounds weight of cotton goods were exported in the same year; but these were for the consumption of the English army and residents. In 1860 this country exported 241,978,364 pounds of yarn and goods to India. Britain has become, or is fast becoming, the clothier of Hindostan; and the cause is obvious. In 1812 we could manufacture coarse yarn cheaper by a shilling a pound than the Hindoo spinner; but in 1860 our manufacture cost only one-fourth the price of Indian. The natives of India will never manufacture with machinery on an extensive scale; their constitution and habits, their climate and their frequent ceremonials render it impossible. One of the best reasons given why the cotton manufacture has not largely succeeded in Roman Catholic countries is, because of its disturbance by the continual recurrence of feast and fast days.

To return to the English manufacture of cotton, which we left in the hands of the Flemings and the Lancastrians of the time of Elizabeth. From that day it grew—it could hardly be said to flourish—until the invention of the spinning-jenny marked the first step in that advance which was to lead to such tremendous results. It will be well, perhaps, to attempt a little explanation here. Cotton has been described by a now eminent writer as the 'flocculous product of a malvaceous shrub;' his meaning would have been more clear, though possibly less 'sensational,' had he simply informed his readers that it was the wool of the seed pod of a plant known as *gossypium* among botanists, growing wherever it is planted under a tropical sun, in a deep fresh soil, and with sufficient moisture. The wool consists of filaments, of cylindrical shape before drying, varying in length from half an inch to nearly two inches. There are equal differences in the diameters of these filaments, which vary from the $\frac{1}{1500}$th to the $\frac{1}{2000}$th part of an inch. It is evident that in spinning this wool into yarn or thread, the most important requisites are the length and strength, the fineness, and the equability of the woolly fibres. Of all substances, whether of animal or vegetable production, cotton has certainly the greatest capacity for textile manufacture. The operation of cotton-spinning may be described in a few words. It is nothing more than making a yarn by elongating and twisting a bundle of cotton fibres. But the history of the cotton manufacture shows that the process by which it has been perfected was slow and laborious. At the first, this elongation and spinning were performed by the hand and the distaff; that is to say, one person worked at one thread, and spun but one yarn. These were the spinsters of the mediæval period. Of all those who are published as spinsters in the modern temples of Hymen, how few are there who have a right to the designation!

Such was the condition of the cotton manfacture when James Hargreaves, a poor Blackburn weaver, invented the spinning-jenny. It was in the power of the jenny to accomplish as much with one man's hands as sixteen or twenty could do with the single spindle. A simple frame contained machinery which, being moved backwards and forwards, produced on several threads the elongating action formerly achieved by the thumb and finger; while a wheel, turned with the other hand, wound the yarns so produced upon as many spindles. By some authorities this invention is ascribed to Thomas Highs, who, it is said, gave to his machine the name of his daughter 'Jenny.' But to whichever of these two the merit of the invention may belong, it is certain that such a machine was produced by Hargreaves in 1764. Can we of this generation, who have broken threshing-machines and opposed free-trade,—can we, conscious of our glass walls, pelt the fools who broke

Hargreave's machine, and drove him out from Lancashire to find a new home? But the fault of the jenny, as of the more simple and more ancient process, was the want of some mechanism to attenuate the cotton into a regular and even yarn. This want was soon supplied. To the inventor of the drawing-rollers belongs of indefeasible right the first place among the fathers of our manufacturing machinery. This was Richard, afterwards Sir Richard, Arkwright. All the minor details of his machine may be forgotten, for the sake of the rollers. If he did not first conceive the plan, to him at least belongs the honour of making public the discovery, that by moving two rollers—the lower one grooved, the upper having a plane surface—in opposite directions, with different rates of rotation, and pressed together with weighted levers, the elongation of the yarn could be produced with a regularity and fineness determined by the speed and pressure of the rollers. Arkwright's spinning machine was called a water-frame, because water-power was by this means first applied to the manufacture of cotton; and the term 'water-twist,' so common in the trade circulars and market lists of the present day, is only the technical name for a yarn made on an improved machine most nearly resembling the original water-frame of Arkwright. The all-important principle in the water-frame was the drawing-rollers. There is, however, one other portion of the machine of great value, and this is known as 'the spindle and flyer,' the use of which is to wind the yarn, as it leaves the rollers, upon the bobbins on which it is removed to be prepared for weaving. The mere action of being drawn through the rollers could not give the yarn the requisite twisting. This is accomplished by the spindle, which passes through the bobbin or reel, having at its upper end two widely extending prongs hanging downwards over the sides of the bobbin. The yarn runs through one of these prongs, called the flyer, which is hollowed for the purpose, and so becomes twisted as it is deposited upon the bobbin. Arkwright deserves to be recognised as the parent of the factory system—at least of the mechanical part of it; for to his genius we are indebted for the greater part of the *modus operandi.*

Like Hargreaves, he was a prophet without honour in

his own country. Born at Preston, in 1732, and apprenticed to a barber, he laboured over his machines until their superior powers began to attract envious attention. But Arkwright was a man of far greater strength of character than the inventor of the spinning-jenny. Hargreaves was to Arkwright as Herschel to Newton—one discovered a member, while the other founded a system. Arkwright's mill, situate at Birkacre, near Chorley, was destroyed by a furious and ignorant mob who, there is too much reason to suppose, were incited to the act by the enemies of the great inventor. Like Hargreaves, he retired to Nottingham; but, unlike Hargreaves, he made a partnership which led him to opulence and honour. In 1773 the firm of which he was a member sold the first cloth ever manufactured in this country entirely of cotton-wool, and it is not long since the peerage of England was enriched by the elevation of a descendant of one of his partners, in the person of Lord Belper.

The constellation of the great inventors of the factory system of machinery will be complete when to the names of Hargreaves and Arkwright have been added those of Crompton and Cartwright. To the first, the manufacturing districts owe that most valuable auxillary the 'mule,' or 'mule-jenny,' so called because, born of the spinning-jenny and the water-twist frame, it is distinct from, while it partakes the qualities of both. The principal events in the life of Crompton would seem to show that he was a man gifted with genius, fired with impulse, but destitute of those solid qualities which, united to the inventive faculty in Arkwright, led him on to fortune and high position. In Nelson Square, Bolton, near where he was born, a statue has been now raised to the man who gave to the world this machine, which in itself united the elongating and twisting principles with that of the drawing rollers, and in such a manner that the finest yarns could be spun by its agency. Such was Crompton's invention. He took no patent, and made little secret of his discovery. But Lancashire had grown wiser since the destruction of Hargreave's machine and Arkwright's mill. Crompton was annoyed by the intrusion of curious visitors, and in consequence he determined to exhibit his invention to any one who would pay a guinea to see it. About twenty years afterwards, when the mule had become very generally adopted, he made a tour of the United Kingdom, to prepare a statement of the extent to which his invention had been made use of. Aided by friends, he laid before Parliament the results of his inquiry, and so established a claim upon the national bounty. The glittering prospect of a recognition and reward for his labours from the august hands of Parliament could not but have been very exciting to the sanguine inventor, and more highly valued perhaps by one of his temperament and habits than the opulence and dignity which crowned the career of Arkwright, or than the royal favour which conferred the patent of rank upon the now all-honoured name of Peel. After much solicitation on the part of Crompton's friends, a Committee was appointed to consider his claims. The present Earl of Derby was the chairman, and the deliberations of the Committee resulted in the recommendation of Crompton as highly deserving of reward. So far everything favoured his expectations. It is said that among the last words uttered by Mr. Perceval—probably in the presence of the assassin whose pistol was to terminate his useful life—was a remark to Sir Robert Peel, 'You will be glad to hear that we mean to propose for Crompton 20,000*l.*'

Whether he was inspired by the Minister's promise, or by a private estimate of the value and importance of his invention, it is impossibe to say; but it is certain that Crompton assessed his due at something like this amount, and was grievously disappointed when, upon the proposition of Lord Stanley, it was resolved that 5,000*l.* should be given in recognition of his services to the cotton manufacture. The House of Commons has held many a beating heart and throbbing brain, many a statesman fearing no one but himself, and many a timid aspirant fearing all else; but surely it never held such another as the gloomy, sanguine mechanic who turned away from watching the passage of this Bill, a disappointed man. At the inauguration of his statue in Bolton, in September 1862, his only son, a poor man aged seventy-two, was present, to whom Lord Palmerston has since sent a donation of 50*l.* from the Royal Bounty Fund.

Cartwright was the inventor of the power-loom. Others, whose name is legion, have brought the machinery of the cotton factories to its present high state of perfection. Many of them have deserved to be, and would have been famous, had they not formed units in a crowd nearly, if not equally, meritorious.

Of the various descriptions of cotton, the most valuable is known as 'Sea Island,' the produce of the islands lying along the shores of South Carolina and Georgia. But it was no uncommon seed from which this cotton was originally produced. The length of its staple and the fineness of its quality are entirely attributable to local influences. Among the constituents of the cotton plant, potash occupies a most important position; and this fact, taken together with the peculiar luxuriance of Sea Island cotton, seems to prove that a saline atmosphere is necessary to produce the finest qualities. Certain it is that Sea Island cotton is unequalled in quality, and that even in the States it cannot be produced at a greater distance than fifteen or twenty miles from the coast. Next in natural quality, though it is not yet marketed quite so well as the American cotton, is the produce of Egypt. During the Cotton Famine, many of the fine-spinning mills have lived upon Egyptian instead of their usual fare of Sea Island cotton, and the rapidly improving condition in which it is brought to market will enable it under any circumstances to maintain a high place in the estimation of manufacturers. The produce of Brazil holds the next rank; then come the inferior sorts of American, 'Upland Georgia,' 'Middling Orleans,' 'Boweds,'—so called from its being cleaned with a bow-string,—but the last, and least valued, is the cotton of India, generally termed 'Surat,' of which the principal sorts are known as 'Dharwar,' 'Broach,' and 'Dhollerah.' Up to the year 1861, Indian cotton was very rarely used, except in admixture with superior growths. It will be necessary to refer more fully to the cotton supply, and to the question of cotton growing in India; but at present the survey is limited to the aspect of affairs in the manufacturing districts.

It is time that reference was made to the cotton mills. But all mills are not alike. Of that large and wealthy class generally understood by the designation of manufacturers, some are spinners only, making nothing but yarn; others are weavers only; but the most important section of this class combines the operations of spinning and weaving. In the language of the trade, a master-spinner is not a manufacturer, but only a master weaver. Yet, as this is neither in accordance with the verbal significance, nor with the general appreciation of the word, it may, here, at least, be disregarded. All, however, may be subdivided into two distinct classes—fine and coarse spinners, and manufacturers of heavy and fine goods. Among the former are included fustians and that large class of fabrics known in the trade as 'domestics,' of which shirting and sheeting form a large part. The fine mills produce muslin, lace, and other yarns for the articles *de luxe* of the cotton trade. A cotton-mill is the perfection of mechanism, both human and metallic; but architecturally, it is a brick box pierced with from four to eight rows of windows; sometimes it is cornered with pilasters, and invariably, at no great distance, there rises one of those tall chimneys, which are so numerous in the cotton manufacturing district, that an imaginative person might almost suppose them to be the natural produce of its soil. Volumes of smoke roll from these tapering shafts, but not to so great an extent as formerly, when the atmosphere of towns and the economy of fuel were so much disregarded.

Of late years there has been a remarkable tendency to increase the size of the cotton factories, and although there must be a point at which there is a greater economy of labour by a division of establishments, that point would seem to be constantly moving under the influence of invention, in a direction favourable to the enlargement of mills. Where there is no practical limit to the capital to be employed, the building possesses enormous dimensions; in fact, it is as big and contains as much brickwork, roofing, and flooring as can be put together for from 30,000*l.* to 40,000*l.* Such a mill would contain two steam-engines, with an aggregate power of 200 or 250 horses, which would keep in motion all the machinery required for cleaning, carding, and spinning the raw cotton, besides from 1,000 to 1,500 power-looms engaged in weaving the yarn into cloth or other commodities. Thus fitted completely, this factory and its machinery would cost from 80,000*l.* to 100,000*l.*, and would employ from 1,000 to 1,500 hands. That which gives such a peculiar character to factory labour is 'the power.' The portion of the mill which the steam-engine inhabits is generally lighted, and indeed indicated, by a long window, through which its bright arms may be seen plunging up and down, and its hot, white breath, puffing from an adjacent waste-pipe. The distribution of its force throughout the mill is a triumph of mechanical art, achieved by spindles, firmly fixed on every ceiling, which communicate the power to other spindles, placed at right angles, by means of pinion-wheels; from these spindles it is transmitted to the machines upon the various floors through the medium of endless bands and drum-wheels.

There is no record of a factory operative having deified 'the power' and done idolatrous worship to it; but we cannot wonder that these beautiful machines have received such honours when exported among populations ignorant of Christianity. In visiting a factory, it becomes a difficult question to determine whether steam-power is the Frankenstein—the master, or whether it is the loyal servant of man,—the slave-driver or the driven. While the operatives are, in the early morning, paying unwilling heed to the tapping at their windows of the professional 'knocker-up,' and are preparing to commence the toil of another day, 'the power' is getting warmer and warmer, until, when the factory bell ceases ringing at six, it becomes endued with motion, and the whole mill is full of inanimate as well as animate life. In the lowest department of factory labour, in the blowing-room, where the scutching-machines open the raw cotton and clean it from the husks, leaves, and seeds, due to the inferior machines—to the carelessness or knavery of growers—though the feeders be absent, there is the power at six o'clock whirring away upon the ceiling. This operation is not one demanding much skill, and the Irish are very often found in the blowing room. The raw cotton having been first loosened out, is passed into the scutching-machine, where it is beaten about by fan-flyers circulating with a speed of 2,000 revolutions per minute; the seeds and husks fall through a wooden rail-sieve, on which the cotton rests, and the dust is drawn upwards through a casing, by draught created by an upper set of flyers. The very best qualities of cotton do not always need such rough treatment, and one reason of the superior value of some growths over others is that they make less waste; in American this is estimated at 12 per cent., and in Surat at 25 per cent. After passing from the attentions of these rotating flyers, the cotton is carried onwards, and issues from between two rollers in a flat 'flap,' generally two feet wide by half an inch thick, and as it issues is wound upon an iron spindle. When this spindle is filled it is removed to the carding-engines, wherein, by means of cylinders revolving in closely-fitting frames, both stuck full of thin, crooked wires, in size about equal to common pins, bent to a right angle, the fibres are gently coaxed into a longitudinal position, and are moved towards the rollers, from which they leave the machine in a transparent fleecy web, which is gathered by a funnel into the softest and most incoherent of ropes. Thus the first stage of spinning is completed, and the 'card end,' as this rope is called, deposits itself in circular tin 'pots,' in the state known to the outside world as wadding.

Then the elongating rollers begin their work. The tender production of the carding-engine is subjected to the drawing-frames, which give a little more consistence and much greater length to the fleecy rope, now become a 'drawing.' In most mills the 'drawing' now passes to the coarse and then to the fine 'bobbin-and-fly frame.' The advantage of this machine, and the great benefit gained by its invention, consisted in the fact that it performs the operation of elongating and twisting the 'roving' —as the 'drawing' is termed after it has passed through this machine—without endangering its fracture by making any strain upon it. The difficulty to be overcome was that the bobbin or reel upon which the 'roving' was wound would not retain the same size while the automaton flyers ran round and round it, depositing and twisting the roving, not yet strong enough to bear much twi ting. As the bobbin became filled, and its diameter increased under the attentions of the flyer, the strain upon the roving became too great. This was obviated by an invention of Mr. Houldsworth, who, by adopting a conically-shaped drum, adjusted the speed of the bobbin and the flyer to a mutual and accommodating action.

These bobbins, when filled with roving, are removed to

the 'throstle-frames' or to the mules, and are there spun into yarn. The 'throstle,' on which that much-quoted commodity 'water-twist' is made, elongates, twists, and winds with one continuous operation. The mule does its spiriting more gently, and elongates the roving by passing it through three sets of drawing-rollers, during which operation the carriage advances, drawing out the yarn; then, while the rollers cease to give out the yarn, the length already drawn out is stretched and twisted by the turning of the spindles; the carriage then returns to beneath the rollers, while the spindles are actively winding up the yarn. When full, they are removed, and the yarn taken from them, resembling nothing so much in size and shape as a 'tip-cat;' in which condition it is thrown into a basket to be sold as 'cop,' or to be taken to the winding-room, where the yarn undergoes the first preparation for weaving.

Yarns are sold in hanks, each containing a length of 840 yards. However fine the yarn may be, the same length is made into the hank; so that the quality of the yarn is indicated by the numbers of hanks which make a pound in weight. The enigma of Indian telegrams is solved by remembering that 20's water-twist means a coarse yarn of twenty hanks to the pound, the product of the 'throstle-frame;' and the announcement, 'mule-twist firm,' is no longer perplexing when it only suggests the invention of Samuel Crompton; nor 'grey shirtings dull' mysterious, when it is remembered that the colour is but a synonym for 'unbleached.'

But if the yarn be not intended for sale it is taken to the winding-room, where it is prepared for 'warp' or 'weft;' warp being the longitudinal, and weft the latitudinal threads of cloth. And in these winding-rooms are often found the aristocracy of the operative class. Prior to the invention of the self-acting spinning-machines, a spinner was a great man in his way. The management of the hand-mule, of which there are still many in use, required considerable skill and great practice. He appointed his own 'piecers' and his 'scavenger'—places generally filled by his younger children. His wife was rarely a mill hand. These were the lawgivers on the subject of strikes. The general adoption of automaton machinery has considerably lowered the pretensions of the spinners. But even now the handicraft required in a cotton mill is very considerable. None will doubt this who have watched the precision and unerring regularity with which, at the summons of the factory bell, the 'hands,' men, women, and children, move to their appointed place in the monstrous building, and with what quiet and assured self-confidence each sets about the work of feeding or attending to the various machines. Nor, being thus acquainted with the drill and order of the factory system, would the observer wonder at the anxiety of the manufacturers to keep their people together, soft-fingered and light-handed, ready for the revival of the cotton trade.

The system adopted for the payment of wages has, under the combined influence of the deliberations and disagreements of masters and operatives, risen to a high degree of perfection. A standard list of prices for spinning and weaving is published in most of the chief centres of the manufacture. Take that of Preston as an example, which is issued as compiled by the 'Cotton-Spinners' and Manufacturers' Association and adopted by the 'Operative Spinners' and Weavers' Associations.' The rate of payment for spinning is calculated upon 100 lb. weight of yarn, and progresses with the number of spindles in the spinning-machine, and also with the fineness of the yarn. According to this standard list of prices, an operative spinning 40's yarn on a mule with from 381 to 400 spindles, would receive 50½*d.* for every 100 lb. of yarn; while, if he were spinning 100's yarn on the same number of spindles, he would have 195½*d.* per 100 lb. of yarn. This would include the wages of a man and boy—a minder and a creeler—engaged in manufacturing with a self-acting mule. But if the machine contained from 981 to 1,000 spindles, another boy—a piecer—would be required, and the payment of the three would be, for 40's yarn, 42½*d.*; and for 100's yarn, 165½*d.* for every 100 lb. in weight. There is therefore a considerable difference in the earnings of the spinner, according as his machine has many or few spindles. The standard list of prices is not affected by fluctuation in wages, any rise or fall being accomplished by the addition or subtraction of a percentage agreed to by employers and employed.

Standing in an atmosphere heated to about eighty degrees—scented and thickened with oil, cotton-dust, and steam—with clothing which is rather a slight homage to decency than a compliance with ordinary fashion, the 'self-acting minders,' their creelers, and piecers earn wages varying, for the men, from 20*s*. to 35*s*.; and for the boys, according to their age, from 6*s*. to 14*s*. per week. The wages on the throstle-frames are rather less than on the mules, and on the former many women and girls are employed. The duties of the spinners on self-acting machines are not very onerous. Besides directing the machinery, they have, in technical language, to 'fill the creels,' to 'piece the yarns,' and to 'doff the cops;' in other words, to feed the rollers with bobbins of roving, to reunite the ends of any broken yarns, and to remove and relieve the spindles of the spun yarn. Piecers—boys and girls—are the attendants upon all the machines used for spinning, from the roving-frames to the fine mules: and it is the addition of the wages of these younger members of his family which makes the earnings of the operative appear so large.

'Winding,' which is the preliminary to weaving, consists in passing the yarn on to bobbins or reels, from which it is 'warped' on to a large polygonal frame; in which condition it is wound in perfect parallelism on to large reels with iron ends of the precise width of the power-looms. The winders and warpers earn about 25*s*. per week, and are perhaps among the best paid and most comfortably placed of the *employés* in a factory. The yarn, which has now become 'warp,' is then 'beamed' and 'twisted'—a very curious and cunning hand-operation impossible to describe—and having been sized, it reaches the loom-shed, which is always on the ground-floor, in order to prevent vibration. The working life of a power-loom weaver is passed amid a noise most resembling that which accompanies an express train through a long tunnel. A weaver, either male or female, attends two, three, or four looms, which produce pieces of cloth varying from 24 to 37 yards in length. Their rate of earnings averages about 12*s*. to 14*s*. per week. The wages of weavers, like those of spinners, are regulated by the standard lists of prices.

This is not a history of the Cotton Manufacture, and

the mills are only thus visited in order to give some idea of how the operative's life is passed, and what is the description of labour in which he is ordinarily engaged. But the manufacture is full of mechanical and general interest to the highest degree; and nowhere more so than in the fine-spinning mills. By means of the self-acting mule, European spinners have at last been able to overmatch the Hindoo in the fineness of their yarns. Messrs. Houldsworths' factory at Manchester is famous for fine spinning. When it is remembered that 32's is a common-sized yarn for weaving calicoes, the delicacy of this firm's machinery will be appreciated by the fact that they can spin 540's yarn, one pound weight of which would contain a thread long enough to reach from London to Newcastle. In the Exhibition of 1862 they displayed 700's yarn, a pound of which would be 588,000 yards in length. According to Hindoo poets, the Dacca looms produced 'woven wind;' but this is something still finer, still more immaterial.

There are many other operations carried on in the various descriptions of factories, such as the preparation of sewing thread, muslin weaving, and fustian cutting; and there are the bleaching, dyeing, and printing works. It would also be an interesting inquiry to look into the occupations of the numerous camp-followers of the great army of cotton workers. Many of these will cross the widened path of this history as it progresses into the depths of 'Lancashire distress.' But the purposes of this Introduction will be accomplished with a concluding glance at the position of the cotton trade in the zenith of its glory at the close of the year 1860.

The dreary totals which Mr. Gladstone's eloquence illuminates, and the rolling numerals of the National Debt, become almost insignificant beside the figures which this statement involves. Arithmetic itself grows dizzy as it approaches the returns of the cotton trade for 1860. One hundred years back and the cotton manufactures of England had been valued at 200,000*l*. a year. Had not French, American, and Russian wars,—had not railways and telegraphs their part and lot in this century, surely it would be known as the Cotton Age. This year 1860 was the '*annus mirabilis*' of King Cotton. In this year his dependents were most numerous, and his throne most wide. There was no Daniel at hand to interpret to him the handwriting on the wall, which within twelve months should be read by all who ran in letters of blood. What cared he? An argosy of ships bore him across every sea, and into every port. He listened to the humming of his spindles, and to the rattle of his looms; he drank of the fulness of his power, and was satisfied; for he was great,—yes, very great.

There were in Great Britain in 1860 some 2,650 cotton factories, worked by a population of about 440,000 persons, whose wages amounted to 11,500,000*l.* a year. Of these workers, 90 per cent. were adults, and 56 per cent. were females. A power, equal to that of 300,000 horses, of which 18,500 was water-power, drove the machinery which these quick eyes and active fingers guided and governed. Among other offices performed by this giant force was the twirling of 30,387,467 spindles, at rates varying from 4,000 to 6,000 revolutions per minute. Each of these spindles could consume 9½ oz. of cotton-wool per week; their required food for the year, therefore, equalled 1,051,623,380 lb. of cotton. The actual consumption for the year, inclusive of waste, was 1,083,600,000 lb., and the total quantity imported 1,390,938,752 lb. About 350,000 power-looms threw their shuttles with unerring regularity, impelled by the strength of these steam and water horses; and, besides supplying the household requirements of this kingdom, which in the article of cotton manufactures then amounted to about 24,000,000*l.* in annual value, and 180,000,000 lb. in weight, this population, these spindles, and these looms, being supported with an invested capital of 65,000,000*l.*, produced for exportation 2,776,218,427 yards of cotton cloth, besides 197,343,655 lb. of cotton twist and yarn. In addition to this, they manufactured and exported hosiery and small wares, valued at 1,795,163*l.* The total declared value of their exports for the year amounted to 52,012,380*l.* If figures can ever be magnificent—if naked totals ever reach to the sublime, surely the British cotton trade in 1860 claims our admiration. Its production for this single year equalled in value 76,012,380*l.*, or nearly six millions more than the gross revenue of the kingdom for the same period.

Of this stupendous trade, the share of Lancashire, Cheshire, and Derbyshire may be judged from the fact, that the number of mills in each county respectively was 1,920, 200, and 75. Of the factory workers, they held respectively 310,000, 38,000, and 12,000; thus engrossing upwards of eighty per cent. of the whole trade. It is not, therefore, without good reason that Lancashire, including the adjoining borders of its southern neighbours, is known *par excellence* as the cotton manufacturing district.

The cotton supply of 1860 presents another array of vast totals.

	lb.
America sent	1,115,890,608
The East Indies sent . . .	204,141,168
The West Indies sent . . .	1,050,784
The Brazils sent . . .	17,286,864
Other countries sent . . .	52,569,328
Total	1,390,938,752

Of this quantity, 250,428,640 lb. were exported, the remainder, 1,140,510,112 lb., being retained for home consumption. And at the close of this year of terrific prosperity—this year of unequalled production, there remained in the country a stock of raw cotton amounting to 250,286,605 lb.

Is it marvellous that a trade like this should have inspired its chief agents with a belief—shall we not say a conviction—that the greatness, ay, the very existence of England as a first-rate power, depended upon its continuance? Is it strange that a county, which in extent is but the thirty-third part of England, but which contained one-tenth of the riches and of the population of the country—is it strange that such a province, the chosen seat of such a trade, should be somewhat vain and overbearing, should become regarded with envy and dislike by many of its neighbours?

There is no marvel in this; the wonder yet remains to be told. The succeeding pages of this history will describe how this great industry was stricken, palsied, and withered; how, in its prostration, those who had made great gains, and those who had been its human machinery, bore themselves and their altered fortunes. They will tell a long tale of privations nobly borne, and of charity that never faileth. They will record examples of management and governance worthy of imitation for all time. But they will fail in doing justice to England if they neglect to show how she rose superior to this crisis: how the loss of this trade, on which she was supposed to lean, made no unsightly gaps in her revenue, and was not suffered to influence her policy.

They will fail, also, in a very important duty, if they do not inculcate, from the events of the past, the lessons of adversity; if they do not point out how this time of trial has been utilised by the fulfilment of duties and obligations hitherto neglected. They will show how, and to what extent, the insecure foundation of this trade has been replaced by more reliable, because more numerous sources of supply. They can be but an unworthy monument to the memory of one of the greatest moral triumphs that ever ennobled a people; but their record will not be in vain, if, by recalling the incidents of this period, it promotes the lasting establishment of a kindlier feeling between class and class,—if it encourages a more practical fulfilment of that most high and sacred command, that men should do to others as they would others should do to them.

CHAPTER II.

APRIL—SEPTEMBER 1861.

THE history of the Cotton Famine naturally commences with the bloodless bombardment of Fort Sumter on the 13th of April, 1861. The event took the world by surprise. No one saw—certainly no warning voice of authority proclaimed, that this most courteous hostility, that this military performance was the overture to the most tragic opera yet placed upon the world's stage. Mr. Lincoln had been elected President on the 4th of March,—on the 30th he had delivered his Inaugural Address—the first and last occasion upon which the chief magistrate of the United States is officially called upon to make a speech. His tone was eminently pacific—indeed, nothing less illogical than the argument of war could reconcile the present doings of the Abolitionist Generalissimo of the Federal armies with his inaugural utterance:—'I 'have no purpose, directly or indirectly to interfere with 'the institution of Slavery in the States where it exists. 'I believe I have no lawful right to do so; and I have 'no inclination to do so.' We must confess in all humility that our purview was small indeed; we neither foresaw the toilsome strife which was about to dye the Central States with human blood, nor did we regard Abraham Lincoln as destined to become the most relentless enemy of the social curse of America. It never even occurred to us that he and his party were dissembling, in order to obtain complete possession of the Republic: and when the 13th of April arrived, and that sound was heard, so new, so startling to young America—when a hostile cannon-shot boomed across Charlestown harbour, even then we persisted in believing that this interchange of iron compliments between General Beauregard and Major Anderson was nothing more than a game of brag.

There are many now, and their numbers will probably be increasing, who would gain a facile reputation for prophecy by the pretended prediction of accomplished facts. There are many whose most mournful recollection will be, that they could not foresee the signs of the times, and share that golden harvest which is ever the strange accompaniment of a modern famine. It is told of one of the kings of England, that he was never seen to smile after the drowning of his hopeful son, and the same perpetual gloom is said to overhang the visage of at least one manufacturer, who, in the temporary absence of his good genius, cancelled speculative transactions made in his name, which, being confirmed, would have raised him to the metallic rank of a millionaire. At this time, fortunes lay ready to the hands of investors; 'Middling Orleans'—the gauge of the cotton market—was selling after the fall of Sumter at 7¾*d.* per lb., which in December, eight months later, was worth a shilling. Where was then the capital of the cotton trade, and where that genius for money-making with which its constituents are not falsely credited?

The fact is, that the Cotton Famine—if this word still means scarcity—did not commence for a year after the period to which reference is now made. April 1861 was a time of gorged markets, both at home and abroad. The India and China markets had been overfed with manufactures until they threatened to burst with bankruptcy. The enormous demand of these new markets had so stimulated the home manufacture, that new mills had sprung up in every town and township in the cotton districts, and, with reckless cupidity, manufacturers had rushed to divide the profits of the increased trade. In the preceding year India had taken manufactures to the value of 17,000,000*l.*, one third of the whole export; but merchants still piled the goods in the warehouses of Bombay, until ruin stared them in the face, and they began to realise the fact that these commodities had become an unmarketable burden. One of the wisest heads in Lancashire had forewarned them of this. Twelve months had passed since they had been told from the chair of the Manchester Chamber of Commerce, not to regard the trade of 1860 as normal, or the increase of exports to the East as continuous; but the cotton trade is not the only one which it would be difficult to turn from markets that seemed to promise high rates of profit.

Such a glut of production had there been in 1859 and 1860, that at the time to which we are referring not a few houses in Manchester and Liverpool felt the severest difficulty in meeting their liabilities. They had plenty of goods in stock, but the enchanter, demand, was not at hand to turn them into gold. In Bombay, 'shirtings' found no buyers; no one cared to inquire after mule-yarns, and water-twist was a drug in the market. There was a larger supply of cotton in England than there had been for years previous to this time. The increasing probability of hostilities in America had induced the shippers of the Southern States to bring forward the crop of 1860 with unusual haste; and before the end of May 1861, the imports from America for the five months of the year amounted to 1,650,000 bales—a supply largely exceeding the total importation from the same source during the whole year of 1857. This unexampled import was superadded to the large stock of 594,505 bales remaining in England at the expiration of 1860. Nor was this all. Cotton was arriving from the East as well as from the West. The rumour of a deficient crop in America, and the murmurs of that coming storm, of which the first flash was seen at Fort Sumter, had roused the feeble energies of the Asiatic planters, and they contributed to augment the cotton supply of Britain. In the first six months of 1861, the Indian supply, which for the same period of 1860 had been 249,000 bales, amounted to 314,500 bales, an increase of 65,500 bales.

But that we know what followed this; were it not that we have since seen a half a million cotton-workers and their dependents become the helpless recipients of Poor Law allowances or private benefactions, we might well think the title of this history a misnomer, and question the existence of a Cotton Famine. A Cotton Famine! In June 1861, the cotton trade was suffering from apoplexy, with a full larder. There was nothing it stood so much in need of as depletion. Come it must, either by an artificial or a forced suspension of trade. Every one was looking out for buyers. The importers of cotton had invested largely, and pressed by the wants of the American planters —patriotic or rebellious, as viewed through Southern or Northern spectacles—they forced their wares upon apathetic speculators and unwilling manufacturers, who, though possessed of much yarn and cloth, may have had but little cash, and less desire to increase their stocks of goods. No one believed in the long continuance of the war. Though Sumter had fallen two months back, though Mr. Lincoln had gathered together his first army, though the Southern States had become a drill-ground and Richmond a barrack, yet the sales to speculators in Liverpool were less in June than they had been in January, and 'Middling Orleans was quiet,' though advanced to 8*d.* per pound.

This rise, forced upon the market by the situation in America, was the means of saving many manufacturers from impending difficulties. In 1859 and 1860, the years of 'terrific prosperity' and over-production, Middling Orleans had been quoted on the last day of each year at $6\frac{7}{8}$*d.* and $7\frac{3}{8}$*d.* respectively. The adventitious circumstance of the American war, had brought profits to those who, but for this outbreak, would have had to suspend payments. Notwithstanding the enormous mass of goods in stock, estimated to value upwards of £20,000,000, the rising market for the raw material galvanised the trade in manufactures into life; and the prices of yarns and cloth having slowly declined since the commencement of the year, now rose languidly, and liberated some of the capital of the cotton trade—set it free to be invested far more profitably in the raw material.

Probably at no one period in the history of the cotton trade was there such a weight of cotton and cotton manufactures in England as at the time of the battle of Bull Run. Production continued at nearly the same rate as it had done in 1860. The exports of yarn and goods for the first nine months of the year 1861 amounted to 537,969,000 lb., less only by 16,250,000 lb. than the exports for the same period of the previous year. But the total production of yarns and goods from January to September, 1861, was 779,279,000 lb., of which therefore 241,801,000 lb. were retained at home. The average home consumption for this period would be 135,000,000 lb.; so that in the first nine months of 1861, at least 100,000,000 lb. of yarn and goods were added to the large stocks then remaining in the country. The overfed condition of the foreign markets, especially those of India and China, may be best judged from the fact that they were subsequently troubled with indigestion and loss of appetite for upwards of two years. The weight of raw cotton and of manufactures at this time in the hands, or at the disposal of the British cotton trade, cannot have fallen far short of 1,000,000,000 lb. This was in their possession when first they welcomed a rising market. They had recklessly pushed production beyond requirement; with all the assistance of low wages, light taxation, and perfect domestic peace, manufacturers had made their spindles revolve faster, their shuttles move more quickly, than they had ever done before. They had done this in fear and trembling—they had been encouraged by the excitement which burned at the prospect of such increasing markets—they had aroused a competition which recognised no duty paramount to that of obtaining the largest share of profits; and at the moment in which they might have expected judgment and execution—in the shape of a large depreciation in the value of their commodities—almost in the very hour when the reaction to which they had given no heed was upon them, the scene shifted—the war in America assumed an aspect of determined continuance, and the blockade of the Southern ports was declared effective. The price of cotton rose rapidly, and immediately a golden radiance of profit hovered around these plethoric stocks which were stored throughout the world.

The first signs of distress in the manufacturing districts appeared in October, when many factories began to run short time. But the American war, to which this distress was then generally referred, had as yet far less to do with it than the overstocked condition of the markets. Speculation had forced the price of Middling Orleans up to 10*d.* per pound on the 30th of September; but even this rate would not have deterred spinners from continuing operations, had it not been for the fact that they must work for stock, there being no demand for goods in the markets. Every one who can pretend to the slightest knowledge of the cotton trade knows that 'short time' must, under any circumstances, have prevailed very extensively during the winter of 1861 and the whole of 1862. Before it became evident that war would ensue in America, many of the great spokesmen of the cotton trade had predicted this necessity. Had there been no war in America, 'hard times' must have come upon all in the winter of 1861. As it was, this event brought relief to the holders of goods, wealth to the speculators in cotton, and a comfortless autumn, with a hopeless winter prospect, to the operatives.

That difficulty which, happily for Englishmen, is experienced in attempting any very accurate division of classes in this country, is nowhere found greater than in referring to the cotton trade. The line between master and operative—between employer and employed—would seem clear and well-defined enough; but practically it is not so. In the course of this history it will oftentimes be necessary to refer to the manufacturers as a class, and to the operatives as a class. It will be well therefore to understand the gradations of each, which meet upon and almost obliterate the line of division. Highest of the operative class are the overlookers and minders, and the lowest of the manufacturer class are men of precisely the same stamp and origin. Backed by some capitalist, and masters only in name, or plodding on towards independence with their mill mortgaged to the top brick of its tall chimney, the position of many of these men during a disturbed condition of the trade is full of danger and anxiety. The easy gains which attend a rising market are not for them. The troubled sea of an excited trade engulfs many, and they drop out from the list of manufacturers unnoticed and unknown. But when Englishmen talk of the manufacturers as a class, it is not of these men they speak; they refer to those who are really the representatives of the class. When they speak of landholders as a class, they do not allude to the shareholder in the semi-political building society, or to the cottier who is squatted upon his patch of waste. If they talk of grocers, they are not including every village huckster with the representative men of that important trade. The most casual view of the manufacturing districts will convince any one that the number of factories of the first class in size is increasing more rapidly than any other. This is the tendency of the trade. From the commencement of the Cotton Famine, and throughout its duration, many of the inferior class of manufacturers have been as nearly irresponsible as employers of labour can be. If here and there they have succeeded in speculation, it has been at a risk more than equally proportioned to their gains. They have had in general a hard struggle to keep their machinery in order, to pay their rates, to live without their ordinary profits, and in many cases to submit to the loss of their cottage rentals. If they have given their time freely to the organisation of committees, and to the dispensation of relief,—if they have never screwed their cottage rents from relief allowances, nor taken advantage of the prevailing distress to press down wages to a starvation-point,—they have done all that could be expected of them.

In alluding to the constituents of the cotton trade, it is necessary to remember that the merchants and brokers, who are neither manufacturers nor employers of operative labour, are an exceedingly wealthy and responsible class.

Some insight into the nature of the division of the manufacturers will be gained by recollecting that at the close of 1861, there were in the three counties of Lancaster, Chester, and Derby, 2,270 factories engaged in the manufacture of cotton. Of this number, 890 were engaged in spinning only; 593 were devoted solely to weaving; 152 were 'miscellaneous' mills; and in 635 both spinning and weaving were carried on. At the same date there were in these three counties 369,452 persons employed in the manufacture, which would give an average of 162 to each factory. Of these 2,270 factories it is estimated that one-third are what may be called 'small' establishments. It has been ascertained by one of the factory inspectors, that in this proportion the working power was less than 'twenty horses.' Therefore the responsible mauufacturers may be taken to be about two-thirds of the whole number. But they employ very many more than two-thirds of the mill hands. Representation therefore upon the principle of numbers falls due to the higher class of manufacturers, as it certainly would if the test of capital were applied.

Having thus analysed the employers of labour, fairness demands that no less should be done for the inferior class. With every desire to do justice to the operatives, it is possible that this history may not emulate those speeches and writings which have but thinly disguised a contemptuous fear beneath the most fulsome adulation. Yet it will not be thought censurable to refuse to be among the number of those, of whom Mr. Disraeli truly said, 'the people have their parasites as well as monarchies and aristocracies.' None can be blind to the virtues of this working class; the almost uninterrupted reign of peace and order throughout this terrible crisis; the readiness with which many have taken advantage of their compulsory leisure to make up for the neglected hours of youth, by diligence in schools and lecture-rooms; the willingness and patience which many have displayed in learning to handle the spade, the pickaxe, or the barrow, preferring to earn their subsistence rather than receive it at the hand of charity, are deserving of high praise. Nor will their goodness one towards another be wasted or forgotten. How much of all this is owing to the beneficial legislation of late years, to the Factory and Free Trade Laws,—how much to the faultless energy with which so many of their superiors in position have served them during this crisis, will be better judged at the conclusion than at the opening of this history. In regarding the Manchester of the present day, it will be well to recall to mind the Manchester of the past. When Johnson made his tour to the Hebrides, his friends looked upon him as a man bent on a desperate enterprise. The Highlanders who have since held fast in a 'thin red line' the honour of England, who are now the favoured, if not the favourite neighbours of our widowed and beloved Queen, were then regarded as a ferocious race of murderers and marauders, addicted to scanty clothing, and universally troubled with the itch.

And the manufacturing districts, were they not supposed even in our own time, to be filled with a population whose loyalty could only be ensured by the material bribe of high wages,—by the constant company of light dragoons, and by the continual indulgence of their self-will and self-interest in the legislation of the country? Happily for England, still more happily for the manufacturing districts, much of this picture which was real, and much that was imaginary, have together passed away. The grey-headed recorder of those troublous times, when he and the century were very young together, when Mr. Deputy-Constable Nadin was the Jeffreys of Manchester, and Peterloo a famous battle-ground, still lives honoured by the class to which he belongs by birth and early association. But now, no longer forced to hide from the strong arm of the law, which is, as it should be, nothing but a terror to the wrong-doer and an equaliser of the weak against the strong, the author of the 'Life of a Radical' has seen Manchester pass through hard times to which those of former years were mild and momentary, free from any serious menace of the public peace, and amid the undisturbed reign of order and authority. Is it not also a happy emblem of improvement that in St. Peter's Square—the scene of that foolish and exaggerated encounter—he may hear, in place of the curses of a crowd and the cries of the wounded, the strains of a choir unsurpassed in sweetness by any in the district?

When William IV. received Dr. Dalton, the King's first question was, 'Well, Doctor, are you all quiet at Manchester?' as though discord were the normal state of this city. And it is said that the highest placed of womankind was not free from this fearful impression on her first visit to this district; and that her astonishment was as great as her delight, when she saw these crowds of working people, which had been the terror of her uncles and the anxiety of her grandfather, linked hand-in-hand to form for her the noblest body-guard a Sovereign can possess. If the result of this time of trial shall be, that England, better informed of the weakness as well as the strength of Lancashire, shall regard the chief industry of this county with greater sympathy and satisfaction; and if, on the other hand, Lancashire—grown wise by experience—shall perceive that her greatness is dependent upon, and cannot exist in isolation from that of England, the lesson of this Famine will not have been in vain, and Charity's true mission—that of uniting hearts and hands—will have been fulfilled. England will not grudge to Lancashire the credit she has gained in this campaign against so dire an enemy; and surely Lancashire will have learned her subordination to the commonwealth, in seeing that even the sudden prostration of her mighty industry, while it brought aid from every quarter, caused none but local difficulties and scarcely affected the general prosperity of the empire.

In speaking of the operative class, it may be almost assumed that their natural acuteness is taken for granted. It is no libel on the working classes in general to say that in this respect the cotton-workers stand to them in the proportion of five to four. But this intellectual superiority is owing to the character of their labour, and not to any peculiarity of race. It is well known that we cannot use the muscles and the brain very actively at one and the same time. In the village *coterie* it is the sedentary shoemaker or the stitching tailor who is the politician or the poet. Hodge comes in miry from his work, with strength only sufficient to fall on to the settle, and to be a listener and a sharer in the recuperative cheer. In these days of automaton machinery, there are many moments in every hour when the varied and immense production of a cotton factory would continue, though ninety-five per cent. of the 'hands' were suddenly withdrawn. The work is exciting, but not laborious. It quickens the eye and the action of the brain to watch a thousand threads, being obliged to dart upon and repair any that break, lest even a single spindle should be idle: and it strengthens the brain to do this with bodily labour which is exercising but not exhausting. It polishes the mental faculties to work in continued contact with hundreds of others, in a discipline necessarily so severe and regular as that of a cotton factory. The bodily system becomes feverishly quickened by thus working in a high and moist temperature. Even the rattle of the machinery contributes to preserve the brain of the operative from that emptiness which so fatally contracts its power. As regulated by the Factory Laws, operative labour in those establishments—and there are many—which are well ventilated and cleanly, is not by any means an unhealthy form of industry. The high and damp temperature will not make rosy cheeks; and the general paleness of complexion is one of the most remarkable features of the people. But with personal cleanliness

—rendered peculiarly necessary by the sudorific effects of their working atmosphere—and temperate habits, the operative has a far better chance of a long life and a merry one than the agricultural labourer. But as to his intelligence, there is no doubt that the prodigies of literature and general 'self-help' which have left the spindle and and the shuttle to astonish even the weary *quidnuncs* of London, have given place to an impression that the standard of education among the factory-workers is much higher than it really is. Curious Cockneys, making their first round of a spinning-room or a loom-shed, have been surprised if they did not find several copies of Cæsar's Commentaries, or stray volumes of works on moral philosophy, lying ready to the hands of learned workmen. There are, as there have been, men among them whose erudition is astounding—linguists and botanists, philosophers and political students; there are women filled with religious zeal, and gifted with a power of expression which is beautiful and almost divine; but this is no more true of the bulk of them than it would be to assert that Trinity College was filled with wranglers, or Christ Church with double-first-classmen.

Indeed, on the contrary, it may well be thought that the previous character of the population of this district was due to their dense ignorance,—an ignorance which, so far from being lightened by comparatively high wages and comfortable existence, was really fostered and encouraged by the hungry demand for labour. It was thus that the cotton districts nurtured a population which was not unreasonably regarded as dangerous. Well fed, and warmly, if not healthily housed, they increased and multiplied, the more regardless of the moral responsibilities of parentage because their offspring were a source of increased gain to them. When the migration of agricultural labourers to the cotton districts was being encouraged in 1834, by the very able letters of the Messrs. Ashworth and the comprehensive reports of Dr. Kay, it was satisfactory, no doubt, to find that the Bledlow peasant, forty years of age, with a family of nine children, could, by the help of these 'encumbrances,' so far better his condition as to advance from 16*s.* 3*d.* in Buckinghamshire, to 41*s.* 6*d.* in Lancashire. And, considering that in one place he was at least an occasional pauper, while in the North he was a cherished acquisition, and 'would rather be transported to Van Diemen's Land than go back to that there bungling parish of mine,' it would seem surprising that the Law of Settlement yet prevails,—a law which, but for the amendments carried by Sir Robert Peel and Mr. Villiers, would have hurried away thousands and thousands of paupers to the different union-houses of the kingdom during the period of the Cotton Famine. But though the Bledlow peasant rejoiced, it is not quite certain that his removal benefited his children equally with himself. In Bucks they might have received some education at the National School, while in Lancashire they had to earn seventy per cent. of the paternal income.

When honest Joseph Brotherton hushed the House of Commons by the simple narration of his own sufferings and privations as a factory boy, he spoke as one of those units who now and then escaped from the general destiny. This speech aided very materially in the passing of one of those legislative measures which struck at the root of the ignorance and misery of the manufacturing districts. By the benevolent provisions of the Factory Laws, it is enacted that ten hours shall be the limit of labour in a factory; that no child under the age of thirteen years shall be allowed to work full time; that no woman, young person, or child shall be employed in a factory for more than five hours before one o'clock in the afternoon of any day without an interval of leisure for at least thirty minutes.

Every manufacturer, before commencing to work a factory, must send notice to the Government Inspector or the sub-inspector of the district. In every such establishment an abstract of the factory laws must be affixed to movable boards, and placed prominently before the notice of the workpeople. To this abstract must be added the names and addresses of the inspector, sub-inspector, and certifying surgeon, and also notice of the allotted hours of work. It is required that every factory shall have a clock, that the machinery in motion shall be fenced as much as possible, in order to prevent accidents, and that the interior of the factory shall be lime-washed once in fourteen months, in order to promote health. Christmas Day and Good Friday, besides eight half-holidays, must be given in the year, and of the latter, four are to be allowed between the 15th of March and the 1st of October.

With reference to employment, the law declares that from eight to thirteen years of age the operatives are to be classified as 'children;' from thirteen to eighteen as 'young persons,' and with unusual deference to a weakness of the fairer sex, women of all ages are placed in this interesting class. The duties of the surgeon consist for the most part in making certificates as to age, and in every factory, registers of the class of persons employed are duly kept for inspection and reference. None of the 'young persons' can be employed before six in the morning, after six in the evening, or after two o'clock on Saturdays. But the law is especially and desirably stringent with respect to children. All the restrictions of the working hours of 'young persons' apply also to children. But besides these, it is enacted that no child can be set to work before noon and after one o'clock of the same day. With the exception of Saturday, children must attend school for three hours daily, and the occupier of the factory in which they are employed, is required to ascertain on Monday morning, from the certificate of the schoolmaster, that such attendance has been duly made. These provisions have certainly had a tendency, which may well be thought beneficial, to diminish the employment of children and young persons. When children are employed, it is necessary to have two sets, one of which works in the before-noon, and the other in the later half of the day, changing their hours of labour every week.

The requirement as to school attendance has led, in the larger factories—which are in every respect the most healthful, both morally and physically—to the establishment of factory schools, in order that when the legislative regulation as to three hours' schooling was completed, the child might be ready to its work. The army of King Cotton is recruited without reference to stature, and as to age, eight years is sufficient. At thirteen the operative attains his majority and becomes a 'full-timer.' From the age of eight to thirteen is therefore the noviciate of the operative. At the age of thirteen he passes from a 'half-timer' to a 'full-timer,' from wages of three or four shillings to three or more times that amount per week.

The ignorance of the elder generation of operatives—so painfully manifested in the adult schools which have been one of the many good consequences of the .Cotton Famine—is not, therefore, continued to the same extent in the middle or the rising generation. Still much improvement is needed here. In many, too many cases, the parents, knowing that their children must attend school from the moment they enter the factory, gives themselves no thought about their mental or moral training. While babes, they leave them during the hours of labour too often in the hands of crones, who preserve the quiet of their 'kindergarten' with the pernicious assistance of 'Daffy's Elixir' and 'Godfrey's Cordial;' and the interval between this condition and their entry upon factory life is frequently passed in the utter absence of all control. The main anxiety of these parents is to push their children from their profitless minority to their profitable majority in their fourteenth year. On this subject it may be well to refer to the high authority of the Factory Inspectors. In Mr. Redgrave's Report for 1861, one of his sub-inspectors 'regrets to say that, when work is pretty plentiful, every effort is made by the parents to deprive the children of the benefits of the educational clauses of the Factory Acts, by getting them passed for full time before they are thirteen.' Mr. Baker, in one of his Reports, finds that in his district there were, in 1861, 21,239 factory workers under the age of thirteen. Of this number he fears that 'at least 14,000 would never have been sent to school by parental affection or consideration unless they had been employed in factories.' The children are in too many cases merely the helots of their parents, who hope to gain as much as possible from their labour, before the time arrives in which they declare their independence. This is true only of the inferior, though it must be said, of a large class of factory operatives. Of the half-timers, who in compliance with the law spend one-half of their working day at school, not fifty per cent. have received even the slightest previous schooling. Boys and girls from eight to twelve years of age have to be taught the alphabet. It is found that those who attend school in the morning, and the factory in the after part of the day, make better progress in their studies than when the operation is reversed. But what a poor hope is there for the education of the half-timer, if he is to be allowed to 'grow' in his own way until he ten or eleven years old,—less cared for even than the immortal 'Topsy,'—and then to pass his one or two years of schooling simultaneously with his entry on factory life! It is said that for the first year the noise and confinement in the mill exercises a benumbing influence upon the children. It may well be so. At all events, if their minds were fortified by a longer education they would be strengthened to resist this influence, and it does appear to be of the highest importance that an amendment of the Factory Laws should require some educational test of the children, in order to compel their parents to fulfil their duty. It has been suggested that the law should be made to bribe the parents by permitting their children to pass for full-timers at twelve instead of thirteen years of age, if at the earlier period they had attained a certain standard of knowledge. But this proposal, although it might possibly succeed in promoting education, has obvious defects. No one would say that to attain this end it was necessary or advisable to condemn a child to ten hours a day of labour at the tender age of. twelve years. Besides, what is most necessary is, that the parents should be compelled to pay some more attention to the bringing-up of their children before they become half-timers. For this reason, many will be disposed to agree with Mr. Baker in his view of this subject, and to join his recommendation that 'a certificate of a certain minimum amount of education previous to employment, and a certificate of a maximum amount thereof on attaining the age of thirteen' should be required, and that in default of this, 'the education begun during half-time employment should be carried on to a period not exceeding sixteen years of age in some night school, until the required maximum amount of education be attained.' But the difficulty lies deeper than it appears to do.

Children frequently leave their parents at a very early age in the manufacturing districts. Girls of sixteen years, and lads of the same age, find that they can enjoy greater liberty, and if not greater comforts, that at least they can have their own way more completely, in a separate home, and these partings cause little surprise or disturbance. As might be expected where labour is in such great demand, juvenile marriages are more common in Lancashire than in any other of the English counties. The census returns of 1861 show that among the population of Bolton 45 husbands and 172 wives were coupled at the immature age of 'fifteen and under;' in Burnley there were 51 husbands and 147 wives; in Stockport 59 husbands and 179 wives in the same category. The same reliable evidence shows that from fifteen to twenty is an age at which a considerable number of the male, and a still greater proportion of the female operatives are married. For the last fifty years the cotton manufacture has given such encouragement to matrimony as never existed elsewhere. And it must be admitted that to the best of its ability the operative class has fulfilled the Scriptural command. They have been fruitful, they have multiplied, and if they have not replenished the earth, they have certainly to some extent subdued it by enwrapping its people in the produce of their hands. No one who has ever attended morning service at Manchester Cathedral will forget the ceremony of asking the banns of marriage. When the happy couples make their appearance after the third publication, it is to be hoped that they are not so confused as are most of those listeners to this long-drawn string of some hundred names. Nineteen to twenty-two in the male and seventeen to twenty in the female sex are the usual matrimonial ages. Boy-husband and girl-wife—themselves often not fully-grown —become the parents of weakly children, specially requiring what they rarely get, a mother's care. The husband and wife can earn at least thirty shillings per week, can rent a house which is wind and weather proof, though a filthy roadway may rise high above the door-sill,—though the paved floor be perpetually damp, and though, through the back door, fever-seeds are wafted from the pestiferous 'midden,' which is 'Lancashire' for that unwholesome combination of an open cesspool and an ashpit, usually to be found at the back of their houses.

But it is the condition of the cotton trade, and of the various classes included in this denomination, which are the immediate subjects of inquiry. It is necessary, however, before plunging into the details of a distress from which we shall not emerge even at the close of this volume, that reference should be made to those laws which existed at this period for relieving want and destitution. It is necessary to examine what legal machinery was available for securing the due and efficient relief of the poor, and what capacity of expansion or adaptation to these peculiar and unprecedented circumstances this machinery contained.

It will be conceded, not readily perhaps, but upon reflection, that of all the legislative institutions of a country, the law relating to the relief of the poor is one of those by which its civilization is most surely tested. The condition of the Poor Law is certainly among the truest tests of the progressive and general diffusion of political knowledge and economical principles which can be found in any state. How slow, for instance, how very slow are the steps which lead from the alms-giving of the single rich noble, or the solitary abbey, to the acknowledged lien of the poor upon the wealth of the country. What costly steps, what cautious progress must be taken, to fix upon whom should rest—not of his own pleasure, but upon compulsion—the duty of maintaining the poor and needy. Then, again, the question, who are the poor and needy—who are they that have the right to be the unbidden claimants of public provision?—opens the door through which, by patience, perseverance, and experience, imposture, indolence, and vice, have been at length cast out. A Poor Law is especially an institution which does not admit of being transplanted from a nation of ripe intelligence to one of inferior civilization; it must grow with the growth, and strengthen with the strength of social knowledge.

Of all home legislation, it is the least popular, though by no means the least important. Nor is this surprising, considering that its mission is to the least attractive portion of the community. To the mind's eye, indeed, there is something more alluring in the largesse-giving, purse-flinging days of old, than in the measured and unwelcome tread of the modern collector of poor-rates. But the old system made many beggars, and starved those who could not, or who were too proud to beg. There is very little that can be called interesting in the Poor Law.

It never exercises the least influence upon the national policy abroad; and though we are an insular and a home-loving people, yet the debates of Parliament would soon cease to have any general interest, if the subjects to which they referred were all within the range of her Majesty's dominions. People are not usually much attracted by institutions which are the result of a long period of legislation, unless privileges and dignities are attached to them, such as catch the eye or excite the imagination. But they would not like to lose them, and any attempt to destroy such institutions will call forth the popular affection and appreciation for them. The English people do not undervalue the Habeas Corpus Act or the Reform Bill, although there have been times when a discussion upon either subject would clear any assembly in the country. So it is with the Poor Law. It is accepted by all, and perhaps languidly admired by some; but few are at the trouble to satisfy themselves that its provisions are the laborious result of three centuries of active legislation, and that, so far as human knowledge, justice, and reason can accomplish, they are based upon right and immutable principles.

The acknowledged foundation of the English Poor Law is the 43rd Elizabeth, c. 2, an Act now more extensively appealed to than any other of equal antiquity upon the statute-book. Due probably to the sagacious and prescient mind of Cecil, it has remained to our own time one of the many honourable monuments of the Elizabethan era. The particular statutes by which pauperism is now relieved and controlled, commence with the 35th George III., c. 101. This Act, passed in 1795, had a special reference to the case of many of those persons who had migrated from southern homes to settle in the manufacturing districts, where they could earn higher wages, and who, by the depression of trade or other unavoidable circumstances, were likely to become temporarily chargeable upon the funds raised for the relief of the poor. It may excite a smile to remember, that this Act was passed to prevent the parochial authorities from robbing a poor man of the position he may have won by honest labour, and from transporting him to his native parish, lest he should become a pauper in their neighbourhood. This was in the days when beadledom was triumphant. Next followed an Act depriving orders of removal of their Median and Persian character, and permitting their suspension. Among the four remaining Poor Laws of the reign of George III., the only one of particular importance is that—the 54th Geo. III. c. 170—which enables justices to excuse poor persons from the payment of rates, upon receiving proof of their poverty.

A revolution in the system of poor-law administration occurred between the passing of the Acts last referred to, and the establishment of that great statute, 'The Poor Law Amendment Act' (4th and 5th Will. IV., c. 76), which was passed in August, 1834. By this Act, the Poor Law Board was established as a separate department of State, became invested with independent authority, and empowered to issue from time to time, orders and regulations relative to matters concerning the relief of the poor. By this Act the union system was organised. It repealed the power possessed by the magistrates under the 36th Geo. III., c. 23, to order relief to be given to the poor at their own dwellings, a power which had led to the most monstrous abuses, and which was really a perversion of the spirit of the more ancient Poor Law. Its mover, Lord Althorp, anticipated as its effect, the raising of the British labourer from the condition of a 'pauperised slave' to a degree of independence. And it will be remembered that it was at this period the agitation took place, with reference to that migration of agricultural labourers into Lancashire, to which allusion has been previously made.

The Parochial Assessment Act (6 & 7 Will. IV. c. 96) is concerned with the area of rateability, the description of property to be rated, and with details relating to these subjects. We pass on to a statute which may be designated as the poor man's Magna Charta. It will probably not be long before the general consent to the principle of this Act, and of that recent statute by which it was enlarged, shall give him also his Bill of Rights by the abolition of the Law of Settlement. The 9th and 10th Vict., c. 66, declares, that no person shall be removable after five years' residence in any parish, provided that during that period they have not been chargeable. By this enactment, which was described by the then Secretary of the Poor Law Board as 'having the rare good fortune of being begun by one administration and finished by another,' the Law of Settlement received a severe blow. It was further shaken by Mr. Villiers in the Session of 1862, who introduced and carried the 24th & 25th Vict., c. 55, which reduced the time of residence from five to three years. With this tendency in recent legislation, the abolition of the law involving compulsory removal may be regarded as certain, if not impending. The 9th & 10th Vict., c. 66, also included the humane provision that no widow should be removed for twelve months after the death of her husband. A year later and it was found advisable to transfer the cost of the paupers rendered irremovable by the provisions of this Act, from the parochial to the common fund of the union, and this was accomplished by an Act (10th & 11th Vict., c. 110), bearing the respectable name of Mr. Bodkin. This brief summary of the chief statutes referring to the relief of the poor, may be closed with a mention of the Small Tenements Act (13th & 14th Vict., c. 99), which permitted vestries to declare, by the vote of a majority, that the owners of small tenements not exceeding 6*l.* in value, shall be rated instead of the occupiers.

Such are the most important of the Poor Laws at present in force, but as these are modified and regulated from time to time by Orders of the Board, it will be necessary to extend this examination, in order to define with any degree of precision the law as it stood with respect to the unexampled amount of pauperism so shortly to be cast upon its resources. It must, however, be borne in mind that in the administration of the Poor Laws in Lancashire and the adjoining unions, the Board has always recognised the peculiar constitution of the district. They have not always been able to relieve themselves of those apprehensions to which earlier reference has been made. This is instanced by the fact that in their annual report for 1840, the reason given for the tardy introduction of the new law into Lancashire, and especially into the unions of Bolton, Bury, Ashton, and Rochdale, is stated in the following terms:—'The depressed condition of the manufacturing population to which we have already adverted, and the disquietude of the public mind occasioned by the Chartist riot at Newport, in Monmouthshire, rendered us extremely unwilling to take any step in the manufacturing districts in Lancashire, which might have even a remote tendency to produce a disturbance, or which might be used by designing persons as a pretext for agitation.' They go on to say, 'The reasons which led us to abstain from interference with these unions seemed not sufficiently applicable to Lancaster,' which union had been accordingly formed and declared. There is yet stronger evidence than this of the discretionary and special power vested in the Poor Law Board, by which they could render local or relax the application of the various statutes they administered.

One of the most important of the orders of the Poor Law Board is known as the, 'Out-door Relief Prohibitory Order.' Upon the evils of an uncontrolled dispensation of out-door relief, it is hardly necessary to dwell. The statement of an Irish peer, that he had seen out-door relief in food being devoured by a pauper's ass, the pauper herself being much too well fed to eat it; or that which confidently asserts that a gentleman's coachman was a recipient of out-door relief, will meet with no discredit from those who know the evils engendered by the existence of this system when free from all control. Perhaps these evils reached they climax in the reign of George III., when the poor-rates were liberally dispensed in aid of wages,—when the farmer could obtain the labour of the men 'on the rounds' for a merely nominal sum, the remainder of their wages being made good by the parish. Jeremy Bentham satirised the Act by which these ignorant practices were sanctioned, as being made up of the 'under ability' or 'supplemental wages,' the 'family relief' or 'extra children,' the 'cow money,' the 'relief extension' or 'opulence relief,' and the 'apprenticeship' clauses. It is not now necessary to argue against this economically immoral system. The country has grown wiser as well as older since George III. was King, and the order referred to, prohibiting the relief of any able-bodied persons out of the union workhouse, is one of the consequences of this improvement. But to this prohibition there are several exceptions, and '1st,

When such person shall require relief on account of sudden or urgent necessity.' In their Instructional Letter which accompanied this order, the Commissioners define 'sudden and urgent necessity' 'as any case of destitution requiring instant relief.' This order, which was issued on December 21, 1844, has however no application to any one of the unions in the county of Lancaster.

The 'Outdoor Relief Regulation Order,' issued on December 14, 1852, is, on the contrary, addressed to every union within the county of Lancaster, and has formed the ruling principle for the administration of outdoor relief during the prevalence of the Cotton Famine. The first article of this order declares, that whenever the guardians allow relief to any able-bodied male person, out of the workhouse, one-half at least of the relief so allowed shall be given in food or fuel, or in other necessaries. There is a conspicuous omission here of any other class than 'able-bodied males,' and the instructional letter sent with this order expressly states that 'the guardians have therefore full discretion as to the description of relief to be given to indigent poor of every other class.' They are, however, specially precluded from bestowing relief to redeem from pawn any 'tools, implements, or other articles," belonging to those persons who are in receipt of these allowances, nor have they power to purchase and give to any persons tools or implements. The importance of these provisions and the necessity for observing them will be clearly seen as this history proceeds.

The order is emphatic upon the point that 'no relief shall be given to any able-bodied male person while he is employed for wages or hire, or remuneration by any person.' In applying this very wholesome regulation to the circumstances of the Cotton Famine, it will be necessary to observe how it is modified by the instructional letter accompanying the order, in these significant terms:—'The board desire however to point out that what it is intended actually to prohibit, is the giving relief at the same *identical* time as that at which the person receiving it is in actual employment, and in the receipt of wages (unless he falls within any of the exceptions afterwards set forth), and that relief given in any other case, as, for instance, in that of a man working for wages on one day and being without work the next, or working half the week and being unemployed during the remainder, and being then in need of relief, is not prohibited by this article.'

This order then goes on to declare in Article VI., that every able-bodied male person, if relieved out of the workhouse, shall be set to work by the guardians and be kept employed under their direction and superintendence so long as he continues to receive relief.' The apparent stringency of this article is relaxed by several exceptions mentioned in Article VII., in which sudden and urgent necessity and sickness are specified and included. But the most important modifications of Article VI. are contained in the instructional letter of the same date as the order. The guardians are therein warned that all their payments should assume the form of relief, not of wages; and they are pointedly reminded, that 'if, however, owing to any commercial pressure or general depression of trade, large masses of people should hereafter be thrown out of employment, that upon such an emergency the board would, upon the representation of the guardians, be prepared at once, as on former occasions, to take such steps, by temporary suspension of this article or otherwise, as might be expedient to meet satisfactorily and effectually the difficulty experienced;' and further, the guardians are told, that any deviation from the terms of this order will not be illegal, provided that report is made concerning it, within three weeks from the date of such departure from the regulation.

The Poor Laws are necessarily thus liberal and expansive when administered by a central authority, from the variety of circumstances perpetually submitted to its arbitrament, and from the number of those which are constantly craving to be made exceptions. Prior to the passing of the 'Outdoor Relief Regulation Order,' the requirement of the Poor Law Amendment Act, that relief should only be given to the able-bodied, within the union-house, had been modified by an instructional letter dated the 30th of April, 1842, which states that when the guardians have not provided adequate workhouse accommodation, or where large numbers of able-bodied persons are often suddenly thrown out of employment by the fluctuation of manufactures, the

Commissioners may, if they think fit, exercise the power conferred on them by section 52 of the Poor Law Amendment Act, of prescribing other conditions for the relief of the able-bodied than admission into the workhouse. The principles and practice of the Poor Laws as affecting the pauperism created by the Cotton Famine are now before us. We now know the legal machinery which existed before the time of its gravest trial arrived. How it supported this strain, when and at what points it showed signs of weakness, and how it was assisted by other organisations, the history of the Cotton Famine will disclose.

Among the other organisations referred to, there is one deserving special mention, on the ground of seniority and long-established character. The Manchester and Salford District Provident Society is an institution, which may be described as the parent of those 170 relief committees which were subsequently at work within the district. Originated in 1833, this society has been conducted and supported since that time by many who are locally notable both in Church and State. Its objects have been 'the encouragement of industry and frugality; the suppression of mendicancy and imposture, and the occasional relief of sickness and unavoidable misfortune.' An excellent programme truly, and it is certain that the moral influence of the society has been very much greater than its material success as a savings-bank. It may have largely inculcated, though it has received but little of the fruits of providence. In this respect the society is an obvious failure, for so at least must a provident society be content to be regarded, when in Manchester and Salford the amount deposited in the most prosperous year, 1860, was but 3,464*l*. In this history, the society is specially noticeable as containing within itself an organisation precisely similar to that which was subsequently adopted by the relief committees throughout the district, among which it always maintained a leading place. Upon its foundation, the boroughs of Manchester and Salford were divided into districts, and these, distinctly traced out on maps of large scale, were each confided to the care of a sub-committee and visitors. The chairmen of these district committees were *ex officio* members of a general committee. The establishment of this society was followed thirty years ago, by the formation of several upon the same pattern in several towns throughout the cotton district, and thus there existed a nucleus for that gigantic relief system which has formed one of the most important features of this crisis.

Since Lancashire had been from the early years of the century a very large importer of population, it would be naturally supposed, as is indeed the case, that her average rate of pauperism was much below that of less progressive counties. But her normal rate of pauperism is yet by no means inconsiderable. Her population in 1860 amounted to 12 per cent. of that of England and Wales, and her wealth, evidenced by the assessments under schedule A of the Property Tax, stood at 10 per cent. in the same comparison. The mention of these assessments suggests a momentary deviation from the precise line of this exposition, in order to note the growth of this enormous wealth centred in one county. Reverting to the time when the cotton trade had not received the impulse given to it by the abolition of the Corn Laws, and comparing 1843 with the halcyon year of 1860, it will be found that the agricultural land in Lancashire had in the latter year decreased in annual value by 32,000*l.*; while the value of tithes had fallen from 39,729*l.* in 1843, to 1,514*l.* in 1860—showing at what a tremendous pace the redemption of tithe-rent charge had progressed in Lancashire. The decreased value of agricultural land is explained by the fact that the value of the 'messuages' within the county increased from 4,777,536*l.* in 1843, to 7,019,978*l.* in 1860. The immense development of the railway system in Lancashire is strikingly exemplified in the rise in value of this class of property, from 593,515*l.* in the former, to 1,564,366*l.* in the latter year; and in this short period of seventeen years the total wealth of 'the cotton county' mounted from 7,756,228*l.* to 11,450,851*l.* Nor does it appear to have declined under the influence of the Cotton Famine. From 1860 to 1863 is not a very long period, yet in these three years the annual value of the agricultural land of Lancashire increased by nearly 61,000*l.*, while that of the 'messuages' increased by nearly 800,000*l.*, and the total gross annual value of the property of Lancashire was higher by nearly 1,000,000*l.* in 1863 than in 1861.

There was at all events something here for pauperism to feed upon, and it is well known that want is never far distant from wealth. It cannot be considered a large demand upon the riches of this county, equalling 10 per cent. of the aggregate wealth of the remaining fifty-one counties of England and Wales, that it should have been called upon in 1861 to pay for the relief of the poor the sum of 429,617*l*., about 8 per cent. of the total amount paid in respect of this charge, while in numbers the pauperism of Lancashire was equal to 7½ per cent. of that of England and Wales. The position of Lancashire in 1861, relatively to pauperism, was therefore extremely favourable. As compared with England and Wales, she had 12 per cent. of the population, and 10 per cent. of the collective wealth; but the number of her paupers was only 7½ per cent., and her expenditure for their relief was 8 per cent. of the amount paid by England and Wales.

We have now glanced at the physical features and the social and commercial condition of the cotton districts at the commencement of the Famine. We are somewhat acquainted with the state of the cotton trade at that period, and have examined at length the legal and charitable machinery which then existed for the relief of distress. The resources of Lancashire, the ways and means of her teeming population, have been to some degree exposed; and now we must proceed to veil this prosperous picture, and draw across the scene those clouds which have for a time obscured the brilliant commercial triumphs of the cotton trade.

CHAPTER III.

OCTOBER–DECEMBER 1861.

In the month of October 1861, the price of cotton advanced at a rate such as had never been previously known in the annals of the trade. Time had been when a rise of a farthing per pound gave cause for more talk, and—unless the causes were self-evident—for more astonishment throughout the manufacturing districts, than would have been occasioned by a continental revolution. But now, the cotton trade was beginning to realize something of the magnitude and probable duration of the struggle which had sealed up the ports of the Southern States of America. The defeat of the Federals at Bull Run, in August, and the hostile proclamation issued by Mr. Lincoln in September, interdicting all intercourse with Secessia, had tended to produce this conviction. Had it not been for this war manufacturers would have been much in the same position, and very many of their mills must have been closed. It cannot be said that the industry of Lancashire was as yet affected to any considerable extent by the stoppage of supplies from America, because the previous over-production had been so great, that a continuance of it would have been found to involve a very large depreciation in the value of manufactures. During the past two years, the excess of production over consumption amounted to at least 300,000,000 lb. weight of manufactured goods; which, in the raw material, would be equal to 842,000 bales of 400 lb. each. With this surplus stock in the hands of the trade, it cannot be a matter of surprise that manufacturers should have become anxious to work their mills 'short time.' Had it not been for this war, the propable consequence of such a policy would have been a fall in the price of the raw material to sixpence per pound. But the Cotton Famine, though not immediately at hand, could be seen looming dark and dreary in a not very distant future. Speculators began to operate upon the Liverpool market, and in this one month of October the price of Middling Orleans rose twopence per pound. One shilling per pound was now given freely for this cotton, which could be grown with profit at threepence halfpenny. And the hitherto neglected Surat, ill-treated both in the land of its growth and in the place of its consumption—the pariah of the cotton trade—the *bête noire* of the factories, actually rose in the four weeks of this month from sevenpence farthing to tenpence per pound.

The immediate result of the American war was, at this time, to relieve the English cotton trade, including the dealers in the raw material and the producers and dealers in manufactures, from a serious and impending difficulty. They had in hand a stock of goods sufficient for the consumption of two-thirds of a year, therefore a rise in the price of the raw material and the partial closing of their establishments, with a curtailment of their working expenses, was obviously to their advantage. But to make their success complete, this rise in the price of cotton was upon the largest stock ever collected in the country at this season. To the cotton trade there came in these days an unlooked for accession of wealth, such as even it had never known before. In place of the hard times which had been anticipated, and perhaps deserved, there came a shower of riches. There were, of course, arid spots whereon this auriferous deposit did not fall. It is not impossible that here and there a large manufacturer could show his losses even at this period; but if so, these were due to his own want of judgment or of capital. At this time there were two classes of men, one on either side of the Atlantic, who were becoming enormously enriched, the one directly and the other indirectly, by the American war. In the New World it was the contractor class, which was rolling in wealth gathered from the tremendous endeavours of the United States Government; in the Old, it was the cotton trade. Towards the close of this year, the excess of production was estimated at 300,000,000 lb., and the stock of raw material in the kingdom had reached the unprecedented amount of 279,207,000 lb. There is good authority for believing that these stocks were consumed at the rate of two-thirds in 1862, and one-third in 1863. But at what prices? The manufacturer, conscious of overproduction in 1859–60–61, had reason to suppose that he would have to submit to a reduction in prices. How must these sad prognostications have been turned to rejoicing throughout the cotton trade, as the price of mule yarn rose from 1*s.* 1*d.* in October 1861, to 1*s.* 11*d.* in October 1862, and subsequently to 2*s.* 9*d.* in the same month of 1863. A similar rate of advance was seen in the value of cotton cloth. Its price rose from 11*s.* in 1861, to 20*s.* in 1862, and to 22*s.* in 1863. If it be conceded that these 300,000,000 lb. of goods were manufactured at the prices of October 1861, it is quite fair to assume that they were sold at those of the same date in 1862 and 1863. Upon this calculation, there would be a profit upon their sale amounting to 8,333,333*l.* in each year, the increase of value in the latter year being exactly cent. per cent. Then, as to the stock of raw cotton at the close of 1861, amounting to 279,207,000 lb., a very large quantity of this had been imported before the month of June, when Middling Orleans was quoted at 8*d.* per lb.; but it may be assumed that it was all paid for at the rates of October 1861, that is, at the rate of 11*d.* per lb. The price of raw cotton rose in October 1862, to 2*s.* 3*d.*, and in the same month of 1863 to 2*s.* 5*d.* per lb. Assuming that this surplus of the raw material went off at the same rate as that of manufactured goods—and the stocks of cotton at the close of 1862 and 1863 would seem to warrant this assumption—there would have been at the above prices a gross profit upon the whole surplus amounting to 19,059,985*l.*

Taking this view of the sale of the surplus stocks of raw cotton and manufactured goods in the hands of the cotton trade, at the close of 1861, there was a gross profit upon the former amounting to 19,059,985*l.*, and upon the latter of 16,666,666*l.*, making together the magnificent total of 35,726,651*l.*! There might be added some more millions for the difference between the price paid to the grower, and by the consumer of the imports since 1861. But here is enough and more than sufficient to repay at least a considerable portion of the loss of wages and profits during the two years of famine. Where this profit rests, cannot precisely be known; in what proportion it has been divided between those who are really exporters, those who are professed speculators, and those who are manufacturers, cannot be told. Spinners have oftentimes been speculators, and speculators have been frequent exporters. All that can be said is that such an amount of profit has palpably accrued to the cotton trade during the past two years. Thirty-six millions of money! Even supposing that all the production of the past two years has been carried on without profit—which it would hardly be less than ridiculous to suppose—there is, at least, something here to have consoled the trade for the diminished production which has been the cause of this accidental prosperity.

But October 1861 brought very different prospects to the needy manufacturers, to the small shopkeepers, and to the operatives generally. Short time means short wages and much compulsory idleness, less food and less pleasuring to the operative. It means to the manufacturer without capital, a serious reduction of income, with no corresponding abatement in his expenditure on account of the fabric and machinery of his mill. It means very short profits, long credit, and perhaps many bad debts to the little, working-class shopkeeper.

At this time, comparatively few mills had stopped altogether, but soon many would do so, and the prospects of labour in the manufacturing districts were never more gloomy. It was known that the distress which was now felt was the consequence of a glut rather than a famine. The impending cotton dearth had, no doubt, its influence; but there was as yet no scarcity of cotton in Lancashire. The results of the 'short time' of 1861 are written in the savings-banks returns for that year, where it is seen that the amount withdrawn in England alone, exceeds that paid in by 834,792*l.*, showing a larger surplus of abstraction than any since the year 1848 of revolutionary memory.

In the latter months of this year, though the Cotton Famine was not evident in the warehouses of Manchester and Liverpool, it began to show signs of its approach in the streets and roads of the manufacturing towns. Groups of idlers, no longer listeners for the factory-bell, were to be seen at every street-corner. In busy times, the operative class is only to be met with out of doors at regular intervals during the day. The clatter of their 'clogs' echoes on the pavements in the early morning, at midday, and in the evening, but now it was heard at all times. Not with the quick step of 'full time,' but with the dropping patter so remindful of their blameless inactivity.

The general feeling throughout the district in the autumn of 1861, was that the crisis would be of but short duration. Even among the operatives, few were willing to look upon the dark side of the prospect. Hard times were upon them, but to these they were not altogether strangers. Now and then a warning appeared in those literary twins of Siam, the 'Manchester Guardian' and the 'Manchester Examiner,' which have done so much credit to Lancashire by their outspoken honesty, no less than by their political morality during her severe trial. No duty is more pleasing to the writer of these pages, than that of acknowledging, from a close study of their columns during the past three years, how much it is owing to these very responsible organs of the public press, that goodwill and order and authority have been so well preserved. Deeply concerned for the honour of their district, they were among the first to rouse the wealthier classes of Lancashire to a sense of their duty, and to call forth their donations. These journals have never failed to do justice to the efforts of the Government or to the intentions of the Legislature, nor have they ever faltered in their resistance to any proposal for relieving the distress by the medium of a national grant, or by any means inconsistent with the wealth and abilities of Lancashire.

Coming events in the manufacturing districts cast but very faint shadows before them during the dying months of this year. At the commencement of November there were but 49 mills stopped throughout the whole county, and only 119 working so little as half-time. There were but 8,063 hands out of work—less than one-fourth of the number which were in this sad position in Blackburn alone at the same period in 1862. One of the most prescient public bodies in the district—the Chamber of Commerce of Manchester—evinced its fears with reference to the future, by summoning a meeting to agitate the question of the cotton supply, and India, too long neglected, received some encouragement to increase her production of cotton. But the enormous stocks of goods on hand, necessarily rendered the consumption of the raw material very languid. Already it had fallen off fully thirty-five per cent. Spinners still bought largely, but oftentimes with the thought, if not the intention, of becoming speculators.

The state of affairs in Lancashire had not escaped the attention of the Government. Fortunately there was at the head of the Poor Law Board a minister who knew and who was known in the manufacturing district. As a prominent member of that famous League, the memory of whose victory is still the pride of Lancashire, Mr. Villiers held a high position in the estimation of the district, before he was called upon to fill the presidential chair of the Poor Law Board. In 1847, the southern division of the county had recognised his services by electing him its representative in Parliament, an honour the more remarkable as it was unsought and declined by him in favour of Wolverhampton, by which constituency he had also been returned. As the author of that well-remembered resolution which declared the abolition of the Corn Laws to be 'wise, just, and beneficial,' and certainly obtained if it did not stand for the national verdict in the great case of 'Free Trade against Protection,' Mr. Villiers possessed a claim on the gratitude of Lancaster, which has not been without its influence in the successful action of the Poor Law Board upon the distress occasioned by the Cotton Famine.

In a letter dated November 11, and addressed by the President of the Poor Law Board to the boards of guardians throughout the district, they were informed that the board viewed 'with some apprehension the effects which may ensue from the stagnation of the cotton trade,' and that the board were then 'considering the manner in which any unusual amount of distress may be effectively provided for.' They were reminded that the 'machinery of the law' was to be tempered 'with judicious management,' and were promised that every assistance and facility should be given to them in the discharge of their arduous and increasing duties.

It not unfrequently happens that distance, which is said to lend enchantment, also gives truth to a view. Time ripens the fruit of history, and the focus in which critical events are most clearly seen and most correctly judged, is somewhat removed from the time of their occurrence. This premonitory step on the part of the Government was met by some of those to whom it was addressed with affected indifference, and by others, even with a tone of lofty disdain, but by all, or nearly all, with a profound conviction of their ability to deal with any circumstances which might arise. Let them not be censured for the confidence they displayed, though subsequent events have made it appear in a great degree misplaced! It is a far less evil in a State that men should despise an impending difficulty,—a frame of mind not uncommon to Englishmen,—than they should weaken their power of meeting it by an untimely cowardice.

Meanwhile, the cotton trade, so far as the manufacture was concerned, was becoming more and more depressed. The necessity for a cessation of production will be readily seen on reference to the condition of the markets. Middling Orleans cotton was selling at about a shilling per pound. Allowing twelve per cent. for waste, and adding the cost of spinning, together with threepence farthing per pound for the expense of weaving, it will be evident that no manufacturer could sell cloth at a profit under nineteenpence per pound, or ten shillings for 'shirtings' pieces of seven pounds weight. But a reference to the price of shirtings pieces of seven pounds weight at this time, will show that they were finding no very ready sale at eight and sixpence per piece, and therefore a continuancy of production with American cotton involved an immediate loss. And the demand was so faint, that there was little inducement to make experiments with Surat cotton, which had hitherto been used in admixture with American, and but very rarely as the sole constituent of cloth. It is some proof of how firmly the markets stood at this time, upon the over-production of the past two years, that with the almost certain prospect of a long war in America, and a strict blockade, the prices of goods were generally the same in November 1861, as they had been in May 1860, though the price of cotton had risen by as much as fivepence halfpenny per pound.

It is not easy to gauge the responsibility of large employers in a country where labour is free from all feudal fetters. Practically, the masters and the 'hands' are mutually dependent on the self-interest of each other. On the one side, a sudden strike may involve the employer in serious loss, and on the other, the unexpected closing of the factories will certainly place many of the employed in deep poverty and distress. Hence it is, that the framers of the Poor Laws have been so careful to make special provision for their widest expansion in the manufacturing districts. Manufacturers, in the working of their mills, must and ought to be guided by their interests, and if they look to these, not without due thought for those they employ, no more can be demanded of them. At the time to which we are now referring, a Wigan firm, employing some 2,500 hands, forewarned them of their intention to close their mill, adding 'that they trusted to the prudence and good sense of their hands to do what they could in the meantime, to prepare for the hard time which is coming.' This humane advice was not given too soon, for shortly afterwards, on November 20, intelligence arrived of the seizure of Messrs. Mason and Slidell on board the 'Trent,' the West India mail steamer, and the cotton trade experienced to its disadvantage the uncertainties attending the prospect of a war between this country and the Northern States of America.

Autumn had passed away into winter with no improvement in the cotton trade. Blackburn, always energetic, was the first to propose a public meeting upon the subject of the prevailing distress. Those who have, with so much credit to themselves, and it must be added, with so much external assistance, carried Blackburn through subsequent difficulties, can now afford to think lightly of their alarm in November 1861, upon finding an access of 829 above the ordinary number of outdoor recipients of relief. An attempt which was then made to effect a partial reduction of wages, affords an opportunity for stating that the operatives do not always display either a filial or an intelligent confidence in their masters. This may proceed partly from ignorance, and may be ascribed in part, no doubt, to the results of experience. The cotton-worker has an almost insane dread of a reduction of wages. An instance of this occurred at Wigan, in April 1862, when 150 people struck work in one mill, upon the rumour that sixpence would be deducted from their wages, although there were several thousand operatives then in receipt of relief in that town. It may be that the operative knows how difficult it is to regain that which is thus lost, but it may well be thought that he would lose nothing in the end, if he were a little more conversant with the true position of the capitalist he is serving. Many of the operatives assume that there must always be a profit on production, and it would be impossible to persuade some among them, that a mill is ever worked with even a temporary loss of capital. Those who at this season threatened to go on strike rather than submit to a proposed reduction of wages to the extent of 7½ per cent., would surely have acted more wisely had they submitted to a sacrifice which might have enabled the manufacturers to defer for a time the closing of their mills.

The first year of the Cotton Famine passed away amid political difficulties and increasing distress. What was to come of the 'Trent' affair no one knew. Would the Southern ports be forced open by the English fleet, or would our peace remain unbroken? On the side of peace, there was the letter of General Scott, who had not then passed into the 'old school' of American generals, in which that massive hero declared that the seizure of Messrs. Slidell and Mason had been made without the the authority of the Federal Government, and in the middle of December there arrived Mr. Lincoln's Message, containing very pacific utterances towards every people but those of the Confederate States. Those who dreaded war, were further reassured by the despatches of M. Thouvenel, who supported the demands of England with *entente cordiale*, which, though not always observable, has yet been a prominent feature in the imperial policy of France. The consequence of all this was that the cotton market remained firm at the close of the year. But manufacturing production was checked only by the prodigious weight of stocks in hand, while of the raw material, there was in stock a larger supply than had been accumulated at this season since 1853.

The distress which was now increasing the duties and responsibilities of the local authorities, and which was felt sorely by the operative class, was not due to an immediate want of cotton. Had the stocks of manufactured goods been lessened by a tremendous conflagration, there would not have been that weekly increase in the number of closed mills which now became so alarming. Of course, the uncertainty which has throughout attended the American war, and which at this time was aggravated by the position of the relations existing between Great Britain and the United States, has always had the effect of making producers fearful of working for stock to any considerable extent. That organised system of relief which has since become so perfect, and of which it may safely be affirmed, that the minimum of demoralisation has been combined with the maximum of good which it is possible to effect by a system purely eleemosynary, had its commencement in this month of December. Several of the boards of guardians, who, probably from having the poor always with them, had conceived that they had a special property in the poor and needy, were inclined to look coolly upon these amateur attempts, and with a weakness to which all officialism is prone, they seemed to take more thought for the symmetry of their administrative system than for the wants of those who now claimed relief. By many, the exigencies of the crisis have been throughout underrated: it is not therefore surprising if, at the onset, boards of guardians here and there deemed themselves something more than competent to meet the extraordinary demands which the fast increasing distress was bringing upon them.

Before another twelve months had elapsed, what reams of appeals for assistance had passed to all the ends of the earth! In the year which followed this, in 1862, the great year of the Cotton Famine, there will be found suggestions, opinions, and advice offered from all quarters, and help invoked from all who had ears to hear or eyes to read. The charitable agency set up by the local relief committees will excite surprise by its magnitude, and admiration by its efficiency. No one with pretensions to sanity will argue that the crisis could have been effectively grappled with in the absence of this agency. It is due to the energy and intelligence of the manufacturing districts to say that this organisation did honour to these qualities, and if ever a similar visitation should afflict this or any other part of the country, there cannot be devised a better mode of meeting the difficulty than by the formation of committees on the pattern of these, which have done their work so well.

The character and composition of these voluntary bodies is deserving of some attention, as is also that of the boards of guardians. The function of these committees being temporary, incidental, and ministerial only, attracted for their members the persons of highest consideration in their several districts. Their popularity has always exceeded that of the boards of guardians, which, it must be admitted, is largely owing to the difference in their duties. But it is certainly to be regretted that the office of guardian has somewhat fallen in the estimation of the public, and does not command the services of many, who are distinguished by education, position, or wealth. We must not overlook the circumstance nor should we omit to inquire how this inferiority has been brought about. Probably all who have studied the question will agree that such a degradation of a very important office is mainly owing to the fact that the local administration of the Poor Laws is regarded as an unpopular and disagreeable duty, in which a public officer must choose either to be the ratepayers' guardian, or to be looked upon as an erratic and unprincipled philanthropist. Is it too much to hope that the time is not far distant when it will seem possible so to blend the duty of a guardian of the poor with that of the due protection of the rights of property, that this office shall be regarded as one pre-eminently dignified by its union of justice with humanity? By the poor, these boards are considered to be established for the repression, instead of the relief of indigence, and as is very often the case when men find a character ready-made to their office, guardians have not unfrequently given fresh currency to this opinion by their proceedings. Rightly regarded, there is no higher parochial duty than theirs: none requiring more especially that authority which gentle manners and good education confer upon their possessors. But it is no libel upon the Lancashire boards in particular, nor does the statement necessarily include the many distinguished personal exceptions, to say that generally their members have not fulfilled this requirement.

The poor are especially sensitive about the treatment which their poverty receives, and to them the board of guardians appears generally to be a repellent, not as it should be, an assistant force. They may be driven to seek its aid, but rarely do they feel thankful, in good times, that this provision against starvation exists. The guardians, in many cases, exercise authority without commanding respect. The probable reason for this is because their practice is contrary to their theory. Practically their chief duty is to keep down the rates of the locality they represent; theoretically it is to relieve the poor. Now that there is a widely diffused knowledge of the principles of a just and equitable Poor Law; now that it has been learnt—and what pungent lessons will not the history of this crisis teach?—that the hand of charity, though pure in itself, rarely fails to demoralise those for whom it is too long held out, is it not possible to inaugurate a better state of things—to take from poverty its seeming criminality, to relieve with discretion, yet without illegality, with kindness, yet closing the door upon indolence and vice, with some view to the redemption of position, yet without injustice to the ratepayer? When this shall be accomplished, these boards will really deserve their most honourable appellation of guardians, and their office will no longer be repugnant to a refined and educated sense; and when this shall be accomplished, then, and then only, would these bodies be thoroughly fitted to deal with such a state of pauperism as that which existed in Lancashire in 1862. The boards of guardians in the manufacturing districts are no worse nor any better than those of other localities. Owing, however, to the redundancy of the lower middle-class population in this part of the kingdom, they have one peculiar feature which is not universal, and which can hardly be described as an excellence. They are composed, for the most part, of men in one and the same position in society. In less densely populated districts there is naturally a greater diversity of class represented at the board, which certainly tends to strengthen the respect attaching to its authority.

There are also peculiarities in the position of other local authorities in the cotton districts which deserve notice, as they have not been without influence upon this crisis. It would be unreasonable to expect that a very strong reverence for municipal government would be found among a people increasing so rapidly, that a few years suffices to alter the particular features and the general aspect of their towns. That most conservative principle—the reverence for constituted authority—cannot be so strong where a trade of enormous production is carried on,—where capital is massed in monster establishments, and where towns are thickly congregated within hearing of each other, as in those parts of the country where the local authority is not menaced by the rival power of capital, nor its dignity lessened by frequent repetition, and where the material additions of a generation are not so great as to efface its local recollections. Compare York and Manchester in this respect, and it will not be found necessary to push the comparison to an invidious conclusion between the relative position of his Eboracean lordship and that of the chief magistrate of the cotton metropolis. So it is throughout the manufacturing districts. The great manufacturers of the cotton towns stand related to the local authority, as do the Daimios of Japan to the Tycoon, not existing in open rivalry nor as an independent authority, but as a great influence not often incorporated in the body in whose name the local government is administered.

The same difficulty afflicts the boards formed under the provisions of the Local Government Act, but in a less degree, for these are most often the ruling power in semi-rural districts, where the rights and duties of the property owner and the necessities of a sparse population bring forward superior men. In all the larger towns of the manufacturing districts, there is discernible among the population a signal want of cohesion; this is only the natural consequence of the multiplication of capital and of that individual energy of industry which is so peculiar to the locality. The cotton towns are beloved by few. It is not in them as in the less active South, where the sequestrated walk within the precincts of the town has been to generations of its inhabitants the child's play-ground—the well-remembered tryst—the sunny strolling place in feeble days of old age. These are the spots in which local affection is engendered and preserved, and these cannot exist where the space between one home of a large population and that of another is in that worse than barbarous condition which ensues when land is anxiously awaiting bricks and mortar. The Lancashire towns are generally regarded by those who, most of all, have the power and the intelligence to improve them, merely as places of business,—as places endurable because they are money-making,—as places, good for nothing but the co-operation of labour and capital, and consequently they are, with few exceptions, places rendered horrible to the artistic eye, by every architectural abomination which possesses the sole merit of saving first cost. A false appearance of poverty is given to the streets by the absence of all but the productive class, until at last, it must be admitted, that for all those external effects which deaden the spirits and harden the heart, these towns have not their equal in the wide world. That they are comfortable is not to be denied. The home of an English peasant is often wretchedly mean, in comparison with that of a Lancashire operative. The cotton-worker is warmly housed, and in good times very well fed; yet it is easier for the garret-lodged denizen of Drury Lane than for him to find the natural beauties of the country,—to look upon the waving cornfields and the russet woods undefiled by smoke, —the rich possession of every man in less wealthy districts. But human nature, especially English human nature, more especially northern English human nature, loves to conquer difficulties, and will have its consolations. Lancashire, a comparative stranger to Nature, is the bosom friend of Art. There would seem to be good reason for supposing that the cultivation of music in English towns is inversely to the purity of their atmosphere and the beauty of their architecture. Nowhere throughout the kingdom is this gentle Art more studied and better appreciated than in the County Palatine. And who are such liberal patrons of the painter's genius as the cotton lords? So, in the economy of all things, there is order and reason in their localising and disposing causes, proving nothing so much as that men are most like to one another in the insatiable wants of the mind,—in all that is highest, and best and noblest in their nature.

CHAPTER IV.

JANUARY—MAY 1862.

THERE was gloom throughout England at the commencement of the year 1862. The good deeds and the wise words of the illustrious Prince, but lately dead, were the talk of a sorrowing people. In the depth of a Canadian winter, English troops were hastening to strengthen the frontiers of the British possessions in North America, for the 'Trent' outrage was as yet unatoned for. In Lancashire, gaunt distress was advancing with rapid strides; and yet the aspect of political affairs was so uncertain, that no one knew but that the news of the morrow might not bring relief. Emigration had steadily declined since the first outbreak of the American war. It soon became generally evident that extraordinary measures must be taken to meet the fast accumulating destitution.

Wigan was among the first of the Lancashire towns to produce a definite organisation. At a meeting held in the Moot Hall on January 3, it was resolved, that a committee should be formed and measures adopted to alleviate the distress. It was stated at this meeting, that the operatives of Wigan were now losing 3,000*l*. per week in wages; and 1,000*l*. was raised in local subscriptions on the day of this assembly. Taking the average throughout the district, the operatives were at this time working about four days a week, and therefore earning two-thirds of their ordinary wages. It will be advisable perhaps to remark upon the use of the term 'losing,' as applied to the falling-off of wages. Throughout the whole duration of the Famine, the words 'lose' and 'loss' have been much wrested from their proper signification. A man cannot be said to lose that which he never had, and both the profits and the wages fund of future are in this category. But if the absence of profit is set down as 'loss,' it is but fair that the same term should be applied to a deficiency of wages, and inasmuch as the ledger-keeping portion of the cotton trade has generally so dealt with the public during this crisis, the impartiality of history demands for the operatives at least a verbal equality.

By January 18 the Wigan Committee had collected 2,000*l.* and divided their town into districts, each having its separate sub-committee. The mode of relief adopted was that of giving cheques of a certain value upon provision dealers, to be expended in such articles as the applicants chose. In looking over their expenditure it is curious to observe how different were the tastes of the relieved. In some, in fact in most cases, one halfpenny went for soap, but few indulged in candles; some invested largely in bread, while others thought that oatmeal was preferable. At Blackburn the distress now began to be great. The cotton manufacture of both these towns consists chiefly of heavy goods, involving a large consumption of raw material. It was therefore to be expected that a stoppage of supplies would afflict them most seriously. A sub-committee devoted itself at Blackburn to the distribution of soup, and the board of guardians largely augmented their staff of relieving officers. The number of paupers in Blackburn was now increasing at the rate of a hundred and fifty per week. Still, nearly one-third of the mills were working full time, and there were not more than 28,000 operatives in the entire district wholly thrown out of employment. Proud Preston was now added to the much distressed towns, and the numbers relieved in this borough during the third week in January were three times as numerous as those on the guardians' books in the same week of the preceding year. The guardians were perplexed how to act between the necessity of granting relief to the many applicants, and their unwillingness to class these unfortunate persons as paupers. In this dilemma they meditated the advisability of making loans, to be repaid when better times arrived,—a plan much more inviting in theory than in practice. The 'labour test' was also beginning to give trouble. The operatives found themselves praised abroad and pauperised at home. They asked for bread, and complained that they should first be given a stone to break. The boards of guardians were placed in a position of considerable embarrassment between the triple difficulties—the letter of the Poor Laws—the stereotyped forms of pauper labour—and the demands of their numerous applicants. Blackburn resolved to memoralise the Poor Law Board to suspend their order relative to the relief of able-bodied men. The Manchester Board admitted a deputation of the District Provident Society to a discussion, without seeming very anxious for their assistance. Oldham, Bury, Rochdale, in fact every place, now began to tell its own tale of distress. In Haslingden, great suffering was experienced by many of the newly-imported population; 'furriners,' as the Lancashire-born operatives call them. In Blackburn there were 7,150 persons in the receipt of relief. The guardians of this union were relieving 5,074, at the rate of about 1*s.* 6*d.* for each person. The Poor Law Board felt it their duty to refuse permission to suspend their order as to the relief of able-bodied men, which required that their relief should be given half in money and half in kind, and that they should be set to work under the direction of the boards of guardians. This order did not prohibit the bestowal of relief in cases of sudden or urgent necessity, nor did it compel the pauperisation in the workhouse, of those to be relieved. It did not necessitate that their houses should be stripped of furniture, nor that they should be naked and homeless before they were fit subjects for relief. For twenty-one days, at all events, the discretion of the boards of guardians were entirely uncontrolled. The chief object of this order was to provide against the demoralisation of the paupers, and hence it was that such anxiety was shown to maintain its principle. The order did not prescribe the stoneyard and the oakum shed as the only labour to be set before the men. Even if the guardians found, as was the case at this time at Oldham, that it was practically impossible to enforce the 'labour test,' owing to the suddenness and extent of the distress, and to the difficulty of devising suitable works, it would still have been very injudicious on the part of the central authority to relax the law, and so to encourage a system avowedly pernicious, which necessity alone could excuse. To suspend this order upon the first pressure of distress, would have been to deprive the guardians of a very wholesome reserve of power; the carefully specified exceptions to it, together with the well-known appreciation of their difficulties by the Poor Law Board, afforded them a sufficient latitude for all the exigencies of their situation.

Had it not been for the general establishment at this time of local relief committees, there might have been occasion to record a great failure on the part of the boards of guardians. Fortunately this charitable agency came to their assistance. Early in February, Rochdale and other places followed the example of Wigan and Blackburn, as they in their turn may be supposed to have modelled their system on that of the Manchester and Salford District Provident Society, which had established a special fund for the relief of the operatives, and had already distributed food and clothing to nearly 6,000 persons. Even in these early days, migration from the cotton districts had commenced. The relieving officer of a Yorkshire parish tendered his resignation to the Huddersfield Board of Guardians, on the ground that his house and his family were in danger from the violence of the wayfarers from Lancashire to Yorkshire, consequent upon his inability to relieve the immense numbers of those who made application to him.

Meanwhile the distress was rapidly increasing, although as yet it had not exceeded that which had been experienced in previous 'hard times.' Everywhere the numbers of relieved were growing. Ashton recorded that she had 2,379 more paupers than in the corresponding week of 1861. In the middle of February a very decided stand was made in the Ashton and other unions against what was incorrectly termed the 'labour test.' The guardians were at their wits end to devise works such as should meet the complaints of the operatives, who pleaded their misfortunes and their soft fingers in bar of stone-breaking and oakum-picking. Rather than enforce an unpopular law, or perhaps to prove that they were acting in this respect ministerially, the guardians in some cases threw the responsibility upon the Poor Law Board. The operatives hated the name of the 'labour test.' Not that they were indolent and averse to work, but they had been so bepraised by those who feared that the general stoppage of the mills would be the signal for pro-Southern riots,—intended to force the Government to a violation of their righteous policy of non-intervention,—that they regarded themselves as the honorary pensioners of the nation, to whom relief was not dishonourable until it was paid for by work. To be subsisting upon the poor-rates did not seem to them to involve pauperism. But this condition, so especially degrading in a locality where the great demand for labour has made pauperism so comparatively scarce, was realized in their minds immediately they had the stone-hammer in their hands or the oakum in their fingers. Had they not received so much uneasy flattery, they might have had less objection to the requirement of labour in return for relief. It would, however, be unfair to the operatives to pass unnoticed their strong repugnance to seeking relief from the guardians. It may be safely affirmed that the severest sufferings of these years of famine have been caused by this honourable pride. This unwillingness can be compared to nothing else than the dislike which the better portion of the superior class has to the Insolvent Court, where it may be said that the Commissioners sit as guardians for the relief of the rich.

The Poor Law Board evinced their sense of the difficulties of the situation, by invariably giving their sanction to any necessary expansion of their order; all that they refused to do was to suspend their order, to abrogate it entirely. As was shown in a previous chapter, the order, or the instructional letter which accompanied it, contains ample provision for an unusual increase of pauperism. To suspend the order would have been to stultify a wise and just principle; to interpret it most liberally and with due regard to the exceptional circumstances, was all that was required. To suspend this order would have been to invite the vagrants of the whole country into Lancashire. There is a wide difference between the effect of a law frequently violated, and that of a law repealed. In one case the principle is maintained, though it may be often trodden down; in the other, the principle is abandoned and the violation is encouraged. No wise administrator of the law would punish a man for working during Sunday, if such labour was necessary to obtain sustenance for himself and his family; indeed, he might applaud such a workman, while he would on no account consent to repeal the legal obligation to respect the sacred rest of the first day of the week. So it was with the relief order and its labour requirement. The Poor Law Board could not urge the boards of guardians to violate a principle of immutable justice. They had told them that urgent and sudden necessity constituted an exception; they had told them that pauperism arising from fluctuations of trade was to be regarded as altogether exceptional, and they certainly did not assume an attitude of indignation when the guardians of the Oldham and of other unions acted contrary to these orders. Let us suppose for a moment what would have been the position of these boards, in the absence of such a central authority. They could hardly have withstood for a moment the demands, whatever they might have been, of the hungry crowds, comprising many who believed themselves to be political martyrs. As it was, they gained strength by leaning upon the Government when they wished to enforce authority, and again by decrying it, when they took a popular course in seeming opposition to its mandates,—a policy, perhaps, more convenient than justifiable. Fortunately, however, for the district, the Poor Law Board preserved inviolate the principle which subsequently received the willing allegiance of all, and without which, it may well be thought that the history of this crisis would not present so fair and honourable a record.

As the spring advanced the distress deepened. At Preston, in April, the cost of relief had risen to 500*l.* per week. At Chorley, which is not far distant, there was no better prospect. It confirms an opinion before expressed, as to the operatives' distrust of a reduction of wages, to find that here, in this month—when there was the terrible example of seven hundred operatives out of work in this small town, existing in a condition only half way between living and starving,—some of the weavers of Chorley 'struck,' on account of an intention on the part of the masters to reduce their wages. If it be conceded that the duties of the manufacturer are not limited to the simple obligation of buying in the cheapest and selling in the dearest market, then, certainly, there is little indeed to be said for any master who availed himself of the circumstances of the time to reduce wages. It by no means follows, that the continuance of production in their mills was purely an act of kindness to those they employed.

How easy it would be to point to many a mill throughout Lancashire, which has done a roaring trade throughout the Cotton Famine, spinning warp for the mixed fabrics of the Yorkshire markets, or manufacturing fine goods, into the cost of which the raw material does not enter to a greater extent than a very small percentage. These poor weavers on strike were not, however, able to hold out long, for their choice was limited to reduction or pauperism.

Blackburn now began to find that her distress more than sufficiently taxed her abilities. Of the 84 mills in Blackburn, 23 were silent and smokeless; of the total number, but 18 were working full time. In the second week in April, the guardians relieved 8,974 persons, being an increase of 350 per cent. upon the number relieved in the corresponding week of the previous year. Before the end of the month, this number had risen to 9,414. The Wigan guardians now consented to meet twice a week,—a very industrious concession. They had a number of men employed in roadmaking, and these men struck upon a reduction being made upon their daily wages from 1*s.* 6*d.* to 1*s.* 3*d.* The Strike system is a valuable and perhaps an indispensable weapon of defence and offence for the labouring class, when their work is closely concentrated; but the ridiculous uses to which their ignorance at times prompts them to turn it, suggests, on such occasions, a comparison with the policy of the hedgehog when urged to move on.

Everywhere the situation was growing worse. At Manchester, a deputation urged the guardians to extend their operations and tendered other advice, but they have never been wanting in self-reliance, and are rather jealous of what they deem interference. To the credit of the members of this board and to that of their chairman it must be said, that they have done very much to preserve the character of the official machinery of relief. If at times they have seemed too unbending, they have erred only by too strict an adherence to legal principles, and if they have not been eager to encourage temporary agencies, their excuse would be a preference for the established organisation, almost pardonable in those by whom it is composed. The Manchester Board of Guardians is distinguished by a resolute following of the letter, and a faithful adherance to the principle of the Poor Law. With less vigour and intelligence, their policy might seem narrow; as it is, they have exercised a most beneficial influence upon the general administration of relief throughout Lancashire.

But, while the cotton districts were thus drifting into the Famine, how fared the homes of the poor? The conventional idea of a famine must be laid aside by those who would understand the position of the operatives in Lancashire during these times. The term itself conjures up such sad pictures as those with which the potato famine of Ireland once made every one familiar. The scene is set with groups of fathers, mothers, and children, ragged, gaunt, and fever-stricken, foodless and fireless, starving to death. There is the miserable hovel on one hand, with the pauper graveyard on the other and more hopeful side. But no such sorrow, no such shame as this, lies at the door of the wealthiest of the English counties. Suffering there was, sad and enduring, but not such as this. Many were the sacrifices made in the homes of the poor. The pawnbrokers' stores were glutted with the heirlooms of many an honest family. Little hoards were drained to meet the exigencies of the time. Many found it the sorest trial of their lives to ask for food, and it is a happy circumstance for all to remember, as it is honourable to those of whom it is recorded, that none suffered more severely than those who had a struggle to overcome their unwillingness to subsist upon food which they had not earned. Rents were falling in arrear, and many a house which had held but one home was now occupied by three or four families, in order to economise rent, fuel, and furniture. The summer was coming, and extra clothing was sold to buy food. Those excursions, which in good times are made with such gusto and with such frequency by the operatives,—these, their most cherished pleasures, were of course abandoned. Less to be regretted was the decrease in the consumption of spirits, though by many this must have been a privation sorely felt. That this decrease actually occurred is shown by the returns of the quantity of spirits consumed in Manchester and Bolton, which was less in the city by sixteen per cent., and in the borough by twenty-nine per cent. than it had been in the corresponding season of 1861. Then it must be remembered that the operative had been accustomed to live well. He had been no stranger to animal food of the best qualities and in large quantities, and the sudden deprivation of this nourishment, the fall from a family income of thirty shillings or two pounds per week to one of about ten shillings, was very trying to his endurance. But there was no helpless starvation ; the numbers of the homeless were not so great as may be found upon any winter's night in London. There was food, though little enough, for all. A fire is not a very expensive luxury in Lancashire, and even among the houses of the poor there are but few that are not wind and water-proof. Above all, there was an intelligent confidence existing between the suffering and the governing class ; there was, it may be said, neither coercion nor duplicity on either side. Lancashire was girding herself bravely for a great struggle ; relief committees were formed or forming in every direction ; order and authority were respected as they had never been before by idle hands and hungry stomachs. Few were the voices raised for an armed interference in America, which though it might have curtailed the profits of many of the rich, would certainly have given work and food to many of the poor. Grandiloquent as the words may seem, the utterance of the 'Manchester Examiner' at this time is worthy of record, though a deduction from the terms of this demand must be made, if only for the holders of goods who had no reason to wish for an increased supply of cotton. 'Let this be said in favour of the political morality of Lancashire, that at a period of great and increasing gloom, when factious counsellors and mischevious politicians told us that war was our only escape from ruin, and urged upon us an act of intervention which would be carried out with the consent and applause of the whole country, we refuse to buy prosperity at the cost of a public wrong, and were willing to suffer rather than to connive at the violation of a great principle.'

The leaders of the operative class are in general strongly favourable to the Northern policy, firm in their hatred of slavery, and firm in their faith in democracy. There can be no doubt that by the majority of this class it was thought that intervention would bring relief, nor that they restrained themselves from agitating in favour of this policy. And it would be unjust to the operatives to question the nobility of their attitude because it had been stated by Mr. Bright at Birmingham in February, that 'if cotton be now one shilling per lb., it could not be got through war at less than five;' for certainly they did not enter into the recondite reasoning by which this proposition was supported, and besides, the cost, according to the estimate of Mr. Bright, must have been borne by the whole country.

But now a demand for help was made to the nation, and England sympathising with Lancashire, anxious that nothing should occur to menace the strict neutrality which she desired to observe towards America, lent a ready ear to the tales of distress from the cotton districts. Early, if not first among the appeals which moved the generous public, were some simple letters, signed, 'A Lancashire Lad.' Mr. Whittaker, the writer of these letters, is now known to many, and by very many more are his services gratefully appreciated. There was a reality, a tender and original sympathy in his appeals, which plainly told that his *nom de plume* was his truest name. The text of his first letter to the 'Times,' was the pathetic entreaty addressed to himself by a factory girl, 'Con yo help us a bit?' How clearly these few words express the struggle between independence and want! A sermon, and not a dull one, might be preached from them. They touched many a heart, they rang sadly in many an ear to which the Lancashire dialect was strange. They opened many a purse, and together with other appeals which now became numerous, caused a stream of 'help' to flow northwards,—a stream which has not since ceased its kindly current.

Early in this year the cotton trade exhibited a novel feature in the export of the raw material to the United States. By the second week in January upwards of 20,000 bales of cotton had been shipped for New York and Boston, a proceeding which at one time would have seemed very like carrying coals to Newcastle. But as the Americans could afford to give 18*d*. per lb. for the cotton which was worth no more than 1*s*. in Manchester, it naturally found its way across the Atlantic. Owing to the plentiful stocks still in hand, and the uncertainty which attended the progress of the American war, there was not yet sufficient demand for the raw material to cause any considerable rise in its value, although greater firmness had been given to the markets by the release of the Southern Commissioners, and the consequent termination of the 'Trent' difficulty. Manchester evinced her knowledge of one of the roads to increased consumption, by holding a meeting to consider the best means of obtaining the removal of the protective duties levied on the importation of cotton goods and yarns into India. These had already been reduced from ten to five per cent. As might be expected, there were many who were warmly eloquent in favour of relief to those large stores of cotton manufactures which were laid up in Bombay, Madras, and Calcutta, and other Indian emporiums. It must be admitted that they had a good case, and that the time for demanding a reform was not ill-chosen. But Sir Charles Wood maintained his tariff, pleading the necessities of the Indian exchequer.

In April 1862, the consumption of cotton was not greater than 25,000 bales per week, about one-half of what it had been in 1860, and the imports had shown a very considerable falling off. During the past six months the quantity received from America had been only 11,500 bales, while in the corresponding period of the preceding year the arrivals from America amounted to 1,500,000 bales, more than one hundred times the quantity which was now received. But a glance at the state of the yarn and goods market at this time, will show that there could be no very great demand for the raw material until the stock of goods was further lightened. Middling Orleans was quoted on the last day of April at 13½*d.* per lb., which was also the average price of 40's mule yarn during that month; so that the spinning of this description of cotton into this quality of yarn, involved the loss of all the waste, and all the cost of the operation. But what a proof it is of the glutted condition of the goods markets, that there had been no rise in price of yarns during the past six months! During these six months production had been very small compared with that of former years; many mills had stopped altogether, and a large majority were running short time. There was a certain prospect, however, or whenever the American war might terminate, of a greatly diminished supply of cotton as compared with that of 1860. But with all these stimulants, and even with a rise in the price of

Middling Orleans, from $11\frac{5}{8}d.$ in November to $13\frac{1}{2}d.$ in April, the quotations for yarn remained obstinately the same. Of course, the rise in the price of goods must come; every holder knew that. Those who were strong enough to carry on until consumption should sufficiently reduce the stocks which the over-production of 1859-61 had accumulated, might reckon on great gains. And they had not long to wait. In four months from this time the price of goods had risen in value by as much as 75 per cent.

There can be no doubt that the Indian cotton, which was now received in large quantities, was of very inferior quality. The native planters had no great faith in the durability of the European market. They had heard of the stoppage of the American supplies, they experienced all the temptation of high prices, and believed that this was but a transient gleam of prosperity, of which they must hasten to take advantage. And consequently most of the cotton was picked before it was ripe, was carelessly ginned, often fradulently weighted, and very generally it was badly packed. In England it found purchasers, as everything that pretended to be raw cotton would have done since the outbreak of the American war. When taken for consumption, it turned out dirty and knotty, full of seeds and leaves. It was short in staple, and its fibres were harsh and brittle. It damaged the machinery, especially the nice adjustment of the carding engines, and so got a bad name among both operatives and masters. To the spinner, who is paid by the weight of spun yarn, it was a sore trial, as his spindles were constantly idle from the breakage of the threads, and their speed had to be lessened in some cases by as much as a thousand revolutions per minute.

The month of May 1862, is for several causes remarkable in the history of the Cotton Famine. It witnessed the foundation of those two great charitable agencies, which will be remembered so long as the recollection of this Famine shall endure. The historian of this crisis should at this point be conscious of the feelings of a dramatist about to introduce two leading characters to his stage. In this history, at least, it would seem that unusual honours ought to usher in the names of the Central Relief Committee of Manchester and the Mansion House Committee of London; and believing that these public bodies, their resources and their performances, are more honourable to our country than the memory of a hotly-contested and well-won battle, we shall not be likely to disrespect them. But nothing in nature, in art, or in society, nothing however wise and great and good it may become, is born full-blown and full-grown. So it was with these committees; they had their origin, their infancy, and their prime. It will hardly be possible to increase the public gratitude to them for the manner in which they have discharged their trust,—it would be as difficult to exalt as it would be impossible to tarnish their reputation; but it can scarcely fail to be interesting to trace their origin.

Precedence must be given to the Mansion House Committee. It is not necessary to inquire whether the existence of this committee stimulated Manchester to the production of the Central Relief Committee, but certainly the London Committee was collecting and disbursing large funds before the local committee was in being. During the past few years the Mansion House has been a favourite receptacle of public subscriptions. It was to the Lord Mayor that the sympathetic contributions of their fellow-subjects flowed in aid of the sufferers from the Indian Mutiny. The Albert Memorial Fund was even at this time in his keeping, and therefore, at the moment when the distress in Lancashire first assumed the appearance of a national calamity, it was not unnatural that a proposal should be made to centralise a relief fund at the Mansion House.

Among the many who have deserved honour in the circumstances which have arisen from the cotton dearth, must be mentioned the originator of the Mansion House Committee, Mr. William Cotton. With an early proffer of money and personal services, he first introduced the subject to the notice of Lord Mayor Cubitt. Subsequently, Mr. Cotton and two or three gentlemen, who have also served as members of this committee, addressed the Lord Mayor upon the bench of the Mansion House Police Court, with reference to the desirability of collecting funds for the relief of the distress in the cotton districts. This proceeding was arranged between them and the Lord Mayor, in order to give publicity to the proposal, and to test the public willingness to make subscriptions. Towards the end of April, the Lord Mayor announced that he had received a 'host of letters' upon the subject, and made the more agreeable statement that money was coming in fast. On May 16 he informed the public, that a meeting had been held of the gentlemen who had interested themselves in the establishment of this fund, and that it had been resolved to send 1,500*l.* to the distressed districts. Of this sum, 500*l.* was sent to Preston, with an equal sum to Blackburn, and 250*l.* was forwarded to Wigan, with an equal sum to Stockport. This was the first instalment of the relief given by 'The Lancashire and Cheshire Operatives Relief Fund,' which is the authorised denomination of the fund at the disposal of the Mansion House Committee. Since then it has transmitted nearly half a million sterling in furtherance of its most praiseworthy objects. The Mansion House Committee has always been essentially executive, at all events its deliberations have not transpired, and its limitation to five or six working members has given great directness and simplicity to its action. Latterly the Central Executive Committee has acted to some extent for both; for it cannot be doubted that the publication of the reports and debates of the Manchester Committee has been of material assistance in directing the councils of the London Committee. Early in June, the Mansion House Committee passed by 'accumulation' from a provisional to an established committee; nominated a secretary, and proceeded to organise that system of grants which, to the great benefit of the cotton districts, has continued up to the present time. The labours of this committee were not interrupted by the retirement of Mr. Cubitt from his two years' tenancy of the Mansion House. He was succeeded in the duties of chairman by Lord Mayor Rose.

Many reasons contributed to strengthen the hesitation of Manchester to form a committee for the relief of distress. In the first place, there was the Manchester and Salford District Provident Society already in existence—an organisation which possessed every qualification for the work that experience and reputation could confer. In the next place, the distress in Manchester was not very severe, and many thought that the crisis might be passed over without calling for any special measures of relief. The trade of Manchester is continually becoming more and more varied, in consequence of its position as the metropolis of the district. Warehouses are driving the mills into the out-townships where land is less costly, where local rates are less oppressive, and where the factories can be surrounded by the cottages of the cotton-workers. Of the cotton factories in Manchester, the majority produce 'high counts' of yarn or fine fabrics, which involve but a comparatively small consumption of the raw material, and in which the produce of Egypt now forms a very satisfactory substitute for the unattainable Sea Island cotton. Manchester with her varied industry and large charitable resources, was very indisposed to believe that famine was at her gates. But at length it was seen, that excellent as was the constitution of the District Provident Society, it was not fitted to act as a central organisation for the relief of the whole, and more than the whole, county. The accounts of the distress now prevailing in Blackburn, Preston, Wigan, Stockport, and other places, evinced unmistakably the necessity for a concentrated effort, which should unite and strengthen the local authorities in their efforts to mitigate the misfortunes of the poor. Accordingly, a conference was summoned by the mayor of Manchester, and at this meeting, which was held on April 29, a Central Relief Committee was appointed. This committee was destined to undergo many changes. It was subsequently reconstructed more than once; it received aristocratic additions which largely increased its influence and dignity, but in one respect it stands unaltered, for the honorary secretary who was first appointed still continues his beneficial labours. It is rarely indeed that honorary duties of such magnitude and importance as those which his position have imposed upon Mr. Maclure, have been so well performed. Zealous and energetic, possessed of many natural advantages, he has never been sparing of his services, though always most conservative of the fund of which he was one of the appointed guardians. The committee having been appointed, the conference adjourned for a week, when a treasurer was nominated. On June 20, the Central Relief Committee was formally established by resolution, and consisted of the mayors and ex-mayors of the principal towns of the cotton district, together with a number of gentlemen, chiefly known in connection with the commercial interests of Manchester. Before the end of this month, the committee was in full working order, and had passed the following resolution, copies of which were sent to the lord-lieutenants of counties, the mayors of cities and boroughs, and other officials throughout the kingdom:—'That the existing distress of the work-people connnected with the cotton trade, in Lancashire, Cheshire, Yorkshire, and Derbyshire, and the well-founded expectation of its increasing in intensity as the winter approaches, warrants the committee in communicating to the various counties, cities, and towns of the country, that it is prepared to receive any sums that may be subscribed for the object in view, and will give its best attention to the proper and judicious distribution thereof.'

CHAPTER V.

MAY—JUNE 1862.

WHILE these charitable agencies were being organised, and were commencing their benevolent operations, the Government was not unmindful of its responsibility, and was fully informed of the position of affairs through the agency of the Poor Law Board, who from their official connection with the boards of guardians throughout the kingdom, are in possession of a source of general information superior to that pertaining to any other department of state. It is worth the consideration of the Legislature whether this important organisation, which is at once so firmly localised by the parochial system, commanding every corner of the realm, and which is yet so easily and so harmlessly centralised in the Poor Law Board—it is well worthy of deliberation, whether this may not be made of further service in the collection of much statistical information of the highest value. Through no other official medium could agricultural statistics be collected with equal facility. By this means, however, the Government was made acquainted with the condition of the manufacturing districts, and it was probably owing to the importance which the boards of guardians had acquired—from the fact that upon them first devolve the duty of meeting the distress—that the parliamentary representatives of Lancashire were induced to seek an interview with Mr. Villiers, early in the month of May, in order to have a conference with him upon the condition of the county.

It was difficult at the time, and perhaps it would be impossible now to define the precise object which led Colonel Wilson Patten and his colleagues in the representation of Lancashire, to the Poor Law Board. It was suggested that they were anxious to discover if the

Government intended to give assistance from the national exchequer, and it was hinted that they would not be indisposed to encourage such a disposition. But considering that not a voice had been raised in favour of a national grant, and that on the contrary, up to this time, the public and the press of Lancashire had ostentatiously disclaimed any such assistance, there is no reason to suppose that such was their object. What passed in the tea-room of the House of Commons—which was their first meeting-place—did not transpire. But it may well be thought, that they acted simply from a feeling of duty towards their constituents in a great crisis,—that they felt it incumbent upon them to do something, and as they were the immediately connecting link between the district and the Government, it was not unnatural that their concern should find expression in Whitehall. Moreover, the questions of outdoor relief and the 'labour test,' were at this moment questions of the day in Lancashire, and these gentlemen felt it their duty to inquire whether it was possible so to combine the principles of the Poor Law with the growing exigencies of the situation, that their constituencies should not be disturbed by contentions between the boards of guardians and those to whom they administered relief.

If it were not that the Poor Law is so unpopular a study, and necessarily so diverse in its operation, it would seem strange that these legislators—the representatives of a county, certainly not the most benighted in the kingdom—should learn, from a minister with whom many of them had long been personally acquainted, much that was new to them in a simple statement of the law, as it stood affected towards the applicants for relief in Lancashire. They came to complain of an enforcement of the 'labour test,' unwittingly adopting an opprobrious term wholly unknown to the law. It was news to these gentlemen to be told by Mr. Villiers that the law established no 'test,' but only made the requirement that the applicant 'should be set to work so long as he continued to receive relief.' These are but a paraphrase of the very words of the Act of Elizabeth. And they are simply another reading of those still more ancient words, 'he that will not work neither shall he eat.' They were left to infer that the description of work is entirely at the discretion of the guardians. The stone-hammer is of rustic origin, and does not, like the lictors' fasces, of necessity accompany the law. They were informed that the guardians were allowed absolute discretion in relieving all classes of persons except able-bodied men; and that the guardians might extend their staff of relieving officers, or increase the poor-rates with no other limit than that of the ability of the ratepayers.

The deputation withdrew, satisfied with Mr. Villiers' explanation, and with his advice that they should 'leave the matter at present in the hands of the guardians, who were performing their duties very efficiently.' This official exposition of the Poor Law had unquestionably a good effect in quieting the fears of those who had hastily formed the opinion that the Poor Law would be found inoperative in Lancashire. But while Mr. Villiers gave this pacific advice, it is very evident from the circumstances which immediately followed this conference, that he was convinced of the necessity of being more closely connected with the district. It may be that in the various constructions which were put upon the Poor Law, he saw the need of having some official expounder of its true principles and objects. The distress was, however, becoming too wide and too serious for the Government to neglect the duty of having a special representation in the locality. A Royal Commission had been suggested, but it is certainly not to be regretted that the idea was abandoned. This very dignified deliberative machine demands the sacrifice of time as a necessary homage to its importance, and moreover, it possesses the disadvantage, which would have been specially felt in Lancashire, that—as becomes its rank—it does its work at second hand. Distress might have been carried into the august precinct of its presence, but could scarcely anticipate the honour of inspection with its official eyes.

It was well that the Government chose a less cumbrous mode of representation. It may be that the national library is by a whole blue book the poorer, but surely the the inch or two of shelf is not the only gain by the absence of this volume. In preferring to be represented by an individual, there was at once the means provided of obtaining confidential information, of imparting advice, and of strengthening the hands of the various local authorities. An individual could, as it were, incorporate himself with these public bodies, while the members of a Royal Commission must have met these local authorities, either in disliked superiority, or in unprofitable rivalry. It was no secret in official circles, that much inquiry had been made as to who should be sent upon this arduous mission. The jealous eye with which Lancashire has always regarded any interference from Whitehall was well known. It was not one of those posts which are sought of many, but one of those which are essentially of that nature that demand the right man. Soon it was whispered that a gentleman of high standing and long experience at the Poor Law Board, had been summoned more than once to attend the councils of the Cabinet, when it was known that the condition of Lancashire formed one of the subjects of deliberation. And upon May 12, Lord Granville announced to the House of Lords, that Mr. H. B. Farnall, 'who for five or six years had been previously engaged in the district,' was specially commissioned for this service.

Mr. Farnall's instructions, which were dated May 12, appointed him a 'Special Commissioner of the Government,' and directed him 'to make inquiry into the operation of the Poor Laws, and the orders of the Poor Law Board at the present time, on the condition and habits of those workpeople who, from a great diminution in the demand for labour in the cotton districts of the counties of Lancaster, York, and Chester, have suddenly and unavoidably fallen into temporary distress.' He was requested to embrace every opportunity of personally communicating with all authorities and special organisations administering relief and succour to the poor; he was to interpret and define the true spirit and breadth of the Poor Law; to create and sustain harmony; to promote liberal and judicious action; to examine into the manner in which the poor were relieved; to find out what labour was required of them, and to suggest the most suitable forms of employment. Finally, he was desired by Mr. Villiers to keep a daily journal of his proceedings, and to give a weekly report of the progress of his labours.

It was not long before Mr. Farnall made his first appearance in public in the North. On May 22, ten days after the receipt of these rather extensive instructions, he had been already some days engaged collecting information in Preston, with reference to the general condition of that town. Preston had the honour of the first visit from the Special Commissioner on account of her unfortunate pre-eminence in the numbers of her distressed population. Mr. Farnall thoroughly justified the selection of the Government by his first address, which was made to the Preston Board of Guardians, and was characterised by a very evident appreciation of the real difficulties of his position, by nice tact and winning courtesy. It is no small praise to say, that of all the subsequent addresses he delivered, this first was by far the best, in arrangement, in style, in balance of argument, and in exposition of facts.

By following Mr. Farnall during his first circuit, a fair and impartial view of the condition and prospects of the chief towns of the cotton district will be obtained. The population of the Preston Union, in May 1861, was 110,488, and of this number 11,665, or 10·5 per cent., were now in the receipt of parochial relief. The town of Preston contained 81,058 of this population; but its rate of pauperism was less than that of the union, being only 6,615, or 8·2 per cent. The gross estimated rental of Preston township was 225,019*l.*, and the net rateable value 217,459*l.*, showing the very moderate difference of 7·8 per cent. Mr. Farnall found that the millowners and large occupiers paid one-fifth of the rates, and that only one mill hand in every 80 was directly rated to the relief of the poor. At the date of his inquiry, he learnt that there were close upon 11,000 operatives out of work, and, allowing to each one dependent, he estimated that this number would represent a destitute population of 22,000. To meet this unprecedented distress, local subscriptions had been raised to the amount of 7,000*l.* The withdrawals from the local savings-banks had exceeded the average amount by 17,500*l.* The trade societies had paid out an extraordinary sum of 700*l.*, so that the total amount which had been available in aid of the rates was about 25,000*l.* But the weekly loss in wages of these 22,000 persons cannot be taken at less than 11,000*l.*

In ordinary years the poor-rates in Preston amounted to 2*s.* 2*d.* in the pound, and produced 20,221*l.* The expenditure of the guardians, 'in and about relief,' had been, in 1861, 8,500*l.*; but at Lady-day, 1862, this had risen to 15,183*l.* It was concluded that a rate of 3*s.* in the pound, with the aid of the relief fund, would enable them to meet all claims until December. The Relief Committee was distributing 2,400 quarts of soup, and 1,500 loaves daily; they had the gratuitous assistance of 120 visitors, whose charitable services were systematically directed by the division of the township into districts.

Leaving Preston with the prospect of a 3*s.* rate, with a relief fund of 7,000*l.* (of which about one-half was already expended), and with 18,200*l.* of hard-earned savings already gone, the Special Commissioner took his way to Blackburn, which was the next town he visited. Here he found that the population of the union was 119,735, which had increased during the past ten years at the galloping rate of 32 per cent., exceeding the general rate of increase throughout the United Kingdom by 20 per cent. The rateable value of the property in the township of Blackburn was stated by Mr. Farnall to be 144,418*l.*, showing an increase of 44 per cent. in the decade from 1852 to 1862. The prosperity of this town was manifested by the fact that its normal rate of pauperism was but 3 per cent. upon the population, while that for the whole union was still less, being only 2·3 per cent. At the time of Mr. Farnall's visit the rate of pauperism in the town of Blackburn had risen to 7 per cent., and there were 8,429 'hands' out of work, who, upon the same calculation as that made in Preston, represented a population dependent upon relief of one kind or another amounting to about 17,000. The operative class in Blackburn numbered in all 27,000, and of these about one-third were working full time, one-third working short time, while the remainder were unemployed. At this time, Blackburn had raised by local subscriptions 5,235*l.*, and the Relief Committee had a balance in hand of 2,242*l.* The savings-bank funds had been drained of 10,000*l.* beyond the amount usually abstracted, and the trade societies had done much to help their impoverished members. In ordinary times, the wants of the poor of Blackburn had been met by yearly rates, equalling 2*s.* 4*d.*

in the pound. The borough rate was included in this amount. Ordinarily the sum expended for the relief of the poor during the whole year was about 3,800*l.*; but for the half-year ending Lady-day, 1862, this expenditure had amounted to 4,900*l.* The rate of relief given by the Blackburn guardians was in excess of the average throughout the district. To single able-bodied men they gave 3*s.* per week, requiring three days' work; to those who had a wife and two children, 8*s.* 6*d.* a week, with perhaps a pair of clogs, if required; and to larger families upon the same scale. It was considered that an additional rate of 3*s.* in the pound would meet the extraordinary demands of 1862.

Wigan was the next place to which Mr. Farnall bent his steps. This town has a very large colliery as well as cotton population. Between 1851 and 1861 its population had increased 18 per cent., and its wealth, as evidenced by its rateable value, 36 per cent. The expenditure of Wigan for the relief of the poor had been 3,316*l.* for the year ending Lady-day 1861, and at the same period in 1862 it had not risen by so much as a hundred pounds, being only 3,403*l.* The present rate of pauperism was 5 per cent. upon the population, and, counting each unemployed 'hand' as two persons, there were 13,600 individuals dependent on relief. Besides this number, there were 400 handloom weavers thrown out of work, and upwards of 3,000 operatives working short time. The out-payments from the savings-banks showed an extraordinary amount of 6,000*l.*, and 4,275*l.* had been received in charitable contributions. The treasurer of the Wigan Union had at this time 6,642*l.* in hand, and it was not thought that any special rate would be needed until September, when it was believed that a 2*s.* rate would supply all requisite assistance.

From Wigan Mr. Farnall went to Ashton-under-Lyne, a union especially devoted to the cotton manufacture, and hitherto conspicuous for its prosperity. In June 1861 the rate of pauperism in this union was 1·3 per cent., being considerably less than that of the model and connubial parish of St. George's, Hanover Square. It contained a population of 134,761 persons, and its total rateable value was 321,502*l.* The expenditure of this union for the year ending Lady-day 1861 had been no more than 1*s.* 0¾*d.* in the pound. In June 1862, the parish of Ashton-under-Lyne contained 66,806 inhabitants, the number of whom had increased very rapidly since the year 1851. In the same ten years the rateable value of this parish had increased 17·5 per cent., and now stood at 154,058*l.* The relief given to the poor of this parish during the half-year ending Lady-day 1861 did not amount to 2,000*l.* But, in June 1862, the rate of pauperism had risen to 6 per cent. of the population, and the cost of relief was about doubled. It was then considered that future requirements would not rise above this rate of demand. Here, as in other towns, the position of the operatives was one of great distress. In Ashton, their weekly loss of wages amounted to 2,120*l.*, and, during the past six months, their savings-bank funds had been drawn upon unusually to the extent of 14,773*l.* But only one in a hundred of the operatives of Ashton were contributors to the rates, so that the amount collected was not to a great extent affected by their poverty. There was but one mill in Ashton now working full time, and there were 4,614 persons directly dependent on public relief. Subscriptions amounting to about 1,000*l.* had been raised in the parish, and expended under the auspices of a relief committee, but the committee had now broken up, and a donation of 100*l.*, which had been received from the Lord Mayor, was consequently in the hands of the chief relieving officer, who made a public communication to Mr. Farnall concerning the 'admirable manner' in which 'the able-bodied men deported themselves,' and their willingness to accept the task of work provided by the guardians.

At Stockport the Special Commissioner found the customary rate of pauperism throughout the union to be as low as 1·5 per cent. upon the population, the expenditure for relief during the year ending Lady-day 1861 being covered by a rate of 7¼*d.* in the pound upon a value of 248,199*l.* A rate of 1*s.* 9¼*d.* in the pound sufficed for the entire expenditure of this union during this year. At the date of Mr. Farnall's visit in June 1862, the rate of pauperism had increased to 6 per cent. In the township of Stockport there were 1,826 persons chargeable as paupers, out of a population amounting to 30,745. The rateable value of the property within the township was

61,833*l.*, of which amount the factories were assessed at 11,945*l.* It was estimated that a special rate of 2*s.* 3*d.* in the pound would carry the guardians through the difficulties of the year. Hitherto the distress in Stockport had been partially met by the withdrawal of 9,321*l.* from the savings-banks above the usual amount. The loss upon the new rate was estimated at 35 per cent., on account of the fact that the Small Tenements Act is not adopted in this borough.

Five days after he had addressed the Stockport Guardians, Mr. Farnall met those of the Oldham Union. The population of this union had increased between 1851 and 1861 by 28 per cent., and the rate of pauperism was in 1861 as low as at Stockport, being only 1·5 per cent. In June 1862 this rate had risen to 2·8 per cent. Even now it was lower than the average rate of pauperism throughout England in times of general prosperity. In the previous year the expenditure of this union 'in and about relief' had been 9¾*d.* in the pound; the total amount levied being 1*s.* 8½*d.* once collected during the year. In the township of Oldham the population had increased at the rate of 37 per cent. in the space of the last ten years, while its rateable value had risen within the same period from 106,225*l.* to 163,446*l.*, being nearly 54 per cent. Of this amount the mill and colliery proprietors were assessed at 71,292*l.* As in Stockport, the number of assessments in this borough is very large, owing to the fact that the provisions of the Small Tenements Act are not adopted. In Oldham there were in 1862 as many as 16,000 assessments in the township only, of which 14,000 were upon the owners and occupiers of small tenements. In the previous year the total amount of poor-rate levied in the township of Oldham had been but 1*s.* 2¾*d.* in the pound, and it was estimated that an additional rate of 9¾*d.* would be all that would be required to meet the extra expenditure of the current half-year.

It may be advisable to refer to these statements again, when we have advanced sufficiently far to be enabled to see by how much the funds, which were now estimated as sufficient to meet the distress, fell short of the amount actually required. But the leading features of these several statements are so similar, and bear such general application to the condition of the whole district, that it would be an error to pass them over without immediate notice. It will be seen that these towns had increased in population at a very unusual rate—not less than 25 per cent, during a period of ten years — while their wealth had augmented still more rapidly. It will be observed, also, that in a purely manufacturing community, the factory proprietors and occupiers are chargeable with about one-fourth of the poor-rates. Nor will it fail to attract attention, that the average amount of poor-rates levied upon the property of these unions throughout the year, was usually less than 2*s.* in the pound. Lastly, coming down to the actual times of the Famine, in June 1862, it will be seen that in no case did the extraordinary provision which was thought necessary exceed the amount of 3*s.* in the pound. In Wigan and in Oldham it was considered that an extra rate of 9¾*d.* would enable the guardians to tide over the difficulty. Of the unusual amount of out-payments from the savings-banks in these towns, the larger sums belonged to the overlookers, to the higher classes of the operatives, and to the small shopkeepers; for the majority of the operatives are not to be found among the investors in savings-banks. These amounts—the highest of which, 17,500*l.*, was withdrawn in Preston, —were taken out in such driblets, that the details of the process alone would have told the sad cause of their abstraction. In good times these banks receive small and pay out in larger sums; for it is the purchase of furniture, the apprenticing of a son, or the dowering of a daughter, which then withdraws the little hoard. But it is some proof of the stubborn and virtuous resistance which many of the operative class opposed to the poverty which threatened them, that up to this time they owed more to themselves than to others; for it will be remembered that these sums far exceed the excessive expenditure which had yet been made from the poor-rates; and more than this, that their amount was greater than that of the extraordinary funds raised by the guardians, and that of the local subscriptions added together.

But these savings once gone were gone for ever, leaving behind them, as a rankling sorrow, the incomplete purpose of many an honest home. Money is never so hard to part with as when it is the savings of a long period. How many of these investors had comforted themselves with the assurance that here was laid up a provision for their old age, sufficient to keep them from descending to the pauper rank, a fate which the operative class generally regards with a repugnance somewhat morbid! Almost invariably they speak of the workhouse as the 'Bastille,' and to be taunted as a 'pauper' would be by many regarded as the most opprobrious of epithets. Indeed, this feeling is too strong to permit any concealment of its origin, which is undoubtedly in the great demand for labour that has existed with very rare intervals, and in the prevailing high rate of wages, together with the fact that a large majority of the pauper class are Irish, for whom the native population of Lancashire have no very great esteem.

In the course of his addresses Mr. Farnall gave an exposition of the Poor Law as affecting the prevailing distress, which, as it exactly accorded with the popular feeling upon the subject, was generally received with great satisfaction. But it was said by some, whose position gave weight to their opinions, that although this tempering of the Poor Law with mercy and humanity was very delightful, yet that it was not the law. Just as the French General exclaimed at Balaclava, when the 'six hundred' rode 'into the jaws of death': 'C'est magnifique, mais ce n'est pas la guerre.' But a closer comparison of what was advanced by the Special Commissioner with the law actually in force, will however convince them that the error existed in their own interpretation of the law. It has been often said that it is as well to hang a dog as to give him a bad name; but in view of recent circumstances, it cannot but be regarded as fortunate that it has been easier to give the Poor Law a bad name than to terminate its existence. It must be plainly stated that many who believed themselves possessed of an intimate knowledge of the Poor Law had in truth acquired their opinions at second-hand from its adversaries, or from those who had but a very superficial knowledge of the subject. This is by no means an unusual occurrence. The Whig of to-day, who rejoices in the highly respectable designation, ignores the fact that it was bestowed as a term of reproach and has its derivation in sour milk. It is the same with the Tory.

So it was the same with many who believed that the Poor Law was revolutionised for the special purpose of meeting Lancashire distress. They had been told that the iron rule of this law demanded that the applicant for relief should dispose of all that he had—that, with no allowance for exceptional circumstances, he and his family must be stripped of house, home, furniture, everything but the clothes in which they stood—before he could become a fit object for relief, and they believed it. They had been told the law required that every able-bodied man who applied for relief should undergo the ordeal of a 'labour test,' which was supposed to demonstrate his poverty in an unmistakable manner; and they believed that this regulation applied without exception to every class in the community.

It had been so often said of the Poor Law, that it forced a poor man under any circumstances to sell his furniture and break up his home, that this view of it actually obtained general credence. The marvel is that if the public thus regarded it, they did not rise and overturn the man-crushing machine of this Juggernaut. Mr. Farnall stated, before he had been ten minutes addressing the Preston guardians, that in the course of twenty-seven years' experience as an *ex officio* Guardian and a Poor Law Inspector, he had never known a single instance in which a board of guardians had called upon a poor person to sell his or her furniture before relief could be afforded. The Poor Law does not concern itself with furniture. Any applicant, unpossessed of real or personal property, and not in receipt of, or at work for, wages, is a fit subject for relief, although he may have a house furnished with the requirements of life. It is true that in the greater part of England he can only obtain relief, unless under certain exceptions, in the workhouse; but this regulation does not apply to those districts where the working class is liable to be suddenly thrown out of employment by the fluctuations of trade. Yet even in the case of such persons, so carefully does the law avoid any invasion of the 'Englishman's house,' that the pauper might, if he pleased, leave his furniture when he went into the workhouse, and, provided his rent was paid, there need be no disturbance of it until he returned to his home upon the approach of better times. It would be absurd to argue that the workhouse, or indeed that the life of a pauper is in any respect elysian; all that can be desired is, that during the period of an able-bodied man's dependence as a pauper, he should not be deprived of any natural rights which do not tend unfairly to increase the cost of his support—that his health should be preserved, and that his position should not be made enviable to the humblest of those who are getting an independent livelihood.

In the manufacturing districts, however, the Poor Law has always had a special operation. Here again the law has nothing whatever to do with furniture, but here it permits relief, with no limitation as to the amount, to be given at the homes of the able-bodied poor, provided they are necessitous applicants, and are willing to work as an acknowledgment and in consideration of the relief afforded. Mr. Farnall's speech at Preston, noteworthy as it was thought to be at the time on account of its humanity, was in truth not less so for its strict legality. He hoped that the guardians, in fixing the scale of their allowance, would not take into consideration the trifling addition which the applicants might be receiving by way of charitable relief. Had not this point been clearly understood, it might have led to a general repulse of the charitable feeling which was now beginning to heap up such stores of relief for the distress of this district. The subscribers to charitable funds would have been directly contributing to the relief of the ratepayers and not to that of the operatives. It was therefore necessary to obtain an assurance upon this point from the guardians.

Then as to the 'labour test,' which would be much more properly termed the labour 'requirement,' it was opposed by many of the operatives on the ground that their poverty and the causes of it were sufficiently patent, and needed no 'test.' This was little less than a ridiculous perversion of the intention of the requirement, which is simply that no able-bodied man shall be maintained in idleness at the public charge. In his addresses to the various boards of guardians, Mr. Farnall laboured to impress upon them that in selecting work they should take into consideration the previous occupation and mode of life of the cotton operatives; that in every possible way they should avoid classing or ganging them with the hereditary paupers, who are the inevitable unit of our social scale. It cannot but be thought that the guardians showed in this respect some paucity of invention at the commencement of the distress. It was a happy idea that subsequently invented the school, wherein mental was substituted for muscular labour, and the wholesome rules and regulations of the Poor Law Board maintained. But this had not yet come to light. There are many other useful employments for such men beside the common expedients of oakum-picking and stone-breaking, both of which are peculiarly unfitted to the operative suddenly shut out from the cotton-factory. His hands are singularly soft, which is desirable to secure the requisite delicacy of touch, and is maintained by working indoors in a high temperature, and by continual contact with oil and cotton-wool. The stone-hammer blistered his hands immediately, and the oakum galled his fingers. Mr. Farnall suggested the selection of more suitable labour. His tone was throughout encouraging; and perhaps to this fact is to be attributed the very great success of these addresses. He reminded the boards of guardians of the large wealth of many of their neighbours, some of whom had risen to opulence from the position of those whom they were now called upon to relieve, and urged the duty of subscription to the lists of charity, without offending those who had not fulfilled this obligation. The good results of his official tour were seen in the fact that the agitation which had hitherto rendered it difficult for these boards to perform their functions became subsequently less violent. The position was arduous, and the part not easy to play. It is very rarely indeed that a public servant stands in a position of equal isolation and responsibility. How often since this time have surprise and congratulation been expressed that these dark days should have been passed so peaceably! How many expected that the autumn of 1862 would be passed amid scenes of continuous riot, and perhaps of frequent bloodshed! That a far happier state of things prevailed is due to no single individual, but is rather the undivided honour of Lancashire and of England. Yet it may be safely affirmed that no one contributed a larger personal share of duty at this critical period than Mr. Farnall, who had to a great extent succeeded in making the law popular without lessening its authority, and who, in the face of a critical and distressed population—whose reputation for disorder was far worse than they deserved—upheld with dignified moderation and successful amiability the great trust with which he was charged by the responsible Minister, who watched with anxious solicitude the development of this most important epoch in the administration of the Poor Laws.

CHAPTER VI.

JUNE—JULY 1862.

During the first half of the year 1862 the condition of the operatives had been passing from bad to worse. The pawnshops were crammed with their furniture and clothing; their funds in benefit societies, in trade unions, and in savings-banks had been heavily drawn upon to support their necessities; and the prospect of the coming winter was not illumined by a single ray of hope. No one supposed that a revival of trade during the latter six months of the year was possible, but all had a firm faith in the charitable agencies which had been established for their relief, and the resources of these were every day increasing by the continuous influx of donations. There was terrible suffering among the operative class, and this was experienced most sorely by those who could not overcome their repugnance to place themselves among the applicants for relief. This distress was greatly alleviated as the local committees got to work, for these bodies could seek out such as needed their assistance in a manner which was not open to the boards of guardians, whose function it is to give relief only to those who apply for it. As a rule, the operatives greatly preferred to be the pensioners of the committees rather than of the guardians; and many, who would have borne even greater hunger and hardship sooner than descend to the low level of pauperism, were anxious to partake of the bounty of the Mansion House Committee. One reason which has induced many Lancashire men to advocate throughout the separate and independent existence of this committee, was that its grants had a peculiarly agreeable character in the estimation of the recipients. By many of the operatives this money was especially regarded as a sort of testimonial to their good conduct under these trying circumstances, and was received as an honorarium due to their sufferings and forbearance. Generally speaking, it might be obtained without any labour being required in return; and justice compels the avowal, that this circumstance may have had something to do with its popularity. Still it was the odious rank of pauperism which made the board-room of the guardians the unwilling resort of the distressed; for as the men came to understand that the labour required of them in return was not a test, but rather a natural requirement on the part of those who administered public funds, honourable alike to both—and as the days were growing longer and the sunshine warmer, very many performed their outdoor tasks contentedly and well. Comparisons were sometimes made between the relative hardness of the stones they were set to break and the hearts of the guardians who put them to such work, not always complimentary to the latter; but these were mostly suggested by those who were desirous to take rank in that very doubtful class, 'the friends of the people,' or by some who, with scarcely less culpable ignorance, regarded this required work as a punishment of poverty, when it was really the redemption from pauperism. The following rhymes, taken from a local paper, express, in native dialect, 'The Operative's Lament:'*—

Eh, dear! What weary toimes are these,
  When scores o' honest workin folk
Reawnd th' poor-law office dur one sees,
  Loike cadgers, wi a cadgin poke;
It 's bad to see 't, bo wus a dyeal,
  When one's sel helps to make up th' lot;
We'n nowt to do, we darno stayl,
  Nor con we beighl an empty pot.

Aw hate this pooing oakum wark,
  An breakin stones for t' get relief;
To be a pauper—pity's mark—
  U'll break an honest heart wi grief.
We're mixt wi th' stondin paupers, too,
  Ut winno wark when wark's t' be bad,
A scurvy, fawnin, whoinin crew—
  It's hard to clem, bo that's as bad.

An for mysel aw would no do 't,
  Aw 'd starve until aw sunk to th' floor;
Bo th' little childer bring me to 't,
  An would do th' best i' th' lond ow'm sure.

* By Joseph Ramsbottom.

If folk han childer starvin theer,
  An still keep eawt, they 're noan so good;
Aw 've mony a toime felt rayther queer,
  Bo then aw knew they must ha food.

When wark fell off aw did my best
  To keep mysel and fam'ly clear;
My wants aw've never forrud prest,
  For pity is a thing aw fear.
My little savins soon were done,
  Un then aw sowd my twoth'ry things—
My books and bookcase o' are gone,
  My mother's picther, too, fun wings.

A bacco-box wi two queer lids,
  Sent whoam fro Indy by Jim Bell,
My fuchsia plants and pots, my brids,
  An cages, too, aw 'm forced to sell;
My feyther's rockin-cheer 's gone,
  My mother's corner cubbert too;
An th' eight-days' clock has followed, mon—
  What con a hongry body do?

Aw 've gan my little garden up,
  Wi mony a pratty flower and root,
Aw 've sowd my gronny's silver cup,
  Aw 've sowd my uncle Robin's flute;
Aw 've sowd my tables, sowd my beds,
  My bedstocks, blankets, sheets as weel;
Each neet o' straw we rest eawr yeads,
  And we an God known what we feel.

Aw 've sowd until aw 've nowt to sell,
  And heaw we 'n clem'd 's past o' belief;
What next for t' do aw couldno tell,
  It wur degradin t' ax relief.
Ther wur no work, for th' mill wur stopt,
  My childer couldno dee, you known;
Aw 'm neaw a pauper cose aw 've dhropt
  To this low state o' breakin stone.

Bo wonst aw knew a diff'rent day,
  When every heawr ud comfort bring;
Aw earned my bread, aw paid my way,
  Aw wouldno stoop to lord or king.
Aw felt my independence then,
  My sad dependence neaw, aw know;
Aw ne'er shall taste those jeighs ogen—
  Aw 'm sinkin wi my weight o' woe.

Such was the feeling of the operatives in their own lyrics, and a painful blush of shame visibly crossed the faces of many of these men as they were ushered into the august presence of 'the board;' while sometimes, the half kind, half patronising—'Sorry to see you here, ——,' only increased the applicant's discomfort. To many, the thought that with the revival of trade, and the resumption of their position, it might be said to them, 'Thee'st bin a pauper,' was a torture hard to be understood by those of superior rank. The better class of Lancashire operatives are perhaps as thin-skinned a race of beings as any among the subjects of Queen Victoria,—as keenly sensitive, as anxiously conservative of their rights and their position, as any that could be named. Of course this includes but a small minority; for the most part, they, like their masters, are busied with selling their labour in the dearest, and buying their wages in the cheapest market.

The following extract from one of the letters of the correspondent of the 'Manchester Examiner,' depicts a scene not unfamiliar to those who, through business or curiosity, were present at the meetings of the boards of guardians:—

'A clean, old, decrepit man presented himself. "What's brought you here, Joseph?" said the chairman. "Why; aw 've nought to do,—nor nought to tak to." "What's your daughter, Ellen, doing, Joseph?"—"Hoo's eawt o' work." "An' what's your wife doing?"—"Hoo's bin bedfast aboon five year." The old man was relieved at once; but, as he walked away, he looked hard at his ticket, as if it was not exactly the kind of thing; and, turning round, he said, "Couldn't yo let me be a sweeper i' th' streets, istid, Mr. Eccles?" A clean old woman came up, with a snow-white nightcap on her head. "Well, Mary, what do you want?"—"Aw could like yo to gi' mo a bit o' summat, Mr. Eccles,—for aw need it." "Well, but you've some lodgers, haven't you, Mary?"—"Yigh, aw've three." "Well; what do they pay you?"—"They pay'n mo nought. They'n no wark,—an' one connot turn 'em eawt." This was all quite true. "Well, but you live with your son, don't you?" continued the chairman. "Nay," replied the old woman, "*he* lives wi' *me*; an' he's eawt o' wark too. Aw could like yo to do a bit o' summat for us. We're hard put to't." "Don't you think she would be better in the workhouse?" said one of the guardians.

"Oh, no," replied another, "don't sent th' owd woman there. Let her keep her own little place together, if she can." Another old woman presented herself, with a threadbare shawl drawn closely round her grey head. "Well, Ann," said the chairman, "there's nobody but yourself and your John, is there?"—"Naw." "What age are you?"—"Aw'm seventy." "Seventy!"—"Ay, aw am." "Well, and what age is your John?"—"He's gooin' i' seventy-four." "Where is he, Ann?"—"Well, aw laft him deawn i' th' street yon, gettin' a load o' coals in." There was a murmur of approbation around the board; and the old woman was sent away relieved and thankful. There were many of all ages, clean in person, and bashful in manner, with their poor clothing put into the tidiest possible trim; others were dirty, and sluttish, and noisy of speech, as in the case of one woman, who, after receiving her ticket for relief, partly in money and partly in kind, whipped a pair of worn clogs from under her shawl, and cried out, "Aw mun ha' some clogs afore aw go, too; look at thoose. They're a shame to be sin!" Clogs were freely given; and, in several cases, they were all that was asked for. In three or four instances, the applicants said, after receiving other relief, "Aw wish yo'd gi' me a pair o' clogs, Mr. Eccles. Aw'd had to borrow these to come in." One woman pleaded hard for two pairs, saying, "Yon chylt's quite bar-fuut; an' he's witchod (wet-shod), an' as ill as he con be." "Who's witchod?" asked the chairman. "My husban' is," replied the woman; "an' he connot ston it just neaw, yo mun let *him* have a pair iv yo con." "Give her two pairs of clogs," said the chairman. Another woman took her clog off, and held it up, saying, "Look at that. We're o' walkin' o' the floor, an' smoor 't wi' cowds." One decent-looking old body, with a starved face, applied. The chairman said, "Why, what's your son doing now? Has he catched no rabbits lately?"—"Nay, aw dunnot know at he does. Aw get nought, an' it's *me* at wants summat, Mr. Eccles," replied the old woman, in a tremulous tone, with the water rising in her eyes. "Well, come; we mustn't punish th' owd woman for her son," said one of the guardians. Various forms of the feebleness of age appeared before the board that day. "What's your son

John getting, Mary?" said the chairman to one old woman. "Whor?" replied she. "What's your son John getting?" The old woman put her hand up to her ear, and answered, "Aw'm very deaf. What say'n yo?" It turned out that her son was taken ill, and they were relieved. In the course of inquiries I found that the working people of Blackburn, as elsewhere in Lancashire, nickname their workshops as well as themselves. The chairman asked a girl where she worked at last, and the girl replied, "At th' Puff-an'-dart." "And what made you leave there?"—"Whau, they were woven up." One poor pale fellow, a widower, said he had "wortched" a bit at "Bang-the-nation" till he was taken ill, and then they had "shopped his place," that is, they had given his work to somebody else. Another, when asked where he had been working, replied "At Se'nacre Bruck (Seven-acre Brook), wheer th' wild monkey were catched." It seems that an orang-outang which once escaped from some travelling menagerie was retaken at this place.'

But though the board-rooms of the guardians were crowded with applicants, whose distress could not be questioned, yet it is probable that the scenes of deepest sufferings were disclosed by the relief committees. Thankfully it may be affirmed, that throughout this famine none were forced to starve; none died, like the unhappy peasants of Ireland, seeking, but unable to find relief; none passed away like many of their wretched fellow-subjects during the Indian Famine, for lack of a power which none but Christ himself could manifest upon earth. Yet truth compels the sad confession that many—yes, many—have been the victims of nakedness and hunger—of the want of those attentions for which human beings are dependent one upon another. It would be too much to suppose that but one secretary to a relief committee could have guided a newspaper correspondent to such information as is contained in the following portion of a letter:—

'He pointed to some of the cases in his books. The first was that of an old man, an overlooker of a cotton-mill. His family was thirteen in number; three of the children were under ten years of age; seven of the rest were factory operatives; but the whole family had been out of work for several months. When in full employment the joint earnings of the family amounted to 80*s.* a week; but, after struggling on in the hope of better times, and exhausting the savings of past labour, they had been brought down to the receipt of charity at last: and for sixteen weeks gone by, the whole thirteen had been living upon 6*s.* a week from the relief fund. They had no other resource. I went to see them at their own house afterwards, and it certainly was a pattern of cleanliness, with the little household gods there still. To see that house, a stranger would never dream that the family were living on an average income of less than sixpence a head per week. But I know how hard some decent folk will struggle with the bitterest poverty before they will give in to it. The old man came in whilst I was there. He sat down in one corner, quietly tinkering away at something he had in his hands. His old corduroy trousers were well patched, and just new washed. He had very little to say to us, except that "He could like to get summat to do; for he were tired o' walkin' abeawt." Another case was that of a poor widow woman, with five young children. This family had been driven from house to house, by increasing necessity, till they had sunk at last into a dingy little hovel, up a dark court, in one of the poorest parts of the town, where they huddled together about a fireless grate, to keep one another warm. They had nothing left of the wreck of their home but two rickety chairs, and a little deal table reared against the wall, because one of the legs was gone. In this miserable hole—which I saw afterwards—her husband died of sheer starvation, as was pronounced by the jury on the inquest. The dark, damp hovel where they had crept to was scarcely four yards square; and the poor woman pointed to one corner of the floor, saying, "He dee'd i' that corner." He died there, with nothing to lie upon but the ground, and nothing to cover him, in that fireless hovel. His wife and children crept about him, there, to watch him die, and to keep him as warm as they could. When the relief committee first found this family out, the entire clothing of the family of seven persons weighed eight pounds, and sold for fivepence, as rags. I saw the family afterwards, at their poor place, and will say more about them hereafter. He told me of many other cases of a similar kind.'

One of the most notable coincidents of the Cotton Famine — though with more literal justice it might be spoken of as a result of it—has been the lessened death-rate throughout nearly the whole of the district, and, generally speaking, the improved health of the people. This rare accompaniment of a famine deserves a lengthened investigation, though when the ordinary habits of the operative class are considered and compared with the enforced regularity and temperance of the pauper or relief dietary, the fact will cease to appear paradoxical or even surprising. Most of the operatives who are family men have, when in full work, incomes exceeding those of many clergymen, who have to feed an equal number of mouths, and in addition to maintain a much higher social position. Of the majority of these persons it may be truly said, that while they are not wasteful, they are not saving. Of food they have the best, which they consume in quantities far larger than the requirements of healthy life demand. Teetotalism is not common among them, and not a few are large consumers of ardent spirits. Then the atmosphere of even the best ventilated of the factories is not to be compared with the open air, in which the unemployed cotton-workers were now generally to be found. The demand for women's labour takes the wives from home at times when their condition requires repose, and at others, deprives their offspring of that maternal care for want of which infant life is so often sacrificed; while the same demand for children's labour forces them into the mill at an age when outdoor exercise is especially requisite for their healthy development.

Of necessity, the Cotton Famine remedied many of these evils. Over-eating was not possible to persons who were receiving at the most but two shillings each per week. No class of tradesmen have suffered more from the suspension of industry in the manufacturing districts than the retailers of beer and spirits. So early in the distress as May 1862, it was stated by Mr. Farnall that the beershops of Preston were not taking one-fourth of the money received in ordinary times, and the statement would have held good throughout the district. The Commissioners of Inland Revenue experienced in 1862 a decline of more than twenty-eight per cent. in the quantities of spirits taken into retail stocks in some of the towns of the cotton district. The labour requirement of the guardians, or the outdoor idleness of the recipients of relief, were both more healthful than the work of the factory. And last, but by no means least among the causes which have tended to produce such good bills of health during the continuance of the Cotton Famine, has been the better attention which mothers have bestowed upon their children, while they have not been torn from these natural duties at the sound of the factory-bell. Many, indeed, have learned the homely arts which tend so much to health and comfort, but of which their continuous working life had hitherto left them in ignorance. It was well said by the sexton of one of the most important towns in Lancashire, when asked how it happened that his lugubrious trade was unusually inactive during the summer of this year, 'Well, thae sees,' he answered, 'Poverty seldom dees. There's far more kilt wi' o'er-heytin' an' o'er-drinkin' nor there is wi' bein' pinched,'—a truth which contains a moral lesson valuable to all classes.

Whatever be the cause, it is certain that the hand of the destroying angel has been unusually light upon Lancashire during the continuance of the Cotton Famine. The death-rate of the Counties Palatine had for many years exceeded that of any other part of the country. Calculations ranging over a series of past years, show that whereas the mortality of Lancashire and Cheshire was 2·550 per cent. of their population, that of London was but 2·363 per cent., while in the south-eastern counties, the rate of mortality was little more than half that of the cotton districts, being only 1·955 per cent. The outdoor work in which the operatives had been employed by the boards of guardians was already improving the stamina and health of many of them. There were few who had not a very troublesome, and, in some cases, a painful probation to pass before they could accomplish their outdoor tasks without unusual fatigue or suffering. 'It was not difficult,' wrote an intelligent observer of one of these gangs, 'to distinguish the trained quarrymen from the rest. The latter did not seem to be working very hard at their new employment, and it can hardly be expected that they should, considering the great difference between it and their usual labour. Leaning on their spades and hammers, they watched me with a natural curiosity, as if wondering whether I was a new ganger, or a contractor come to buy stone. There were men of all ages amongst them, from about eighteen years old to white-headed men past sixty. Most of them looked healthy and a little embrowned by recent exposure to the weather; and here and there was a pinched face which told its own tale. I got into talk with a quiet, hardy-looking man, dressed in soil-stained corduroy. He was a kind of overlooker. He told me that there were from eighty to ninety factory hands employed in that quarry. "But," said he, "it varies a bit, yo known. Some on 'em gets knocked up neaw an' then, an' they han to stop a-whoam a day or two; an' some on 'em cannot ston gettin' weet through—it mays 'em ill; an' here an' theer one turns up at doesn't like the job at o'; they'd rayther clem. There is at's both willin' an' able; thoose are likely to get a better job, somewheer. There's othersome at's willin' enough, but connot stn th' racket. They dun middlin, tak 'em one wi' another, an' considerin' that they're noan use't to th' wark. Th' hommer fo's leet wi' 'em; but we dunnot like to push 'em so mich, yo known, for what's a shillin' a day? Aw know some odd uns i' this delph at never tastes fro mornin' till they'n done at neet,—an' says nought abeawt it, noather. But then, they'n families. Beside, fro wake lads, sich as yon, at's bin train't to nought but leet wark, an' a warm place to wortch in, what can yo expect? We'n had a deeal o' bother wi' 'em abeawt bein' paid for weet days, when they couldn't wortch. They wur not paid for weet days at th' furst; an' they geet into their yeds at Shorrock were to blame. Shorrock's th' paymaister, under th' guardians. But, then, he nobbut went accordin' to orders, yo known. At last, th' board sattle't that they mut be paid for weet and dry, an' there's bin quietness sin'. They wortchen fro eight till five; an' sometimes, when they'n done, they drill'n o' together i' th' road yon, just like sodjurs, an' then they walken away i' procession." '

While the operatives were thus doing battle with their

distress, and living without much complaint upon one-fourth of their ordinary income, their masters were watching with anxious eyes the fluctuations of the cotton market. In Preston and Blackburn, as well as in other towns, production had virtually come to a standstill in the month of June. These two towns had been the largest consumers of the inferior qualities of American cotton; their manufactures are coarse, and contain three times the weight of raw material which the same number of spindles would require if engaged in spinning the finer qualities of yarn. The consequences of the Cotton Famine came therefore most heavily upon them. The cotton trade was at this time much confused between alternations of panic and reaction. In May it had seemed that the fall of New Orleans into the hands of Farragut and Butler, and the surrender of Yorktown, one of the most historic spots of American ground, to the then victorious and all-praised M'Clellan, foretold the speedy annihilation of the young Confederacy. But when no cotton came down the Mississippi, but only tales of how the much-coveted staple was used for ramparts and bonfires, then again holders grew bold and the price of the raw material still gained upon that of manufactured goods. Not unfrequently did hundreds of bales make their way from the manufacturing districts to the ports of England. It would be useless to censure individuals for selling the raw material while their 'hands' were out of work; yet it is beyond doubt that as many as fifty thousand bales of cotton were resold by manufacturers during the year, to say nothing of the quantities which they bought and sold on speculation. But this is noticeable, rather as proving the convulsions of the trade, than as forming a basis for any accusation against these single-minded traders. There were some among these manufacturers whose productions were in constant and indeed increased demand. These were mostly the 'hard' and the fine spinners, who supply cotton yarns to the Yorkshire weavers and to the lace and stocking manufacturers. There were a few whose manufactures were not in demand, but who yet preferred to work up their stocks of cotton rather than to sell them. By this course they incurred loss only if they were compelled to market their goods before the course of time brought the certain increase of their value. Yet it may be said that the uncertainty which overhung affairs in America made working for stock seem then to be a very hazardous proceeding, and one which no one would be disposed to undertake unless actuated by the most humane feelings. But it is not safe to calculate upon what is called humanity as the motive power of any large class of men. There were many among the manufacturers, men without capital, to whom a continuance of production was impossible, because cotton could not be purchased and spun into yarn for immediate sale without incurring a heavy loss. They might have been as anxious as their more moneyed neighbours to keep their 'hands' together; and the wondrous economy, the perfect division of labour, which is observable in a cotton-factory, will suggest of what tremendous importance is this to the success of the manufacturer. The deterioration of machinery is a very serious item in the cost of a closed mill, in some cases involving a net damage estimated at 100*l.* or 150*l.* per week. The loss of the skilled 'hands' involves great waste of the cotton, inferiority of production, and often serious damage to the machinery—each and all being hindrances to profit which the manufacturers cannot afford to overlook.

There was much complaint at this time that the larger manufacturers were not doing their duty; that while they shunned the subscription lists on the one hand, they were, on the other, not indisposed to prolong the inactivity of the cotton manufacture. Indeed, it was said that they saw with no sorrowful eye the difficulties of their smaller competitors, and were not unwilling that these, having fallen as victims of the Famine, should leave the trade to become their own monopoly. To some extent they were slandered by these insinuations. That they were not ready with their subscriptions for the relief of the distress is beyond denial. Half the newspapers in the country, and none more strongly than those of Manchester, urged them to be heedful of the sufferings of others, and of their own duty. And both whip and spur were to a large extent applied in vain. But there is no reason to suppose that they looked with any satisfaction upon the ruin of others. The worst that can be imputed to them is that they were intent upon their own business, when a regard for others should have been made to form a large part of it. Those who possessed stocks of goods—and there were many such—could not have desired the rapid renewal of production. Their interests, in a sordid sense, were best served by the present condition of the trade, and their profits must have been enormous. Some behaved nobly to those with whose assistance they had made their great wealth. Some worked their factories when it was not directly profitable, and when it was certainly hazardous to do so. Some subscribed, not large, but considerable sums to the relief funds. Others gave their 'hands' daily meals and established soup kitchens. Many lost considerably by the non-payment of their cottage rentals, and all paid many times over the amount of poor-rates they had been accustomed to pay. But to generalise the profit and loss, it may be said that the scarcity of the raw material benefited the trade and occasioned the evils of a famine among the workers. And as is ever the case in such a calamity, there was but little sympathy on the part of the gainers for those who were the sufferers. Manchester and Liverpool men made their millions and subscribed their thousands. The inference from their conduct is, not that any other community would have been more liberal, but rather that the commercial spirit does not encourage generosity to overgrow the other sentiments of human nature. Such behaviour will not however have been without its moral if it should dispel that most absurd illusion that liberality is the corollary of affluence.

But this class does not comprise the considerable number of needy manufacturers who were now stricken with fear at the position of the cotton trade. No man who had the bulk of his fortune invested in one of those huge boxes of bricks and mortar, fitted with machinery, known as a cotton-mill, could be expected to be otherwise than engaged with selfish thoughts regarding the depreciation of his property. It seemed as though any restoration of a healthy demand for goods was impossible. The war in America had lasted for a whole year, and production had greatly decreased, but even now the price of 40's mule yarn was only ½*d.* a lb. higher than that of Midling Orleans cotton. And inasmuch as mill property is at such a time perhaps the most inconvertible form which a man's possessions can assume, some share of that consideration which all will be ready to grant, must be given to the class of millowners whose entire substance was thus bestowed.

During this summer East India cotton began to take a much higher place in the total of sales, and the spinners, submitting to inexorable necessity, largely adapted their machinery to its manufacture. It is beyond a doubt that strong and unwarrantable prejudice opposed the use of Surat cotton. The believing operative, who lifted up his voice in chapel, and added to his pastor's prayer for increased supplies of cotton, the rider, 'O Lord, but not Surats!' spoke the sentiments both of masters and hands generally. The even quality of the cotton, and the sureness of the supplies which all had been long accustomed to draw from the Southern States, made these to seem the natural if not the only legitimate habitat of the cotton plant. Moreover, Indian cotton was universally associated with hard times, for nothing but a failure of the American crop had ever induced spinners to take notice of so despised an article. To what degradation it had fallen may be gathered from the circumstance that a firm of Lancashire brewers considered themselves so grossly libelled by the epithet of 'Surat brewers,' as to have resort to an action at law. Certainly this cotton was naturally short in staple, harsh and brittle in fibre, while the sudden demand and the rapid rise in price made the profits of fraud by adulteration too great for the weak consciences of those by whom it was packed. But it was not fair to call the wretched stuff which was now flung upon the English market, Indian cotton—it was to a great extent the waste, the scrapings, the sweepings of the Indian crops. It is true that there were men who toiled all the week in the endeavour to spin this cotton into yarn, and in these long, weary fifty-five hours, barely earned more than enough to satisfy the demand for the weekly rental of their cottage. But even this did not trouble them more than the irritation caused by the continued stoppages of the machinery, consequent upon the frequent breaking of the yarns and the general inferiority of the raw material. Yet, at this time, there were lying among the treasures of the International Exhibition, specimens of cloth woven with Surat cotton, of which the most experienced eyes could not detect the inferiority, and concerning which the calico printers to Her Majesty declared they had never met with any cotton cloth better adapted for receiving the most delicate colours.

It is not unreasonable to suppose that there was but little desire on the part of the leading merchants and manufacturers in the cotton trade to promote the consumption of Indian cotton. Clearly it was against their interest to do so, while their warehouses were choked with stocks of cloth, or while their looms were producing more, which nothing but an improbably increased demand could render saleable at a profit. Still, as American cottons were rapidly becoming more scarce, Indian must be employed; and invention, which is never long at fault in the cotton manufacture, was even now busy in devising how best to use this inferior material. The difficulty was mainly experienced in the earlier processes. From being badly baled and packed, from careless cartage and long exposure to the weather, even the best samples of Surat came to hand so matted and wadded as to require unusual labour in preparing it for the carding-engines. Unlike the produce of America, much of it had been badly harvested, and seeds and seed-pods added weight to bales that should have contained nothing but cotton-wool. The saw-gin, the invaluable gift of Whitney's mechanical genius, was not much used by the Hindoos, and their rude processes made but a very partial separation between the valuable export and the worthless refuse. Hence the great waste in the use of Surat cotton, which may safely be estimated in 1862 at double that of American cotton.

But during this year, Indian cotton was rarely used as the sole material of any extensive manufacture, and consequently no very considerable alteration of machinery was requisite. It was not until a much later period in the duration of the Cotton Famine, that the steaming process was made use of, by which the matted cotton was loosened for passing through the scutching-machines. The length of the fibres of Surat and that of the inferior descriptions of American cotton do not differ so greatly as to preclude the possibility of using a large admixture of Indian cotton in the comparatively coarse machinery used for spinning yarns under 40's. But Indian cotton contains a troublesome quantity of very short (many of which may be broken) fibres, necessitating greater draught to carry them away, which of course increases the amount of waste. It would be impossible to card Indian cotton with the engines used for carding cotton-wool of the longest staple. And in making any considerable use of Indian cotton, even in the well-adapted factories of Blackburn, Burnley, Preston, and Wigan, it was found necessary to card more lightly than had been the wont of manufacturers. When Surat cotton was pressed too quickly into the engine, the wires tore the fibres which they should have separated and ranged in longitudinal order. But this did not amount to a prohibition of its employment, nor did it to any very serious extent increase the cost of manufacture. A more important hindrance was found in the spinning process, from the difficulty of imparting sufficient strength to the yarn, made from cotton unusually short in staple and greatly inferior in textile capacity and strength. The series of rollers, by means of which the mere bundle of fibres is gradually elongated and twisted into yarn, are among the most important as well as most delicate ministrants in the cotton manufacture, and the extensive employment of Surat cotton rendered necessary certain alterations in their relative diameters and positions, which formed the most considerable item of expense in the adaptation of the mechanism of the cotton-factory to the use of this description of raw material. The expense of this alteration varied with circumstances. But while some were thus making every effort to recommence production with profit, there were adverse circumstances which tended to depress the English market for manufactures. The injury caused to our trade by the blockade of the Southern ports of America was aggravated by the new tariff adopted by the Northern States, which amounted to a prohibition of the import of English goods. The United States protected the manufactures of Lowell by the imposition of a duty of twenty-five per cent. Still, as the home consumption of this country would be the last of all the markets to show falling off in consequence of a rise in price, the result of the great diminution of production had been to decrease very considerably the weight of manufactured goods in stock, and the English was now the dearest market throughout the world. India and China were still immensely overstocked, but then they were being enriched by the increased price of cotton. Russia found it profitable to spin yarn for sale in Manchester, and the fall of Sebastopol was partially avenged when the shrewd merchants of Muscovy effected these transactions, so promising to the industrial progress of Holy Russia. One circumstance which tends to make the home market the dearest, at a time when overproduction has caused a general stagnation of trade, is the greater convenience for forced sales afforded by the foreign markets. It now and then happens that the holder of large stocks of goods is pressed by the want of ready money. His mercantile name and credit will be injured if he forces his goods upon a dull market, and, impelled by his necessities, submits to an obvious sacrifice. But he can make these goods over to a foreign agent without the transaction appearing more suspicious than one of ordinary speculation, and by this means he can at once obtain an advance upon their value, and will in due time receive the balance of the foreign market-price.

The stocks of cotton in England had by Midsummer become so seriously reduced, and there was so little prospect of large importations, that much revival of the cotton trade during this year was not to be expected. At the commencement of the second half of 1862, the stock of cotton in Liverpool had fallen to 180,450 bales; at the corresponding period of 1861 it had been 1,108,650 bales, while in 1860 it had been as large as 1,297,030 bales; nor was there any likelihood of an increase of stock, for the expected arrivals did not equal the average consumption and export. It was all but certain that the stock of cotton in Liverpool would be still further diminished; and although the very gloomiest prognostications upon this subject were not fulfilled, yet in September there were no more than 17,000 bales of American cotton in Liverpool, a supply insufficient for three days' consumption had all the mills been fully engaged in its manufacture. Under these circumstances, it is not surprising that the price of cotton should have shown such a rising tendency towards the end of June and in the beginning of July. In the former month, American had risen 2½*d.* and Indian cotton 3*d.* per pound. By the middle of July this rise had been increased to nearly 6*d.* per pound on each description of cotton. Of course, this rendered production still more impossible, and the number of 'standing' mills and 'hands' out of work was rapidly increased. If many of the holders of cotton, who had purchased with the intention of spinning, now found it impossible to withstand the temptation of the times, and returned their cotton to Liverpool, such conduct can excite but little reprehension. Raw cotton had risen one hundred and fifty per cent. in value within a year, while the price of manufactured goods had not risen more than fifty per cent., and there was no immediate prospect of a rise in value of the latter equivalent to that in raw cotton, nor any certainty that even the present prices would be maintained. Markets fell, therefore, into a speculative condition, being fed, as it were, from hand to mouth. The advance of 2*d.* a pound upon the value of the cotton sold in Liverpool during one week enriched some persons to the extent of half a million, but no one stayed to inquire who shared the plunder, for all were racing towards the next heap of gains. The enormous profits which were realized during this excited condition of the cotton market were not confined to Liverpool. The inland capitalists of Lancashire were gainers, as well as their amphibious neighbours upon the banks of the Mersey. About this time there began to be observed a growing discrepancy between the reported sales to spinners and the actual quantity taken out of stock for consumption. At the close of the year, it appeared that at least 121,000 bales had been so dealt with, showing that manufacturers had done not a little speculation on their own account. To what extent they speculated as 'speculators' cannot be known. They were free, also, to deal with the stocks of cotton which they had accumulated in their warehouses in the manufacturing towns; and that these were not unimportant, was also manifested at the end of the year, when the estimated stock of cotton in the kingdom was suddenly found erroneous by upwards of fifty thousand bales, which were held in store by the manufacturers, and, owing to the unusual intricacy of cross-transactions, this was unknown to the brokers by whose agency the statistics of the cotton trade are furnished.

At this time there were many manufacturers who could not open their mills, if they would have done so. Being without sufficient capital to hold goods until their value should rise, they could only have worked at a very serious loss. A few, possessed of larger means, ran their mills, determined to risk a loss in order to keep their 'hands' together, and in work. Many mills were still active, of which it was said, in newspapers and in magazines, at the dinner-table and on 'Change, that they were working at a loss to their masters of 250*l.* or 500*l.*, or even more, per week. So they might have been, but it by no means follows that their masters realized this loss. The loss was estimated upon the basis of supposition, that as fast as the goods were manufactured they were forced upon the market, and sold for whatever they would fetch. But did these manufacturers do so? Would it not be a calumny to suppose that Lancashire capitalists were capable of such quixotic actions? Of course, they did not do anything of the sort. It is true that they had to run the risk of a sudden reopening of the American ports. They knew that there were 3,000,000 bales of cotton stored in the Southern States, which might be let loose at any moment upon the cotton markets of the world; but if they were secure from this, they were perfectly safe against any other contingency. Profit must come, even upon the manufacture of cotton at 18*d.* per pound. It could not be long before consumption should tread upon the heels of supply, and then they would have kept their machinery bright, their workpeople in full skill and complete order, and there would be a comfortable margin between the cost and the selling price of their manufactures. And surely it required no very great political foresight to be aware that the American struggle was an affair of years, not of days;—surely it needed no ghost to tell those who had learned the alphabet of the cotton trade, that the supply of cotton must for some time to come be very much below the ordinary rate of consumption. If every pound of raw cotton at this time in Europe, and if every additional pound which was expected to arrive within the next six months were worked up, the total product of manufacturers would not have equalled one-half the consumption of Europe alone for that period. Surely such a reflection must have suggested to many a producer the advisability of keeping his factory at work throughout this summer. Newspaper correspondents informed the public of men who were losing 1,000*l*. per week by continuing production. It would have been as reasonable to declare that a man wastes his labour and capital by making in one day food sufficient to last him for a week. Both require the possession of capital, and neither can be accomplished without it; but it would be unutterably absurd to argue that either necessarily involved a loss. The actual profit or loss incurred by those who continued to manufacture cotton during this unprecedented crisis, it would be impossible to ascertain with any degree of certainty. But now that we are in possession of the broad fact, that from this time the price of manufactured goods continued steadily to rise until it exceeded by more than one hundred per cent. their value in June 1862, it is not perhaps unfair, while it is an unalloyed pleasure, to assume that these accounts of losses were to a great extent illusory.

Meanwhile that charitable agency which was destined to exercise such an important influence upon the Cotton Famine was being matured and established. In June 1862, the Central Relief Committee of Manchester was principally composed of the commercial and municipal representatives of Lancashire, of whom some of the most notable were connected with the Manchester and Salford District Provident Society. In this same month, another stream of charity had its commencement, which subsequently ennobled and expanded that already located in Manchester, by becoming confluent with it. The representatives of Lancashire in the Houses of Parliament did not permit the gaieties of the Exhibition season wholly to divert their attention from the distress which prevailed in their home county. Colonel Wilson Patten, whose loyalty to Lancashire forms no unworthy or inconspicuous portion of his public character, took the most active part in bringing them together, and a meeting was held at Bridgewater House, which however produced no immediate results. The opinion of this meeting was that local efforts had not yet been sufficiently strained,—that no good would result from arousing London to the rescue of Lancashire,—that for the present it would be well 'to rest, and be thankful' that matters were no worse. It is impossible entirely to acquit these noble and honourable gentlemen of blame for this proceeding. It was a mistake on their part to delay the substantial token of their personal sympathy. They were the largest property owners in the distressed districts, but the weight of the calamity was not falling upon them. They did not pay the heavy poor-rates, nor were theirs the cottage-rentals which could not be collected. Yet no local exertions could be demanded of Lancashire which it was not their duty to share. They had heard of the sufferings of the operative population; it was not possible to doubt the existence of a very extraordinary amount of poverty after the publication of Mr. Farnall's speeches and reports upon the condition of several of the most distressed towns. The mere fact that a Special Commissioner of Government was at the present time engaged in an inquiry as to how this unemployed and unpaid population could best be maintained, with the least hardship to themselves and the least disturbance of salutary enactments, was of itself a sufficient indication of the plain duty which lay before them. Though it be true that they had not shared the exceptional profits of the recent years of prodigious trade, of which it was stated in the circular of an eminent cotton firm, that 'Manchester is dazzled by the splendour of such a state of things,' yet they had made solid gains by the progress of the cotton manufacture; and indeed it would be unfair to deny that they subsequently showed, by personal assiduity and very liberal contributions, an ample recognition of their responsibilities. It may well be thought difficult to believe that the brilliant company of statesmen, scholars, and gentlemen who assembled in the drawing-room at Lord Ellesmere's, on the 19th of July, could not have foreseen a month earlier what would be the condition of affairs in Lancashire at this occasion of their second meeting. However, when they did put their shoulder to the wheel, their impulse was immediately felt. The great abilities and unrivalled influence of their chairman, the Earl of Derby, gave weight to their deliberations, and materially assisted in afterwards placing the promoters of this assemblage so prominently in the Manchester Executive. Eleven thousand pounds were subscribed in the room. Colonel Wilson Patten became the treasurer of this fund, which was distinguished by the title of 'The Cotton District Relief Fund,' and Sir

James Kay-Shuttleworth found congenial occupation as the secretary to the committee of management.

It must have been obvious to many, that the constitution of the Manchester Executive Committee was not at this time such as would insure for it the confidence of the empire at large, and that at all events it was most unwise to have one committee of landowners, and another of mercantile and business men, sitting to further the same objects, but without current or responsive action. The committee which had its head-quarters at Bridgewater House, naturally attracted the support of the wealthy classes of the metropolis, and money flowed fast into its coffers. By the 8th of August its funds amounted to 40,000*l.*, while those of the Central Committee of Manchester had reached only to half of that sum. It had been arranged between the two committees, that on the 8th of August a conference should take place, in order to provide for the expenditure of the Cotton Districts Relief Fund by the Central Relief Committee. Colonel Wilson Patten was the mouthpiece of the Bridgewater House Committee, and offered to pay over 4,000*l.* monthly to the credit of the Manchester Committee, upon receiving a guarantee for the fulfilment of several conditions, the chief of which was that relief should not be given from this fund to any who were receiving assistance from the guardians. The intention of this stipulation was as obvious as it was humane. In the first place, the directors of the Bridgewater House Fund were anxious that it should not operate merely in alleviation of the poor-rates. They desired that this relief, collected by their agency, should be devoted to the class for whose benefit it had been given—they did not wish to subsidize the ratepayers. But, further than this, it was their intention that this fund should be applied in prevention of pauperism. The trials endured by those who were too proud to apply for parochial relief had not passed unnoticed, and it was especially for the benefit of this class that it was desired the Cotton Districts Relief Fund should be expended. It cannot be doubted that this was the course suggested by all the dictates of prudence, economy, and humanity,—the best at once for the recipients, and for the ratepayers. But one or two members of the Manchester Committee did not think so, and evidently considered that all subscriptions should be applied to supplement parish relief,—a doctrine especially dangerous at this early period of the distress, when the rate of relief given by the guardians was so low and the unwillingness to apply for it so strong, and it was an objection which it may be thought contained two words for the ratepayers and but one for their distressed clients.

The relations between the two committees were thus drawn more close, and the necessity for some amalgamation became more evident. There was danger lest the public sympathy for Lancashire, now becoming so pronounced, should not be utilized to the greatest possible extent while the division existed. There was danger lest the relief funds should be maladministered, if three committees were to exist in simultaneous and totally independent action. It was felt to be very desirable that the co-operation of Mr. Farnall should be secured, but it was obvious that he could not effectively lend the weight of his official position to more than one committee. Liverpool had raised a large sum—inconsiderable only when contrasted with the enormous profits she had derived from the recent fluctuations in the cotton trade—and through the chairman of her committee had expressed willingness to make the Manchester Committee her almoner, if that body were remodelled, and included the Special Commissioner. Accordingly, a list of names was prepared, of members to form a central executive committee. It matters not by whose hand the selection was made. With the exception of two names, it comprised those of the gentlemen who have since for so long a time formed the hebdomadal council of the district. Death has removed Lord Ellesmere, and Lord Derby has been installed in his stead; and Mr. Millar, who was nominated to represent Preston, has been replaced by Mr. Goodair, of that town. At a meeting of the Central Relief Committee, held in Manchester, August 22, several resolutions were adopted, and among them one constituting the gentlemen included in this list of names, the Central Executive Committee. The selection was admirable. Together with the official representative of Government, were nominated men of the highest rank, of the greatest wealth,—great landowners, great capitalists, great employers of labour.

Nor was there more variety in the social condition and occupation than in the religious profession of the members of this committee. The bent of their minds and their general scope of intellect was equally various. It would not have been possible, looking to the localities from whence they came, to have collected a fairer representation of the whole district, and it is much to the credit of the original Manchester Committee, that it should have thus unanimously agreed to vote away its executive functions by the election of this committee. But it is certain the General Committee never performed a more salutary duty, or one which exercised a more beneficial influence, than in this most justifiable suicide. In consequence of the election of the Executive Committee, the three relief funds collected respectively at Manchester, at Bridgewater House, and at Liverpool, in fact, all the relief funds excepting that administered from the Mansion House, were placed at its disposal. It was resolved that the Central Executive Committee should meet every Monday at twelve o'clock, and it was arranged that notice should be then received of the grants which had been made during the previous week from the funds of the Mansion House Committee, who now seemed determined—in spite of several overtures for amalgamation—to remain a separate and independent organisation.

Of that complete system of local relief committees, which subsequently left no corner of the district unvisited and no deserving person unrelieved, the few which were yet established existed, as might be supposed, in the great centres of distress. The operatives were yielding unwillingly to the grip of poverty, retreating inch by inch to that inevitable but unwelcome time when they must ask for bread. One of them, strangely gifted with a voluble and erratic eloquence, had told in Stevenson Square how, under the pressure of these hard times, he had parted with books which he valued at 100*l*. And of those who stood round him in this Manchester Forum, many would be reminded of how they too had parted with household treasures, the more prized because they were the reward of very narrow savings. But these were unavoidable sacrifices. Throughout the district a good deal was being done by private charity—more, in fact, than has ever been accomplished at any subsequent period. Considerable difficulty had been experienced in dealing with the large number of girls who had been thrown out of work, and were during the early months of the year to be seen idling about the streets and lanes of the cotton towns in listless groups,—in some cases singing in the streets to obtain the alms of passengers. These Lancashire lasses attracted much sympathy; it was easy to recognise the danger to which their situation exposed them; they could not dig, they were ashamed to beg, and it was a happy thought which led to their employment in sewing-schools, wherein they acquired facility in another and more domestically useful description of cotton-work than that to which they had been accustomed in the factories, and, what was of equal value, they were submitted to order and discipline, and learned not a few lessons the benefits of which will endure to their life's end.

With reference to these establishments, Mr. Redgrave, one of the Factory Inspectors, subsequently reported to the Home Secretary:—'In many of the sewing-schools I was told that one-third of the females knew nothing of sewing upon their first attending the classes; that when they first took a needle in their hand, they pushed it through their work by pressing it upon the table; and that many had no idea of mending or patching their clothes. I saw a mother, for instance, who until she attended a sewing-class, had never used a needle, making a frock for her sixth child; and I have seen even and regular work done by girls after three months' training, and they have been taught not only to sew but even to make clothes. When it is remembered how many hundreds of women and girls have been taught to sew well, it is a matter of the greatest gratification that so many will possess for the future in their homes a greater power of increasing their domestic comforts, and of economising their household expenses.'

To the Manchester Board of Guardians belongs the high honour of having been the first to promulgate officially a recommendation in favour of the establishment of sewing-schools for girls. And this board of guardians also has the distinction of having been the first to recommend that educational exercises should be accepted as the labour required in return for relief. Later in the year, these beneficial systems were very generally adopted, and 'children of an older growth' pored over their spelling-books, their arithmetic, and their writing exercises, who had passed many a year regretting that they had never time to master even the rudiments of schooling. Continuing his remarks upon the relief schools, Mr. Redgrave reported with reference to these establishments generally:—

'At the male adult schools I have occasionally thought there was an appearance of weariness; but this is not surprising; the employment of females in sewing and knitting was a proper and congenial occupation for them, and though the attendance of classes might have been somewhat irksome, yet upon the whole they were all doing something which had a practical result: in some schools they made shirts for the Militia, in some they made all kinds of clothing for distribution by the Relief Committee, and in others for sale; but in the male adult schools it was not possible to set the men to work upon an occupation which would be equally congenial to them; whereever it was possible, the men were taught trades, as shoemaking and mending, carpentering, mat-making, etc., but the number was comparatively small, and the great bulk of the operatives attended school merely as a condition of relief. The life of a labourer is monotonous. He rises at a given hour, goes to work, to the same work every day, does to-day as he did yesterday, but that which makes his life a cheerful one is that he receives the value of his labour. In these schools it was impossible not to feel that the time spent there was, compared with their former labour. unproductive: and I was therefore the more impressed with the attention of the men in these classes, and the anxiety of so many to improve themselves, especially in arithmetic. It sometimes caused a shade of melancholy to see an old grey-haired man leaning over his desk and poring through a sum in Reduction or Practice; but even this was relieved by being told by a frank-spoken spinner in his own hearty manner, while showing the sketches of geography and what he was reading, "They could not give us work, and so God put it into their hearts to give us the next best to it." These men cannot return to their families and homes without feeling that instruction is one means of adding to happiness, and to the purpose of life. They frequently expressed their conviction that they had lost much from not having had more instruction in their younger days, and their desire for their children to attend school and to improve them has certainly been shown favourably.'

And though it be impossible to do justice here to the exertions of those good men and kind-hearted ladies who devoted themselves to the superintendence of these schools, yet they have the satisfaction of knowing that the fruits of their endeavours are not only for to-day or to-morrow, but enduring always with those who received their attentions; nor can they be without that high reward of an approving conscience which nothing external can increase or diminish.

The condition of Lancashire was anxiously watched by the Government during the summer of this year. They were kept fully informed of the dimensions and rate of increase of the distress; but as the season advanced, there was evidence that it would be necessary to invest the guardians with further powers in order to relieve the pressure upon some of the most severely distressed towns. London was sweltering in the dog-days, when the member for Oldham put a question to the President of the Poor Law Board, as to whether he was prepared to bring in a Bill for the purpose of enabling boards of guardians to borrow money to be expended in relief. The reply of Mr. Villiers showed an anxiety to avoid if possible the establishment of any new precedent—a view of the subject to which the House of Commons was evidently favourable. It was not that he or the House grudged the bestowal of any provision which the necessities of the cotton districts might require, or that either failed to do justice to the patience and fortitude which the operative class was manifesting, but that they desired, if possible, for the sake of national interests, to avoid the concession of an unprecedented power, which it would be difficult to revoke and impossible to withhold in the future upon the occurrence of any similar calamity, however temporary might be its duration. Yet it cannot be supposed, that in suggesting the sufficiency of the Act of Elizabeth, Mr. Villiers was even at this time satisfied that enough had been done, or that no extended powers would be needed. It is true that that Act provides that 'if any two justices perceive that the inhabitants of any parish are not able to levy among themselves sufficient sums for the purposes aforesaid, then they shall tax, rate, and assess any other of other parishes, or out of any parish within the hundred, to pay such sums to the churchwardens and overseers of the said poor parish, as the said justices shall see fit.' But Mr. Villiers must have known Lancashire far too well to suppose that this provision could be put in force throughout the manufacturing districts. It is rather to be thought that in suggesting this, he was putting forward the principle upon which he had resolved to propose legislation, if the consent of the Cabinet to such a measure could be secured. This provision of the Act of Elizabeth had been brought to light for the relief of the parish of Bedworth, near Coventry, which had suffered great distress subsequently to the ratification of the recent French Treaty. But the order of the justices had never been enforced; and it is obvious that so long as this power was discretionary with them, the provision could never be effective. Mr. Cobden followed up the subject, and Mr. Villiers' reply to him left little doubt upon the mind of the House that his proposal to Parliament would embody the principle of the rate-in-aid.

Of the three courses open to Mr. Villiers, it cannot be doubted that he chose the best. He had to select between national grants, the bestowal of special borrowing powers upon each parish, and the rate-in-aid. It must be said that the first course found as yet but few advocates, and none of any note. The experience of the Irish Famine, when large sums were misspent, if not wasted in this way; and the general conviction that charitable grants from the public treasury are demoralising both to the dispensers and recipients, forbade the mention of this mode of relief. Parochial loans found many respectable advocates; but the large majority, acting on the principle that to be out of debt is to be out of danger, preferred the rate-in-aid, confident that a county, the rateable value of which already exceeded 8,000,000*l.*, could without difficulty meet its liabilities, provided that they were distributed over a sufficiently wide area. The rate-in-aid is unobjectionable, both in theory and practice. It operates upon the common principle that the heavier the pressure, the wider should be the area by which it is supported. As the prosperity of a town increases, so do the wealth-increasing influences extend which its neighbourhood imparts. While a flood is stayed upon a small space, its deep waters will destroy vegetation, and may seriously damage the power of production. But if it be shallowed out over a wide extent of land, its waters will soon be harmlessly absorbed. The rate-in-aid was in like manner an equalizer of the distress.

In bringing his measure before the House of Commons, Mr. Villiers did not conceal his apprehension that the distress would seriously increase; but at the same time he was unwilling to admit that the ordinary sources of relief were as yet inadequate. He was careful also to show that his proposal was not entirely new, but that it aimed at giving vitality to the existing law. When first laid on the table of the House, the Bill proposed that the rate-in-aid should come into operation in any parish in which the expenditure for the relief of the poor exceeded by two-thirds that of previous years. At first, it was only proposed that in case of a union becoming insolvent, the parishes of the county should be liable to a rate for its assistance. The power of putting the Act into operation was to remain with the Poor Law Board, who were to be invested with authority to recommend the issuing of an Order in Council, directing the levy of the rate-in-aid. The Bill was received with much favour in the district, the chief organs of public opinion expressing their grateful appreciation of Mr. Villiers' proposals. The 'Manchester Examiner' manifested its confidence in the Minister by saying, 'If the unemployed of these districts wish for a guarantee that their wants will not be neglected by the State, in this season of bitter distress, they have it in the fact that Mr. Villiers is the President of the Poor Law Board.' But in the House of Commons a somewhat different feeling was evinced by several of the Lancastrian Members, who were perhaps not overanxious that the burden should be borne locally.

It is both instructive and amusing to watch what may be termed the manufacturing idea at work in the Legislature. A very busy people, whose business makes much noise both at home and abroad, are always liable to the supposition that everything they have to do with exists for themselves alone. Hence they are apt to strain a principle to which they are favourable, and to fail to recognise one when its incidence is contrary to their wishes. It may well be doubted, without any disrespect to Mr. Cobden, if he would have thought this measure insufficient had the circumstances to which it was applied occurred elsewhere than in the cotton districts. Mr. Potter, who estimated the present weekly loss of wages at 140,000*l*., was of the same opinion as to its insufficiency; and the members for North Lancashire and Oldham expressed their preference for a public loan. Mr. Cobden thought the legislation of the Romans equally relevant with the Act of Elizabeth, and urged that the Government should allow the guardians a power of contracting loans to be lent to the distressed operatives, who, he stated, would gladly repay every farthing upon the return of good times. This but ill accords with the very anxious desire expressed by so many of the better class of operatives, to avoid anything like a mortgage of their future; and without going the length of saying that the men would have repudiated these loans, it may be safely affirmed that considerable difficulty would have attended their repayment, while the precedent thus established would have been most unfortunate. Probably, Mr. Cobden will not now regret that his advice was not accepted; and could he have foreseen to what a small extent the guardians would be called upon to avail themselves of any extraordinary powers, it is possible that Rochdale might at least have given a silent assent to the introduction of the Union Relief Aid Bill.

It will be useful to review the circumstances attendant upon the introduction of this measure, in their relation to the subsequent operation of the Act. The recollection of them will give increased interest to the account of this operation, and incidentally it will be further effective as a commentary on the value of parliamentary utterances. In the committee upon the Bill, Mr. Villiers introduced amendments, fixing the amount of rates upon payment of which the parish might call for a rate-in-aid upon the union, and the union upon the county, at five shillings in both cases; and substituting a special order of the Poor Law Board for the proposed Order in Council. It was so obviously desirable that the point of pressure at which the operation of the Bill commenced should be a fixed sum, that the omission suggests something like an oversight in its preparation. Upon Mr. Potter's suggestion, Derbyshire was included, and with these improvements the Bill rose into higher favour with the Lancashire members. But some were still discontented, and expressed their fears that the local poor-rates would be unbearably oppressive. No doubt they would have preferred that the casual profits of the calamity should be received by the cotton trade, and that the cost of relieving the poor should be borne by the nation. But the justice of Parliament would not suffer this. While the House was in Committee upon the Bill, Mr. Cobden reproved Lord Palmerston for his want of appreciation of the millowners' sympathy with their unfortunate 'hands.' He stated, roundly, that ninety-nine out of every hundred of the manufacturers were working at a loss. This may have been correct in the present tense, and within the technical definition of the term manufacturer, but he would be very reckless of truth who should now assert that these ninety-and-nine were actual losers by their industry. Besides, there was a class of cotton-spinners whose goods were even then in very active and profitable demand.

The Bill was destined to undergo further alteration. It was suggested that it would be much more easy to pay the extra burdens of these hard times upon the return of prosperity, and that therefore a power of raising loans would be preferable to that of calling for a rate-in-aid. It was further contended that,—as the excess of rates above the average amount would be incident upon the occupier without imposing any charge upon the property-owner,—by deferring the time of payment the burden would be borne with more proportionate equality. These suggestions were both plausible and just. When it was seen to be the desire of the Legislature to grant this borrowing power, no objection was raised on the part of the Government. Their endeavour in framing the measure had been to adhere as closely as possible to the principle of the existing law. As an alternative for the rate-in-aid, it was conceded that the boards of guardians, with the sanction of the Poor Law Board, might raise loans to be secured upon the common fund of the union. Three shillings in the pound was subsequently fixed, in lieu of five shillings, as the amount of rates which a parish must bear before calling for the rate-in-aid. Finally, a clause was inserted giving the chairman and vice-chairman of a union power to appoint a guardian to represent the union in the extraordinary administration of relief under this Act, a privilege which, it may be said, was never made use of.

In the House of Lords the Union Relief Aid Bill received some discussion, but no amendment. On the second reading, Lord Fortescue spoke of Mr. Farnall's speeches in the North as 'bunkum,' and from them made the rather startling deduction that the Poor Law Board was a superfluous institution. It is perhaps too much to expect that the dignified occupants of those red benches, which support the hereditary senators of the Upper House, will often condescend to join in the battle of life and learn the difficulties of keeping an outpost. It is far easier—though far less honourable—to rise from those cushions and criticise the workers; careless, to all seeming, of the personal feelings of those assailed, and of the more important interests of the service in which they are engaged. As an ex-secretary of the Poor Law Board, Lord Fortescue might have been expected to be conversant with its rules and regulations, as well as with the letter and spirit of the Poor Laws. The conviction is inevitable that he had not this knowledge; otherwise he would have known that the speeches to which he referred not only contained nothing contrary to the law, but threw a clear light on its provisions, and probably for the first time made it popular.

On the third reading, the Bill was subjected to much comment. Opposition Lords blamed it for coming so late in the Session, and expected that Lancashire would have borne rates of ten shillings in the pound before appealing to the Legislature for assistance. They assumed that the present annual charge for poor-rates in Lancashire was under two shillings in the pound, which, though true, if the total amount collected had been charged upon the assessment of the county, was by no means correct in respect of certain townships and parishes. In support of the measure, it was shown that its introduction at the commencement of the Session, would have had the effect of lessening the national sympathy for the distressed population of the cotton districts, and of diminishing the local ability of self-help. It was also shown that the poor-rate of Preston was at this date seven times greater than it had been in the previous year, and a Lancashire peer gave his opinion that a five-shilling rate would be in fact a fifteen-shilling rate upon those who could pay the demand of the overseers. Three days after this debate, and but five before the beginning of grouse-shooting, the Bill became law by receiving the Royal Assent, and Parliament was prorogued with a flattering recognition in the Queen's speech of the manner in which Lancashire was bearing her trials—Her Majesty trusting that this Act woud tend to mitigate the distress. So the Session of 1862 passed away, conspicuous by the absence of any very important national legislation, leaving Europe in peace, America in the midst of war, London lounging in the International Exhibition, and Lancashire deeply plunged into a distress which was borne with dignity and fortitude, and supported by the active sympathy of the Government and the nation.

CHAPTER VII.

JULY—SEPTEMBER 1862.

'The Duchess of Lancaster' sent a donation of 2,000*l.* to the Cotton Districts Relief Fund in July 1862. By this title the Queen claimed her right to contribute towards the relief of the sufferings of her subjects in and about the County Palatine. A homily upon the duties of crowned heads might be read from this simple action. While it reflected honour upon the Sovereign as the graceful expression of her sympathy, and upon the nation over which she ruled, it also implied a homage to the principle of local responsibility,—a principle next dear to that of their country's honour in the minds of Englishmen. The gift was well-timed, for the autumn and winter prospects of Lancashire were the worst that had ever been known. Nor is it likely that the example given by the Queen, as Duchess of Lancaster, was lost upon the property owners of less degree in the cotton districts. As yet the manufacturers and commercial classes had not done very much to swell the subscription lists. It had been proposed that a guarantee fund should be established, payable by instalments, to be called up by a committee; but this proposition met with no very favourable reception. It is possible that now, looking back upon events which are past, and obligations which have been incurred, there are many of the capitalists of Lancashire who regret that this mode of meeting the distress was not adopted. And though it is not to be denied that the Cotton Famine was a national calamity, nor can it be asserted that England has done more than her duty as the mother of Lancashire, yet it may well be thought that the character of the manufacturing districts for wealth and independence would have been supported in a manner more satisfactory to local pride, if a guarantee fund of 2,000,000*l*. had proved the self-reliance of the cotton trade.

As the year began to wane, the amount of pauperism increased, notwitstanding the operations of the relief committees and the repugnance of the cotton workers to become applicants for relief. The 'labour test' was still unpopular, but this was rather a consequence of the character of the labour required than of the requirement in the abstract. To some extent, the operatives regarded themselves as political martyrs, who had a right to demand of the State a peculiarly delicate treatment. Some assistance towards forming an estimate of this section of the class may be gathered from the resolutions adopted at a meeting of the deligates of the Operative Spinners' Association, which declared that Mr. Villiers' Bill was insufficient, and that no labour, and nothing but a statement of the time and place of their last employment, should be required of those who applied for relief. At a monster meeting held subsequently in Stevenson Square, complaint was made that these paupers upon compulsion were set to weed a macadamised road, and that they who had been used to work in an atmosphere of 80° of heat should now be forced to labour in the open air of a dying summer. The unusual presure upon the machinery of relief involved, if it did not necessitate, great hardship to individuals. Some suffered temporary want from the tardiness with which their claims were adjudicated upon, others felt aggrieved because the obligations of the law could not bend to the exceptional circumstances of their case. It is difficult not to sympathise with the poor man who, upon asking for bread for his starving wife and four children, is told that he, necessitous and famished, must work before he can eat, which, though not the actual requirement of the law, may have occurred by force of circumstances,—or with the overlooker, who, being allowed to retain his place with the nominal pay of five shillings per week, is told that he cannot be relieved unless he throws this up and takes to work upon the farm-lands of the union. Yet neither the guardians nor the Poor Law Board could abandon those principles which at such a time were the only barrier that preserved the property of the ratepayers from confiscation, and the poor themselves from rapid demoralisation. Hop-picking was suggested as a diversion for these unfortunately idle hands. This was certainly the least promising of all the migratory schemes that were now or subsequently proposed, but this, like the next, which was that of Miss Rye, for rectifying the inequality of the sexes in Australia, met with little favour—the first requirement of any scheme of relief being, so far as the manufacturing interest was concerned, that it should not involve the removal of the cotton operatives.

All the modes of co-operation for political, social, educational, and productive purposes, are familiar to the people of the cotton districts. Memorials and mechanics' institutes, deputations and debating clubs, resolutions and reform associations, are as household words in the mouths of all, from the millhand to the millionaire. Set a party of operatives to work, which for some reason or other they dislike, and it is more than probable that either before or at dinner-time, they will hold a meeting and adopt a memorial. If the authority is distant, they will send a deputation, such as that which waited on Mr. Villiers from the Operative Spinners' Association at the beginning of August. They came to denounce the 'labour test,' and they were told as the guardians of several of the unions had been already told by Mr. Farnall, that the labour should be such as is the most suited to the person of whom it is required. It may be said that the guardians had not sufficiently considered this in devising labour. To pack these men together in an oakum shed, was to force them to a comparison the most repulsive to minds both sore and sensitive; and while this work is stamped with peculiar degradation as the common occupation of convicts, stone-breaking is but little better, being always associated with hereditary paupers, a class next to that which by the commission of crime has forfeited liberty.

It was not until the end of August that the office committee of the Manchester Board of Guardians recommended the employment of men, women, and children in schools. That this and other valuable suggestions should have emanated from this board justifies its superor position as the metropolitan board of the cotton district. The history of the next three months will exhibit the distress continually deepening, with no corresponding effort to meet it on the part of the wealthiest classes in the cotton districts. On the part of all classes there was manifested a generous and intelligent recognition of the duty of the Government to persevere in their policy of neutrality, and a liberal sympathy with the suffering population of Lancashire was expressed, not only in words but also in hard cash, by Englishmen throughout the world, and by the peoples of many another nation. The press at this time was deservedly severe in alluding to the apathy with which the moneyed classes in Lancashire regarded the distress.

But it is a more agreeable task to record the fulfilment than the neglect of duty, and a view of the cotton districts at this period will be all the more acceptable because its foreground is most pleasing. If what was now done by a few of the wealthy manufacturers had been done by all who had it in their power to follow these good examples; if a united organisation had determined, that even if it were not possible for them to be the masters of this crisis, they would at least be foremost in the struggle, they would have earned a very high place in the gratitude of the sufferers and in the estimation of their countrymen. That they did not lack example is evident from the public announcement made by Sir Elkanah Armitage and Sons, who were by far the largest employers of labour in the populous borough and district of Salford, and who took upon themselves the responsibility of relieving the 'hands' in their employ, justifying the publication of their liberal intention, by stating that it was made in order to guard the public funds 'against misrepresentations from any parties saying that they are suffering through our suspension of work.' But it is impossible to concede all that was advanced by this distinguished firm in the letter which contained this statement. It may be allowed that the manufacturers were not morally culpable for a policy which had narrowed their supply of the raw material to a single source, but that the operatives had no stronger claim upon their employers than generally upon the owners of property, cannot be maintained, unless the responsibility is confined within the strictest limits of the law, in disregard of moral and equitable rights and duties.

In Preston, the most northern of the much-distressed

towns, the numbers receiving assistance from the Relief Committee had doubled in the period from March to September. There are now nearly 24,000 persons on the books of the committee; their weekly expenditure amounted to little less than 500*l.*, while in this township the guardians were also relieving upwards of 10,000 persons. The material assistance given by the committee in the first week in September was 15,130½ loaves of 3 lb. 10 oz. each, besides 54,848 lb. of bread, 11,716 quarts of soup, and 4,860 quarts of coffee. At one industrial school there were 505 females employed, at a weekly cost of 50*l.*, and all went smoothly in this establishment until the ruling powers decreed that these women and girls should sing the Doxology before leaving, to which harmless performance the Roman Catholics objected. This was the beginning of the religious difficulties which subsequently not a little affected the distribution of relief.

The Preston guardians were giving nearly 1*s.* 5*d.* per head to the distressed population, which was about 2*d.* above the average given by the Lancashire unions generally. The Relief Committee augmented this allowance by the addition of 5*d.* per head, given wholly in kind, while the guardians' relief was, according to regulation, given half in money and half in kind. On September 1 Preston presented the strange contrast of a carnival and a famine. The Preston Guild,—an incorporation as ancient and honourable as those of similar origin and constitution, which are better known to fame in the City of London,—assembled this year according to immemorial usage, and for several days the town was filled with scenes of gaiety. The gaunt grim spectre of famine which had stalked about the streets was laid by the appearance of gay processions, of famous singers, and of the prince of tight-rope performers. The value of local festivals such as this, and the strong attachment which people have for their celebration, must be considered before the wealthier classes of Preston are blamed for feasting while they were surrounded by so much want. Indeed, it cannot be doubted that this gay ceremonial actually tended to mitigate the sufferings of the people of Preston by a welcome increase to the ability of the ratepayers. And something must be set down for the advantage of the 'shows' in raising the spirits of the people. No one would be at a loss to understand the policy of amusement, so much adopted by continental rulers, who had seen how the looks of listless depression, so commonly worn upon the faces of the sufferers by the Cotton Famine, would pass away at the sight of a few booths, merry-go-rounds, and peepshows. The Preston carnival caused a large influx of visitors to the town, and a consequent expenditure of money, which benefited the shopkeepers both small and great, who were at this time much pressed by the increase of the poor-rates, and still more by the withdrawal of the custom of the operatives. In contradiction of the proverb with reference to corporations, that of Preston evinced its possession of a conscience by sending 500*l.* to the relief fund at the same time that it resolved to hold the Guild. And there can be no doubt that Preston, which is said to be 'proud,' but which is certainly rich, could afford to celebrate this ancient usage without involving of necessity any neglect of other duties.

There were seventy-six mills in Preston, and a moderate estimate set the wealth of the manufacturers at between four and five millions sterling. As the number of cotton workers in this township was about 25,000, and as this was also the number of persons receiving relief, it is evident that there could have been but little work going on in the cotton-factories. The number relieved, of course, included infants, aged persons who were past work, and paupers, who had never been employed in the manufacture of cotton. The guardians were expending 800*l.* a week in relief. Of this, the manufacturers of Preston probably paid one-fourth. But as they were not generally working their mills, it might have been expected that their names would stand for large sums in the subscription lists of the Relief Committee. Yet such was not the case. The operatives had pawned their furniture and exhausted their savings, the small ratepayers were pressed with rates grievous to bear, but the manufacturers of Preston had, up to this time, given no more than 1,842*l.* 15*s.* out of their abundance to the relief fund, rather more than one-tenth of the sum which the hard times had forced the Preston operatives to withdraw from the savings-banks.

Sophistry may defend, but justice cannot excuse, this

most painful exhibition of covetousness in its worst guise. Much the same was the case at Blackburn, and in other towns throughout the cotton district. All that can be said for these men, some of whom were actually at this time amassing prodigious wealth, and who yet refused to give liberally to their famished neighbours, is that their minds, expanded with but one idea—that of gain—were paralysed by the extraordinary uncertainty of the time, and by finding a large portion of their fixed capital rendered suddenly unproductive. The perusal of the names of these niggards would not give the pleasure which is felt by the sight of those of the few who acted uprightly and upon a due sense of responsibility. By the censures of the press, they were afterwards, to some extent, flogged into a recognition of their duty, and the subscription lists made progress. But subsequent events will show that external charity took the task to a great extent upon itself, and supplied the wants of their poor with unceasing beneficence.

In Blackburn the weekly loss of wages, owing to the Cotton Famine, at the beginning of Sepember amounted to 10,000*l.* In place of this, the 15,000 operatives who were out of work received 676*l.* from the guardians, whose scale of relief was a little over 1*s.* per head. Besides this, the Relief Committee distributed 28,000 lb. of bread, with 24,000 lb. of oatmeal. Of 74 mills in Blackburn, 18 were running full time, 16 short time, and 30 were entirely closed. At this time, and throughout the duration of the distress, Blackburn had been singularly fortunate in the number of its energetic and charitable friends. A great deal has been done by the untiring perseverance and irrepressible zeal of some of the leading townsmen. The privations endured by the poor of Blackburn had been very great, and their sufferings might have passed beyond the point of endurance but for the external aid which they have received. The subscription lists had here made but little advance. The guardians and the Relief Committee were together simply preserving the lives of the people, while their behaviour—at one degree above starvation-point—was irreproachable. The operatives had pledged goods to the amoount fo 30,000*l.*, which it was said were now lying in the pawnshops of the town, to the distress of the pawnbrokers as well as that of the mortgagors of all this furniture and apparel.

Private charity was busy in Blackburn. Many of the clergy and a large number of ladies distinguished themselves by their benevolence; but private charity—implying that kindly, neighbourly giving which supplies a meal but does not keep a hundred households—could not save 15,000 paupers from starvation. If the people of Blackburn had intended from the first to cope with their own troubles, their more than ordinary acuteness should have taught them that this could only be accomplished through the agency of large relief funds. But in this respect they had done almost nothing. In addition to the 30,000*l.* worth of goods which have been spoken of as being pawned, the suffering classes had withdrawn upwards of 15,000*l.* from the savings-banks, and may be fairly said to have done more for themselves than had been done for them. Of the 9,037*l.* which had been received into the relief funds, 1,940*l.* had been subscribed by the outside public, 2,300*l.* had been sent by the Lord Mayor of London from the funds of the Mansion House Committee, 600*l.* had been received from the Manchester Committee, another 600*l.* was specially given for the payment of labour upon the union-grounds, and the local subscriptions amounted to 3,597*l.* To this paltry sum the manufacturers of Blackburn had subscribed 700*l.* Some were running their mills, possibly at a loss, others were giving food occasionally to their workpeople. Among them no one was more attentive to the poor than the mayor, and none more liberal than Mr. Hornby, the member for the borough. It will be seen that afterwards the subscriptions were increased; but it cannot be said of the manufacturers of Blackburn that they from the first evinced that energy, for which in the pursuit of profit they are so remarkable, or that they showed a generous determination to grapple boldly with their local difficulties. They had had their good times, and not a few were even now making large gains. 'For years before the Cotton Famine,' wrote the 'Times' correspondent in September, 'cotton manufacture flourished so exceedingly in Blackburn, and such fabulous fortunes were amassed in a short time, that there was a general rush to get into it. Cotton was everything, and every man, no matter what his business, who had realized or could scrape together a little capital, made haste to turn it into spindles and looms wherewith to convert the precious staple into cloth for man's use. The operatives here have an odd way of perpetuating the remembrance of the origin of some of their wealthiest employers, by nicknames applied to their mills. One mill is familiarly known as "pinch-noggin," its owner having once been a publican; a second is the "lather-box," to remind people of the time when its owner was a barber; another is "physic," from the former profession of the gentleman who now works it, and so on.'

Dorsetshire might have done well to come to Lancashire during this autumn, and learn how to keep a family upon 1*s.* 2*d.* per day. The sewing-schools were of great service; in Blackburn there were now 900 girls employed in this way, and throughout the district many thousands were engaged in a similar manner. The girls were paid 6*d.* or 8*d.* a day for sewing and reading, or for learning to sew and read. In some of the largest of these excellent institutions it was found that 75 per cent. of the girls could not read, and that 80 per cent. had no knowledge of sewing—facts which go to show how much they and their future husbands and families will be benefited by this compulsory suspension of factory labour. Each class had a male superintendent, a female cutter-out, and lady instructresses. The least popular of the regulations was the enforcement of silence; but this was not universally adopted, and where it was the rule the seamtresses were allowed at intervals to sing hymns and to hear readings. These schools have always needed considerable funds to maintain them, and were to a great extent supported by the funds of the Central Relief Committee. Money was required to pay for materials, and for the wages of superintendence; and in addition, the amount earned by the girls had to be supplied from charitable funds, inasmuch as the garments they produced were almost invariably given away. Every religious denomination in Blackburn had its sewing-school, so that the directors of each were at liberty to mingle spiritual exercises with the regular work. The mayor of Blackburn was active in every direction for the benefit of the borough. South, east, and west his voice was heard supporting the claims of Blackburn to be the most distressed of cotton towns. Flattering resolutions encouraged the generosity of the Mansion House Committee, which has always been so good to Blackburn. But the local relief funds did not make much progress, until the tremendous increase of distress and the example of other places induced the mayor to convene a meeting for raising a second subscription. The large amount of 9,000*l.* was collected at this meeting, and among the donations were considerable sums from the members for the borough, who had not hitherto been the most neglectful of their duty One of them, Mr. Hornby, had been assisting his 'hands' for some time past by the voluntary remission of their rent; he had also given them a daily dinner, and a small weekly payment. Mention was made of a Blackburn manufacturer who had paid 26,945*l.* in wages since the commencement of the distress, —an amount nearly equal to the whole sum distributed by the board of guardians and the Relief Committee. But this gentleman did not estimate his loss at 5,000*l.*, and as it may be supposed that his calculation was based upon the relative prices of cotton and manufactures, it is reasonable to hope that he, like a good many others, counted his losses without realizing them. The public were loud in criticizing the conduct of the capitalists in the cotton trade, and angry manufacturers referred them, by way of correction, to this or that man who was working his mill at a loss, or to another—and of both there were specimens in every place—who was charitably assisting his workpeople. But the cause of public dissatisfaction lay deeper than this. It was well known that there were numbers of the Lancashire capitalists who were making such gains this year as they had never made before, by sales of goods, by cotton sales and speculations; and the public looked—and it must be added looked in vain—for those who would share this accidental wealth with the class by whose sufferings it was in some measure produced.

Blackburn indeed had an anxious prospect in the coming winter. Thirty-six thousand of the population were now dependent on legal and charitable relief, and their weekly loss of wages amounted to 13,000*l.*, in lieu of which they were receiving about 2,500*l.* At Over Darwen, in the neighbourhood of Blackburn, a determined spirit of independence has been manifested throughout the whole period of the Famine. In the autumn of 1862 subscriptions were liberally and promptly made, and in the month of October, Darwen, rated to the relief of the poor at 33,000*l*., had gathered as much in local subscriptions as the neighbouring town of Blackburn, of which the rateable value is 144,000*l*. Darwen is one of the mushroom towns of the cotton district, and has increased with extraordinary rapidity during the last ten years. There were now upwards of 1,000 persons wholly unemployed in this place, and nearly 4,000*l*. had been subscribed to the local relief fund. Like Blackburn and other towns, Over Darwen was divided into districts, to which visitors were appointed, and it may be said that throughout the whole cotton region of the Palatinate it is to these visitors and to the committee-men that the first honours of this trying campaign belong.

Organisations similarly constituted were dealing with distress of the same character in all the towns, and in many of the remote villages throughout the district. Through the humane exertions of Sir James and Lady Kay-Shuttleworth with those of other charitable persons, schools, both sewing and educational, had been established at Burnley, where great distress prevailed. These were attended by persons of all ages and both sexes. In many unions the guardians were paying the school-fee of twopence a week for each of the children of those parents who were in receipt of parochial relief; and by this excellent provision of that Act of Parliament which bears the honoured name of Denison, these little ones were kept from idling away their time, and forfeiting their schooling in the streets.

Great progress in education has been made during the period of the Cotton Famine. Guardians, relief committees, manufacturers, the clergy, and last, but not least, the schoolmasters, have exerted themselves, in order that the children should benefit by the cessation of factory-work. Mr. Redgrave has reported that the number of children in attendance in the schools—in the district over which his supervision as a Factory Inspector extends—increased from 16,692 in 1861, to 18,028 in 1862, and the concurrent testimony from all sides is that the children were more regular in their attendance and made better progress than in previous years. For the most part, the educational fees of these children were paid from the poor-rates and charitable funds, though to a large extent by individuals, in some cases by the very praiseworthy self-denial of their distressed parents; while in some they may be said to have been the voluntary contributions of the schoolmasters, who remitted them rather than turn away their pupils.

No township in the manufacturing district has felt the consequences of the Cotton Famine more severely than Glossop, and none could be less prepared to meet such a calamity, for Glossop is almost as much dependent upon cotton as though it were one great factory. The population, speaking generally, consists of cotton workpeople and the tradesmen dependent upon the wages of the operatives. Of its 14,000 inhabitants, 5,300 had been employed in two of the fourteen cotton-mills which were in the township in the autumn of 1862. In ordinary times the Glossop Union can boast that it has less pauperism than any other union in the kingdom. One per cent. is the usual rate of pauperism upon the population in this union. But this rate had increased to thirty per cent. in September, and in October there were forty per cent. of the population of Glossop subsisting upon relief. The weekly circulation of money in the town had diminished by three-fourths, and the miserable condition of the shopkeepers may be imagined, from their having suffered so large a withdrawal of the custom upon which they were dependent. The signs of distress soon became visible in the long rows of shut-up houses—in the frequent bankruptcies—in the knots of unemployed operatives standing about the streets. The Relief Committee and the board of guardians were active, and provided an ample scale of relief. But Glossop has been most fortunate in possessing a resident landed proprietor, who with practical benevolence has been anxiously energetic for the welfare of its impoverished population. Lord Edward Howard has been the good genius of this much-distressed place,—not by throwing down a sum of money and leaving this mass of pauperism to be dealt with by others, but by unfailing readiness to supply whatever was wanted,—by personal intercourse with the suffering population, and, most of all, by his unceasing endeavours to provide work for them, at which they could earn wages and enjoy an honest sense of independence. A liberal subscriber to the local and general relief funds, he was also foremost among the landholders in promoting outdoor works for the employment of the distressed operatives. The manufacturers of Glossop made a donation to the relief fund, and then closed their mill-gates. By Lord Edward's assistance the Market House was fitted up as a school, with stoves, desks, forms, and other requisites for the accommodation of 1,500 pupils, who received relief upon the condition of attending school for five hours daily. Probably in one point of view the operatives of Glossop were never working so entirely for their own benefit as during this time of distress. There were 313 unmarried girls at a sewing-school. Besides a large attendance of men and boys at the industrial and educational schools, it was made compulsory on all parents receiving relief, that their children between the ages of six and thirteen should be sent to school, which was done at the cost of the guardians.

Unlike Glossop, Oldham is a place of rather multifarious industry. Even in its cotton manufacture there is much variety, and in October there were not more than 4,817 persons wholly unemployed in this town. But the distress was not dealt with here in a masterly manner, though this was rather the fault of circumstances than of individuals. The Relief Committee reassured the Mansion House Committee by an opinion that in no instance had their funds been injudiciously applied. But the subscription lists filled slowly, and loud were the complaints of the rate of relief given by the guardians. They on their part, could not, or would not, devise work for the unemployed, and were rather inclined to favour the agitation against the so-called 'labour test.' The unemployed operatives resolved, in a public meeting, that the relief given was inadequate to the requirements of human nature, and from the speech of their chairman, it seems to have been taken as certain that their rent would be exacted from the amount they received in relief. At the end of the month the guardians were relieving 9,411 persons, at a weekly cost of 512*l.*; the majority of these received additional assistance from the Relief Committee, which divided between 9,881 persons the weekly sum of 643*l.*

Although Rochdale is largely engaged in woollen as well as in cotton manufacture, yet the distress was very considerable in this town. There is a great deal of public spirit in Rochdale, a more perfect admixture of classes of society than in most of the manufacturing towns of Lancashire, and a more effective local authority than perhaps in any other borough of equal importance in the district. Much of this may be due to individuals, but it may be thought that much is also accounted for by the natural features of the vicinity, and the comparatively isolated positon of Rochdale. Local attachment is always stronger where the neighbourhood is hilly or otherwise marked in its scenery—where the landscape is not materially altered by every new expansion of the town. Rochdale is famous for the extent and success of its co-operative associations, and as the residence of one of the most popular orators which this age has produced. There was more evidence of system in the administration of relief, and a more thorough mastery of the distress in this borough, than was general. In October the Rochdale guardians were relieving 9,813 persons, at a weekly cost of 754*l.* while the Relief Committee was assisting some 10,000 persons who received no help from the guardians. But the rate of relief given by the guardians—1*s.* 6*d.* per head—did not altogether satisfy the recipients, and at one of their meetings, an old woman expressed her troubles and those of her class in this homely language :—'Sisters and brothers, I thought I would say a few words, as in reality we are clamming, and very near starved to death. There's five of us in a family, and we are only getting 1*s.* 6*d.* a head, and we have to buy coal, pay the rent, and pay for our "bagging," and I don't think it is right to think a body can do it. I think those great men for whom we've worked ought now to try to keep their "warkpeople" from starving, as they'll want us again. As to the gentlemen in the country giving, they'll weary of giving if they don't see our masters giving "summat."'

In Ashton-under-Lyne the prospects of the operatives were exceedingly gloomy. Nearly 20,000 were unemployed, and receiving relief from the guardians and the relief committees. The expenditure of the former was 1,128*l.* per week. At the close of October there was but one mill in this populous borough working full-time. There was rivalry between the relief committees of Ashton, where religious jealousies run higher than is common even in the cotton district. The manufacturers' and the Nouconformists' party in Ashton do frequent battle with the representatives of the Church and the landed interest. The first benefits by the rare and restless intelligence of a resident cotton-spinner, while the latter is somewhat damaged for the fight by having in its chief pastor an aged absentee, and in its principal landowner a most devoted sportsman. It is not likely that the conflicting existence of two committees was productive of very serious injury to the poor, but it is certain that in the conduct of their differences, that which professed to represent the Church was not distinguished for superior humility. As distress is of no creed, it must be thought better that the local authorities should head a movement for relief, rather than any ecclesiastical or religious functionaries. The ostentatious activity of a clergyman provoked the hostility of the dissenting body, and the consequence was a formation of a Borough Relief Committee, which aimed at universal representation, in opposition to the General Relief Committee, which was certainly somewhat tinctured with a clerical and manorial character. There were schools in Ashton-under-Lyne in which a thousand girls were taught sewing and reading, and were kept from idleness. Schools were also established for men and boys. But the local subscriptions barely amounted to one week's loss of wages. Many of the mill-owners had opened schools in connection with their factories, and attendance in these was accounted by the guardians as entitling to relief.

Out of a population of 54,000, there were 23,000 receiving relief in Stockport in the month of October, and every prospect of a large increase in the numbers of the destitute. The guardians relieved 8,000, and the Relief Committee 15,000 persons. The relief given by the guardians, about 1*s.* 6*d.* per head, was not supplemented in any case by the committee. There were nearly 1,500 girls employed in sewing-schools, who had already turned out some 2,000 articles of clothing. Up to this time the local subscriptions had not amounted to 6,000*l.*, and although the organisation for relief was here, as in other places, admirable,—though there were troops of charitable visitors, who were performing a most Christian duty under very trying circumstances,—yet it must be said that here, as elsewhere, there was manifested a marked inability to deal with the crisis, and a totally inadequate provision for the distress which has fallen so heavily upon all.

The difficulties which beset the administration of the Poor Law in Manchester and the adjacent townships are always very considerable. The city and suburban operatives have acquired many of the most innocent vices of a parliament, and possess an armoury of verbal weapons easily reducible to resolutions, memorials, and suchlike, but very embarrassing to the administrative power, and not always used with sufficient consideration. Yet, although there has been much 'bunkum' talked in the Manchester Forum, which is commonly known as Stevenson Square, it must be admitted that nothing but the prevalence of a strong sense of injustice can gather a successful meeting even there. The rate of relief given by the Manchester Board of Guardians at this time was about 1*s.* 6*d.* per head. They had always made great efforts to secure the due return of labour for relief, in accordance with the regulations of the Poor Law Board. Nearly 1,000 of the unemployed were set to work upon the farm which the guardians maintain for this purpose. But here an indignation meeting was held in September, because the bailiff had the assistance of policemen in his duties of superintendence. Sewing and educational schools were early established in Manchester and the neighbourhood. These gave general satisfaction. But this was not the case with the labour in which the able-bodied men were employed. At one large meeting held in Stevenson Square, the 'cursed labour test' was loudly exclaimed against. 'All money and no stuff!' was the cry of those who disliked the regulation which gave their relief half in money and half in kind. There was another cry, 'How can we pay our rent if we receive no money?' which, as it sounded not only here but in many other places, suggests that the remission of rents was not so universal as was supposed by many liberal donors to the relief funds.

The Report of Mr. Redgrave—one of the Factory Inspectors—for the half-year ending October 31, contained the most favourable evidence that could be collected by dint of the most friendly perseverence, of what the manufacturers were doing to support their hands through this terrible crisis. Through the agency of his sub-inspectors, he had collected, in every neighbourhood, instances in which mills were kept running for the benefit of the operatives, in which schools were being maintained, food, clothing, and gifts of money distributed. And this evidence, so far as it goes, is irrefragable. It shows that throughout the district many of the principal manufacturers were doing very much for those who had been in their employ, but still the number of cases recorded does not amount to fifty, and there are 2,109 cotton-factories in the district over which Mr. Redgrave's survey extended.

Of some of the masters it was truly said, that the donation of 500*l.* or 1,000*l.* to the relief fund would be as nothing compared with what they were doing in other ways to mitigate the distress. The sub-inspector of the Ashton district referred to one who, while his mill was standing, was expending no less than 180*l.* a week in feeding and educating 452 males and 609 females. In addition, this gentleman gave 50*l.* a month to the local relief funds, and remitted 60*l.* per month in the rentals of his cottages. Perhaps under these circumstances it is not altogether surprising that this quaint song should have been heard in his improvised school-rooms:—

You factory folks of Lancashire, a song we'll sing to you,
Of a school now formed at Higher Hurst, and every word is true.
Our masters are determined to care well for their hands,
If they will only come to school, and there obey commands.

CHORUS.

Then old and young, attend the school, your teachers there obey;
There's military exercise, and military pay.

Our mules and looms have now ceased work, the Yankees are the cause.
But we will let them fight it out, and stand by English laws;
No recognising shall take place until the war is o'er;
Our wants are now attended to, we cannot ask for more.

Potatoes, ham, and bacon are now to us being sold;
With comforts such as these we have no fear of winter cold;
Every one seems hearty glad, and sings with joyous glee,
For men and masters now do meet in love and unity.

Amongst our scholars there are some whose age is past threescore,
Who have for learning, wages, which they never had before;
The pencils, slates, and copybooks are free for us to use,
And every morning on each desk is laid the daily news.

A system of good order rules supreme from morn till night;
There's grammar and arithmetic, and nearly all can write;
Reciting too, with moral songs, to suit the gay or brave,
And often do we close our school with singing 'Sailor's Grave.'

Now old and young, forget your cares, and join in singing praise;
The time is not far distant when we shall have better days;
Then comforts soon to everyone, with joy we shall abound,
Contentment, peace, and plenty may we have on British ground!

The Central Executive Committee was now firmly established, and the Central Relief Committee, to which it rendered a merely nominal allegiance, had sunk into a respectable retirement. The part had become greater than the whole, and the executive held its position not only by right of rule over the purse-strings, but also by its unrivalled composition and its intelligent administration. As described by one of its most distinguished members, it was composed of 'noblemen, gentlemen, and the most considerable capitalists' of the district. It included also the representative of the Government, but its diverse elements had never interfered with the utility or the harmony of its action.

At its installation this committee inherited large funds, and these were continually augmented as the winter approached and the distress increased. The colony of Victoria—one of the youngest of the daughters of England—was among the earliest in testifying her sympathy with the parental distress. The telegram which announced the first instalment of her donation was short, but sweet as the best sentiments of patriotism could make it. 'From Victoria Relief Fund to the Mayor of Manchester:—For relief of the distress, we send you 5,500*l.*' This was quickly followed by a further donation of nearly equal magnitude, accompanied by a most touching expression of thankfulness on the part of the colonists for their own prosperity, and of sympathy with the sufferings of their fellow-subjects in

Lancashire. In forwarding these funds the colony expressed the high-minded wish, that they should be distributed in a manner best calculated to relieve the want, at the same time to promote social progress among the operative classes. The merchants of London sent their thousands; the committee were already the appointed almoners of Liverpool; five thousand tons of coal were placed at their disposal by one proprietor, and stores were opened for the reception of whatever gifts in kind the charitable might be disposed to send.

One of the earliest difficulties of the committee had reference to the scale of relief generally adopted by the boards of guardians. They were anxious that the assistance given by the funds at their disposal should, in the first instance, relieve the destitute and not the ratepayers. Humanity prompted the bestowal of a rate of relief high enough to maintain as much comfort as could be secured, with a due regard to the numbers requiring aid and the extent of the resources in the hands of the committee. But had they established a scale of relief much above that of the guardians, and refused in all cases to supplement the relief given by the poor-law authorities, it is obvious that the expenditure of the guardians would have been very light indeed. And the same evil must have occurred had they shown too great readiness in supplementing the relief given by the guardians before this was raised to a sufficiently high standard. Accordingly the committee, in a carefully-prepared circular, addressed the boards of guardians upon the subject of their responsibilities and resources. Nothing could be more deferential, not to say obsequious, than the language adopted by the committee. Avoiding all dictation, they submitted to the guardians the gravity of the crisis, and the legal definition of their duties. They reminded them that, in twenty-four unions, they were relieving in the first week in September 140,165 persons, of whom 129,536 were receiving outdoor relief, at a cost of 7,922*l.* 5*s.* 1*d.* per week. The ordinary charges of these unions amounted to considerably more than one-fourth of this sum. The committee pointed out that, supposing the guardians' present rate of expenditure to be maintained for a whole year, it could be met by a rate of 1*s.* 11½*d.* in the pound, once collected upon the net rateable value of the property chargeable to the relief of the poor. They then ventured to suggest that 1*s.* 2⅞*d.* per week, per head, was not a sufficiently high scale of relief. This circular was certainly written with rose-water, but though so mild in its expressions, it was not altogether ineffective. Probably the committee were becoming conscious of the auriferous power of their touch, and relied upon the hidden influence of the balance at their bankers'.

The Central Executive Committee failed in one attempt to increase their power, and it is the only failure with which they can be charged. Inspired with a well-founded belief that, from their local knowledge and representative constitution, they could administer the charitable funds with greater efficiency and economy than a committee unconnected with the district, it was resolved to make a proposal to the Mansion House Committee, to the effect that the funds at their disposal should be distributed through the agency of the Central Executive Committee. Colonel Wilson Patten was deputed to conduct this delicate negotiation. That it failed was no fault of his, but was simply attributable to the fact that the Lord Mayor and his friends were unwilling to abdicate their functions.

The determination of the Mansion House Committee is not to be regretted. If it somewhat deranged the symmetry of the general organisation, it certainly tended to increase the supplies for the benefit of Lancashire. Every churchwarden knows that two plates will collect more money than one, and it was undoubtedly far better for the interests of the cotton districts that both the Mansion House and Manchester should each be the depository and the dispenser of relief. It is more than likely that the Mansion House Committee has been now and then deceived into making grants to places which have not been entirely deserving of its liberality, and it is quite certain that, but for the ample information which the nice machinery of the Central Executive Committee subsequently placed at the disposal of its London coadjutor, this would have occurred with much greater frequency. But it may well be thought that even this drawback has been far more than compensated by the increased energy and importance given to the London Committee by the circumstance that it was directly engaged in conveying aid to the sufferers by the

Cotton Famine. When its first chairman, Mr. Cubitt, passed to an honoured grave, the muffled bells of many a Lancastrian church, and the silent prayers of many a thankful heart, bore witness to the gratitude which the labours of the Mansion House Committee had eminently excited and deserved.

But while the Central Executive Committee thus pleaded with the guardians, it was only by very slow degrees that any rise was made in the rate of relief administered by these boards. They excused themselves by urging the present oppressive increase in the rates; they submitted that they could not in justice to the customary paupers exceed the usual scale of relief merely because the applicants were cotton operatives. Manchester was giving about 1*s.* 6*d.* per head, and it was said that to raise this to 2*s.*,—the sum which was held by the advocates of the poor to be the minimum allowance which should be made,—would involve a rise of the poor-rates from 3*s.* 3*d.* to 4*s.* 6*d.* in the pound. The Central Executive Committee were anxious that 2*s.* should be the scale generally adopted. To those who suggested that the pressure on the small ratepayers would be intolerable, and that the required increase in the rates would pauperise the little shopkeepers and small-property owners, it was objected that their case was not proven. The committee foresaw the injustice of too widely opening their purse before the guardians had raised their rate of relief to a sufficient standard. Nothing could be softer than the tone of their address:—

'We feel assured that each case upon your books is relieved according to its individual merits; and that you administer relief to the destitute poor with care and judgment, and with a due regard to their necessities; but we take the liberty, with every submission to your descrimination and experience, of expressing our doubts whether this weekly sum of parochial relief (1*s.* 2$\frac{7}{8}$*d.*) is sufficient to meet generally the great necessities of the unfortunate mill-hands in this peculiar distress.

'We have every reason to know, up to the present time, the pressing wants of the mill-hands have been met, to a very great extent, by the mill-hands themselves; their savings, their furniture, their clothes, their investments have all been converted into ready money to buy bread;

but it is now well known that their private resources are almost wholly exhausted, and, as you must yourselves be aware of this significant fact, you may be at this moment determining to adopt forthwith a more adequate scale of parochial relief.

'The action of our Central Relief Committee, in disbursing aid to local relief committees, must necessarily be altogether regulated by the county of Lancaster and by the benevolence of England generally; but we must very explicitly request every guardian of the poor to remember that the Central Committee will not feel justified in so appropriating their grants as to make them compensate for any deficiency occasioned by a low standard of parochial relief.'

There is just the suspicion of a threat observable in the last few lines. But for all this the rate of relief made very slow upward progress. With a half-indignant expression, one of the most energetic members of the committee demanded, 'Would the collective opinion of the manufacturers of this district hesitate an instant to decide that a poor-rate of 2,000,000*l*. a year would be a small price to pay to prevent the dispersion of a population without which their capital is valueless, or to prevent the proportionate loss consequent on a reduction of the strength, health, and contentment of their workmen; or to avert the horrors of their decimation by disease?' But Sir James Kay-Shuttleworth put his pungent question in vain, for in the first place there is no collective opinion among manufacturers upon subjects of this character, and in the next, because the individual opinion of the majority was that it would be better that anybody rather than themselves should provide the requisite aid.

Shortly after the publication of this circular, the Central Executive Committee lost its chairman by the lamented death of Lord Ellesmere. Largely interested in the district as a landowner, he was also eminently fitted for the situation, by the possession of great amiability of temper and polished courtesy of demeanour. Had his successor been less distinguished, it is probable that his untimely vacation of the chair would have been more loudly regretted. But the acceptance of this position by Lord Derby was felt to be an event so fraught with benefit to the conduct of the business of the committee, and so calculated to insure for its operations the further confidence and support of the people of England, that congratulations somewhat overpowered regret. In these days, when earls have no retainers, when there is no royal or noble road to public estimation but that which all may tread with equal favour, Lord Derby holds a position in the empire hardly second to that of any other subject of the Crown. He is a great lord in Lancashire by right of lineage and property, but neither the splendid annals nor the wide domains of his house would have won for him the position he holds by the higher right of personal genius and character. Politically, it was an immense advantage and support to the action of the Government in Lancashire, that the chief of the Opposition should lend his assistance in so conspicuous a part. To Mr. Villiers, whose department was more especially charged with the responsibility, the accession of Lord Derby must have given great satisfaction; while the Special Commissioner could not but have felt his work materially lightened by the enrolment of so distinguished a coadjutor in a committee of which he was not an unimportant member. To Lord Derby himself the position must have afforded sincere gratification. In the active life of a statesman, it cannot be rarely that the mind is beset with doubts as to whether the path of policy towards which he is led, often by the considerations of party, is that which is certainly the wisest, the best, and the most patriotic. No such question overhung this good and great work. Lord Derby has, by his occupancy of the chair of the Central Executive Committee, materially increased his claims to the respect of his countrymen; nor can it be doubted that he himself enjoys the sweet reward which is the sure attendant upon the fulfilment of such a disinterested duty. Those who have benefited by his labours and liberality, will remember with interest that two hundred years have passed away since the seventh Earl of Derby, then also king in the Isle of Man, attacked the town of Bolton at the head of a host of his retainers. It was his sad fate to be beheaded in the town he had so rashly invaded. Another seven Stanleys have since borne the illustrious title, and the fourteenth earl has ministered with devoted attention to the wants of the suffering cotton-workers, the descendants of the stern Puritans who stood around the scaffold of his ancestor. How happy a circumstance it is,—how sure a proof of the advance of civilisation, that nobility is now thought to be ennobled rather by the performance of peaceful duties than by the doughtiest feats of arms!

One of the first acts of the committee after the election of its new chairman was to address a circular to the magistrates and chairmen of petty sessions, warning them of the probable danger of an increase of mendicancy and vagrancy, and suggesting that they should take steps to discourage and suppress it. Especially they recommended, that indiscriminate almsgiving should be discountenanced, as likely to attract hordes of beggars into the district, who would trade upon the existing distress. The committee had now also to acknowledge large additions to their funds. The Bridgewater House Committee had increased their monthly payment from 4,000*l.* to 8,000*l.*, and wisely permitted the relaxation of the condition they had annexed to this grant, that no part of their funds should go to supplement relief given by the guardians. Undoubtedly a serious aggravation of the distress would have been caused if this policy had been rigorously adhered to: for instance, it was shown that no less than seventy-eight per cent. of the families relieved by the Manchester and Salford District Provident Society, including many of the most deserving cases, were also in the receipt of parochial relief.

Local relief committees were now becoming very numerous. Their formation was encouraged by the circumstance that the grants of the Central Committee were made only to those places in which such organisations were existing. Early in September the Central Executive Committee addressed a circular to these bodies, which they were anxious should, where convenient, represent the landed proprietors, the clergy, the ministers of religion, and the chief employers of labour. In language equally moderate with that which they had used to the guardians, they assured the local committees that no neglect of duty on the part of the superior classes would forfeit the claim of the indigent poor of their district to participation in the national bounty, yet that the committee would feel themselves justified in taking strict observance of the fulfilment of local duties. It was declared to be a necessary qualification for participation in the grants of the committee that an efficient local relief committee should be appointed, having at least the sanction if not the co-operation of the principal employers of labour, and of the chief subscribers to the local relief funds. The local committees were anxiously urged to develop labour schemes; to establish sewing-schools for the women and girls, and educational schools for the children. They were urged to send to school the children of parents who were in the receipt of relief, and to pay their educational fee, which generally amounted to twopence a week. With more invention than had been shown by the guardians, the committee suggested the most suitable forms of labour for the able-bodied; yet, in this respect, it must not be forgotten that they profited by the experience of these boards. Their activity was untiring, and their well-directed ambition limited only by the magnitude of the work before them. They laid themselves out in every possible way to catch the popular sympathy for the benefit of their distressed clients; establishing clothing stores, dépôts for gifts of all sorts in kind, and for the distribution of coals. With thoughtful ingenuity, they gave notice that they had even provided package labels, in order that no losses might occur through misdirection.

In October, the financial position of the charitable associations, appeared to be in a very hopeful condition. The Central Relief Committee were masters of funds amounting to 150,000*l.*, and these were every day augmented. The Mansion House Committee held 50,000*l.* The local subscriptions amounted to 98,000*l.* The present rate of expenditure throughout all the unions in Lancashire did not exceed, for in-maintenance and outdoor relief, 1*s.* 2*d.* in the pound upon their rateable value. Fifty local committees had been formed, and were now in action. Taking the number of cotton-workers at 360,751, there were now 58,638 in full work, 119,712 working short time, and 182,401 wholly unemployed. The appeal of the cotton districts for aid from without was being nobly responded to, not only by the rest of the kingdom, but from every quarter of the globe. In shameful contrast to the illiberality of many who were at this time making enormous gains by the actual circumstances which had caused the distress of their poor neighbours, came princely donations from districts connected only with the suffering population by the common tie of humanity. Looking around the manufacturing area at this time, it would be seen that the local subscriptions had utterly failed to meet the requirements of the occasion, and it was feared that this source of relief would not be likely to increase very largely, now that the nation was placing such considerable funds at the disposal of the great committees. Up to this time it may be safely affirmed that the operatives had at least contributed as much to their own maintenance as they had received from the charity of others; while, if the sacrifices of those who gave and of those whose savings and household treasures were dragged from them, are measured by a truer standard than that of actual pecuniary value, the losses of the employers will bear no comparison with those of the employed. The richest class in the cotton districts had been benefited by the forced suspension of production; and now, before the burden of maintaining the 'hands' had been fully cast upon them, they found themselves liberally assisted in this responsibility by the people of England. Their poor-rates were not excessive; and though, with regard to those who were manufacturers, their machinery was standing still, yet the value of any cotton or goods they were possessed of was continually rising; and even if they had none, they might at least congratulate themselves upon the fact that the locality was not now, as formerly, charged with the entire cost of the maintenance of their operatives. Some, who had stored a large stock of cotton before the outbreak of war in America, continued production, preferring to keep their hands together and employed, rather than to realize immediate profits by a sale of the raw material. The only risk these manufacturers ran was the sudden restoration of peace between the North and South. Had the differences between the Federals and the Confederates been patched up, they would have endured that regret which assails the producer who has missed the time when he might have realized large profits. But the course taken by these gentlemen—among whom were the largest spinners and manufacturers in the district, whose chimneys have never ceased to smoke, nor their spindles to turn, during the period of Famine—is one deserving of the credit due to the exercise of prescience and courage, of commercial acumen and social justice. They resisted the temptation to sell their cotton, but there is no reason to suppose that any loss accrued to them by this policy. It was not in the power of all to act as did these few, for all had neither their capital nor their opportunity. But, as a class, it must be said of the manufacturers and merchants, that they had not rightly appreciated their responsibilities and duties; that they had made no effort to master the difficulty in any way commensurate either with their commanding position or their reputation for wealth and independence. On the other hand, too much praise can hardly be given to the conduct of very many individuals throughout the district, whose obligations were not those of large capitalists, and whose alms not unfrequently formed a considerable portion of their income. Many a tale of distress was poured into their kindly ears, by sufferers to whom even their attention was a valuable relief, and many a luxury was voluntarily resigned for the sake of those who were now brought nigh to starvation. Brotherly kindness and sisterly love are not exotics in any English community; and all know how much more effective, in the relief of distress, are the willing alms of the visible giver than the donations of those who cannot transmit the gift's most cherished accompaniment. Nor can it be doubted that one of the best results of this time of trial has been the establishment of greater sympathy between class and class, which the meeting of the givers and receivers of relief has occasioned. Many a factory lass will date her first faint notions of the real value of graceful courtesy allied with personal charm, of what is meant by delicacy and what is implied by refinement, from her recollections of the sewing-schools. Many a mother and infant owe their existence to the nourishment which, in the sorest hour of their need, they obtained from some kind matron, who was herself distressed at the limitation of her powers of giving. Many a man, who now looks back upon the dark days through which he has passed, can trace his rescue from awful want—and, it may be, from crime—to the large-hearted fellow-man who interested himself in his behalf, and either supported him in his difficulties, or sought out for him, and assisted him to reach, a new sphere of labour. All this has been done, and done willingly and thankfully, by the men and women,—the ladies and gentlemen of Lancashire.

CHAPTER VIII.

OCTOBER—NOVEMBER 1862.

LANCASHIRE DISTRESS had now fully won national sympathy. Ungrudgingly the country was prepared to share the calamity with the cotton districts, and that such was England's duty cannot be denied. But this enlargement of the area of responsibility had been contended for by some upon very illogical grounds. The arguments advanced upon the conduct of the operatives had been well supported by their demeanour and their sacrifices. Perhaps it was not too much to say that no other working-class population would have been possessed of sufficient intelligence and self-control to bear such privations with equal fortitude and resignation. They had done more than this; they had to a very great extent shown themselves masters of the opportunity afforded for self-improvement by their compulsory inactivity. There was good ground also for urging that the shopkeeping class was suffering greatly from the depression of trade consequent upon a withdrawal of wages amounting to 136,000*l.* a week; and that the superior classes were heavily burdened by the demands upon their charity, and by the unusual pressure of the poor-rates. But there was no legitimate support for the proposition which was made and repeated for national assistance in the form of a grant of money, though this policy was advocated by many, not without a character for unselfishness, prudence, and experience. By some it was whispered, and muttered by others; with some it was the panacea for the distress; with others, the equitable right of suffering Lancashire. By no less a voice than Mr. Cobden's such national aid was sought, upon the principle, that as the distress was a consequence of national policy, its relief was therefore a national responsibility.

We may rejoice that the nation charged its private purse with the responsibility, while we condemn the principle thus laid down as utterly unsound and fallacious. Nor is it easy to resist astonishment that it should have been advanced by one, who of all men in England has been, more than any other, the cause of distress in particular trades, by his influence upon the national policy. To question that the abolition of the Corn Laws was a wise, just, and beneficial measure, or that the French Treaty has tended enormously, and most advantageously, to extend the commerce of England, is to doubt evidence the most plain and convincing. Mr. Cobden has done the State much service, and the country knows it; but the magnitude and suddenness of these commercial reforms have beggared many a man, whose claim upon the public funds he would have been the first to ignore. Suffering possesses an eternal claim to relief, on the grounds of humanity, of nationality, and of the complex construction of society. And the legitimate, unquestioned claim of Lancashire upon the public at large rested upon the unparalleled extent of her distress, upon the fact that her entire industry was paralysed, and upon her confessed inability to meet the difficulty by her own resources.

England was proud to show that she could bear this heavy blow without swerving from the political path which she believed to be founded upon principles of truth and justice: proud of the men and women who, though of the working classes, had been accustomed to a high degree of social comfort and respectability, to warm houses and good food, and who now struggled against the loss of their independence, and when forced to accept charitable aid, did so with behaviour as honourable as had been their reluctance; and it must be said that the result of the struggle justified her pride and rewarded her generosity.

It was because the distress had exceeded a certain limit, because it was so overwhelming in its incidence, that it was acknowledged to be national. Local distress is in the first place a local responsibility, because the presumption is warranted by experience, that labour produces wealth, and that the district which has profited by the labour of a population should bear the pressure of bad times. It was once advanced, by way of excuse for the inactivity of the landowners of Lancashire, that they were not so very wealthy, because the value of agricultural land in the county had only increased thirty-three per cent. since 1800, whereas in the easternmost of the English counties the value of such land had increased one hundred per cent. With reference to an argument so transparently fallacious, it would be sufficient to say that the landowners of Lancashire know the reason why; and probably they do not regret that their land produces minerals and stone, and bricks and mortar, instead of bringing forth corn and hay. A better reason for extending the responsibility is found in the indissoluble interests of all classes of producers throughout the country. While the cotton manufacture languished, the woollen looms of Yorkshire drove such a rattling trade as they had never known before. While Manchester was under a cloud, the sun of prosperity was shedding unusual rays upon the flaxen industry of Belfast. India consolidated the foundations of a glorious commercial future through the very circumstances which distressed the English cotton district; while, nearer home, Birmingham forged, at large profits, the very arms which maintained the strife that was desolating the States of America and causing the privations of Lancashire.

At the November meeting of the Central Relief Committee, the condition and prospects of the cotton manufacturing districts were thoroughly exposed. Nothing could be more cheering than the response which had been made from all quarters to the energetic appeals of the committee. The funds at their disposal had now reached the goodly sum of 180,714*l.*, and they felt able to promise aid to the extent of 25,000*l.* per month for the next five months, a period which would carry them far into the spring of 1863. The bishops had issued pastorals to their clergy upon the subject; Cardinal Wiseman had penned mellifluous sentences to the same effect; nor were the Dissenters of every shade of religious opinion behindhand. The Army and Navy had their share of acknowledgment from the committee, for they also had come forward, not in person but in purse—a manner which, in this war against starvation, was far more effective. The colonies had sent of their abundance, abundantly. The thanks of the committee were wafted to Buenos Ayres for a donation of 415*l.*, and to far Bangalore for half that amount. Egypt had her acknowledgments for value received, and many cities and towns of the United Kingdom —Belfast and Newcastle, Dublin and Tunbridge Wells, with many others—partook of the same reward. Oxford had opened her mythical chest; Birmingham had sent her moneys; wealthy firms had made large donations: one had forwarded three thousand needles, and another two thousand tons of coals. But the appetite of the committee grew stronger upon their generous supplies; their cry for help grew bolder and louder, and even at the meeting in which these acknowledgments were made, it was said that nothing short of a million of money would be sufficient for the necessities of the case.

And the case was certainly bad enough. Already there were 208,621 persons in receipt of parochial relief, an excess of 163,184 over the number which had been relieved in the corresponding week of the last year. October had added 45,437 to this hapless total; and, besides this large number of paupers, there were 143,870 persons relieved by the local committees. The average percentage of pauperism in the twenty-seven unions of the cotton district was now 10·8, while last year it had been only 2·4. But in Ashton-under-Lyne, the darkest spot of all, there was 20 per cent. of the population in the receipt of parochial relief, besides the many who were relieved exclusively by the committees, by the manufacturers, and by what may be termed irregular charity. In outdoor relief the expenses of twenty-four of these unions exceeded by more than 10,000*l.* the cost of the corresponding week in the previous year. This was the sad story which Mr. Farnall had to tell the committee; and while it cannot be said that his reports were ever pleasant reading—seeing that they have always been made up of such facts and figures —yet it must be acknowledged that they have invariably possessed the merit of utter truthfulness—extenuating nothing, and setting down nought in favour or in malice.

The whole country was now aroused, and zealously bent upon succouring Lancashire. Lords-lieutenant were beating up their counties. The clergy were preaching moving sermons, and their efforts were rewarded by many a well-filled plate. Mayors convened public meetings, and provincial eloquence was strong on behalf of the suffering thousands. Money and money's worth poured into the coffers of the great committees, by whom it was retailed with the most honourable avoidance of that subtraction not altogether unknown even among honorary financial mediums.

Nor were the local committees idle: they had considerably increased the amount of their subscriptions. But if there were among them more willing and kindly visitors than liberal givers to the relief of the distressed, it must be said that the constant flow of assistance from without had somewhat disproved the necessity for great sacrifices within the district. Still, it must be remembered that the distress was spreading fast. Its increase had been aptly likened—by one who had anxiously watched its course from the commencement—to the circling ripple on water, extending its area with remorseless precision, as it passed from the operative to the small shopkeeper, and from him to the larger ratepayer. Men's hearts began to fail them with fear of what might be coming upon the district. Was it famine—the famine not of food for machines, but of food for men; or was it pestilence, or both? The wavering began to importune for pecuniary assistance from the Government. With anxious abasement they compared the Cotton Famine with the Irish Potato Famine; but many were determined in their opposition to any such relief, and, fortunately for all, the press of Manchester and of the whole country gave no uncertain negative to any proposals of this nature.

The distress was sorest in Ashton, Blackburn, Preston, and Wigan. It is observable that one of the agencies, most powerful in its moral influence, and by no means insignificant in its material contributions in aid of the distress, was not so firmly established in these as in other towns of the district. Unquestionably, co-operation is the most important movement now at work among the lower classes of society. Slowly but steadily the true principles of co-operation are permeating the working classes, casting off the old dross of communistic Owenism, and exhibiting results such as must ensure their rapid development. There are now but few townships in the cotton districts without a co-operative store, and nearly all are modelled upon the pattern of that patriarch of such societies, the successful and well-established association known as the 'Equitable Pioneers' of Rochdale. Co-operation is the oldest of the discoveries of civilisation, but yet it may be said that largely to the founders of this society belongs the honour of opening a new future to the working-men of England. So recently as 1844, a handful of Rochdale weavers clubbed their pence together with the intention of establishing a co-operative store. Such was the origin of this association, and how great results may flow from small beginnings is to be learnt from the history of this undertaking. They started in business with a capital of 28*l*., purchasing articles of food at wholesale prices, and retailing among themselves at the current prices of the neighbouring shops. 'No credit,' was the first and most necessary of their rules. All the members were expected, but not compelled, to deal at the store. Their most successful discovery was the mode of dividing their profits, in accordance with the true principles of co-operation. Customers, upon making a purchase, receive a ticket, stating the amount expended; and the dividend is paid upon the aggregate sum of these tickets in the possession of each member at the time of a division of profits. From time to time the members change these tickets at the store for 1*l*. cheques, to avoid confusion at the settlement. So that the man who has a long family, and is a large purchaser of goods, is, concurrently with his expenditure, laying up for his own benefit a larger share of the profits. Year by year this society has progressed—always well managed, always growing richer, always extending its operations, and including some new undertaking for the profit of its members. The accounts are audited once a week by members of the society, and stock-taking is performed quarterly. The narrow hilly street in which its principal storehouses are now the chief object of attraction, is lined on both sides by these establishments, of which it possesses sixteen in all, each being devoted to a different branch of trade. But whether a member of this association buys at one a measure of flour, at another a pair of clogs, or at a third a pound of meat, he receives the price-ticket upon which his dividend of profit is assured. At length, by a process as marvellous as it is honourable to the conductors of the

Equitable Pioneers' Association, its yearly sales of goods have amounted to upwards of 158,000*l*. How largely the habits of prudence, temperance, and economy, fostered by the influence of this society and similar associations, may have tended to produce that self-respect and good conduct among the operative class, which have been so observable during the Cotton Famine, it would be impossible to determine; but some notion of the extent to which this association has contributed to the support of the unemployed, may be gathered from the fact that during the year 1862 the number of its members was lessened by 399, and the excess of withdrawals over receipts of capital was 15,766*l*.; while its profits, which were mainly expended in the same direction, amounted in this most disastrous year to no less than 17,564*l*. Nor is all this by any means the measure of the support which this association afforded to its members, many of whom existed upon funds obtained by the mortgage of their shares, while some were helped by its weekly donation of 10*l*. to the general relief funds.

In order to prevent the capital of the association from passing into the hands of moneyed men, no member is permitted to hold more than 100*l*. worth of shares. And for the promotion of self-education and the intellectual employment of leisure hours, one of the standing rules declares that 2½ per cent. of the profits shall be assigned to the purchase of books and the maintenance of news-rooms. This association is possessed of a library of about six thousand volumes, and its news-room tables are covered with fifteen daily and sixteen weekly newspapers and periodicals, besides twenty-one monthlies and four quarterly reviews. The strongest proof of the substantial character of this society is afforded by the fact that it has weathered the trials of the Cotton Famine, uninjured in credit or reputation. The quarterly report for September 1862, showed that its shares were held by 3,700 members; that, in spite of the withdrawals and difficulties of the time, the quarter's profits amounted to 4,422*l*., and that a 'divvy'—as the reward of co-operation is sometimes familiarly termed—of 2*s*. 5*d*. in the pound had been declared. The report for the first quarter of 1863 showed an increase both of members and of trade, the total number of the former having risen to 4,000.

The Equitable Pioneers' Association is the acknowledged model upon which, at this period, some three hundred similar associations were known to exist. Their profits upon business done, to the extent of something like two-and-a-half millions sterling, amounted to nearly 100,000*l*. for the year, which was divided among the members at an average of 6*s*. in the pound, after payment of interest at the rate of 5 per cent. to 77,000 members upon a capital of 349,000*l*. Many co-operative associations have originated in a feeling on the part of their promoters somewhat more fanciful than that of appropriating the ordinary profits of retail trade, or even than that of improving the social and moral condition of the working classes by the encouragement of provident and temperate habits. That these advantages result from such co-operation is as certain as that apple-trees produce apples. But there are not a few among the most active promoters of this movement, who are still believers in the doctrines of Owen and St. Simon—who see in this movement an advance towards that millennium, in which there shall be an equal distribution of this world's goods, and when, like the Apostles, men shall have all things in common.

If it were not certain that the progress of the co-operative movement will clear away this nonsense, it might be expected that the rate of its advance would be seriously checked when it had attained such dimensions as to attract the general attention of the superior classes. Communism was possible to monastic institutions, but Communism without celibacy becomes Mormonism, or worse. Unless human society is to be reduced to the moral level of a rabbit-warren—unless it is prepared to annihilate the mutual responsibilities of father and mother, of husband and wife, of brother and sister—in fact, to make all people the common care of all, there can be no communistic fellowship in labour or its produce. The future of co-operation is not clouded by these absurdities; yet in its future is involved, as surely as night follows day, and year to year, such a change in the condition of society as some may wonder and some be startled to contemplate. But it must be understood that all co-operation must be of capital, and capital must be understood to include all the productive powers of man, whether it be body-power, brain-power, or money-power, or one or all, separate or in conjunction. The lever of self-help is capital, and the surest, as well as the safest road to its further acquisition, is beset with those gifts, which, being rightly used, lead to the possession of credit, and power, and wealth. The co-operative store suggests a means to increase the capital of the working man so sure and easy, that their general establishment may be regarded as certain. Notably they have failed in London; but this has been owing to the fact that the few instead of the many appreciated their advantage, and that the supporters of the movement were too widely separated for successful co-operation. Yet the store is but the whisper, the beginning, the first step of a peaceful revolution, from which results may be expected far more important than the retailing of apparel and food. The co-operative store is the agency by which the working man may most quickly and with the greatest benefit to himself acquire the possession of savings. Setting aside its valuable moral results, this is the sum of its accomplishment. And it is to be remembered that, as a rule, men who save do not save to spend; they save capital in order to employ it in assisting their power of production.

What, then, will the provident and industrious working man, few or many, do with his savings? He has abandoned the public-house for his own fireside; he is accustomed to some trade, familiar with the news and events of the day; tradition or experience will have taught him that his privations, as a man set to work by the assistance of another's capital, occurred during a depression of trade; that such hard times must recur, and that nothing but the accumulation of savings can then keep him from a forced dependence on legal or charitable relief He will know that there are times when he can only maintain the wages rate against the combined action of masters by the painful agency of a strike. He will not fail to perceive that the most productive use to which he can put his little capital is that in which it shall be a partner in his own handicraft. He will have learned by the fate of the handloom weaver, by the penury of the small shopkeeper, by the disappearance of the little yeoman-farmer, that capital must be employed in masses, in order to reap the greatest profits; and wide-spread co-operative production will be the consequence, encouraged and made secure by such legislation as the Limited Liability Act and the Provident Societies Act of 1862.

There are many co-operative manufacturing establishments now existing in the cotton district. One of the first was started by members of the Rochdale Association. In this undertaking, which now numbers about sixteen hundred proprietors, it is provided that no one shall possess a larger interest than 200*l*. Up to a very recent date, these companies were not formed under the provisions of the Limited Liability Act, and consequently the shareholders were exposed to unnecessary risks. But in most cases they had a shrewd regulation that their brokers and dealers should not be shareholders, and so avoided the danger of any rash speculations on their part. The Manufacturing Society of Rochdale commenced business in shops and sheds in various parts of the town, one operation being carried on in one place, and another in another, on the primary principles of co-operation—the whole of the profits being divided among the workers. But soon it became evident that they must have a factory, built and fitted after the manner of the factories of the cotton lords. And before long there grew up, near to the river's bank, a co-operative mill, from foundation to roof of the most approved form and construction, with its towering tall chimney, with all its appointments the best calculated to secure the health and comfort of the workers; and its cost was not less than fifty thousand pounds.

It would have been impossible to effect this by means of the capital possessed by those who could or would be the factory hands. It was therefore resolved to set apart a portion only of the profits, to be divided amongst the operatives, in addition to their wages; the remainder being paid as dividend, after satisfying the demand for interest upon capital. But a large number of the *employés* were not shareholders, and it was soon objected that they had no right to a participation in profits. The result of this was the demise of the primary principle of co-operation, which is the division of the entire profits among the actual producers, and the establishment of the joint-stock principle with limited liability, which is co-operation in its most beneficial form, after being transplanted from the retailing store to the production of commodities in competition with capitalists of unlimited wealth. This is co-operation advanced two steps from the store.

If co-operation be not understood to be the co-operation of capital, it cannot succeed in its more important objects. It is and can be nothing else. By limiting the share which a member may possess in the enterprise, the same principle which binds the shareholders of the London and Westminster Bank may unite with equal facility and safety the thousand partners of a cotton factory. In the eastern part of Lancashire, especially in and about the town of Bacup, and throughout the union of Haslingden, these co-operative manufacturing companies are very numerous. In 1859-60 they realized large profits, and in some cases paid dividends of fifty per cent. A considerable portion of the capital thus accumulated is invested in new mills, many of which are now in course of erection. Towards the close of 1862, the shareholders of seventeen such companies, formed in the Haslingden Union, memorialised the Central Relief Committee, stating that their paid-up capital, from six thousand shareholders, amounted to about 300,000*l.* They submitted, with a good show of reason, that the great bulk of this, 'apart from the co-operative stimulant, would either not have been earned, or would have been spent uselessly, if not injuriously.' Their complaint was that the local committees would not relieve them unless their shares were mortgaged to their full present value in the market, or were unsaleable. It is some proof of the effect which, to the extent of their adoption, these societies exercised upon the distress, that the memorialists stated that, though 478 of their shareholders were entirely out of work, and had been so for periods varying from seven to fifty-two weeks, and though, besides this number, there were 800 of their shareholders working short time, from two to four days a week, yet there were but 69 obtaining relief from either the guardians or the relief funds. They feared the destruction of their companies by the ruin of their shareholders; they complained that many of the members of local relief committees were opposed to the principles of co-operation, and consequently dealt unfairly by them. The same cry was to be heard from co-operative societies on all sides; and one of the most painful duties of the committees must have been the refusal of relief to these unhappy shareholders. But it was clearly incumbent upon the administrators of public charity, as upon those of poor-law relief, to view with one eye all the possessors of property, whether invested in benefit or co-operative societies, in cottages or other real property, or in the stock-in-trade of small shopkeepers. Upon the suggestion of Lord Derby, the Central Executive Committee subsequently adopted, as an appendix to their report, the following memorandum, written by himself, relative to the claims of co-operative shareholders:—

'The co-operative societies stand upon a peculiar footing. The societies known by this name comprise provision and clothing stores, and flour-mills, which are conducted to a great extent on co-operative principles; but cotton manufactories called co-operative are generally, if not universally, simply joint-stock companies of limited liability, the capital of which has been subscribed in small shares, chiefly by workmen in the cotton districts, and which are often built and conducted with the aid of loans. They have arisen out of motives which do the highest honour to the operative classes; and there is no question but that they have induced habits of frugality, temperance, and self-restraint, which have operated greatly to the benefit of the working classes, morally and physically. But it is indisputable that the shares in some of these co-operative societies are at the present moment greatly depreciated, and in some cases actually valueless. Is, then, the possession, say, of one or more shares in one of these societies, to exclude the holder from a title to relief? On the principle applied to the savings-banks, the answer should be in the affirmative; and the more so as the investment has hitherto yielded a larger interest. But it is to be remembered, on the other hand, that whatever has been invested in the savings-bank, realizes, on its withdrawal, the whole of its nominal amount; whereas the co-operative shares are in many cases not only depreciated, but, if compelled to be sold, would realize little or nothing to the possessors. The utmost, therefore, which can fairly be required, is that the holder shall have mortgaged his share, and that he is not, at the present moment, deriving any pecuniary benefit from it. In such a case, I think the holder might fairly be entitled to relief, as having, for the time, no other resources.'

Upon the active revival of the cotton trade, it may be expected that co-operative manufacturing will be largely extended. For how great is the incentive to an operative, who is already a member of a co-operative store, to invest his savings in these shares, and to transfer his labour to a co-operative mill! In addition to his wages, he knows that he is increasing the profits on his capital. But besides this, he is working among men socially and morally the flower of the district—men, too, of whom at least a great number are stimulated to exertion by the same hope that invigorates his energies.

As the number of these mills becomes greater, so will the number of operatives who are shareholders increase also; and it may well be thought that the stimulant of self-interest will give such an impulse to production, that yarns and goods will be manufactured more cheaply in these factories than in the establishments of capitalists. Nor must it be forgotten, in estimating the future of this movement, that of the inventors very few are not members of the operative class. And if the most thoughtful and industrious members of this class are to be found in the co-operative mills, there also most assuredly will be found the largest number of inventors, and the greatest skill in the application of inventions. And what, in this respect, applies to the cotton manufacture, bears equal relation to every other industry, even to the cultivation of the soil, especially now that farms have become manufactories of food.

In the autumn of this year the Poor Law Board determined to suspend their regulation requiring that outdoor relief should be given in kind to the extent of one-half. At first sight the advantage of this change is not very obvious, seeing that the food furnished by the guardians is generally of better quality than that purchased by the operatives. But the distress had sharply attacked a class above the operatives, and the small shopkeepers were complaining bitterly that their means of livelihood were taken from them by the guardians and the relief committees. They had given 'strap,' as they term credit, to their customers, until their debts were their only possession. The change thus sanctioned by the Poor Law Board exercised a most beneficial influence upon their business.

The manufacture of clothing in the numerous sewing-schools must have been exceedingly large, for there were now twenty thousand girls thus employed. Usually they sat back to back, and stitched away for sixpence or eightpence a day. 'Yon wench wi' a white feather in her cap,' was the expression used by one of these honest Lancashire lasses to designate the young lady who was the teacher of her class. There was no coarseness in this remark, only the simplicity and utter plainness of speech which marks the character of very many of these girls. In general, they were quiet and tractable, very ignorant of domestic matters, but by no means averse to learn of their kind instructresses. But for this mode of collecting them and giving them occupation, their condition would have become most dangerous and demoralising. The increasing numbers of both sexes out of work excused any suggestion for their employment, however visionary and unpractical it might seem to be. Still it is rather startling, even now, to read of a proposition to hire the 'Great Eastern,' and send a shipload of 10,000 operatives to Queensland. Voluntary and independent emigration is no new idea in the United Kingdom; but wholesale emigration, planned by the State, for the relief of distress at home, is tolerably certain to lead from bad to worse. The only attempt made by England to found a colony at one stroke was suggested by expediency, and left behind it the likeness of a crime. The occasion was when Lord Mansfield's judgment in the Somersett case induced the black servants—so numerous in London a century ago—to claim their freedom. After they had attained this boon, hundreds of them hung about the streets of London, in the most pitiable state of want and destitution. Some died, and about five hundred were shipped, with a number of women of loose character, for Sierra Leone. The intention was that they should establish a colony—they quickly found a grave.

The condition of most of the cotton towns was now very

like what it had been during the latter months of the summer, except that the numbers in the receipt of relief were continually increasing. The allowance made by the boards of guardians showed symptoms of increase, and though in some unions the prospective advantages of the rate-in-aid stimulated their liberality, yet the scale of relief made very slow advance. The winter of 1862 was regarded with the most anxious forebodings, both in the district and throughout the country. 'Typhus and starvation would be upon Lancashire,' said one; frost and famine were promised by another. The correspondent of the 'Times,' who veils a noble name under the well-known initials, S. G. O., though he is not equally successful in hiding the warm and generous heart that dictates his appeals, besought the aid of Government, deeming the strain upon optional benevolence greater than it should be made to bear. But it must be said that this heresy was corrected in the editorial columns of the 'Times.' Not less determined was the 'Daily Telegraph' in its efforts to stimulate charity on behalf of the men of Lancashire. The 'Daily News' foraged out Count Rumford's Essays, and taught from them how, by co-operation and good management, 1,000 or 1,500 people might be well fed for 2*d.* apiece per day. But a more useful contribution was that announced by Lord Lindsay, when, on the part of his father and himself, he promised the mayor of Wigan, for the local relief funds, a donation of 100*l.* a week for five months, and an immediate gift of 500*l.* to provide clothing or bedding, or for other necessary demands.

Considering the very large sums already subscribed for relief, and the unbounded resources upon which demand could be made on behalf of the distressed population, it will now seem imprudent, if not inhuman, that the allowance of 2*s.* per head, instead of being only partially reached by the guardians, should not have been universal. Undoubtedly they must have raised the scale of relief very considerably, had it not been for the fact that, where not supplemented by the relief funds, it was in most cases assisted by private charity. Clothes of all kinds were being distributed from the stores; hogsheads of soup were made and given away at the cost of private individuals; and, besides this, there was very much stray almsgiving.

But none could fail to observe that, during the winter of 1862, London was far more busy in collecting aid for Lancashire than the County Palatine herself. One cause of this was, it may be thought, the inferior strength of the observing faculty to that of the imagination. The mind of London pictured to itself scenes of misery unthought of by the ordinary passenger through a Lancastrian town, and it is doubtful if any dweller in Lancashire would have written upon the subject of the distress in the manner of some writers in the London journals.

Yet the distress was very great, and at the second weekly meeting of the Central Executive Committee, in the month of November, it was stated that destitution was advancing at the rate of 3,000 persons a day. The committee voted 30,000*l.* in relief, a portion of which was to be applied to the purchase of clothing and bedding, for which purpose it was stated by Mr. Cobden that 300,000*l.* would be wanted before Christmas. In the next week the committee had the grateful duty of acknowledging many gifts. Edinburgh had sent 2,000*l.*, and Melbourne had made up her subscriptions to 10,550*l.* Lord Ducie had provided, gratuitously, office and warehouse room for the committee. Practical sympathy was shown by a London firm of egg-merchants, who offered 1,000 cases for packing clothing, and placed a vehicle for their conveyance at the service of the committee. Mr. Ansdell had given his picture of the 'Hunted Slave,' and the Wesleyan Methodists' Committee had sent 5,000*l.* Lincoln's Inn gave 50*l.* a week, and Colonel Wilson Patten announced that the Cotton Districts Relief Committee would increase their contribution from 8,000*l.* to 12,000*l.* a month for three months. Mr. Farnall's report to this meeting showed a rapid increase of pauperism. The 27 unions to which he referred were expending 15,672*l.* weekly in outdoor relief; but, even now, the rate of relief was in the case of one union as low as 1*s.* 0½*d.*, the highest being Glossop, which gave 1*s.* 10½*d.* per head.

It having been understood that the New South Wales Fund, which would probably exceed 15,000*l.*, was to be devoted to educational purposes, Sir James Kay-Shuttleworth, whose knowledge and experience upon matters relating to education is widely known, drew up the following estimate for the guidance of the committee in their expenditure of this sum:—

'If, as was too probable, 250,000 factory operatives were out of work at Christmas, and one-half of them were dependent on the Relief Committee for support, they would consist of the following classes: Five-tenths of that half, or 62,500, would be women; about three-tenths, or 37,500, boys and girls; and about two-tenths, or 25,000, men and youths.

'If 35,000 females attended the sewing-classes, 27,500 would be left at home to attend to the families of 125,000 factory workmen, which, taking into account the fact that many mothers and some daughters are not at work in factories, would provide for domestic service.

'If 35,000 females were divided into 230 classes of about 150 on the average, the superintendents would require stipends of 18*l.* 15*s.* for six months, or 15*s.* per week, making a total of 4,312*l.*

'Twenty-four weeks' schooling for an average attendance of 30,000 boys and girls, at 2*d.* per week, would cause an outlay of 6,000*l.*, and 1,000*l.* might be granted towards the cost of the schooling of younger children of families in the receipt of relief.

'The stipends of masters of 100 schools containing 15,000 youths would, at thirty shillings per week, amount in six months to 3,750*l.* 10*s.*

'These schools would also each require eight assistants, selected from well-qualified youths out of work, and remunerated by an extra rate of relief.

'The superintendence of the work of 35,000 women, the schooling of 30,000 boys and girls and of 15,000 youths, might thus be provided for 14,062*l.*, and 1,000*l.* applied towards the school-pence of children too young to work. The anticipated further remittances from New South Wales would provide, at least partially, for any increase of these forms of dependence beyond these limits during the next six months.'

This estimate was accepted by the Executive Committee and acted upon, the fund being set apart as 'The New South Wales Fund,' and grants were made from it especially for educational and scholastic purposes, and for the sewing-schools.

November of this year was signalised by an active revival of the controversy as to the pressure of the poor-rates in Lancashire. On the side of the county, it was said that the rates had already reached the highest point to which they could be raised without inflicting as much pauperism as their increase would provide relief. Southern England exposed its perennial burdens, to which the North replied by referring to the peculiarity of its condition. Both parties used every wordy weapon which ingenuity could devise or research suggest, yet the result was a drawn battle, for 'famine was sore in the land,' and Englishmen preferred to give, and give at once, rather than to quarrel as to whose was the duty of giving.

Yet the question is one of considerable moment, and one which may now be discussed on grounds of ordinary inquiry. The charge made by the South was that Lancashire, in reference to the poor-rate, cried out before she was hurt; that the Famine-rates of the cotton county were only equal to their ordinary imposts, and that many years' previous immunity from heavy poor-rates ought to have reconciled Lancashire to the exceptional burden consequent upon this crisis. It was not denied by the County Palatine that her taxation had been light and her prosperity great, but she submitted that her high wages-rate must be set against the heavier poor-rates of the South; that her assessments to the relief of the poor far more nearly represented the annual value of her property; and, lastly, she boldly declared her poverty, protesting that the Cotton Famine had prostrated her abilities, and turned her wealth into a worthless encumbrance—in fact, she pleaded the poverty of her riches.

When the Union Relief Aid Bill was debated in the House of Peers, it had been angrily demanded by Lord Malmesbury, why Lancashire parishes should object to pay two shillings in the pound, when some others were paying ten shillings, and his own, 'one of the best cultivated and most prosperous parishes in rural England,' was paying three shillings, and occasionally four shillings, in the pound. To this Lord Egerton of Tatton—whose seat is in the neighbourhood of Stockport—submitted, in reply, that a five-shilling rate upon that town would in reality be a fifteen-shilling rate upon the few who were able to comply with the demand of the overseers. During the long vacation the controversy had slept, to be now suddenly awoke by a letter from Professor Kingsley, published in the 'Times,' which stated that 'Wessex' would give 'grumblingly and grudgingly' until assured that the cotton districts had in this respect fulfilled their duty.

The first subject in this inquiry is naturally the earliest point in dispute. It was asserted, and not disproved, that during the seventeen years anterior to 1862, the charge in respect of the poor-rate upon the population of Lancashire, as compared with equal numbers of the population in the south-western counties, had been less by 8,373,000*l.*; that is to say, that the 2,469,260 people of Lancashire had retained this sum in their own possession, which the less fortunate people of the South-west had been obliged to spend in the maintenance of unproductive pauperism. 'Why not feed your starving thousands with these accumulations?' asked the South.—'We have spent them in wages,' was the reply of Lancashire. 'While you have been giving your peasants nine and ten shillings a week, and keeping all the sick and the destitute, the unemployed and the aged, in your union workhouses, we have been paying higher wages, and have consequently been exempt from pauperism.' 'Where the wages-rate is high there will pauperism be low,' was held to be a very effective reply to the pertinacious queries of southern ratepayers. But was it really so? Was there no fallacy in this argument? Certainly there was, on the side of Lancashire. Unless the higher wages-rate of the cotton districts bears a greater proportion to the margin of rents and profits than the lower wages-rate of the South does to the agricultural margin of rents and profits, then the excess of poor-rates of the latter is, *pro tanto*, an addition to the rents and profits of the former. Unless the amount of poor-rate is actually a deduction from the wages of labour, it must be paid by rents, or be a charge on capital, or on both. If the argument of Lancashire was sound, the higher poor-rate of the South-west must be paid by a deduction from the peasants' wages. And this might be the case if the poor-rate was charged upon the capital employed in husbandry. But being assessed upon the rental, actual or estimated, and with little or no fluctuations in amount, its incidence is entirely upon the land,

and poor-rates, in their average amount, consequently become a deduction from rents. It is obvious that a farm free of poor-rates would command a rental larger by the precise amount of the unusual exemption.

Then, to continue the inquiry, if the poor-rate be not a deduction from wages in the South-west,—where wages must rise, as by means of invention and improvement labour gains greater productive power,—are the higher wages of the North a charge upon rents and profits, in lieu of poor-rate? Most certainly not. The wages-rate is simply the consequence,—the cost of an actual demand for labour following upon the existence of an unusual rate of profits, and to a large extent upon the uncertainty of employment. The price of labour is undoubtedly higher in the North than in the South. Large profits make it in greater requirement: therefore there is less pauperism. Wages are higher in the North; therefore the sick and the aged are maintained without difficulty by their families. But suppose that inhumanity prevailed universally, and that the operatives refused to bear any charges from which they could escape; assume that vagrants, who could but would not work, and men, women, and children, who were unable to work, flocked into the manufacturing districts,—and that so it came to pass that orphaned children, destitute and friendless persons, the sick and the imbecile, as well as the idle and the dissolute, had been forced by thousands, even in the good times of 1859-60, into the union workhouses, and on to the parish-books,—their pauperism would not have affected wages in the slightest degree, but its cost would have been charged upon rents and profits, because the demand for labour, to which its high price is entirely owing, would not have been interfered with. The manufacturing capital of the North, owing to the activity of the district, receives so much larger a rate of profit than that of the South, that after creating a more active demand for labour,—chiefly from the accidental circumstance that the labour of women and children can be made available,—it still retains the ordinary profits of capital, exceeded at least by the amount of the local burdens to which, in less productive localities, it is liable.

Before the argument can be concluded on the side of

Lancashire, and before she will submit to be credited with a bonus of more than 8,000,000*l.*, owing to the bare fact that she is manufacturing and not agricultural, it would be suggested that advantage on the part of rents and profits could not exist in one part of the kingdom without being speedily equalised by the inundation of capital, eager to share these exceptional benefits. But surely no one, upon taking thought, will maintain that capital has been backward in this respect. The freeholders of the cotton districts may be regarded as the most fortunate body of landowners in the world—that is, if fortune consists in a rapid increase in the value of their property. In no county is land more difficult to buy, in none is it so difficult to obtain a lease of any considerable extent of surface, and in none is the rental of real property so free from those charges which stand between the cost to the tenant and the actual receipts of the landlord, while the profits upon the capital of the wealthier class of occupiers are sufficiently attested by the marvellous increase in the cotton manufacture.

There is yet another point advanced for decision before irrefragable proof can be established, that in the years before the Famine, Lancashire, as compared with the South-west, added to her capital the difference between the average of poor-rates in the South-west and her own light expenditure in that behalf. It is contended that the scale of assessment being heavier in the North, the pressure is equalised. But if it be assumed that this objection is valid, the argument which would be based upon it at once falls to the ground when the pressure is not determined by the actual rate in the pound upon the value of the assessment. All that is founded upon the fact, that the ordinary poor-rate throughout the unions of Lancashire did not much exceed one shilling in the pound, may for the moment be surrendered. But the rate of pauperism and the actual expenditure in the relief of the poor will give precisely the same evidence. Glossop, with its pauper rate of 1·5, or Stockport, with the same rate upon its population, may be compared with the much higher average pauperism of the South-west. The normal rate of pauperism in the unions of the cotton-manufacturing district is considerably less than that of the average for all

England, while the pauperism of the south-western counties would be four times as heavy as that of these prosperous northern unions.

Yet, upon examination, it will be found that the difference in the scale of assessment is by no means considerable. The customary deduction from the gross estimated rental may be ten per cent. in the North and fifteen per cent. in the agricultural parishes of the South. Certainly there are instances in which a still greater reduction has been made, but they are to a great extent historical, and are undoubtedly very rare. Allowing five per cent. in favour of the ratepayers of Lancashire on this account, they would still have been in a better financial position, to the extent of nearly 8,000,000*l*., than the equal population of the south-western counties, which had borne during the past seventeen years a pressure of poor-rates greater by one hundred and twenty per cent. than that with which Lancashire was taxed.

But the most important question has yet to be answered. What was the ability of the cotton districts with regard to the payment of poor-rates at this period of the Famine? It is beyond a doubt that the profits of capital had been greater, by the virtual remission of poor-rate, than those which it received in other parts of the kingdom. Glossop, with its near approach to freedom from poor-rates; Ashton-under-Lyne, with its 1·3, and Stockport with its 1·5 per cent. of pauperism, had certainly increased their manufacturing capital by the considerable sum which in less laborious districts would have been unproductively expended in the relief of the poor. And it is proved that this saving had not been expended in providing a higher rate of wages than that paid in the South-west. But when 'Wessex' called on Lancashire to look to her poor-rates, it was not suggested that she should refund her savings, but that she should increase her payments.

Now, there are a great number of very good reasons which induce the owners of property in the cotton districts to hold strong objections to the payment of heavy poor-rates. In the first place, such rates can never be required when trade is active; they can only occur at a season when the mills are closing, and when profits are uncertain. To the extent of one fourth or fifth, the rateable value of the larger towns is usually made up by the assessments of factory property, which are calculated upon an estimate of the net annual value of the fabric, together with the motive power—the machinery other than 'the power' being regarded as the fixtures of the tenant. The closing of a mill does not affect its liability to poor-rates, so long as the manufacturing machinery is in position.* This is obviously an equitable and necessary provision, inasmuch as no heavy pressure of poor-rates is unaccompanied by the closing of factories. But the anxiety to economise the expenses of manufacturing is so great, that nearly all of the larger factories are the property of the occupiers, being held at a ground-rent only. An agricultural lease is almost a curiosity in Lancashire, for landowners are unwilling to resign for a term of years the power of dealing with their property. Except in Oldham, where a mill is often tenanted by three or four occupiers, it is very rarely indeed that a factory is rented. And as a natural consequence, the estimated rental of cotton-factories for rating purposes does not amount to a high percentage upon the cost of their erection. Six per cent. for the gross estimated rental, with a deduction of seventeen per cent where the assessment is rigid, is a much-adopted scale. But the average is considerably lower than this, and the net rateable value of factory property would range from three to five per cent. upon the cost of erection. This cannot be regarded as a high scale of assessment, nor can there be any doubt that factory property in the North is assessed at a much lower percentage of its cost than business premises in the South of England.

There is another peculiarity in the assessments of Lancashire which is worthy of attention. Of the larger towns, Stockport and Oldham are distinguished by repudiating the benefits of the Small Tenements Act. Each has many thousand small assessments; in the latter of these two boroughs there are as many as 14,000, of which the majority are upon houses of about 8*l.* to 12*l.* yearly

* By a recent decision of the Court of Queen's Bench, in the case of 'Stayley and another *v.* the Overseers of Castleton,' it would seem that if a mill thus occupied is 'standing' for a whole year, it can only be assessed as a warehouse for machinery.

value. It might seem that these were two places which of all others would be most benefited by the adoption of provisions so well calculated to simplify collection, and to prevent the occurrence of distraint upon the working-class occupiers. But in Stockport and Oldham a large number of these small tenements are owned by their occupants, to whom the adoption of the provisions of this Act would be, in fact, the remission of one-third of their liability. The equivalent for this reduction allowed to compounding landlords, is the greater security which is thereby obtained for the payment of the rate. But this security is not in any way increased in respect of an owner who inhabits his only property, which he may have acquired by independent savings, or through the instrumentality of some local building society. Even in those townships of the manufacturing districts wherein the Small Tenements Act is adopted, the number of assessments is still very numerous and deceptive, as to any estimate made by averaging the rateable value throughout their whole number. This is owing to the fact that, with rare exceptions, the operative enjoys the English luxury of a separate house, though he is not unfrequently the owner of one or more of these habitations. The major portion of the rateable value of these townships is commonly made up by comparatively few assessments.

Therefore the weakness of the cotton districts in respect of the payment of heavy poor-rates consists in the fact that they are never pressed for them until trade is stagnant, and the rates are paid in respect of standing mills; while the ability of these districts is increased by a virtual exemption from these charges during the ordinary times of prosperity. In reviewing this controversy, it must be borne in mind that Mr. Villiers' Union Relief Aid Act was now in force, and that consequently parishes could obtain from their unions their quarterly expenditure in relief of the poor, in excess of ninepence in the pound on their total net rateable value. And the unions were possessed of borrowing powers, or could obtain from their county any quarterly excess of expenditure above fifteen-pence in the pound.

Besides the fallacies to which reference has been made, there were statements circulated upon partial information which seriously confused the questions in dispute. Mr. Cobden stated that a five-shilling rate in Rochdale would amount to confiscation, while by others it was asserted, that a rate nominally of three shillings upon a distressed parish would virtually be a rate of four or five times that amount upon the solvent portion of the community. The plain fact, that in every poor-rate levied during the period of the Cotton Famine, the nominal rate in the pound represented the entire charge in respect of that poor-rate upon any property, carries the inquiry forward a considerable distance at a single bound. The deficiency caused by the excusals on account of poverty, or the temporary deficiency caused by the amount held over as uncollected, were in no case surcharged upon the wealthier portion of the parishioners.

It was sometimes assumed that the proportion which the number of ratepayers who were excused from payment, or with respect to whom collection was deferred, bore to the total number of the assessments, was very near to that which existed between the amount of rate uncollected and the whole amount of the levy. Such a suggestion was made with reference to Oldham, where there were 16,000 assessments, of which it has been said that 14,000 were in respect of small property. But these 14,000 small assessments, taken at 6*l.* each, only amount to 84,000*l.*, while the rateable value of the township of Oldham is 163,446*l.* And while it is a matter of fact, it is also a matter for congratulation, that the amount of rates collectable was very generally under estimated. It very rarely happened that the amount really lost upon any rate exceeded twenty per cent. of the entire value of the rate. The inability of a portion of the ratepayers has tended to raise the original poundage of the rates, because this was fixed at a sum calculated to meet the immediate wants of the overseers, who had previously estimated the deductions which the prevailing distress would occasion. But the obvious effect of this was to make the pressure of the rates appear greater than it really was. For if the parish officers estimated that their expenditure required funds equal to three shillings in the pound upon the rateable value of the property assessed, and that one-third of the proceeds of this rate must be carried forward as uncollected, or to be excused, the course they adopted (to which no objection can be taken) was to lay a four-shilling rate in place of a three-shilling rate, on account of the difficulty of collection.

In November 1862, the Lancashire rates were, however, heavy enough to satisfy the most jealous southerner, and it is beyond denial that their pressure came at a time when many of the manufacturers were enduring serious losses from the closing of their establishments, and, in some cases, were making considerable expenditure in charitable relief. Yet it was not fair, when the climax of the distress was so nearly attained, and visibly so, because almost the entire cotton-working population was now dependent upon the boards of guardians and the relief committees, to answer the complaint of Mr. Kingsley and others with an estimate of annual rates founded upon an expenditure which was only just entered upon, and which it could not be supposed would be long maintained. During the winter of 1862-63 it will be found that the payments of the distressed unions, in respect of poor-rates, were exceedingly heavy. But this excessive taxation was only of short duration. The normal condition of these unions may be regarded as one of happy immunity from such burdens; nor had their charges in this respect been as yet very materially increased. Taking the seven of the unions which at all times contain the largest percentage of pauperism of any in the cotton district, their annual expenditure for the relief of their poor, based on that of the week ending November 22, 1861, a time of year when the rate of pauperism is in excess of the average, and a time not wholly unaffected by the Cotton Famine, was:—

	£		s.	d.	
Ashton-under-Lyne . . .	8,268	or	0	7	in the pound.
Blackburn	12,012	„	1	0	„
Manchester . . .	37,752	„	1	0¼	„
Oldham	8,320	„	0	9½	„
Preston	17,264	„	1	1¼	„
Rochdale	8,840	„	0	8¾	„
Stockport	8,632	„	0	8⅞	„

For the year ending Michaelmas 1862, the expenditure of these seven unions, 'in and about the relief of the poor,' had largely increased, and stood as follows:—

	s.	d.	
Ashton-under-Lyne	1	6¾	in the pound.
Blackburn	3	2	"
Manchester	1	2½	"
Oldham	1	6	"
Preston	3	0¼	"
Rochdale	1	10	"
Stockport	1	8¾	"

From the circumstance that some of the rates were levied just within and others just outside the year thus taken, this statement is valuable in its general rather than in its particular features. But the deduction may safely be drawn that no union had made an expenditure in relief exceeding 3*s.* 2*d.* in the pound in the year, while in the majority of the unions of the cotton district the expenditure had been considerably less than 2*s.* in the pound. It cannot be said that this was a disbursement calling for the interference of the Legislature. Hereafter the Union Relief Aid Act will be seen in operation, preventing the parochial expenditure from rising above 3*s.*, and that of the unions from rising above 5*s.* in the pound. But even then it will be apparent that not a very large number of parishes made the expenditure entitling them to call for a rate-in-aid from their unions, and that the unions which exceeded the limit of five shillings were never more than those of Preston, Blackburn, Ashton-under-Lyne, and Glossop.

From all this it will be gathered that while the poor-rates in the cotton districts had not become very oppressive, and had not exceeded the amount customarily paid by many other parishes in the kingdom, yet that they were, at this time, paid in respect of property which was suffering temporary depreciation, and by persons many of whom were enduring losses from the same cause which had occasioned the unusual rise in the poor-rates. In the latter months of 1862, it was currently rumoured that the Lancashire unions would be charged with poor-rates exceeding 15*s.* in the pound; but, thanks to Mr. Villiers, their liability could not henceforth exceed 5*s.* in the pound, for all the charges incidental to the relief of the poor. Yet when this rate, or even a less rate, has to be paid by a people who have lived and prospered with poor-rates averaging 1*s.* in the pound, it may be regarded as certain that they will complain more loudly of the excess than a much poorer people would do, who had been accustomed to larger sacrifices. Nor could it be expected that much heed would be taken of previous exemption; for if there be one action in this world which, more than another, habit makes easy and disuse renders more difficult, it is the payment of money for unselfish purposes.

CHAPTER IX.

DECEMBER 1862.

THE 2nd of December beheld a great event in the history of the Cotton Famine. Hitherto the class which had suffered least, and had contributed the least assistance, had been the landowners. Many of them had subscribed liberally, but they had not been called upon for any remission of rents, such as was common throughout the agricultural counties in the temporary depression of agriculture consequent upon the abolition of the Corn Laws; neither had the sudden and considerable rise in the poor-rates affected them in a degree proportionate to their responsibilities. Rates, in their average amount, are unquestionably a charge upon property, because the tenancy is entered upon with a full knowledge that such charges form a part of its liabilities. But an unlooked-for rise of rates involves a charge upon the profits of the occupier to the extent of the excess beyond the average amount. Yet there is an allowance to be made for the Lancashire landowner, owing to the peculiar condition of his property in the manufacturing districts. Agricultural leases are extremely rare, and therefore, in respect of agricultural land, any long-continued increase of rates finds its way more quickly to the purse of the landowner than in districts where leases are the rule, and not, as in Lancashire, the scarce exception.

That principle of the Irish Poor Law which claims from the landlord one-half of the extraordinary poor-rate, might, with some justice, have been applied at this time in Lancashire; but it is always inadvisable to introduce exceptional legislation when by voluntary effort it can be avoided. And it must be said that the tenantry of Lancashire are generally very small farmers, possessed of but little capital, and that even in good times losses of rent are by no means so uncommon as in more highly-farmed districts.

These were among the causes which induced the public to hail with much satisfaction the meeting of the county of Lancaster on the 2nd of December. It was a brave gathering. Poverty, it is said, makes strange bedfellows, and certainly it has been a result of the Cotton Famine to bring together, with a good and common object, men who had not hitherto been seen acting in co-operation. From so much that is estimable it is not easy to select that which is most worthy of admiration, or to decide whether it be the young lord-lieutenant generously acknowledging his responsibilities, as did Lord Sefton; or Lord Derby, with ancestral chivalry, and with his own splendid eloquence, defending his county against the charge of backwardness in duty; or the mayor of Manchester, himself a Radical of Radicals, thanking the Tory earl for his hearty compliments to the working classes; or the strong local feeling of Lord Egerton of Tatton, due to an impulse honourable to himself, and one of the invaluable characteristics of Englishmen. All these, and many more personal incidents claim admiration; but the great fact of this meeting was, that it resulted in a subscription list amounting to 130,000*l.*, of which sum 70,000*l.* was subscribed in the Town Hall. And, like some great fight which is a standpoint in a nation's history, valued beyond estimation either from a review of the contending armies or of the battle-field upon which their blood was spilt—held of far more importance than other events fraught with even more destructive or painful results, yet neither so uncommon nor startling—so this donation was held, and justly held, as a satisfactory and conclusive reply to those who had reproached the magnates of Lancashire with a too-willing avoidance of their proper obligations.

Yet, large as this sum was, and unparalleled as the result of a single effort even in the rich annals of British almsgiving, it is true that it did not represent more than one-third of the sum already subscribed in and around the county of Lancaster. When this meeting separated, the county had contributed to the relief funds upwards of

450,000*l*.; it had paid as much more in extraordinary poor-rates; and besides all this, much had been given in private unrecorded charity. The 5,000*l*. now put down by Lord Derby had been preceded by the donation of 1,000*l*. to the Cotton Districts Relief Fund; the 1,000*l*. of Lord Crawford followed a promise of 5,000*l*. to the special resources of Wigan; the 1,000*l*. given by Lord Edward Howard was but an instalment of what he proposed to do, and did accomplish, for the relief of the deep distress which prevailed in his own neighbourhood. And as much might be said for many of the names which stood upon this golden list.

The artistic survey of the calamity made by Lord Derby was not taken for the benefit of his audience; the picture he painted was for exhibition to the country. He was the eloquent counsel for the defence of Lancashire. In a black foreground he sketched the outline of the distress, filling in the shadows with the terrible totals culled from Mr. Farnall's reports. Then he lightened the scene with the virtuous struggles of the suffering population to resist the weight of distress which forced them towards involuntary pauperism—the withdrawal of savings—the sacrifice of furniture—the noble independence which strove and strove against reduction to the level of the idle, the dissipated, and the improvident—the stout proud heart which, seeing the inevitable, declared, 'Nay, but we'll clem first.' Then he drew in the giant cotton trade, showing what it had been and what it now was; and lastly, like a great master, he relieved his picture with the more cheerful representations of what had been done and what was doing to mitigate the trials of the district.

He defended the Central Executive Committee from the charge of illiberality, by showing that it was not expedient that their allowance should much exceed that given by the guardians. As to the pressure of the rates, he repeated the statements which were current at the time, but which the operation of the rate-in-aid and subsequent experience have happily, to some extent, contradicted. It was stated that the rates in Ashton-under-Lyne exceeded 11*s*. 11*d*. in the pound; the inference from which would hardly be the fact that at this time—the crisis of the distress—the temporary expenditure was at that rate. The calculation was made that the rate of 4*s.* 6*d.* just levied in Ashton would not be realized by 33⅓ per cent. But this rate was collected within 10 per cent. of its total sum. Yet it may be taken as certain, that Lord Derby was well informed in stating that any large increase upon the rates paid at the time at which he spoke was absolutely impossible, and certainly very undesirable. The eulogists of this meeting were justified in saying that enough had been done and was now doing by Lancashire, fully and sufficiently to exonerate the county from all claim by the nation, which was now legitimately her partner in the burden. Looking at the condition of affairs at this moment of deep distress, the most captious critic could but say that local effort had been somewhat long delayed; that this county meeting might have preceded instead of following similar assemblages; that the relief administered by the guardians might from the first have been more liberal, and the rise of poor-rates less graduated by time. But even to him it might be answered that the evident uncertainties of the calamity excused some irresolution; that had Lancashire been more ready, she would certainly have received less external assistance; and if apology were sought for those confirmed niggards whose covetousness was their nature, who had done and would do nothing, it would be certainly found in any neighbourhood from John-o'-Groat's to the Land's End.

On the 6th December, Mr. Farnall's returns of the numbers relieved by the guardians reached their highest point. Week by week it had been for eight long months his toilsome duty to collect and record these swelling totals. Throughout the district the influence of his useful labours had been widely experienced. By personal communication with all classes in every quarter, with an energy which won the admiration of a people whose peculiar pride is the possession of this English quality, he had achieved the great success of rendering the Poor Laws popular, and had broken down that obstinate indifference with which the population of the cotton district had been accustomed to regard official assistance. But he had done more than this. As his list grew heavy and heavier—as the prospect grew dark and darker, and his mission became more crowded with difficulty, he had manifested a hopeful and buoyant spirit that encouraged all who came within the sphere of his influence. He had never been a croaker; he had never wavered in a firm faith in the strength and power of the organisations for relief. He had never, either privately to the Government or in public, advocated the surrender of local independence and the resort to aid from the State. He had hopefully, and not unsuccessfully, urged upon the boards of guardians the paramount duties of humanity and liberality in the performance of their functions; and now the weight of his charge had reached its heaviest, and he announced to the Central Relief Committee that 271,983 persons were receiving parochial aid, at a weekly cost for outdoor relief of 18,728*l.* In one year the increase of pauperism in the unions to which his report referred had been 214,448, or 372 per cent., with a corresponding increase in the cost of relief. The rate of pauperism had risen from 2·9 to 13·7 per cent. upon the whole population. Of these 271,983 paupers, there were 12,527 in the union workhouses; so that the cost of outdoor relief and in-maintenance together exceeded 20,000*l.* per week. But as the returns of the Central Relief Committee were made monthly, the maximum of recorded distress occurred in the week ending 27th December, when Mr. Farnall's returns had fallen to 260,506; the cost of outdoor relief being also reduced to 17,934*l.*; the number of outdoor paupers being 248,179, whose rate of relief averaged 1*s.* 5⅜*d.* per head. A large number of these were receiving supplementary aid from the relief committees. But the number maintained by the relief committees alone, for this week, was 236,310; making, together with those receiving poor-law relief, a total of 496,816 persons supported by parochial or charitable funds. The weekly expenditure of the committees was—for general relief, 24,579*l.*; for clothing, 20,332*l.*; and in expenses, 1,775*l.*; making a total of 46,356*l.* Adding the amount of general relief to that expended in outdoor relief by the guardians, the total is 42,513*l.*, which, being added to the expenditure for clothing, amounts to 62,845*l.* But the estimated loss of wages was 168,544*l.* a week, or at the rate of 8,764,288*l.* yearly, so that the operatives were receiving rather more than one-third of their ordinary income.

This enormous host of sufferers from the Cotton Famine, numbering close upon half a million, occupied, it may be estimated, upwards of 100,000 cottages, representing a rental of at least 500,000*l.* a year, but a small portion of which found its way to the pockets of the owners of these habitations. To every one of these poor homes relief in money and in kind had to be conveyed, in most cases by their occupants. That all this was performed with such regularity and order, with such perfect arrangement and charitable supervision, that none suffered starvation, and but few made complaints of inattention, is the highest testimony which can be adduced to the disinterested labours of those unpaid almoners by whom it was accomplished. Nor could it have been achieved had not the conduct of the recipients been equally praiseworthy: there were cases of fraud, but the fact that they came to light is some proof of their rarity. It was publicly said, that at this time there were demands for 'hands' unanswered, and that instances were known of girls who preferred attendance at the sewing-schools to an engagement in domestic service. Such a statement made at such a time is sure to catch the ear, and is too likely to be repeated without inquiry into the facts. But, even admitting its truth, it must not be supposed that these men refused to return to their ordinary employment with its customary remuneration.

Some of the manufacturers, rather than keep their machinery standing, were using a very indifferent description of Surat cotton, and offering 'short-time' employment upon this inferior raw material. By accepting such an offer, the 'hands' would have lost their claim to relief; while they could not have earned so much as they received from the charitable funds, nor indeed sufficient to support the laborious life which would be required of them. Under these circumstances, they were hardly blameable for declining such work. Until human nature undergoes a material alteration, the majority will prefer idleness to labour, unless the reward of labour is sufficient to overcome their tendency to inertia; yet, the fact that such offers were actually made in vain proves the necessity for maintaining the wholesome regulation, that labour shall be given in return for relief. The case of the girls is somewhat different. Yet, it is a fact, that a considerable number of these girls did leave the cotton districts to undertake domestic service in other parts of the kingdom. More than a hundred left Blackburn and the neighbourhood, being assisted in doing so by Mrs. Gerald Potter, whose humane efforts on behalf of the poor, and especially the women of Blackburn, have been of a most signal character. But when it is asked why these girls were not more numerously provided for, it must be remembered that a factory-girl has more of the 'professional' about her than any class of men, excepting perhaps the soldier. The mill is her only possible. If she does not love its oily floors and noisy rooms, she has, at least, but very little idea of any other mode of life. She is introduced to the cotton-factory at a very early age; from morning till night she works in it, as girl, woman, and mother, till old age or good fortune interferes. The romance of her life, her friendships and her love, are associated with the tall chimney, with the long rows of windows, and with her busy fellow-workers. She is one of a caste, and the suggestion to her of another mode of life is by no means welcome. To be associated with her well-known companions in a sewing-school—to be tended there by well-dressed ladies—to be thus kept from hunger and misery, and yet to live in her old home, all this is tolerable enough: but her idea of household service is, that it is a sort of domestic slavery, and she is not more ready to accept such an ivitation than a Red Indian would be if he were asked to be a 'help' in some New York household. The cherished independence of these girls, resulting from the demand for their labour, causes them to rely one upon another rather than upon their parents or relatives; and the following sketch, by the correspondent of the 'Manchester Examiner,' is very characteristic:—

'Three young women stopped on the footpath in front of the inn, close to the place where we stood, and began to talk together in a very free open way, quite careless of being heard. One of them was a stout, handsome young woman, about twenty-three. Her dress was of light printed stuff, clean and good; her round ruddy arms, her clear blonde complexion, and the bright expression of her full open countenance, all indicated health and good-nature. I guessed from her conversation, as well as from her general appearance, that she was a factory operative in full employ, though that is such a rare thing in these parts now; the other two looked very poor and down-hearted. One was a short thickset girl, seemingly not twenty years of age: her face was sad, and she had very little to say. The other was a thin, dark-haired, cadaverous woman, about thirty years of age, as I supposed; her shrunk visage was the picture of want, and her frank childlike talk showed great simplicity of character. The weather had been wet for some days previous, and the clothing of the two looked thin and shower stained; it had evidently been worn a good while, and the colours were faded. Each of them wore a poor shivery bit of shawl, in which their hands we folded, as if to keep them warm. The handsome lass, who seemed to be in good employ, knew them both; but she showed an especial kindness towards the eldest of them. As these two stood talking to their friend, we did not take much notice of what they were saying, until two other young women came slowly from townwards, looking poor, and tired, and ill, like the first. These last comers instantly recognised two of those who stood talking together in front of the inn, and one of them said to the other, "Eh, sitho! there's Sarah and Martha here!" . . . "Eh, lasses! han yo bin a beggin' too?"—"Aye, lass, we han," replied the thin dark-complexioned woman. "Aye, lass, we han. Aw've just bin tellin' Ann here. Aw never did sich a thing i' my life afore—never! But it's th' first time and th' last for me—it is that! Aw'll go whoam, an' aw'll dee theer, afore aw'll go a-beggin' ony moor,—aw will for sure. Mon, it's sich a nasty, dirty job; aw'd as soon clem! . . . . See yo, lasses! we set off this mornin'—Martha an' me; we set eawt this mornin' to go to Gorton Tank, becose we yerd that it wur sich a good place. But one doesn't know wheer to go to these times, an' one doesn't like to go a-beggin' among folk as they know. Well, when we coom to Gorton, we geet twopence hawpenny theer, an' that wur o'. Now, there's plenty moor beggin' besides us. Well, at after that twopence hawpenny, we get twopence moor, an' that's o' at we'n getten. But eh, lasses, when aw coom to do it, aw hadn't th' heart to ax for nought, aw hadn't for sure." . . . "Martha an' me's walked aboon ten mile iv we'n walked a yard; an' we geet weet through th' first thing, an' aw wur ill when we set off, an' so wur Martha too; aw know hoo wur, though hoo says nought mich abeawt it. Well, we coom back throught t' teawn, an' we were both on us fair stagged up. Aw never were so done o'er i' my life w' one thing an' another. So we co'de a-seein' Ann here, an' hoo made us a rare good baggin', th' lass did. See yo! aw wur fit to drop o' th' flags afore aw geet that saup o' warm tay into me—aw wur for sure! Aw'neaw, hoo's come'd a gate wi' us hitherto, an' hoo would have us to have a glass o' warm ale apiece at yon heause lower deawn a bit; an' aw dar say it'll do me good, aw getten sich a cowd; but eh dear, it's made me as mazy as a tup, an' neaw, hoo wants us to have another afore we starten off whoam. But it's no use, we mun' be gooin on. Aw'm noan used to it, an' aw connot ston it; aw'm as wake as a kittlin' this minute."

'Ann, who had befriended them in this manner, was the handsome young woman who seemed to be in work; and now the poor woman who had been telling the story laid her hand upon her friend's shoulder, and said, "Ann, thee's behaved very weel to us o' roads'; an' neaw, lass, go thi ways whoam an' dunnut fret abeawt us, mon. Aw feel better neaw. We's be reet enough to-morn, lass. Now, there's awlus some way shap't. That tay's done me a deeol o' good. . . . Go thi ways whoam, Ann, neaw do, or else aw shan't be yezzy abeawt tho'." But Ann, who was wiping her eyes with her hand, replied, "Naw, naw, aw will not go yet, Sarah!" . . . And then she began to cry. "Eh, lasses, aw dunnot like to see yo o' this shap—aw dunnot for sure! Besides, yo'n bin far enough to-day. Come back wi' me. Aw connot find reawm for both on yo; but thee come back wi' me, Sarah. Aw'll find thee a good bed; an' thae'rt welcome to a share o' what there is—as welcome as th' fleawers i' May—thae knows that. . . . Thae'rt th' owdest o' th' two; an' thae'rt noan fit to trawnce up an' deawn o' this shap. Come back to eawr heawse, an Martha 'ill go forrud to Stopput (Stockport)—winnot tho', Martha? . . . . Thae knows, Martha," continued she; "thae knows, Martha, thae munnot think nought at me axin' Sarah, an' noan o' thee. Yo should both on ye go back iv aw'd reawm ; but aw hav'n't. Beside, thae'rt younger an strunger than hur is."—"Eh, God bless the, lass!" replied Martha, "aw know o' abeawt it. Aw'd rayther Sarah would stop, for hur'll be ill. Aw can go furrud by mysel', weel enough. It's noan so fur, neaw."

'But here Sarah, the eldest of the three, laid her hand once more on the shoulder of her friend, and said, in an earnest tone, "Ann, it will not do, my lass. Go aw mun. I never wur away fro whoam o' neet i' my life—never! Aw connot do it, mon! Beside, thae knows, aw've laft yon lad, an' never a wick soul wi' him! He'd fret hissel' to death this neet, mon, if aw didn't go whoam! Aw couldn't sleep a wink for thinkin' abeawt him! Th' child would be fit to start eawt o' th' heawse i' th' deead time o' th' neet a-seechin' mo—aw know he would! . . . Aw mun go, mon: God bless tho, thae knows heaw it is!"'

Such a conversation might have been overheard in any part of the district throughout which the distress was now so sore, reducing some to beggary, and leading others to become itinerant musicians. The love and practice of music are very widely diffused among the Lancashire population, and in the winter months of 1862 there might be heard in many of the streets and lanes of the county, the plaintive wail of some wandering psalmists, half shy and half surprised to hear the sound of their own instruments and voices in the open daylight. The correspondent just quoted, also wrote this description of such a party of unaccustomed minstrels :—

'The company consisted of an old man, two young men, and three young women. Two of the women had children in their arms. After I had listened to them awhile, thinking the time and the words a little appropriate to their condition, I beckoned to one of the young men, who came "sidling" up to me. I asked him where they came from, and he said, "Ash'n." In answer to another question, he said, "We're o' one family. Me an' yon tother's wed. That's his wife wi' th' chylt in her arms, an' hur wi' th' plod shawl on's mine." I asked if the old man was his father. "Ah," replied he, "we're o' here, nobbut two. My mother's ill i' bed, an' one o' my sisters is lookin' after her." "Well, an' heaw han yo getten on?" said I. "Oh, we'n done weel; but we's come no moor," replied he.

Another day, there was an instrumental band of these operatives playing sacred music close to the Exchange lamp. Amongst the crowd around, I met with a friend of mine. He told me that the players were from Stalybridge. They played some fine old tunes by desire, and among the rest they played one called "Warrington." When they had played it several times over, my friend turned to me and said: That tune was composed by a Re . Mr. Harrison, who was once minister of Cross Street Unitarian Chapel, in Manchester. And one day an old weaver, who had come down from the hills many miles, staff in hand, knocked at the minister's door, and asked if there was "a gentleman co'de Harrison lived theer?"—"Yes." "Could aw see him?"—"Yes." When the minister came to the door, the old weaver looked hard at him for a minute, and said, "Are yo th' mon 'at composed that tune co'de Warrington?" "Yes," replied the minister, "I believe I am." "Well," said the old weaver, "give me your hond, it's a good un."' He then shook hands with him heartily again, and saying, "Well, good day to yo," he went his way home again, before the old minister could fairly collect his scattered thoughts.'

There was many a cotton-worker with more time than anything else upon his hands, whose back was now covered with clothing which had evidently 'seen better days'—days perhaps when it had adorned some London dandy, or covered the comfortable proportions of some wealthy country gentleman. The business of Moses' establishment was as nothing when compared with that of the clothes-stores of the Central Relief Committee during this month, where a score of packers laboured from morning till night, dividing, sorting, packing, and forwarding the various articles sent from all parts of the kingdom for distribution. There were coats of many colours, and of every cut; the castaway of the 'Melton man' was there, and the faded brilliancy of the soldier's uniform; the shiny sleeve of the man of business, and the once warm familiar friend of the shivering traveller; hats of every shape,—the good beaver of old times, the modern and more glossy silk, the fluffy *chapeau*, the low-crowned waterproof, the billycock, the wideawake, the travelling-cap—all were to be seen, reminding anyone who had leisure for the thought, how much more suggestive of the character of the wearer than any other article of dress, is that which covers and takes the shape of his head. There is sentiment in old clothes. One little cap, for example, contained a volume. Upon the lining was stitched a note, to this effect:—'My darling child wore this: he is gone to heaven; may the little head that shall wear my sweet child's cap be blessed!'

But that which was most worthless here would have won the affections of a continent of savages, whose dusky princesses would have maddened with delight as they contemplated the ball-dresses and the little satin slippers, which had now passed from *l'allegro* to *il penseroso*, and were doubtfully turned over as being more fit for sale than for the wear of those for whom all this labour was performing. One thousand bales of blankets and clothing were sent out weekly from the central stores for distribution by the local committees, and but for the assistance thus afforded, cold and nakedness would have carried away many a sufferer beyond the reach of human charity. Nor was the bedding less valuable; for it was said by one who at this time saw much of the distress,—and the statement could be corroborated by many a district visitor,—that 'a bed' too often 'meant simply a ragged counterpane, a sheet, and a ticking, from which all the straw had long since dropped away through many a hole.'

Of the clothing received by the Central Committee, much that was not suitable for distribution was sold, and the proceeds devoted to general relief. Of that which was distributed in the district, there is no doubt that much found its way, and by no very indirect or long-delayed process, to the pawnbrokers' shops. But it was unjust that the circumstance should have been referred to in terms of very censorious accusation against the distressed borrowers upon this secondhand clothing. Was a satin gown or a dress-coat of so much use in an operative's household as the five or ten shillings which could be borrowed upon each of them? The bounty was not wasted, even though it had all been thus dealt with. It is absurd to suppose that a famished people will have respect to their backs while their bellies are empty, or to doubt that at this time, as eighteen hundred years ago, 'the body is more than raiment.'

Among the resources now collecting for the relief of the distressed, the 'Daily Telegraph' Fund deserves very honourable mention. Originated by the conductors of a journal which, with persistent eloquence, had forced the claims of the indigent cotton-workers upon the public attention, it afforded to every giver, however small, the satisfaction of a gratuitous acknowledgment of his donation, together with the consciousness that his contribution was directly forwarded to the manufacturing districts without the least deduction. With the strictest fidelity, the children's pence or the product of the working man's self-denial, the larger gifts of associated *employés*, the collections of churches and chapels, or the subscriptions of wealthy individuals, were all duly recorded and passed onward to the realization of their charitable mission. During the month of December this source alone contributed a thousand pounds a week to the relief funds. It is no wrong to the generous donors, but simple justice to the conductors of this fund, to say that to the method they established this assistance was chiefly owing. The little rills of charity which together formed this useful stream—the many 'mickles' that made up this 'muckle,' would have run away in profitless expenditure but for the powerful hands that guided them through these liberal columns into so direct and beneficial a course northwards. The total amount of this fund was 6,302*l.* 10*s.* 5*d.*, the deduction for collection and transmission being only 27*l.* 7*s.* 9*d.*

It was only to be expected that while there were so many helping hands outstretched towards Lancashire, some would wish to give increased action to their religious opinions at the same time with their alms. That the sewing-schools would have been comparatively ineffective for good without the attendance of ladies cannot be denied: but the ladies were not always of one mind as to the religious exercises which should be performed by the scholars. Nor was this difficulty confined to the sewing-schools only. For instance, it was one day decided by the Preston Board of Guardians that the Protestants should not be separated from the Roman Catholics in one of the industrial schools to which their relief allowance was made. But no sooner had they come to this decision than the lady-manageresses waited upon them to complain that the

Catholic scholars would not sing the Doxology. It may be difficult to understand how this popular verse of praise could offend the most ultramontane prejudice; but the probability is, that the good Protestant ladies of Preston wished to carry their religious instruction somewhat further than these two very catholic rhymes, and that while they were supported by the ministers and clergy, the contumacious Catholics were backed by their priests. Undoubtedly it was better for these schools to take a denominational character, rather than that the zeal with which they were conducted should grow cold, and that the kindly co-operation of the ladies should be wanting. The sex which is governed—and may it always be so—rather by the impulses of what is called the heart than by the reason—which is supposed to reside in a more elevated quarter of the human structure—cannot take part with full strength in any work of this nature unless it engages the most powerful of their instincts. On the side of the Confederates in the American war, ladies have performed frequent deeds of heroism at least as great as those which have been done in front of gleaming bayonets or at the cannon's mouth. What they will do at the call of patriotism, they will also accomplish for the sake of charity. But when these schools were fully set in order—when throughout their long ranks there was no thought of starvation—when the day's work was secure, and the day's wages not less so, then it appeared there was something more to be accomplished, and that these victims of the Cotton Famine, being safely rescued from the fiends, hunger and idleness, must be further benefited by the indoctrination of religious principles. At least, it will be conceded that they were not to blame who thought so: and the separation of the scholars into their respective religious denominations was, under these circumstances, not only unobjectionable but beneficial, so long as it did not interfere with the due administration of relief. Want and misery are not sectarian, but are the unhappy lot of those who are brought low by physical inability, by vicious habits, or by misfortune, and are then neglected by their more happy and comfortable neighbours.

Yet there were some irreligious enough to found their charity altogether upon religious qualifications. In Blackburn, the clergy have always been, as becomes their office, most active among the benefactors of the poor, without distinction of creed or no creed. But their example did not prevent the fanaticism of others. The local almoner of some 'Christians' at Wimbledon was intrusted with funds for the special relief of 'distressed Christians.' How these persons would be coloured, or what would be the length of their hair or their faces, does not appear to have been in the instructions; but as they must have possessed many pecularities, and as their would-be benefactors had mislaid the first principles of His teaching, whose followers they professed to be, it is not, perhaps, surprising that their agent could lament the addition of but one or two more to the list of her recipients, giving as the reason, 'For I never visited a town where I have met so few who know and love the Lord Jesus Christ as in Blackburn.' That an object of charity should be wanted in a town where some 36,000 persons were maintaining a feeble partnership between body and soul through charitable agency, almost transcends belief. But it is simply shocking that the many should be overlooked in the name of Him who warned His followers not to wait till they saw Him hungered and naked, but to be mindful of their nearer duty to one of the least of these His brethren.

That unlovely collection of houses and factories, gar nished with collieries and wreathed in smoke, which is known by the name of Wigan, was pre-eminent in what were officially denominated as 'strictly local subscriptions.' The local subscription lists of this town contained a larger sum of money than those of any other town at the time of the crisis of the Cotton Famine. Not that the need of Wigan was the largest. It is true there were 9,310 operatives out of work, whose weekly loss of wages amounted to 5,000*l.* But this was not more than two-thirds of the number which were in this unfortunate condition in Preston, and much less than two-thirds of the number out of work in Blackburn. The distress of Wigan, thus estimated by numbers, was not more than equal to that of Stockport, and rather less than that of Rochdale. But the local subscriptions of grimy Wigan exceeded those of 'proud Preston' by nearly 1,000*l.* Wigan had collected 18,000*l.* while Blackburn had got together no more than 16,759*l.*, while

Rochdale had raised 7,550*l.*, and Stockport 12,000*l.* Preston had already received twice, and Blackburn nearer thrice as much aid from the great committees of London and Manchester. But, on the other hand, it must be said that the pressure on the poor-rates of Wigan had been of the lightest. So far from looking to relief from the provisions of the rate-in-aid, Wigan had no other fear than that of being called upon to contribute to more heavily rated unions. There were but 3,415 persons even now relieved by the guardians of the Wigan Union; and during the year, there had been but 2*s.* rates levied, and only a portion of the second had been collected. The Wigan sewing-schools have always been very successful institutions, and there were now 2,000 girls so employed. Here also the Doxology was a source of trouble, but the difficulty was surmounted without being suffered to denominationalise the schools into religious sections. The girls received wages amounting to three shillings for four days' work per week, and were permitted to vary the monotony of their employment with conversation and singing. The rate of relief given in Wigan was generally about two shillings per head, decreasing for large families. It was usually given in the form of provision tickets, which had the advantage of distributing much-needed relief among the poorer shopkeepers. How, in the most frugal housekeeping, to make both ends meet—upon how little food life was sustained during these hard times, may be learnt from an account of the purchases of a family of three persons, who exchanged their tickets for a week's provision, consisting of 3 loaves of bread, 3 lb. of meal, ½ lb. of butter, 2 ounces of tea, 1 lb. of treacle, 1½ lb. of sugar, a shilling's worth of potatoes, a pound of bacon, and a bit of soap. The clothing for the distressed population of Wigan was being rapidly manufactured in the sewing-schools, as was indeed the case throughout all the towns in the district. Upwards of 10,000 articles of bedding and clothing were distributed in one week in Blackburn. The trials of the year had completely bared the homes of the poor, and the whole population was virtually being reclothed and bedded.

Many causes—of which however insufficient food and clothing, mental depression, and overcrowding to avoid the payment of rent, were the principal—had tended to lower the health of the population. To some extent this would have been averted if the guardians had from the first given a sufficient rate of relief, and could have provided suitable outdoor labour for the able-bodied. The aged and weakly were of course among the first to feel the privations incident to the period, and many of these fell easy victims to disease. Mr. Farnall issued circulars to the medical officers of every union in the district, and while the replies gave no cause for serious alarm, yet they evidenced that typhus-fever had made its appearance in these unions, though it was, as yet, chiefly confined to Preston and Manchester. One hundred and eleven out of one hundred and forty-one districts were wholly free from this fever, the origin of which had been imperfect sanitary arrangements, together with the predisposing debility to which so many of the working classes were now reduced. Still, it was the general opinion that much of the sickness and mortality which existed was incident to the season, and common to a population which has always maintained so unfortunate a pre-eminence upon the black lists of the Registrar of Deaths; and this view was verified by subsequent returns.

Christmas was looked forward to as the time at which the provisions of the Union Relief Aid Act would come generally into operation, and when the whole cotton district would be practically joined in one union for the relief of the distressed. For a few weeks before the expiration of the Christmas quarter, Mr. Farnall had appended to his hebdomadal reports upon the state of pauperism throughout the district, a detailed statement of the financial condition of some one of the principal towns, as it stood with reference to expenditure in relief of the poor.* Among the towns to which these statements referred, none was more distresssd than Ashton-under-Lyne. The parish of Ashton, which for the purposes of the poor-rate includes the borough, was pauperized to the extent of 24·4 per cent. upon the population. At the termination of the Michaelmas quarter, five parishes of this union were in a

* With reference to the calculations upon the subject of poor-rate, it is to be observed that they are for the most part based upon the value of the property assessable to the relief of the poor in the yea- 1856.

position, from their expenditure in relief of the poor having exceed 9*d.* in the pound, to charge the surplus over and above this sum upon the remaining parishes of the union, and they did so. But the township of Ashton-under-Lyne was not one of these. Between the periods of Michaelmas and Christmas, complaint was made that the provisions of the Union Relief Aid Act were ineffective before the expiration of the Christmas quarter, although the expenditure of this township already exceeded the required amount. It was thought that immediately upon the expenditure in relief attaining an excessive rate, the provisions of the Act should come into operation, without waiting for the termination of the quarter. Probably a more unpractical suggestion was never made, and it may well be thought that it could hardly have been propounded for a much better reason than that of mere fault-finding. Even supposing that the rate of expenditure during this interval had been maintained at the maximum stated by Mr. Farnall when the distress was at its highest point, the temporary payment required would have been at the yearly rate of 11*s.* 9*d.* in the pound for the relief of the poor. But, in making this calculation, Mr. Farnall made a deduction of twenty-six per cent. in respect of a rate, which in fact was collected within ten per cent., so that the actual incidence of the poor-rates, upon those who could pay upon demand, was less than the amount at which it was assessed by the Special Commissioner. And although it was not ultimately found necessary to exercise the power of excusal to anything like so great an extent as it was supposed would have been necessary, yet the possession of this power was amply sufficient to prevent the immediate pressure of the poor-rates from being the direct cause of an increase of pauperism.

But in reference to the incidence of the poor-rate, and to the mode in which it was effected by the provisions of the Union Relief Aid Act, it must be borne in mind that. as no rate-in aid could be levied until the expenditure of the parish in relief exceeded ninepence in the pound, or that of the union fifteenpence in the pound upon the entire net rateable value of the parish or union, those of the ratepayers who could immediately satisfy the collector's demand must have paid considerably more than their proper share of the nine or fifteen pence. It is not, therefore, strictly correct to say that upon this measure coming into operation, no ratepayer could be called upon to pay more than nine or fifteen pence in the pound towards the relief of the poor. The fact is, that his payment was liable to be increased by a sum equal to the proportion existing between the amount of the rate uncollected and the total value of the rate. But as the amount uncollected rarely, if ever, exceeded twenty-five per cent., it is evident that his payment in respect of relief could not from henceforth rise to a very high figure. Whatever was expended by the ratepayers of any union, in respect of the relief of the poor, in excess of five shillings in the pound, would be repaid to them by contributions from other unions in the county in aid of their ensuing liabilities, or they could defer the immediate payment of their excessive rates by raising loans under the provisions of this Act.

Stockport—where the prevailing distress had been very well managed—was, in reference to poor-rates, in a very similar condition to Ashton-under-Lyne. But in Stockport it had been the invariable rule of the guardians to allow no supplementing of their relief allowances; and as the Small Tenements Act is not in operation in this borough, a heavier loss upon the rates might be expected to ensue. But here the total amount of rates imposed had been about the same as in Ashton-under-Lyne, being 7*s*. 6*d*. in the pound for the year. In estimating the produce of a five-shilling rate in Stockport, which was in process of collection at the time his statement was made, Mr. Farnall allowed the large deduction of forty per cent. Sixty-four per cent. of the rate was at once collected, the remaining thirty-six per cent. being in part carried forward as recoverable, and in part excused or declared to be irrecoverable. But so far as the immediate expenditure is concerned, entitling to the advantage of the provisions of the Union Relief Aid Act, it is evident in this case that those ratepayers from whom the sixty-four per cent. was collected, paid, over and above their nine or fifteen pence, to the extent of thirty-six per cent. of the amount of a nine or fifteen penny rate upon the rateable value of the entire township. Following this five-shilling poor-rate as an example, the amount uncollected, which Mr. Farnall estimated at forty per cent., was not all lost to the exchequer of the Stockport Guardians. When the rate was finally made up, the amount set down as excused and irrecoverable was not more than twenty-seven per cent. of the entire value of the rate, and this in a purely manufacturing township, where, in the absence of the provisions of the Small Tenements Act, every occupier is assessed.

By making a yearly estimate upon the basis of the expenditure at the moment of the deepest distress, the Special Commissioner gave some currency to an opinion that ten, twelve, or even more shillings in the pound had been, or was likely to be, the actual payment in poor-rates by these heavily-burdened centres of pauperism. But, in fact, he referred to the rate of expenditure at the time of making his reports, and without taking into his calculations the provisions of the Union Relief Aid Act. With the provisions of this Act in operation, it was impossible that their taxation for the relief of the poor could equal these amounts, unless by some convulsion of Nature the real property of Lancashire had been swept away, leaving no traces of her wealth save the redundant population; or, what was almost equally improbable, unless the owners of two-thirds in value of the property assessed became insolvent.

For the week ending November 22, the rate of expenditure, for the relief of the poor only, upon seventy-five per cent. of the rateable value of the unions contained in the following list (which were the most distressed in the district) had been :—

	s.	*d.*
Ashton-under-Lyne	11	4¾
Blackburn	7	7½
Burnley	5	4½
Bury	4	6
Glossop	12	8½
Haslingden	9	3¼
Manchester	5	8¼
Oldham	8	2½
Preston	8	2
Rochdale	6	5¾
Stockport	6	8⅛
Todmorden	6	4¾

The highest rate of expenditure had therefore been reached by the Glossop Union, generally the least pauperised in all England. But even this weekly rate of expenditure could hardly have been sustained, and perhaps would never have been incurred, but for the provisions of the Union Relief Aid Act, of which advantage had already been taken by the Glossop Union, upon the termination of the previous Michaelmas quarter. The rate-in-aid was a godsend to Glossop, for by means of it this union could draw contributions from the rich brewers of Burton-on-Trent, and from the wealthy manufacturers of the county town of Derby.

It is unnecessary to take up singly the towns of the manufacturing district, in order to show precisely to what extent they had each been burdened with poor-rates; the instances given are generally applicable. And, moreover, the fact that upon the termination of the Christmas quarter, but thirteen of the twenty-seven unions in the cotton district had made a sufficiently high rate of expenditure to entitle them to take advantage of the provisions of the Union Relief Aid Act, is undeniable evidence of their true position. Of these thirteen unions, which by their expenditure during the last quarter of 1862—a quarter in which the distress was greater than at any other period—were empowered either to borrow the excess above 9*d.* in the pound, or to charge that above 1*s.* 3*d.* upon other less-rated unions in the county, Ashton-under-Lyne could claim 8,037*l.*; Preston could borrow 7,316*l.*, or charge the county with 7,925*l.*; Blackburn could borrow 5,229*l.*, or charge 4,794*l.*; Rochdale could borrow 5,663*l.*, or charge 236*l.*; and Stockport could borrow 4,653*l.* Of the twelve unions (excluding Manchester) which possessed these powers, five made application for leave to borrow, and four both for borrowing powers and for authority to levy a rate-in-aid. But in only one of these unions—in Glossop—had the rate of expenditure for this quarter amounted to 1*s.* 11*d.*, a union of which the rateable value would be very inconsiderable but for the purely manufacturing town of Glossop and the Manchester Waterworks. Preston had reached an expenditure of 1*s.* 9½*d.*; Ashton had expended 1*s.* 9*d.*; Blackburn, 1*s.* 8½*d.*; Haslingden, 1*s.* 7¼*d.*; Rochdale, 1*s.* 3*d.*; and Stockport, 1*s.* 1*d.* in the pound.

Such was the rate of union expenditure upon the relief of the poor during the severest period of the distress. The worst had been realized, but that the crisis was past could not then be so generally known as it is now. Making an allowance of thirty per cent. for uncollected rates, it will be seen that the charge upon manufacturing establishments—now to a very great extent standing unproductive—was exceedingly onerous, and equivalent to an addition of thirty per cent. upon their assessment to the relief of the poor. Nor can it be doubted, that upon a fair and impartial review of the very depressed condition of the industry and trade of the cotton district—regarding the severe though temporary depreciation which the value of manufacturing property was at this time enduring, and the fact that these rates were for the most part paid in respect of such property, out of capital and not from profits, or upon cottages from which but little rent could be collected—the honest verdict of unbiased minds will be, that the incidence of the poor-rate was never so oppressive over an equal extent of the kingdom as in the cotton districts during the months which included the crisis of the Famine.

CHAPTER X.

JANUARY—FEBRUARY 1863.

At the beginning of 1861, the consumption of cotton in Great Britain was estimated at 50,000 bales per week; at the close of 1862 it had fallen to 20,000 bales, of very inferior weight. The question of the cotton supply was now all-important. During the Famine, Lancashire has been subject to repeated accusations of negligence of this question. But there is much less ground for the imputation of neglect than is commonly supposed; and this may be said altogether apart from the fact that it is generally the practice of the consumer to trust to the interests of the producer for the provision of supplies. For years before the secession of the Confederate States was imminent, this question had engaged the attention of many of the leading men in Lancashire. They observed how the increasing competition for the American crop had enhanced the price of the raw material, enriching the Southern planters at the expense of manufacturing profits. They had not failed to remember that in 1845 cotton could be bought at 4*d.* a pound, and that no subsequent year had witnessed a return to that low price. Long since, it had been remarked by Mr. Bazley that mills were growing faster than cotton. In 1847, at the instance of Mr. Bright, a Committee of the House of Commons had inquired into the subject of the cotton supply. In 1850 he had endeavoured, but without success, to obtain a Royal Commission for the purpose of investigating the question of cotton cultivation in India; and from that time to the present the matter had engaged the earnest attention of the Manchester Chamber of Commerce and the Cotton

Supply Association. Mr. Henry Ashworth, the President of this Chamber, who is deservedly respected as an authority upon the subject, had never been inactive in promoting the establishment of more reliable and extensive sources of supply. For years past he had seen that the growth of manufacturing power was fast outstripping the increase of the supply of cotton, and thereby creating a competition most injurious to the interests of his neighbourhood. In 1857 he addressed the then President of the Manchester Chamber from Cincinnati, predicting that the planter would continue to absorb the manufacturer's profits until the yearly product of America should rise to 4,000,000 bales. It is some proof of how this question of the cotton supply is beset with difficulties and uncertainties;—it is some evidence with how little accuracy its future can be predicted, that this increased production should so soon afterwards have been more than accomplished, but without the realization of Mr. Ashworth's calculations. The crop of 1858 produced 4,370,000 bales, while that of the succeeding year amounted to 5,500,000 bales; yet the price of Middling Orleans, which had been $6\frac{1}{4}d.$ in 1857, rose to $7d.$ in 1858, and made a still further advance to $7\frac{3}{8}d.$ in 1860.

When, upon the occurrence of a deficient crop, attention was periodically diverted to the resources of India, and Government periodically urged to take measures for increasing the production of cotton in that vast dependency, Manchester was always told by those who have no sympathy with the cotton trade, to do it herself—to transplant some of her surplus energy and capital to the soil of Hindostan, and by the unaided exercise of her abilities to raise an Indian supply. Yet it was not from want of will, but from absolute want of the necessary opportunity, that so little progress had been made in this direction by the Lancashire capitalists, when the outbreak of the American war forbade the possibility of further delay. Hitherto it had been a question of price. It was not possible, even to English energy and capital, to revolutionise Indian agriculture—to introduce new plants, with improved methods of cultivation—to establish irrigation works, and means of easy communication with the coast—to do all this upon land of which but an unsettled tenure could be obtained, and at a time when they must compete with a supply from the neighbouring shores of America, already sufficient for the demand of the world,—with a climate and soil equal in natural adaptability to the cultivation of cotton and superior in facilities,—with a long-established system of production, aided by slave-labour, and assisted by a peculiarly ready access to the seaboard. On the other hand, it was not possible for the East India Company to force the native farmers to produce cotton, which, for ten successive years perhaps, must be allowed to rot, in order that in the eleventh it might rescue Lancashire from the consequences of a deficiency in the cotton crop of America. The whole population of the Indian peninsula must have been enslaved before they would have submitted thus to labour only for the benefit of the English cotton districts. Nor had the financial position of the East India Company ever been so prosperous as to enable them to carry out very extensive public works, such as would materially cheapen the cost of production, of conveyance, and shipment of cotton. It was partly for this reason they had called upon private capital to do that which they were powerless to accomplish. On the other hand, Lancashire would not submit to the imposition of a protective duty upon the import of American cotton, such as should make cotton an equally profitable crop to the ryots with coffee or tea or jute; and the inevitable consequence was, that though India had always been a large producer of cotton—second only at any time in this respect to the Southern States—yet her products could not maintain a competition with American cottons in the European markets.

So long as the Southern States could increase their production of cotton with all the advantages they possessed in 1860, and so long as their slave-labour market did not fail them, it was indeed impossible for India to compete with them successfully upon equal terms in the cotton markets of Europe. The cost of cultivation in Broach was certainly less than in Louisiana; but this was as nothing in comparison with the fact, that while one acre of American soil produced 300 lb. of clean cotton, the production of India amounted only to 70 lb. of very inferior quality; and so imperfect were the means of conveyance, that it has been estimated that an extra product of 2,000,000 Indian bales would require the services of 5,000,000 bullocks and 1,000,000 attendants.

Whether or not India would now become to any great extent a source of supply depended upon the power of the Government to assist in developing the resources of the country, and the continued stoppage of supplies from America. Fortunately for India, one of these circumstances had fallen upon the other. The Mutiny, by a cruel but decisive process, had performed the necessary ophthalmic operation upon English statesmen, and they were now fully awake to the importance of public works. The sequel of this tragic event was the transfer of the Empire of India from the enfeebled hands of the 'Coompany Bahadoor' to the crown of 'the Great Ranee of the Sahebs,' and for the first time in the world's history, a European monarch reigned over all Hindostan. So it happened, that when the American war gave a premium to the growth of cotton in India, vast sums had already been spent in establishing those means of communication so necessary to rulers who hold by conquest a wide territory with an inferior force. Railways were now pushing their lines across India from Calcutta to Bombay. But want of water is the main difficulty of Indian cultivation, and hence it is that in Dharwar, which is moistened during both monsoons, the growth of the American species of cotton has been most successful. The cardinal faults of Indian cotton are that it is short in staple and harsh in quality; but with the choice of that broad peninsula for soil—with the energy of the British people to facilitate production—with their untold capital to promote its cultivation and improvement—with the assurance that for years to come America cannot be a producer to the same extent that she was in 1860, there is not room to doubt that India will establish a firm and abiding place among the cotton-exporting countries of the world. But the error of that influential class which makes up the English cotton trade, with reference to Indian production, has been one to which a very prosperous and important industry is always liable. They have regarded the world as being composed of producers of the raw material and consumers of their manufactures, and have beheld themselves as the central ornament of this simple design.

With individual and most honourable exceptions, they have shown but little anxiety upon the subject of the cotton supply while plenty was to be had from America. Yet, having succeeded in cheapening the production of manufactures as much as possible in England, with but scant acknowledgment of the temporary sacrifices on the part of others by which this process was achieved, they were quite ready to agitate for a reduction of the indirect revenue of India, when the import duty on manufactured cottons opposed their interests, and to denounce the adoption of the Morrill tariff by the United States, when the war policy seemed to recommend that measure; while one of their chief spokesmen had no hesitation in proposing to sacrifice the direct revenue of India by a five years' exemption from land-tax, nor did he object thus to stultify a free-trade policy when the accident of war had for a time made the operatives of the cotton manufacture to a great extent dependent upon charity.

But the pressure of the Cotton Famine had not, however, been without its immediate effect. The proceedings of the Cotton Supply Association deserve a history to themselves. This association has done much to extend and to improve the cultivation both in India and Egypt. The latter is becoming a peculiarly valuable source of supply for the long-stapled qualities of cotton, such as are used for spinning lace and muslin yarns in the factories of Manchester and Bolton; and it is not improbable that the production of Egypt may in time be drawn from an area of 1,500,000 acres, and amount to upwards of a million of bales. Hitherto, the production of Egyptian cotton had been much impeded by the prevailing system of forced labour, under which no less than sixty thousand men were engaged in making that desert ditch, which is to be known by the name of the Suez Canal. But it is impossible, within the necessary limits of this history, to deviate widely into the very fertile question of the cotton supply; it must be sufficient to notice the accomplished results of the newly-arisen demand, as they arrived at the chief seat of the cotton manufacture. Yet it is difficult to pass without remark the notable absence, throughout the continuance of this unprecedented demand for the raw material, of any discovery even of an inferior substitute for cotton. At one time indeed, during the autumn of 1862, it was thought that an article obtainable in sufficient quantity, and possessing sufficient of the textile qualities of cotton to render its manufacture profitable, had been found to reward the patient endeavours and the anxious researches of this association. But the *Zostera marina* proved only a nine-days' wonder. Its sanguine and disinterested patron, Mr. Harben, had conceived the humane but rather unpractical design, that the unemployed operatives, with their children, should be transported to the coasts, where they could be engaged during the winter months in collecting the fibre. The Manchester Chamber of Commerce lent its important ear to the suggestion, but the result is told in the fact that no lively trade in the amphibious weed followed their inquiry into its merits as a substitute for cotton.

The Customs returns, which are generally assumed to be the surest test of the national wellbeing and comfort, had shown continued improvement through all the quarters of the great year of the Cotton Famine. The amount of receipts for Customs during the year ending March 1862, had been 23,692,00*l.*; at the end of September the year's receipts had risen to 23,863,000*l.*; while at the close of the year a further increase had taken place, and the twelve months' receipts of this department of the revenue had been as much as 24,036,000*l.* On the other hand, the value of the imports and exports is supposed to be the truest index of national prosperity. And certainly no stronger proof could be advanced of the irrepressible commercial activity of this country, than that which is afforded by a comparison of the imports and payments for raw cotton in the zenith of 1860 and the nadir of 1862. In the former year, the United Kingdom received from all sources the unequalled supply of 1,390,938,752 lb. of raw cotton, the value of which was 35,756,889*l.* Of this supply, 1,115,890,608 lb. came from America. During 1862 the total supply was only 535,001,500 lb., of which but 13,524,224 lb. was derived from America, while more than two-thirds was supplied by India. But means were found to pay 31,093,045*l.* for this diminished supply, being only four millions and a half less than the sum which two years before had been paid for a supply of more than twice the quantity. The lion's share of this enormous payment found its way to India. It is, however, to be said, that the export of raw cotton in 1860 did not greatly exceed in weight that of 1862, being in the former 608,260 bales, and in the latter year 564,920 bales. A much larger portion of the supply of 1862 would have been retained for home consumption had not the stocks of manufactured goods been so large throughout the year. At its close, the stock of cotton remaining in Great Britain was 160,561,870 lb., being the least amount held in stock, at the close of any year, since 1858. But for the over-production of previous years, there might certainly have been twice as much employment as there had been in 1862. The total amount of the home consumption of manufactures during this, the great year of the Famine, was provided from stocks manufactured before its commencement; at least, it may have been so, for the quantity of yarn and cloth produced in 1862 did not equal the actual weight of exportations in that year by 100,000,000 lb., which, added to the estimated home consumption of 180,000,000 lb., would show that the demand for 1862 was supplied to the extent of 280,000,000 lb. from stocks of manufactured goods existing before the beginning of that year. The enormous profits which must have been realized upon the sale of these goods have already been referred to; but had they been manufactured during this year of deep distress, the operatives would have received at least 1,500,000*l.* more in wages. The loss of manufacturing profits, and the more serious loss of wages by the operatives, is evidenced by a comparison of the margin between the cost of the raw material and the value of goods produced in 1860 and 1862. In 1860, the value of productions had been upwards of 76,000,000*l.*, while the cost of the raw material had been under 36,000,000*l.* But in 1862, notwithstanding the greatly-increased price of commodities, the total value of the cotton manufactures of this kingdom were estimated at 56,000,000*l.*, while the raw material imported during that year was valued at 31,093,045*l.* Though this is but a very rough method of determining loss of profits and wages, yet the margin of 40,000,000*l.* in 1860, when compared with that of 25,000,000*l.* in 1862, explains some at least of the features of the Cotton Famine. Happier they, who were reselling their cotton or disposing of their surplus stocks of goods during this year! For months past, cotton of average quality had been dearer than the manufactured yarn, and calico could be bought for less money than good cotton of equal weight. To the manufacturer of heavy goods there was certainly no possibility of immediate profits by running his mill; consequently, the distress was peculiarly severe in those towns which manufacture for the Eastern markets, especially in Blackburn, where as many as 30,000 power-looms had been devoted to the service of the Asiatics, and where but few of these were now active.

The opinion of the cotton trade no longer wavered upon the subject of the American war. When the year 1862 had closed, there was no longer any doubt that the conflict would be an affair of long duration, and that the Federals and Confederates would be left to fight it out between themselves. The cotton market had, indeed, been somewhat disturbed in October, by the speech of the Chancellor of the Exchequer at Newcastle, in which he declared his opinion that the South had made itself 'a nation.' But any suspicions as to a wavering in the policy of neutrality which this speech may have excited, were tranquillised in November by the refusal of the English Government to join with that of France in a combined proposal of mediation between the belligerents. Then, in December, had followed the famous proclamation and message of President Lincoln, which, being directly aimed at the abolition of slavery,—at nothing less than the complete destruction of this Southern institution, made the conduct of the war more fierce, and indefinitely postponed all prospect of its termination. And at the termination of the year the cotton market was firm; the price of Middling Orleans being 25*d.*, and that of Indian Fair Dhollerah, 18*d.* per lb.

Indeed, the prospects of supply for 1863 were not calculated to decrease the confidence of the holders of raw cotton in a still further advance of prices. Mr. Edmund Ashworth, whose opinion upon the subject had every claim to attention, estimated the forthcoming Indian crop at 1,250,000 bales, or 25 per cent. in excess of that received in 1862. In this opinion he was subsequently supported by the semi-official authority of Mr. Laing, who had but recently returned from India, where he had been engaged in carrying out financial reforms. Mr. Ashworth estimated the increase from Egypt, Brazil, and the West Indies at fifty per cent., and the total supply from these sources at 1,372,675 bales. Allowing for the decreased stock of cotton in Liverpool, as compared with that remaining at the end of 1861, the estimated increase of raw material available for manufacture amounted only to 134,650 bales. In making this statement to the Central Executive Committee, Mr. Ashworth was careful to remind the committee of the difference between the weight of Indian and American bales; the latter averaging 415 lb., while the former did not weigh more than 370 lb. The views which he expressed concurred with those of the committee, and induced them to regard the future with some anxious glances at the condition of their funds; it being evident that no more than a sufficient supply of cotton for working half-time could be expected during the whole of the ensuing year.

No sooner was 1863 raised to the throne of Time in place of the departed year, than the committee issued a financial statement and balance-sheet, of which it may be said that arithmetical figures were never employed in a service more honourable. It not unfrequently happens, even in the case of charitable funds, that some considerable portion is detained by the administrators on account of 'expenses.' Of course, it must not be assumed that anything more serious than mismanagement is here alluded to: it would be impossible to associate the suspicion of dishonourable conduct with any one of the names of the Central Executive Committee, yet they might have been guilty of mismanagement—they might have adopted expensive modes of obtaining information, and they and their honorary secretary, instead of setting an example of the most jealous surveillance of their funds, might, presuming upon their magnificent proportions, have blamelessly spared themselves, and not their charge. It is to their honour that they did not do so; it is to their honour that when this golden tide of wealth was rushing in upon them—when their receipts in one day alone amounted to 24,000*l.*—they were the faithful, unselfish almoners of the benevolent, and the no less faithful guardians of the best interests of those unfortunate persons for whose sake their labour was bestowed. And it may be safely affirmed that they had accomplished what as yet had never been achieved in the history of finance; for they had received, acknowledged, and to a large extent had administered a sum close upon 600,000*l.*, at a cost for general expenses of 2,708*l.*, or less than one-half per cent. But it is to be observed that more than a moiety of this charge for general expenses was paid for advertising, and that a large portion of the remainder was incurred for labour and expenses in the distribution of clothing.

This document did not realize the statement made at the county meeting with reference to the amount contributed by Lancashire alone to the relief funds. It must, however, be borne in mind that this account of receipts applies exclusively to those of the Central Relief Committee. At the close of 1862, the county had given 258,769*l* to the resources of the committee. But the local relief committees, of which there were now about a hundred and fifty in operation, had received, for their independent expenditure, sums amounting to 228,995*l.*, which raises the total contingent of Lancashire to 487,764*l.* —a contribution only inconsiderable when compared with the wealth of the cotton trade and the loss of wages which was now borne by the working classes of the district.

On the list of foreign and colonial subscriptions, Australia stands for nearly eighty per cent. of the total amount, having sent 46,639*l.*—a practical acknowledgment of filial duty which will increase the pride of England in the splendid prospects of her offspring in the South Pacific. The amount received from India was not equally creditable to the possession which is not without good reason distinguished as 'the brightest jewel in the English crown,' and the smallness of her contribution is the more noticeable, because one of the first effects of the Cotton Famine had been immensely to increase the wealth of India. For of all places where the British Crown has rule, and British law has right, India was that which would be most enriched and permanently benefited by the events which had brought adversity to the manufacturing districts. But it was the native community and not the English in India who had gained most by the advanced price of cotton. Hindoos, whose savings-bank is not unfrequently a shovelful of earth, and whose extraordinary expenditure is almost invariably confined to personal ornaments, were not likely to be much concerned for the sufferings of Lancashire. Still, the amount was not such as the English community can regard with pride, though it was afterwerds augmented.* There had been a considerable accession to the funds of the Mansion House Committee, which indeed was transmitted from India, though it was due to English charity. A large surplus yet remained in the hands of the trustees of the Indian Famine Relief Fund, and after much correspondence, the Lord Mayor of London had been authorised by Lord Eglin, the Governor-General of India, to draw, for the benefit of Lancashire, upon the Indian Government for 20,000*l.*, in respect of this surplus. The Mansion House Committee had been actively engaged in receiving money and remitting grants to the manufacturing districts, and at the close of the year 1862, the receipts of this committee amounted to 335,843*l.*, of which sum they had disbursed no less than 252,157*l.*

Before returning to the proper history of the distress, it is worthy of observation, that during this year of unexampled suffering in the cotton districts, there had been no important increase in the number of emigrants from England. To some extent the war in America had checked emigration to the United States, which has always been the most favoured resort of English exiles. From the United Kingdom there had gone in 1860 to these States 87,500 persons, but in 1862 the number resorting thither had fallen to 58,706 persons. Nor was the emigration to other places increased by this deficiency. The total number of emigrants in 1860, when every cotton 'hand' was in urgent demand, had been 128,469, while in 1862 the number was only 121,214. This fact alone would be sufficient proof that the effect of the Cotton Famine had not yet been to make the operatives leave their country. Some migrated to other counties, and a few were removed by poor-law orders to their legal place of settlement; but these latter were not more than two per cent. upon the

* Since this was written, I have been informed that most of the Indian subscriptions were made to the Mansion House Fund. R. A. A.

amount of pauperism, and with but very few exceptions these removals were from parish to parish within the cotton district. It cannot be doubted that many would gladly have escaped from their present hardships, and from the anxious prospect which saddened their lot at home. But how could they go? Their money was all spent or fast locked up in shares, or in a cottage, which was equally unsaleable; and as the cotton-workers have not generally been an emigrating people, they were not, like so many of the Irish, possessed of friends ready to forward the means of joining them in a new country. But it is quite certain that thousands would, with dry eyes, have left the shores of England had they but been provided with the means of conveyance.

Yet surely it cannot be necessary to defend the manufacturers from the charge of having done all in their power to discourage emigration. Was it to be expected that they should break up their machinery, dissolve their establishments, and render valueless the enormous capital which, with so much thrift and so much self-denial, they had invested in the cotton manufacture? It would be as reasonable to expect that a tradesman should knock the bottom out of his till. These thousands who were now combating all the physical wants of life with an allowance of two shillings apiece per week, were skilled workmen and workwomen, a people highly trained in a manufacture most delicate and difficult. This skill of itself formed not an inconsiderable part of the wealth of England, and anyone sincerely and intelligently interested in the welfare of this country, could hardly have been satisfied to see it scattered and lost to its proper and most efficient uses. It would not be by any means difficult to prove that it would have been to the pecuniary advantage of the country generally to maintain these persons in any required amount of comfort, rather than allow them to take their handicraft elsewhere. But that the manufacturer, whose partners they are in the vested capital of Lancashire,—that he should be expected to lend a helping hand to shove them off from the shores of their country, is past comprehension for absurdity. Like Pharaoh, he would have borne much, rather than let the people go;—he would have raised the total sum required for their relief;—he would have paid three or four times as much in poor-rates as he was called upon to pay;—he would have bought cotton and have manufactured it so long as he ever was able to do so. But would it have been right that he should thus alone bear this burden? Could Englishmen of the South and of the West and of the East have held their generous hand, while their brother of the North had such need? Surely not. Who does not feel that this chapter in our national annals is one which pre-eminently records a long advance to that practical brotherhood of mankind, which, but yesterday, was thought to be nothing but such stuff as dreams are made of? Not the brotherhood of a ridiculous social equality, to which Nature gives the lie by making men unequal in mental as in bodily stature; but the brotherhood which assures the poor and the weak and the destitute of support and comfort, and promises to the ignorant that he shall not be without the opportunity of learning the wisdom of the wise.

With the dawn of the new year, there became visible a decided improvement in the state of employment throughout the cotton districts. The slender production of the previous year, and the demand for goods, unchecked by the rise in their price, had seriously told upon existing stocks, and to a considerable extent had cleared them off. Mr. Farnall's reports invariably commenced with the pleasing announcement of a decrease of pauperism. But with the commencement of the new year, the Central Executive Committee were drawn into a quarrel, which had long been inflaming Ashton-under-Lyne, but which for their connection with it, would hardly have attracted much public notice. It is however the more worthy of attention, as being the only instance in which their dealings with their numerous dependents were ever publicly questioned as being other than fair and straightforward.

It has been mentioned that there existed two committees in Ashton, which, without being exactly rivals, were certainly not animated with friendly feelings the one towards the other. The General Relief Committee was the older of the two. But when the Central Committee commenced operations in Manchester, it found both the General and the Borough Relief Committees in action at Ashton-under-Lyne. The former professed to take charge of the parish, while the latter confined its attentions to the borough. The General Committee owed most of its fame and not a little of its funds to the zeal and the pen of a clergyman who was its secretary and frontispiece. The Borough Relief Committee had collected the larger amount of local subscriptions, and its chairman was the mayor. In these two particulars, therefore, it was pre-eminently entitled to the patronage of the Central Executive Committee. It was not denied that the General Committee was largely tinctured with Church principles, and though the mayor was a Churchman, yet it was true that the most influential member of the Borough Committee was also the most active opponent of the Church Establishment in Ashton. Such was the position of affairs when the Central Executive Committee had to take action, and to decide to which of these committees their grants should be made for the relief of distress in Ashton. Their regulation compelled them to recognise but one committee in each place, and both the justice and expediency of this rule are too obvious to need suggestion. The success which had attended their administration of the relief funds was, as they well knew, largely owing to their discouragement of religious or sectarian influences. At their own board were Churchmen of every shade of opinion—high, broad, and low—the Roman Catholic Church had a dignified and moderate representative, Protestant Dissenters had their spokesmen, the Society of Friends and the Unitarians found a place, but yet nothing could exceed the harmony of their discussions and the unanimity of their decisions. And this resulted because their single aim and object was the relief of distress, regardless of the religious opinions of the sufferer. The more neutral was the constitution of the local committee, the greater were its claims to the support of the Central Executive; and it cannot be doubted that the best evidence which a place could give of this neutrality, was to make the secular local authority the nucleus of the relief committee. It was a *primâ facie* objection to the General Committee of Ashton that its secretary was an active clergyman, and that it had an exclusively Church reputation. The present object was not to promote Church principles, but to relieve distress. On the other hand, it was an objection to the Borough

Committee that it was formed exclusively of lay elements. But, upon the suggestion of the Central Executive, there were added to this committee the senior members of the clergy, of the Roman Catholic priests, and of the Dissenting ministers in Ashton-under-Lyne. And, having failed to consolidate the committees—though Mr. Farnall undertook a special embassage for this purpose—the Executive Committee determined to recognise the Borough Relief Committee, and from that time forward it was the only recipient of their grants in the town of Ashton-under-Lyne.

That this was an error in judgment on the part of the Executive Committee, there can be little doubt, and it was one of those many fortunate circumstances which have attended their operations, that this departure from their rule of action did not result in similar divisions in other parts of the district. They had the power of enforcing compliance with their wholesome regulation, and it may well be thought that they would not in this case have failed to prove its efficacy, had they not been fearful of introducing a still greater evil, by permitting a division of the district between the Mansion House Committee and themselves. The Mansion House Committee has done too much good service throughout the duration of the Cotton Famine, to be harshly judged for those rare occasions when from their lesser knowledge of the district they have somewhat clogged the action of the more ubiquitous executive at Manchester. The administration of relief in Ashton-under-Lyne would have been less liable to suffer from fraud—less provocative of those local jealousies which are for ever on the surface in that borough, if the two great committees of London and Manchester had flatly declared that they would withhold their assistance until a fair amalgamation had been made of both the local committees, or until such a division of their labours had taken place as to preclude the possibility of injurious rivalry. The paradox that 'exceptions prove the rule' is essentially true in this case, for, although the result has been favourable to Ashton in a pecuniary point of view, yet the existence of two committees has seriously thwarted the economical administration of relief, and has placed this town in a somewhat invidious position as regards the other claimants upon the charitable funds. The existence of 'competing agencies of relief,' as these rival committees were aptly termed, was estimated in the depth of the distress to have caused the waste—if so strong a term may be used in respect of charitable disbursements—of 500*l.* a week, which would seem to be proved by the fact, that though the poor-rates in Ashton-under-Lyne were at least as heavy as those of Preston, yet these committees had together received as much assistance from the London and Manchester funds as that which had been given to Preston, though there the numbers of unemployed were nearly twice as numerous as in Ashton-under-Lyne. And it may be that the baneful results of this demoralising competition have yet left sad traces in the scene of its occurrence.

The long continuance of the distress pressed with peculiar severity upon many of the owners of cottage property, who had maintained a struggle against beggary with but little assistance from their customary rentals. Indeed, it not unfrequently happened that the houseowner suffered greater privations than his non-rentpaying tenant, who was not disqualified by the possession of property from partaking in the relief funds. Among this class, and also among the small shopkeepers, the distress was now greater than ever. And now also trouble had fallen upon that rather numerous class of manufacturers whose factories and loom-sheds had been conducted with the assistance of borrowed capital. Though the cotton supply tarried, their interest became due; and though there were no profits to be made, yet rates must be paid and machinery must be kept in order. Among the poor—among those who had now become the regular pensioners of the relief committees—there was certainly less distress than there had been during the previous month. It was something or them to have become thoroughly acquainted with the machinery existing for their relief. There were many cases of actual and many of attempted imposition—sufficient of both to show how vicious impudence and brazen lying would have obtained a very large share of the relief funds, had it not been for the omniscient, omnipresent agency of the guardians and relief committees. Fraudulent imposition was next to impossible in small places, where the relieving officer, or one or another member of the local committee, was personally acquainted with every applicant. But in the larger towns—in Manchester especially—this was not possible. In many cases applicants for relief obtained aid in respect of children who had no existence; in others, they asserted that their children were out of work, when inquiry proved that they were at present earning wages. In large centres of population, where all cannot be known—where the influence of the poor upon the moral character of each other is not great—the administrators of relief will always find their duties to include surveillance as well as sympathy. In such places, to give liberally and without supervision, is not only wasteful but demoralising, for the scale of relief is watched by many quite willing to become applicants when it affords sufficient encouragement. To obviate this difficulty, the system of inspection must be particularly minute in such localities, which should in the first place be subdivided into districts sufficiently small to insure facility of observation.

There is, however, in the cotton manufacturing districts a large population living in a condition never very much above the level of pauperism; while, fortunately for itself, the law does not permit that it shall fall below this standard. To what its degradation is to be ascribed, it would be difficult exactly to state. Certainly it has a bad name; and this, it is known, has not, in a moral sense, an elevating influence. By some its faults are imputed to the accident of race; and by others, who are more charitable, to misgovernment—to existence in the midst of unwholesome social laws—to a want of self-respect, and a lack of power to gain the respect of others. Yet the friends of the poor Irish population of the cotton districts praise only their docility, their generosity, and their courage. It is generally said of them that they are thriftless and improvident; that they do not possess that sober perseverance which is so marked a characteristic of the English operatives; that they have none of that stubborn pride which cherishes independence—though it be ragged and hungry—as the greatest of treasures. The history of the Cotton Famine does not contradict this view of their condition; for they, be it their fault or their misfortune, have always been the first to swell the relief-lists and the last to leave them; they are not among the promoters of co-operative stores, nor are they found, but in rare instances, among the more highly paid classes of factory workers.

It would be absurd to argue that they suffer any external disability on account of their religion. Generally the working-classes of Lancashire are Protestant, but religious toleration is more practical in this county than in any other in the kingdom. Were it not for the fact that many thousands have been domiciled in the district for generations without evincing many symptoms of improvement, it might be thought that they suffered from being denationalised and expatriated. Though generally without cultivation, their natural intellectual faculties are of a very superior order. There are Irish working-men in Lancashire who are fluent speakers, adroit, and well-read men of the world. There are no braver soldiers than the Irish, but they are not distinguished as seamen, nor as merchants, nor as inventors, nor as the best of workmen; and the cause of this can only be ascribed either to their religion or to their born nature. Their religion—differing far more from that of an educated and liberal Roman Catholic than does his faith from the Church of England—suppresses that self-reliance which comes to most men who know themselves to be, under God, the arbiters of their own destiny, and to whom the responsibility of their own opinion is a serious and educating influence. Rather than stimulating 'self-help,' it encourages dependence upon others. This may, in some measure, account for the fact that the uneducated Irish are only great when marshalled in obedience; or if not, it must be that—the born children of impulse—their quicker and less enduring temperament can fight the battle which lasts only a short time and is all-exciting, but can with difficulty comprehend how a more phlegmatic race gird themselves to fight the long battle of a life, never doffing their armour of perseverance, patience, and hope till they pass beyond the need of such defences and assistance.

Early in January there was a satisfactory increase in the numbers employed and a corresponding diminution of the responsibilities of the relief committees. Several mills were reopened in Preston. Hundreds who had been dependant on the relief funds found employment in Blackburn.

In Stockport 4,600 were added to the numbers working full time. The same reports came from Ashton-under-Lyne, from Staleybridge, Oldham, and Bury. Mr. Farnall's lists showed a decrease of pauperism to the extent of 11,477. Cotton was becoming a little more plentiful, and its price somewhat reduced. The two-shilling rate of relief per head was general, and there was no observable deterioration in the health of the population. Wigan was the only place that had adopted a systematic medical supervision; there the town was divided into five districts, with a medical man allotted to each, who gave gratuitous service to the pensioners of the Relief Committee, from the funds of which these gentlemen received an honorarium of twenty-five pounds apiece. The system was found to work admirably, and with great benefit to the sick poor of Wigan. The advantage of this precaution would, however, have been more evident and more acknowledged, had the ravages of such an epidemic as many, whose opinion was entitled to respect, thought but too likely to occur, added the horrors of deathly disease to the existing distress. In many places the sick received the nourishment required by their condition from private charity, and through benefit clubs. A woman, who knew more of the qualities of the famous febrifuge than of its orthography, was heard to say, speaking of a sick neighbour: 'Hoo's got a bit of "Queen Ann" (quinine?) 'as they co'w it, an' some red wine, for hoo's in a bit of a sick club, from wheer hoo gets four and sixpence a week while hoo's ill, an' aw'm sure that's welly as much as hoo'l get eawt o' t' skoo wages.'

The local subscriptions made little or no increase; the difference in their total in the last week in December and in the last week in January being less than four thousand pounds. In most places they had never been large, and, in fact, the burden of the distress was now borne by the central funds. In Oldham, a place of great wealth—the manufactories in which contain a larger number of spindles than those of any other town in the district—the amount of the local subscriptions was 8,500*l.*,—a poor representation of the capital of a borough which has built twenty new factories within the last three years. The Relief Committe regretted to find 'that out of a large number of firms of cotton-spinners in Oldham, only about one-half had contributed to the relief funds.' But it is to be said for Oldham, that it is not a place of large capitals. Many of the mills are occupied by several manufacturers, each renting a portion of the building with a share of the power. This system is peculiar to Oldham, and these masters are very little above the rank of operatives. Generally, the manufacturing wages paid in Oldham are higher than elsewhere, and there is a local belief, probably well founded, that here the operatives do more work than in other places. The guardians were expending 671*l.* and the Relief Committee 832*l.* weekly. These sums together did not represent a third of the loss of wages, which was not less than 7,000*l.*; but many of the Oldham operatives were still supported by their savings, or by the proceeds of mortgages of their little property in shares or in their cottage.

In Stockport, the Relief Committee and the guardians divided the charge of 24,000 persons, by the former taking eighteen and the latter six thousand, each acting without supplementary aid from the other. Under this arrangement, the burden upon the local rates was not very oppressive. But the average allowance of these indigent people was from 2*s.* 2*d.* to 2*s.* 6*d.* per head, so that there was little danger of actual starvation in Stockport. The committee were expending 1,815*l.* in food and 450*l.* in coal and clothing weekly, while the guardians were paying in outdoor relief at the rate of 660*l.* a week. And as the estimated loss of wages did not exceed 6,500*l.*, the Cotton Famine had thus brought nearly the earnings of half-time on the wings of charity. Some portion of this undoubtedly went to pay rent; but even this sum is not by any means the measure of the total relief which the unemployed population of Stockport was now receiving. Congregational relief was very much practised here, and it was said that there were as many as three hundred families, with whose maintenance charitable and non-resident persons had charged themselves. Here, as elsewhere, there were soup-kitchens, full of savoury odour and thankful feeders. Many obtained sustenance by this means, who, if they happened to be dependant upon improvident persons, might otherwise have run great danger of starvation. The time for the delivery of the soup never arrived without having attracted a crowd around the entrance to the kitchen. Often for hours did the patient holders of soup-tickets await, in the cold of a winter's day, the opening of the doors. Crowding to secure the best place and the earliest attention, they came of all ages and sizes. Jugs, cans, and kettles were all in request to carry away the steaming comfort to the houses of the distressed. Some few, usually distinguished outside by having their hands in their pockets, preferred to drink on the premises, and stood by blowing their hot bowls, while the distribution proceeded. A rare preventive of starvation is a soup-kitchen! It is by far the most economical mode of distributing relief in kind, almost precluding the possibility of waste; and while the soup nourishes in a very eminent degree, it is also useful in maintaining the heat of the bodily system. The materials used for making the soup were almost all that could be used; but though the contents of many cauldrons were put to the test of nice palates, the compound was always praised as being very good.

The labours of the local committees were at this time enormous, and the marvel is, not that they were in some places accused of partiality and in others of parsimony, but that they gratuitously performed such a vast amount of work, and spread out their relief with so much regularity and success. The weekly bill of fair of the Preston Committee now included 26,759 sixpenny loaves, weighing 47 tons 15 cwt.; 29,703 quarts of soup; 11,012 quarts of potato hash; together with 500 tons of coal and 1,000*l.* worth of bedding. In addition to this, the 'sick kitchen' served out 862 lb. of cooked meat, 832 quarts of beef-tea, and 35 quarts of gruel. But this was not too much for the 36,078 persons who now looked to them for their daily bread. The weekly relief given by the Blackburn Committee included 37,200 lb. of flour and 19,680 lb. of meal, together with 390*l.* in money. Blackburn had numbers of good and some great persons in attendance upon its wants. It had gained, through the untiring activity of its mayor and other local notables, a reputation as a show-place for 'Lancashire distress,' wherein the charitable and the curious from all parts could mark the action of the Cotton Famine with most precision. The published receipts of the Relief Committee exclude large sums spent here in unrecorded charity. A private clothing store was established, and several 'mothers' kitchens,' institutions in which mothers, with their newly-born infants, received the extra nourishment required by their condition.

What was doing at Preston and Blackburn was also being accomplished in Ashton, Burnley, and other centres of the distress. The condition of Manchester and Salford, and their satellite townships, is so peculiar, that they cannot be classified with these towns. They contained more than 70,000 operatives, but yet their character is not that of manufacturing towns. Their stationary wealth, and consequently their resources, are far greater than those of their neighbours; and so much of the general business of the district is carried on in them, that their agency is equally great with their productive business. In fact, the township of Manchester can no longer be regarded as manufacturing.

In January there were nearly 90,000 persons receiving relief in Manchester and Salford. With the District Provident Society and the board of guardians there was no lack of first-rate distributing power. But it cannot be said that the liberality of the rich in Manchester and Salford had been equal to their means. Indeed, it was not said so. Many who were best acquainted with the immense wealth of the mercantile community of Manchester, did not fail to express their dissatisfaction with their conduct. Yet there can be little doubt, that if the distress had been confined to Manchester and Salford, no appeals would have been made for external assistance. They accepted help which they might have provided for themselves; but they would not have asked for it. By the end of January, Manchester and Salford had each received twice as much money from the Mansion House and the Central Funds, as their inhabitants had subscribed for local relief. They had raised 33,144*l.*; they had accepted 71,690*l.* The profits they had gained by the Cotton Famine cannot be accurately fixed, but to set them at ten times the total of these sums will be sufficient to point the moral of this statement. A more liberal community is not to be found in England than exists in Manchester; nor is there a city in the kingdom which local charity has supplied more amply with associations and establishments for promoting the social and moral well-being of its inhabitants. But even a slight acquaintance is sufficient to show that this most wealthy and influential population is one of the least homogeneous, and that charity and its absence are as much the distinct features of its particular classes as wealth and indigence. Both the Manchester Board of Guardians and the District Provident Society had the will to be independent of all external assistance, but the ways and means were not found.

Transition periods are never productive of great efforts, and it may be that Manchester has repudiated provincialism without having yet attained to metropolitan dignity. Too important for its opinion to be disregarded—too large for its opinion to be without complexity—its action is at present rather embarrassed than assisted by its greatness. To a visitor, the public opinion of Manchester will appear to be a confusion of ideas, not because opinion is individually unsettled, but because it is not, as in older cities of equal magnitude, so definitely represented by locality and class. Year by year, however, Manchester is becoming less manufacturing and more metropolitan. Among the lower orders of the population of this city, there is also a great admixture of species. Among them will be found hard-headed, thrifty, and ambitious artisans, democrats by instinct, but by the stronger bond of nature, lovers of time-honoured English customs and of national institutions;—steady, pious, harsh religionists, ready to fasten the Main Liquor Law and any amount of Sabbatical restraints upon their neighbours;—quiet, docile, domestic folks, enjoying the real happiness of a working life;—lazy, drunken, dissolute, to whom the Cotton Famine has been a season of luxury, when food without work was more easy to obtain.

Yet those who wish to see this central heart of the cotton manufacturing districts in its most remarkable aspect, must look deeper than this. Then it will be found that civil and religious liberty is not so conspicuous in any European city of equal extent, and then it will be discovered that in no city of equal population is so much done for the education of the people. Then, perhaps, it may be asked,—is it impossible to blend progress with good manners, and liberty with refinement? Must the most precious influence of authority in matters of opinion, grow fainter, as in the development of freedom, individuality becomes more perfect? And possibly, the reflection will follow, that, if so, it may be thought even such progress can be purchased at too high a price. But these questions are yet to be answered by modern civilisation in the fulness of time. The facts remain, that in this city the Church does a great work, side by side with the not less zealous labours of the Roman Catholic and the Dissenter; that in Manchester and Salford there is one-sixth of the whole population on the books of the Sunday schools, belonging to the various religious denominations. It is estimated that there are 77,000 Sunday scholars in these establishments, of whom 26,000 are attached to the Church of England, 15,000 to the Roman Catholic, and the remaining 36,000 to the Dissenting schools; while the libraries attached to these schools contain almost as many books as there are scholars.

Returning to the history of the Cotton Famine, it could not but be expected that the very extensive system of relief, which was in full operation at the commencement of 1863—which was so well tended and so amply supplied with funds—should be entrely free from abuses. As a matter of course, they came on both sides. Some of the manufacturers attempted to take advantage of the prevailing distress and the state of employment to reduce wages below the customary standard of prices, in order that they might recommence production with profit. What the international treaties are to Europe, such is the list of prices in the cotton district—the abiding public law, which both master and operative are bound to recognise, and, with here and there exceptions, to adhere to, until alteration is made by their respective plenipotentiaries—that is, by their committees. So that the attempt which was now made to effect a reduction of wages to the extent of ten or twenty per cent. was regarded as the blackest criminality by the operatives, most of whom would submit to very severe suffering rather than accept other terms of employment than those of the standard list. Of course, the desire to recommence production, and the difficulty of doing so with a profit, was at the bottom of these malpractices. The privations of the times made many ready to work for the smallest recompense; but it will hardly be believed that there were two persons who worked five days, or fifty hours a week, in a factory, for pay amounting to 1*s.* 5*d.* for one, and 9½*d.* for the other. Yet such was the fact. Letters found their way into newspaper columns showing that in some cases, after working hard all the week for little more than this, mill-hands had been met on pay-day with a demand for rent, which left them almost penniless. But what is all this, more than saying that the manufacturers were men, and some of them bad ones and heartless —a record neither new nor strange concerning any class?

On the other hand, it was stoutly affirmed by many well qualified to judge, that of the number receiving relief in Manchester, twenty-five per cent. were not fit objects of such charity. Probably this was an exaggeration; but inasmuch as the guardians and the committees of the district Provident Society worked with but little consentaneous action, and as a large number of those receiving relief were of that class which is never so well off as in times like these, when assistance is liberally given, it is quite likely that much money was misspent. It was said that one committee reduced its responsibilities by as many as two hundred and fifty cases, by the simple announcement of an intention to send 'the relief cards' of these pensioners for the inspection of two or three large employers in the neighbourhood. If there were localities in which imposition was thus practised *en masse*, it would be puerile to doubt that single instances were by no means rare. Indeed, the following extract from a report made by their assistant clerk to the Manchester Board of Guardians, affords irrefragable proof that fraud was neither uncommon nor undiscovered:—

'Almost every conceivable variety of fraud, it would appear, has been practised upon the officers of the board, as the reports of the special visitors now employed prove every week. Children recently dead have been booked as living; children that never existed have been booked; children have been borrowed to make up families; concealment or misrepresentation of wages seems almost to have been the rule in some districts of the city; men, whose regular work was at night, have obtained relief for want of work in the daytime; sick men have been found drunk in bed; men discharged by employers for drunkenness have obtained relief as decent, respectable artisans, persons have left employment avowedly because they could get a living easier by charity and parish relief than by work; men have been found who, having work at home, were attending the school or the farm; men have been found who were working, but not at their homes; and the short hours required of those sent to the school or to the farm, have enabled many to secure wages of which they gave no account whatever; and, to finish this most unpleasant recital, the reports referred to have made the guardians acquainted with the existence, in one district at least, of an amount of immorality of which they had not before heard of, a large number of persons living in adultery having obtained relief as married people.'

Disputes occasionally arose between the payers and receivers of relief, which caused in some places temporary tumult, and angry words or threats. Among the latter, one of the most curious and original specimens was addressed to a member of a relief committee in the north of Lancashire. The communication was as follows:—'D—— hypocrite and friend, thy time is short; get thee ready. Long hast thou been hated by hundreds. Hundreds will be glad when thy blood has been spilled. D—— tyrant, beware!' Pleasantry of this character, was however, very rare, and indeed it ought to have been so, considering the immense amount of gratuitous and purely disinterested labour bestowed by the members of the local committees and their officers in the work of relief.

Some told of domestic servants having left their places from a preference for the sewing-schools, and others, of girls, the daughters of well-to-do parents, who took advantage of these excellent institutions. But no one harmed themselves by getting into a sewing-school, and no establishments were more successful. It was well that it was so, for the hard times had seriously affected the prospects of many of these girls. The first prose of matrimony comes from Somerset House, and that unromantic but infallible calculator, the Registrar-General, gave notice of a great fall in the Lancashire marriage-rate during 1862. Neither the death-rate nor the birth-rate told the presence of the distress so plainly as the marriage-rate. The return for the last quarter of 1862, compared with that for the corresponding period of 1860, showed that the number of marriages in Ashton had fallen from 342 to 245; in Bolton, from 344 to 249; in Blackburn, from 412 to 181; in Rochdale, from 237 to 166; and in Stockport, from 332 to 198. With cruel brevity, these figures tell the tale of many a hope deferred, and many a young heart made sick, by the shadow of the cloud which was now over-hanging the manufacturing districts.

Looking back on these days, assisted by all the light of subsequent facts which the progress of time has revealed, it seems unaccountable that so little manufacture should have been going on. Only here and there was to be found a mill working full-time, and even short-time was not much more common. In this respect, the knowledge of the present obstructs to a great extent an equitable judgment of the past. It is hardly possible now to divest the mind of the political knowledge which has since been acquired. Then, it did not appear absolutely certain—at least to but few men—that the American war would seem as interminable in 1864 as it did in the first month of 1863, and the manufacturer had then but a very imperfect knowledge of where should be the future sources of the cotton supply. There was cotton in Liverpool and cotton in Manchester; but where was the end of the American war, and when would the 3,000,000 bales stored in the Southern States be let loose on European markets? These were the unanswered questions which locked the mill-gates and continued the distress. The stocks of goods in the home and the eastern markets were becoming very much lightened, but even now the prices of goods in China and India were twenty-five per cent. lower than in Manchester. And now it began to be found that the rise of prices affected the demand; if it did not actually lessen the quantity consumed, it caused the substitution of a cheaper class of goods. 'Bradford worsteds' in many instances took the places of calicoes; and linens and woollens to some extent replaced the heavy class of cotton goods. So the ill wind that brought doubt and distress to Lancashire, blew prosperity to Belfast and to Yorkshire. One circumstance that increased the difficulty of recommencing work was, that in the majority of mills the machinery was empty. The value of the stock in process of manufacture is an important item, and would have amounted in some mills, at the prices of this time, to 10,000*l*. And at this time it is probable that not less than from eighty to a hundred thousand bales of cotton would have been required to fill the manufacturing machinery of the cotton districts.

The question of emigration was revived in the early months of 1863. At the January meeting of the Central Relief Committee a letter was read from the Secretary of the Province of Canterbury, in New Zealand, announcing a vote of 10,000*l*. to assist in promoting the emigration of distressed operatives to that settlement, and placing one-half of that sum immediately at the disposal of the Government Emigration Board for the despatch of a ship in April. It was proposed that the number to be sent out should be made up equally of single and married persons; but that of the unmarried, two-thirds should be women and but one-third men. It was estimated that this 5,000*l*. would provide passages for three hundred statute adults, counting children between the ages of one and twelve years as half-statute adults. It may have been that this letter resuscitated the movement, and that Mr. Bazley's suggestion for the foundation of a new cotton-producing industry in Queensland and New South Wales, assisted its progress. At all events, operatives' meetings subsequently became numerous, at which resolutions in favour of emigration were unanimously adopted. The working-men of Blackburn requested a grant of 5,000*l*. from the relief committees, 'to enable those who were wishful to emigrate to do so, and thus preclude the necessity of their being longer dependent on poor-rates or public donations.' America was generally the El Dorado which these unfortunate persons wished to reach, and at one of their meetings a memorial to the New York Relief Committee was adopted, asking for assistance from them in order to reach the United States. Philanthropists, unconnected with the cotton trade, gave impulse to the movement, advocating on every ground of expediency and humanity the good of lessening the numbers at home, and of exporting energy and industry, with the hope of a prosperous future, to a new country.

This was not the view generally taken by the manufacturers, nor indeed by any class which looked beyond the immediate pressure of the difficulty. But those who discouraged emigration were not blameable—indeed, apart from their personal interests, they may be said to have been the faithful guardians of the national wealth. These men, whom it was proposed to remove, were not starving at home, and the colonial demand for labour was not such as they were best calculated to supply. The colonies asked for men who, on arrival, would be fitted for hard, out-door, spade-work, which does not exactly meet with the qualifications of an operative cotton-spinner. That large numbers of the best 'hands' in the district would have gone, if they could but have obtained the means, there can be no doubt; but it would be ridiculous to censure the manufacturers for withholding, to the full extent of their power, any assistance to a movement which so directly imperilled the value of their capital Mr. Haywood, the secretary of the Cotton Supply Association, estimated, by a division of the margin of wages and profits in 1860, that the sum of 81*l.* would be lost to the trade for every working-hand that emigrated. The emigration of fifty thousand hands would at this rate involve a loss to the cotton trade of 4,000,000*l* a year. He maintained that it would be better to keep six hundred thousand 'hands' at a weekly cost of 2*s.* 6*d.* each, for three years, with a total expenditure of 12,000,000*l.*, than to incur a direct loss in that period of 147,000,000*l.* in wages and profits. 'To encourage the emigration of our operatives,' he continued, 'is therefore to the last degree suicidal, and especially so of any large proportion of the class of spinners. The emigration of one spinner involves the stoppage of probably ten additional hands; and it is far more difficult to train a hand to the work of spinning than to any other manipulation in a cotton mill.'

All this is very true, and points not only to the manufacturers', but also to the national interest in the question. Yet, was sufficient thought taken for the individual interests of the operative? This must be the question which thoughtful men will ask of the history of the Cotton Famine. When those who can bring themselves to make excuses for slavery, contend that it is the man's labour, and not the man, which is the chattel of commerce in the

Confederate States, besides overlooking the fact that the man's labour and himself are inseparable, they altogether ignore his natural rights, which are the free disposition of his labour and—so long as he can maintain them—the undisturbed possession of his home and family. With regard to the operatives who were suffering privations at home in consequence of the Cotton Famine, of course, no one would have a right to interfere with the liberty of the individual: if he possesses or can acquire the means of doing so, he has an inalienable right to remove himself and his labour wherever he chooses. But it cannot be said that there was a moral obligation on the part of those who would be positively injured by the expatriation of these cotton operatives, to promote their departure. And, under these circumstances, it is not surprising that the emigration movement languished, nor that, with the exception of the schemes organised with colonial funds, no considerable number of the distressed population were assisted in leaving the country.

Had any one of the British colonies taken to cotton-growing on a large scale, with white labour, it is possible that the cry for emigration might have become much louder. But not one of them did so. The Lancashire and Queensland Co-operative Emigration Society was organised and was very much supported by resolutions and votes, but neither one nor the other will float a man round Cape Horn, and of material support this society found but little. Its design was admirable. One thousand members were to subscribe *5l.* each, and when this was done, one hundred families were to be chosen by ballot, and forwarded to the colony. Then, by means of a loan upon their colonial estate, which would be allotted to them upon arrival, others were to be brought out, and so on, till as many of the subscribers as desired to emigrate were provided with a passage. But many of those who were anxious to go could have swum across the Atlantic as easily as they could have found *5l.* A considerable party of overlookers did emigrate to Queensland, but their way was paved with colonial funds, supplemented through the exertions of some charitable persons.

No considerable contribution in aid of the cotton supply was expected from the colonies. The samples from

Queensland, which had been exhibited at Brompton, were declared to be of very fine quality, almost equal to Sea Island; but the hopes of the manufacturers could not rest here, nor upon the northern island of New Zealand, the only other cotton-producing colony. Failing America, India and Egypt were regarded as the main sources of the future supply. British and Dutch Guiana, the Bahamas, Jamaica, the Comachian coast of the Mediterranean, part of Asia Minor, the eastern portion of Ceylon—all these would be contributories to some extent; and it was certain that the high prices would stimulate them to increased production. But at one blow 80 per cent. of our cotton imports had been cut off. It was said that Queensland and New South Wales might be made in a short time to supply this deficiency. But very few people believed such a statement, and, moreover, who could guarantee the continuance of the demand? In India and in Egypt there was the population and the soil ready for production. In Egypt the cultivation was hindered by the system of forced labour, by means of which the Suez Canal works were being pushed forward, while it was but languidly encouraged by the sensual and extravagant Saïd Pasha, who only loved wealth so that he might have the spending of it. There was and had always existed a great prejudice against Indian cotton. Some thought that India could only by an active demand, continued through a long course of years, afford relief to the starving cotton trade, forgetting how, in 1814, under the influence of demand, the Indian supply rose from 17,000 bales in that year to an average of nearly 200,000 bales a year during the three years 1815–18—a supply nearly equalling that which was then received from America. Demand had already accomplished very much. Considerable improvement had been made in the quality of Indian cotton, and much of that grown in the Dharwar district was estimated to be quite equal to Middling American. But the bulk of the Indian cotton received in this country during the winter of 1862 had been very inferior indeed. Its worst fault was the quantity of dirt, seeds, and husks with which it was matted and entangled. But the native consumer had made no requisition for improvement. Cotton was cultivated in India as a rotative and not as a special crop.

The customary price obtained by the producing ryots had been but 2*d.* a pound, and the consequence was that they took but little care in selecting seed, and little in cleaning and preparing their crop for sale. But the inferiority of the Indian supply is not entirely due to removable causes. The climate of the larger portion of India is not equally favourable with that of the Southern States of America for the growth of cotton. The Indian rainfall is sudden and periodical, and there are sanitary difficulties opposed to planting under English superintendence, and with English labour, which are not altogether surmountable. Yet, though India be not the most favourable country in the world for the production of cotton, it may furnish a very considerable amount of the supply. That it will continue to do so as long as the American war lasts, there can be no doubt; but to what extent India will be an exporter of cotton upon the reopening of the Southern ports must depend upon whether slavery holds its ground or falls before the victorious arms of the North, and upon the advance which, upon the restoration of peace, shall then have been made in improving and facilitating the production. If it should ever happen that America can supply five-and-a-half millions of bales of cotton, as she could in 1860, at litte over 6*d.* a pound, and so again reduce the value of Indian to 4*d.*, it would be more than probable that India will again fall out of the market, and relinquish the position which the Cotton Famine promised to open for her advantage. But it may well be doubted if America will ever again be so large and cheap a producer as she has been. Among other preventing causes will be the extensive home manufacture which the blockade has encouraged, and the certainty that the Southern treasury will impose an export duty for revenue purposes. While if the South should fail in achieving its independence, slavery will be abolished, and Northern policy will not be opposed to the interests of India.

But, however great might be the expectations of the future with regard to the cotton-producing power of India, even the most sanguine did not look for a very large increase during this year. The proceedings of the first meeting of the Central Executive Committee in Febrnary, were marked by a desire on the part of all its members to prevent the public from supposing that the end of the Cotton Famine was yet nigh at hand. Money was still coming in freely, and, influenced by these forebodings for the future, the committee were anxious that the flow of charity should not be checked. The 'George Griswold' was bearing her friendy freight across the Atlantic, having been laden with flour and bacon, and other stores, for the relief of the distressed population of Lancashire, by the New York International Committee. Together with this noble and memorable contribution the committee recorded the addition of 1*s*. to their banker's balance of 391,268*l*., being the gift of James Chapman, a Coventry weaver, through the Earl of Derby. Their financial position was affluent, but the immediate prospects of trade, according to the well-informed members of the committee, made even this seem none too good. The Cotton Famine had been severely felt for a whole year, and now Mr. Edmund Ashworth foretold great irregularity of manufacturing production, and increasing distress among the working trades dependent on the cotton manufacture. Mr. Robinson Kay saw nothing encouraging in the prospects of trade at Bury. Mr. Hutchinson warned the committee against supposing that the slight improvement which had taken place at Blackburn would be enduring. Mr. Roberts said the same for Burnley. Mr. Stern stated that 'the fluctuations in the cotton trade prevented any increase in production.' Mr. Robert Gladstone promised no permanently improved demand till prices were lower, and mentioned that production was now interfered with by the importation of yarns from Russia, Germany and Sweden. Mr. Ashton believed that the Indian and Chinese markets were still overstocked. Mr. Platt foretold impending distress among the machinists and engineers, in consequence of the reduced demand for the cotton machinery. Mr. Hugh Mason drew a gloomy picture of Ashton, and Mr. G. L. Ashworth feared that Rochdale would again retrograde in pauperism. Sir James Kay-Shuttleworth anticipated the reduction of the small manufacturers to indigence, and Mr. Maclure could promise nothing more hopeful than his monthly return of the numbers in receipt of relief.

Such sadly coincident opinions from such high authority, induced many to think that the cotton manufacture of this country was doomed to annihilation. They doubted whether it would be prudent or possible to keep, for a much longer time, so vast a population in compulsory idleness. The winter was passing away, but the coming spring bore with it no signs of improvement. What was to be done? Could Lancashire pass another year with her vast capital lying unproductive; could half a million of persons be supported for another year upon the poor-rates and charitable funds? Could useful employment be devised for them? Would the American war come to a speedy end? and, if it did not, would other countries make rapid increase in their production of cotton? Such were the questions that agitated the public mind with reference to Lancashire at the opening of the Session of 1863.

CHAPTER XI.

FEBRUARY—MARCH 1863.

Again, the Speech from the Throne contained an allusion to the cotton-manufacturing districts. Her Majesty expressed heartfelt grief at the severity of the distress, and acknowledged the noble fortitude and exemplary resignation with which it had been borne. She referred with gratification to the abundant generosity with which all classes of her subjects, in all parts of her empire, had contributed to relieve the wants of their suffering fellow-countrymen; and spoke of the liberality with which her colonial subjects had given their aid, as proving that although their dwelling-places were far away, their hearts were still warm with unabated affection for the land of their fathers. The Royal Speech also made well-deserved mention of the relief committees, as having superintended, with constant and laborious attention, the distribution of the funds intrusted to their charge.

Upon the motion for the Address, Lord Derby spoke at length with regard to the condition and prospects of Lancashire. He said that 'the cutting off of the material of a manufacture which had risen to such an unparalleled height was, however, expected to produce worse miseries than those which have overwhelmed the manufacturing districts.' And with graceful depreciation of his own exertions, he referred in terms of eulogy to those of the men of business who, 'engaged in transactions on which it was necessary for them to bestow constant attention, gave hours and days and weeks and months of their time, gratuitously and without the slightest recompense, except the consciousness of the good they were doing, to the alleviation of the distress around them.' He pointed out the hardship, while acknowledging the necessity, of making no distinction in the distribution of relief between those who had been earning 30*s.* and 40*s.* a week as wages, and those who had only earned 7*s.* or 8*s.*, and the natural consequence, that, while the distress had been severely felt by the higher class of workmen, by the lowest it had scarcely been felt at all. He foretold the increasing difficulties of the small capitalists, and predicted that two or three years must elapse before the cotton trade would revive to an ordinary degree of prosperity.

All this tended to confirm the mind of Parliament that the condition of the manufacturing districts was such as would call for their anxious attention throughout the Session. And only a week had passed from its opening, when Mr. Villiers rose to move for leave to introduce a Bill for the continuance of the Union Relief Aid Act. For many reasons the President of the Poor Law Board found his task lighter than it had been at the original introduction of the measure. The Act had been completely successful. It had removed from the minds of the ratepayers the fear that they would be overwhelmed by the pressure of the rates; it had relieved the boards of guardians from any doubt as to the resources they administered, and as to the ability of the Poor Law to bear the unusual strain. The benefits of an Act of the Legislature are not however to be tested, so much by the extent to which it is made use of, as by its proved capability to meet the case for which it was designed. A poor law is not beneficial in proportion to the number of paupers who avail themselves of its provisions—nor a law establishing rewards for good conduct by the number whom it decorates—nor a flogging law by the number of lashes which are annually received in consequence of its enactment. The Union Relief Aid Act had now an established reputation as a thoroughly workable measure, well adapted to the special wants of the district, and certainly preventive of a disastrous pressure of the poor-rates.

That but only a few of the unions in the cotton district had taken advantage of its provisions, was entirely owing to the liberality with which the public had poured in their donations, and was in every way a fair subject of congratulation both to the country and the Government. But something more than the success of his measure supported Mr. Villiers upon this occasion. He had proved himself master of the situation, and had won the confidence of Parliament and the public. It was felt that all that was in the power of the Government, or of the department over which he presided, to do for the mitigation of the distress would certainly be attempted, and that whatever measures were introduced would be such as would not compromise the foreign policy of which the nation approved, nor establish a precedent which might lead to future embarrassments. He had had the satisfaction of seeing the principles with which, during his tenure of office, he had laboured to inspire the Poor Law, working efficiently under extraordinary circumstances. He must have known that many of the opponents of his amendment of the Law of Settlement in 1861, were now thankful that that Act had prevented the transportation of thousands of the distressed northern population. Nor could that policy which he had done more than any other statesman to promote—of equalising the burden of poor-rates—have received a greater impulse than had been given to it by the unbroken success of the action of the Poor Law in the cotton districts. He was further supported by the knowledge that those proposals for money grants from the national purse—which he had refused to sanction or to second—had through all the unparalleled distress of the now departing winter, grown fainter if they had not entirely died away. Throughout this most trying season the ears of the country had not been shocked by accounts of starvation among the distressed population, nor startled by deeds done in violation of law and order. The peace of the district had remained unbroken, the authority of the law had been supreme, relief in money, food, and clothing had been liberally dispensed to all who had claims upon the public bounty, and even the sufferers themselves joined in the general approval of the policy of the Government.

On its second entry into Parliament, the Union Relief Aid Bill derived material support from all these circumstances. The operation of the Act had been such as to prove its utility, with at the same time a minimum of pressure upon those who, though within the sphere of its incidence, were not within the immediate neighbourhood of the cotton manufacture. The total amount which had been borrowed in or charged upon the three counties was but 63,675*l.* The rate-in-aid contributed by Derbyshire had not exceeded one farthing, nor that by Cheshire one halfpenny in the pound on the net rateable value of these counties. The charge thus imposed upon Lancashire had not been greater than one penny in the pound. Seven unions had availed themselves of the provisions of the Act, five of which had borrowed money, while four out of the seven had borrowed and had also charged a portion of their expenditure upon the counties. For the Michaelmas quarter, Preston and Blackburn had borrowed respectively 3,800*l.* and 3,500*l.* For the Christmas quarter, Ashton had borrowed 8,000*l.*, Blackburn 10,000*l.*, Glossop 1,000*l.*, Haslingden 1,000*l.*, Preston 7,000*l*, Rochdale 8,000*l.*, and Todmorden 1,000*l*, making a total of 43,400*l.* borrowed. There had been charged upon the counties—by Ashton 8,000*l.*, by Glossop 1,700*l.*, by Haslingden 2,000*l.*, and by Preston 7,000*l.*; so that the total of the rates-in-aid had amounted to 19,750*l.* The anticipated strain upon the ratepayers had not been felt in its expected severity, and an additional charge of 9*d.* in the pound upon the rateable value of the property within the district would have met all the extraordinary requirement of the three months during which the distress occasioned by the Cotton Famine had been deepest. But for the assistance afforded by this measure the burden upon the chief centres of the distress would have been very grievous, and perhaps intolerable.

In the course of the debate which followed the reintroduction of the Bill, it was mentioned that as many as four thousand persons in Oldham had in one fortnight changed their condition from ratepayers to rate-receivers. But, if the inference from this statement was that they were pauperised by the pressure of the poor-rates, it was entirely fallacious, because these persons would under any circumstances have found no difficulty in getting excused, or at least in being allowed to take indefinite time for the payment. Most, if not all of them, were operatives living in houses of about 6*l.* rateable value, who were destitute of accumulated resources, who had been thrown out of employment by the stoppage of the factories of which they were ordinarily employed, and whose pauperisation was probably not even hastened by the pressure of the poor-rates. During its passage through the House of Commons, the Bill was voluntarily amended by Mr. Villiers, in two valuable respects. The time for the repayment of loans was extended from seven to fourteen years, and the Bill was so altered as to prevent the possibility of the misconstruction which had presumed that the charges made upon unions under this Act, were not to be accounted as part of their expenditure, 'in and about the relief of the poor.' With these amendments, the Bill passed through committee, and was accepted by the House of Lords.

Two days after he had obtained leave to bring in this Continuance Bill, Mr. Villiers moved for and obtained returns of the average rate of weekly earnings of agricultural labourers in the unions of England and Wales. His object was to facilitate migration from the cotton districts, and to direct the emigrants to the best markets for their labour. The returns exhibited a material rise in the wages of agricultural labour as compared with those of a few years back, indeed the average wages earned for task-work in the agricultural districts, appear to equal the average of men's wages in the cotton factories; but the operative is as strange to outdoor work as the rustic would be to factory labour, and while the rate of outdoor relief given to men with families was quite equal to the wages they would have earned in agricultural districts, where children's labour is in very small demand, it was not to be expected that they would be disposed to wander into southern England.

The Central Executive Committee continued their good work, and the number of local committees dependent on their funds were steadily increasing. Though nearly 40,000 persons had been removed from the lists of poor-law relief since the last week in December, Mr. Maclure's voluminous return for the corresponding week in January, had shown that the numbers solely maintained by the relief committees was not lessened by a single thousand. The guardians were in fact being relieved by the formation of additional relief committees. Of the 235,741 persons now receiving relief exclusively from the committees, there were no more than 84,155 who worked or were engaged in educational or sewing-schools in consideration of this relief. Of this 84,155, half were women, who, together with a large proportion of the men or boys, were deriving educational instruction provided by the special fund which had hitherto borne the name of the colony of New South Wales. But, early in February, there came accounts from Australia of serious discontent at the mode in which this colonial fund had been set apart for these special purposes. Sir James Kay-Shuttleworth had been the acting manager in this matter for the Central Executive Committee, in concert with the Sydney Commissioners, Sir Daniel Cooper and Mr. Hamilton. Both Sir James and Sir Daniel had repute for their familiarity with educational topics, and it was assumed on one side and accepted on the other, that such an appropriation of the funds would meet with the approval of the liberal colonists. But it was not so; and when the arrangement came to their ears, they angrily declared that the funds had been handed over to Sir James Kay-Shuttleworth in order to promote certain educational crotchets. The rather unfortunate style of composition in which the minutes and correspondence had been framed —and with the authorship of which Sir James was credited —still further incensed the plain-spoken colonists, who of all people are the least taken by pedantry. Certainly, the Central Executive Committee ought to have known that 'colonials' have an ignorant impatience of long words, and should not have stiffened their reports with sentences of this order, which is not exactly tuned to catch the Australian ear:—'Your committee are of opinion that these schools for men and youths have been eminently useful in maintaining order, in promoting cheerfulness, and in preventing the contraction of evil habits during a period of unwonted leisure, as well as in communicating rudimentary knowledge.' The result of the difficulty was however, that the sum which had already been expended in educational grants, amounting to 7,791*l.*, was debited to the general fund, and the subscriptions from New South Wales were from henceforth declared to be merged in the general account.

If this expenditure had hitherto been the consequence of a blunder, it was one of the most fortunate and salutary errors that ever were made. If Sir James Kay-Shuttleworth was the author of this mistake—and it certainly rested between himself and Sir Daniel Cooper—he is well entitled to the gratitude of all who have been interested in the sufferers by the Cotton Famine. If, as is more than probable, the Central Relief Committee would have delayed to make educational grants had they not been thus led to establish a system, which now they could not abandon, Sir James has the pleasant consciousness of knowing that he has been directly the means of improving the minds, and therefore the future lives of many thousands of the population among whom he resides, while the enraged colonists enjoy the double satisfaction of having had their own way, and also of having indirectly worked out this great good. The committee determined upon continuing their payments to the educational establishments, but extended the purpose of these special grants; and in order to preserve the uniformity of their proceedings, they established an 'Employment and School Fund,' and resolved 'that all grants be restricted within such limits as are required to prevent the evils which might flow from the prolonged relief of the population without work or instruction, and that it is expedient to extend such grants to the superintendence of suitable manual work for 'able-bodied men and youths in receipt of relief.'

The question of employment was now one of most serious concern. The relief committees had been, from the time of their establishment, utterly unable to provide manual labour for all the able-bodied men whom their funds supported, and the guardians, not unnaturally, neglected a requirement which the committees did not make. There were now some sixty or seventy thousand girls employed in sewing-schools, and twenty thousand men and boys being taught and teaching themselves, all of whom were accounted to be working for their relief allowances. But there were upwards of twenty-five thousand able-bodied men and boys who were now receiving the means of subsistence without labouring in any way in return for it. The reduction observable in the numbers receiving relief was rather owing to a resumption of outdoor labour on the part of those who were accustomed to such work, than to the increased production of cotton manufactures. It had been evident during the debates on the Continuance

Bill, and notably in what had fallen from Lancashire members, that the subject of providing employment was one calculated to give great uneasiness to those who were best acquainted with the district and its population, large numbers having now been maintained for a whole year in virtual idleness. It could not but be expected that this should have demoralised many, and together with this reflection came recollections of outrage and violence, of which the experience of former times ominously suggested the recurrence. The labour question now rested at the bottom of the difficulty in the councils of the Government, as well as in the minds of those who were locally engaged in dealing with the distress. How these thousands of unemployed could be set to work for wages, and not relief, was now the subject of most anxious concern to Mr. Villiers, as President of the Poor Law Board, who had especially directed Mr. Farnall's attention to this point. And in one of the Special Commissioner's private reports there occurs the following reference to the subject:—

'I have been unremitting in my endeavours to stimulate boards of guardians and local committees to find manual and useful work for the able-bodied men whom they relieve; and it is a gratification to me to state, that both the boards of guardians and the local committees have cordially adopted my suggestions. That, however, which would be acceptable to the workpeople, advantageous to the ratepayers, and serviceable to the interests of the community at large, would be to supply the unemployed hands with work for wages; they have no interest in work which they are forced to perform in return for parish relief or charitable aid, and they long for remunerative employment.

'I am fully aware that the counties of Lancaster and Chester, and the towns in the cotton district, present available and profitable resources for the employment of the people on public and private works of utility; but, hitherto, no corporation, no public body, no great landed proprietors have attempted to convert these resources into a means of setting the able-bodied men to work for remunerative wages.'

The valuable fruit of this consideration and inquiry was subsequently manifested in the Public Works Act.

Well-intended endeavours to promote emigration still continued, and offers were made to the Central Executive Committee, through colonial agents, to facilitate the emigration of the unemployed operatives; but the Committee could only just feel themselves permitted to become the medium of communications upon the subject, and did not consider themselves at liberty to apply any portion of their funds to promote emigration. There can be no doubt that if they had done so, they would have been acting in direct contravention of the wishes of nearly all their local supporters. As yet, the emigration movement had been chiefly made by the colonial agents, who, both from Victoria and Queensland, were supplied with funds to the extent of 5,000*l.* each for defraying the cost of passage. There were many persons out of the district who thought that the idle hands ought to be no longer kept in the neighbourhood of the empty factories, but they were content to be silent upon the subject while the difficulty was being passed over so peacefully. Those whom reflection or experience had made masters of the question, very well knew that any stream of emigration which, with due regard to the arrival as well as to the departure of the emigrants, could be collected, would fall miserably short of affording that immediate relief which was the really urgent demand. They knew that the wholesale emigration of a population utterly unused to outdoor labour, and debilitated by a continued low dietary, was certainly a questionable, and might be a cruel remedy. These considerations were added to the vested interests of the cotton manufacture, of which the proposed emigrants held in their handicraft a considerable share. The operatives were not starving, all that was needed was employment. There were schemes in plenty, but none fructified into a large requirement of labour. At one of the meetings of the Central Committee, a circular was read, disclosing a proposal for producing an instantaneous supply of cotton 'as fast as the clouds of heaven will grow it.' The committee listened and laughed, and addressed themselves to the serious charge which still pressed with scarcely diminished weight upon their resources. February had witnessed the establishment of ten additional relief committees, and the total number of these local associations now amounted to one hundred and sixty-two. But there had been a further transference of the indigent population from the guardians to the committees, which in a great measure accounted for the decrease of numbers dependent on the guardians, now lessened by upwards of 50,000, and also for the very slight improvement in the returns of the Central Executive Committee.

The 'George Griswold' had arrived safely in February, and discharged her cargo, which, among other stores, included 15,000 barrels of flour. Unnumbered contributions in support of the distress accompanied 'the relief ship.' Laden with generous gifts, she was herself the kindly offering of the distinguished firm whose name she bore. The services of Captain Lunt, her commander, were gratuitous. At the mouth of the Mersey she was welcomed by tugs, contending for the honour of towing her into dock. Dues of all sorts were remitted; her freight was discharged and conveyed to the stores of the Central Relief Committee free of cost. Addresses were presented to the captain and officers at Liverpool and Manchester. There was nothing in the speeches or the conduct of these gentlemen calculated to lessen the value of this practical expression of international sympathy by giving to it a political significance. But upon the day of the Prince of Wales' wedding, an incident occurred which showed that there was no disinclination on the part of Northern partisans to use them for a political purpose. In celebration of the event, a meeting of operatives had been convened in Stevenson Square. They were promised by the promoters of this assembly a distribution of fifteen thousand 2lb. loaves, and the attendance of the chaplain of the 'George Griswold.' They were to follow the bread in procession to Kersal Moor, and a prominent part of the pageant was to consist of two boats drawn on lurries: one from 'the relief ship,' flying the stars and stripes, manned with sailors; the other, a black and suspicious-looking craft, with a crew of men in the stage-dress of pirates. Here was all the paraphernalia of a political demonstration, if a crowd could but be induced to give it importance by their presence and co-operation.

The crowd was in the square, the boats were there, the orators were there, and the bread-carrying waggons were there also, when it occurred to the assembled operatives that there was something derogatory in being drawn after these bread-laden waggons, like donkeys after a bunch of carrots, in order to assist indirectly at a political demonstration. It also appeared to them that if the flour—which however was no part of that brought by the 'George Griswold'—had been provided for their relief, it was not intended that they should earn it by walking to Kersal Moor to see the 'Alabama' burnt in effigy, for this was the designation and the doom of the piratical craft. A row ensued. Loaves were thrown about, were trodden upon, were appropriated in armfuls by the least respectable and probably the least necessitous portion of the crowd, and the meeting broke up. The officers of the 'George Griswold' were not implicated in this curious but unsuccessful attempt to compound a political triumph by such a use of an auspicious national holiday and a kindly expression of American sympathy.

An effort had been made throughout the district to increase the amount of employment given in return for relief, and the local committees had succeeded during the month of February in employing 11,235 additional persons. The rate of expenditure of the Central Executive Committee was now 120,000*l.* a month, and this made even their balance of nearly 400,000*l.* look small and insufficient. The crisis of the distress, so far as the numbers dependent on relief were concerned, was felt to have been past, but there were signs that the time of greatest difficulty had yet to be encountered. The new year was opening full of hope and promise to all but those who were the victims of the Cotton Famine. None predicted an early revival of trade, and the mention of other forms of employment was not loud enough to be heard by those who were brooding over their unimproving condition and their long-enduring pauperism. Some preferred idleness, relief, and unlimited lying in bed, to industry, wages, and the quick summons of the factory-bell. But these were just the persons who were most ready and likely to create disturbance, if by intimidation they could expand the liberality of the relief committees.

The relief committees had now settled to their work, had become plain-spoken, and business-like in their dealings with the poor; sometimes they may have been harsh, but they had been often imposed upon, and this will have its effect upon outward demeanour. Many of the members of these committees were vulgar, ill-bred men, proud of the brief authority with which their duties invested them. But the unemployed had no reason to fear long-continued injustice; the proceedings of these committees were watched by their neighbours, and appeal could at all times be made to the Central Committee at Manchester. It is, however, absurd to suppose that nearly half a million persons could be relieved through the gratuitous agency of a hundred and seventy relief committees without grievances arising on both sides. The wonder is, not that such did arise, but rather that they were of so rare and transitory occurrence. Men were growing sick with hope of regular employment so long deferred; the school exercises had at first in all their novelty been popular, but now the men wearied of poring over the same books and slates day after day, and called their education a 'labour test.' At first, they had been flattered by the praises of public men, but even this sweet food had become somewhat tasteless, and perhaps the supply had somewhat fallen off. Nothing new had been devised to wile away these long hours, in which the only indulgence they could have was idleness. The discovery of much incipient discontent among the operatives at this time, was thought by some who were unacquainted with the district, to throw confusion upon those who had long given themselves to the work of relieving the distress, and to have proved the failure of their influence. Yet it almost passes comprehension that any sane man should have supposed at such a time, when the relief system, with its inevitable evils, had continued so long and so largely in operation, that anything but the thinnest partition divided order from disorder, and maintained over all the semblance at least of quietude and contentment.

To men who are in the receipt of means of subsistence to which they have no claim but that of want, the first question which arises is, 'How will their want be determined, and by what standard will it be measured?' To them, the argument of economy, and, still more, the argument founded on a fear of disturbance of industry, by giving too liberally, seem recondite and unreasonable. The more ignorant of them make to themselves two propositions, and, having answered these to their own satisfaction, accept no others. 'Is not the money sent for us?' they say; and 'do we not want it?'—'are not we the best judges of how it shall be distributed?' Thereupon such men regard the relief committee as intruders and middlemen—as jobbers, standing between them and their rights. Of course, all this is very absurd; but no one can be surprised that it should occur with all the force of inspiration to a half-tipsy lad who has spent his relief allowance in bad gin and worse company, and who in that condition meditates upon his ways and means for the morrow. Who could be surprised to find grumblings and discontent, complaints and recriminations in the manufacturing districts in March 1863? Let any class of persons be thrown out of their customary mode of life, and be given over to very moderate compulsory exercise, and to one-third of their customary expenditure for their maintenance—let them try this for a year, and let the hope of an improving future be fading from them—let them in their desponding moments see nothing before them but insolvency or pauperism, according to which class they belong. Then let them add to this helpless condition the fact that debt is slowly increasing around them, threatening their liberty and mortgaging their future earnings: would they not become discontented? Perhaps it would be said of them that they were fools if they suffered their discontent to move them to acts which would tend still further to lower their condition, and to remove them from the benefits of sympathy. But were they the wisest of men, they could do no more than bear their lot with resignation. To say that the Lancashire operatives belonged wholly to the wise or to the foolish, would be ridiculous on one side and libellous on the other. But to say that the vast majority of them did, at this most trying time—for the pressure of distress was felt most sorely after the lowest point was passed—display intelligent confidence and continued self-respect, is no more than simple justice demands. Yet such were not all, and by this least responsible class was the rioting made which stains the history of the Cotton Famine.

Staleybridge, in which disorder commenced, is one of a group of near-lying towns of which Ashton-under-Lyne and Dukinfield are the most important. The reputation of these towns for order has never been first-rate. The religious differences which so unhappily divide Ashton-under-Lyne may have afforded some example, even to those who are ignorant of polemics; while at Staleybridge, the Irish are, without doubt, the cause of much bad repute. Unquestionably the condition of these towns would be much improved if those public duties, which can alone be performed by the residence of a wealthy and refined middle class, were not delegated to a few individuals, who, however they may exert themselves, become little more than the chiefs of a party. In such a district especially, it cannot be a matter of surprise that there should at this time have been found the elements of a riot. In Ashton, relief had, for some time past, been administered by rival committees, and it was said that the extravagant rate of relief now given at Staleybridge was, to some extent, a consequence of their contention. In the 'relief schools' of this town there were upwards of seventeen hundred men and boys, who were receiving, about Lady Day 1863, relief amounting to 3*s.* 4*d.* per head.

The grants of the Mansion House Committee to Staleybridge had certainly been liberal, but now that the funds of this committee were ebbing fast, and the supply was falling off, Staleybridge, among other places, received notice that less support would be forthcoming from this source; and as the rate of relief given by the local committee of this borough far exceeded the average throughout the district, reduction was determined upon. Instead of 3*s.* 4*d.* per head, 3*s.* was to be the reduced scale, and in order to avoid a wasteful expenditure—for it had been discovered that some of the scholars were given to intoxication and gambling—it was resolved that this should be paid in 1*s.* tickets upon the shopkeepers, who were to give in exchange 7*d.* in goods and 5*d.* in money. This was the ostensible cause of the riots at Staleybridge.

But riot is never caused by so reasonable a proposition as this, nor would there have been an outbreak at Staleybridge, if the discontent of the 'scholars' had not been excited by a greater intelligence than their own. The happiest accident of the Cotton Famine has been the scarcity of demagogues, and the best title of the suffering operatives to the political estimation of their countrymen is that there has been no demand for these pests of society. Had they come forward they might quickly have made bad into worse, and the peaceful action of voluntary committees might perhaps have been superseded by the harsh reign of martial law. But a demagogue is not always conscious of the effect of his language, and as the individual, whose inflammatory harangues excited the people of Staleybridge, had been consistent for five-and-twenty years, it may well be thought that he was guiltless of the consequences of his words. Yet indiscretion is too mild a censure for the use, at such a time and in such a place, of language such as he addressed to these irritated and despondng men. To tell them that 'they were the innocent and guiltless victims of a commercial policy,' was true enough; but to add, that it was the duty of the Legislature to have restrained and checked this policy, was ridiculous. These men had received fair wages for their work while cotton was plentiful, and they had been well supported when the supply failed and the mills were standing. Because those among them who were vicious and dissolute had been found to pawn the clothing given to them, it had become advisable to stamp the garments distributed by the committee. The Relief Committee were the lawful trustees of the charitable funds, and the moneys they received were theirs, until they passed them on at such a rate as they thought most compliant with their duty. But who can wonder at what followed, when these circumstances were, in a crowded meeting of the recipients of relief, alluded to in such language as this:— 'Why then, should they treat you with all this disrespect and cruelty? Why should you be told that you have no right to what you must either have or die? Why should they brand the clothes you must either wear or go naked? Do these garments belong to you or to them? Are you serfs, or thieves, or vagabonds, that your wives and daughters cannot draw on a stocking, or tie a petticoat, or cover their new-born offspring, without a blush of shame, when they look at the infamous brand that is stamped upon every article of their apparel?' The bread of charity is bitter indeed, and naked independence shrinks from contact with clothes thus obtained; doubtless, hard to bear was the necessity that forced honest hard-working men to be classed with, and to some extent to suffer for those whom his misfortunes alone made his fellows. But this style of exposing grievances is not the straight road to their removal; it leads to crime, violence, and bloodshed.

When the Staleybridge Relief Committee offered to pay their schools with tickets at the rate of 3*s.* a week, keeping a day in hand, and so giving 2*s.* 5*d.* per head, the scholars refused to receive these tickets. The men were not riotous in their refusal, and in only one school, which was established at the Castle Street Mills, did they commit wanton damage. But in the streets, mobs, chiefly composed of boys and girls, collected rapidly. Their first outrage was to break the windows of a cab in which two members of the Relief Committee were passing. Then, hooting and shouting, now chasing and now chased by the meagre police force of the borough, they ran about from point to point, smashing windows and inflicting wounds with stones and missiles of every description. Cheered on by their 'colleens,' the Irish boys of Staleybridge damaged the houses of the members of the Relief Committee, smashed the windows of the police office, and thoroughly enjoying their wild licence, gained possession of the town. Then, forgetful of the degradation of stamped clothing, a more personal interest led them to the stores of the committee, which they broke open. The rooms were soon crammed with plunderers, and jackets, trousers, waistcoats, stockings, chemises, calico, and flannel were flying out of the windows, and appropriated by the crowd. Girls and boys, staggering under huge bundles of clothing, were making their way to their homes, and still the loot continued, until a troop of hussars galloped into the streets, and *sauve qui peut* was the word among the rioters. The rollicking invaders of the stores tumbled one over another at the door in their eagerness to escape, and consequently fell victims to the police, who now reappeared. A local magistrate read the Riot Act, the hussars cleared the streets, special constables were sworn in, and the police began to pay domiciliary visits in order to find out the depredators, which led some to trouble, others to hide their spoils, and many to throw them into the river. There was no serious encounter, and the soldiers had little more to do than to frighten the people to their homes. One broken leg and a few bruises among the police, many bruises and some broken heads among the mob, comprised the casualties. Sixty prisoners were secured, most of them boys and girls, who spent the night dancing and singing in the lock-up. As might be supposed, their appearance before the magistrates the next morning was much more pitiable than terrifying. Very few exceeded thirty years of age. The majesty of the law was faced by two or three benches filled with half-blown Irish sluts, behind whom were a rather larger number of ragged boys, and a few men. These were the prisoners. As their names were called over, there were few that were not decidedly Hibernian. The result of the inquiry was, that twenty-nine of the male sex were committed to take their trial at the ensuing Chester assizes.

But while this was going on at the town-hall of Staleybridge, the streets were thronged. Crowds collected round the hall, curious as to the fate of the prisoners, half-awed and half-proud of the attentions of the hussars, who kept guard with drawn swords and loaded pistols. Hundreds of sight-seers had poured into the town to look upon the results of the riot, which for the most part consisted of broken windows and the wreck of a grocer's shop. The clothing store had been damaged, and about 1000*l.* worth of goods had been abtracted. The removal of the prisoners was accomplished by a feint. But the disappointed mob showered the police with stones, and were in turn charged by the cavalry, to whom they always paid the homage of running away. Throughout the day, the crowds continued to be riotous, and as night came on, commenced a series of attacks upon the provision shops. Shutters were forced down, and the appropriation of the stock in trade immediately followed. Unwilling hosts were made to tap their beer-barrels for the thirsty rioters, who ate and drank while the hussars drove them from place to place. Later in the evening a company of the 49th Regiment and a reinforcement of police arrived, and order reigned in Staleybridge.

Sunday followed, bringing thousands of excursionists, who amused themselves by looking at the broken windows, at the placards which declared that the Riot Act had been read, and especially at the soldiers. The streets were their own for this day, but the riot recommenced on Monday morning, and an attempt was made to extend the disorder to Ashton-under-Lyne, where shop-breaking and stone-throwing were also perpetrated. Dukinfield and Hyde were visited by crowds of marauders. In Ashton, it was computed that there were at one time ten thousand persons in the streets. The cavalry rode hither and thither, but the mobs dispersed on their approach and reformed while they were engaged in an opposite direction. The police received many severe blows. Individual magistrates displayed that presence of mind and personal power of command which is so often possessed by the leading manufacturers. Mr. Cheetham, at Staleybridge, had exercised an influence as strong as that of a troop of horse, and Mr. Hugh Mason, at Ashton, had faced the rioters and denounced their conduct with great courage and success. The police officers had been the greatest sufferers; they were provided with cutlasses, but upon one of them wounding a collier in the head, it was decided that they should be disarmed. A few public-house keepers were kicked and maltreated for their unwillingness to afford gratuitous entertainment, and many tradesmen were subjected to considerable losses. The rioters, after being driven about by the soldiers and police, and after a good deal of contention, and swearing and fighting among themselves, gradually dispersed, and the riot was at an end.

Every riot in the cotton districts is very much the same in all its features. At the commencement, there is the sense of injustice acting upon those who are the natural leaders of the working classes, whose influence is always sufficient to maintain order or to create disturbance. An important, though not always a prominent actor, is the inflammatory speaker, who was not wanting in this case. Discontent and insubordination among the more intelligent become licence and riot among the thoughtless and brutally ignorant. Those who proposed the 'turn out,' or the first disobedience to orders, have lost command over what is now becoming a lawless mob. Fearful and half-ashamed, they watch the development of the riot. Having cast off their own allegiance to order, they can claim none from their followers. The doings of the mob are as yet but half comic; how the riot shall end depends upon how they are opposed, and in what spirit the original grievances are discussed. Time has been, when these soldiers at Staleybridge, now so forbearing and good-hnmoured, would have shot and cut down these foolish creatures. There were some who even now advocated such a treatment. But happily wiser counsels prevailed. Such a policy would have converted this riot, as it has done many, into an insurrection, which is a much more formidable affair. A riot is senseless, purposeless, because the minds from whose discontent it originated are not co-operating. Full of the justice of their case, or blinded to the folly of their opposition, they can almost despise their own mob, while authority does not show fear or respect by the exercise of severity. When it does so, then it is that half-educated, impulsive, brooding men rush on in what they believe to be the defence of their order, and then a nation's history receives a blot, always dishonourable, always ineffaceable, because it is made with civil blood.

Such were *not* the riots of the Cotton Famine. It is needless to speculate upon what might have been the consequences of severity. Order would have been maintained, but it must have been at a fearful cost. As it was, many towns in which no outbreak occurred were infected with the agitation. The actual conductors of the dispute at Staleybridge took no part in the riot. On the day following the disturbances in Ashton and the neighbouring towns, an open-air meeting was held at Staleybridge, which was attended by three thousand persons. Deputations had been passing between the discontented 'scholars' and the Relief Committee, but the latter wisely refused to give way. The 'scholars' were to be paid with tickets at the lower rate, or they must be content to look to the guardians for assistance. The speakers at this meeting were moderate in their tone, and condemned the disorderly proceedings which had taken place. It dissolved peaceably, after a unanimous resolution had been passed to return to the schools, and all seemed content with the assurance that some of the leading men of the town would consider the points of their case. Men were seen to shake hands with deep emotion as the meeting broke up. Joyful shouts of 'th' riot is over!' 'bravo!' were raised, while the comic element was preserved by the speech of a girl to a passing soldier,—'Aw, owd chap, thee mit goo whoam, th' riot's done.'

The Relief Committee cannot be held blameless as to the origin of the dispute. It could not have been unavoidably necessary to make so many alterations in their payments at the same moment. Their rate of relief was too high, and there was good reason for reducing it. The reduction they suggested, from 3*s.* 4*d.* to 3*s.* per head, was unobjectionable; but the proposal to commence payment by tickets simultaneously with this reduction was not wise. Still less was it prudent to add to these alterations that of the holding back a day's pay. All these changes occurring at one time were at least very liable to misconstruction by the recipients of relief, and indeed the conduct of many of them supported the defence, that they did not understand the policy of their paymasters. The alterations were in themselves reasonable enough — the reduction, the keeping a day's pay in hand to ensure the performance of the day's work, the payment by tickets to protect the drunken and improvident against themselves. But however impolitic the Local Relief Committee may have been, this was soon forgotten in the imprudence of a much more consequential body. In his weekly report to the Central Executive Committee, Mr. Farnall had expressed a hope 'that the benevolent people of England will not conclude that the portion of the workpeople of Staleybridge which has been misled represents the operatives of the cotton district.' The Central Committee had recorded their entire approval of the reduction of the scale of relief, and of the distribution by tickets; the press had condemned the riot as foolish and unprovoked, and had praised the humanity and forbearance with which order had been restored. Yet, just at this critical moment, it became known that the Mansion House Committee had voted a special grant of 500*l.* for the benefit of the distressed population of Staleybridge, and to defeat the determination of the Local Relief Committee. This splendid sop to the rioters almost choked the relief committees, who, whatever their individual faults, had ungrudgingly given much time, and had worked hard in the difficult, and occasionally dangerous duty they had undertaken. This grant, which cost the Mansion House Committee much loss of respect, was made in consequence of the representations of three clergymen of Staleybridge, who, with a moving representation of the condition of their town, impressed the committee with the severe privations, the probable outrage and bloodshed, which would result should their prayer be unsuccessful. There is no doubt that these gentlemen believed all that they stated; but why the Mansion House Committee should have acceded to their petition is not equally clear. It was their established rule to make grants only to local relief committees, and these clergymen came with a confession that they wished to thwart the policy of the Staleybridge Committee, of which they were not members. The 500*l.* was sent to the chairman of the Local Relief Committee, who, with a commendable display of dignified prudence, briefly acknowledged the donation, significantly observing that he should hold the cheque in hand until the modifications for the distribution of relief, which were considered judicious and expedient, had been introduced. With no further outbreak the terms of peace were concluded, the 'scholars' agreeing to accept 3*s.* per head, to be paid half in kind and half in money. They consented also to the deduction of 4*d.* per week, without any diminution of the hours of school work. So ended the Staleybridge riots. Had the Local Committee displayed more forbearance and tact, the riot might never have commenced. Had they shown less firmness towards the conclusion the riot might have been prolonged and seriously extended. The interference of the Mansion House Committee was dangerous, yet no harm came of it. The actual riot was contemptible, though that it maintained this character was much owing to the discretion of the magistrates and to the forbearance of the military and police.

The immediate effect of this disturbance was to revive with great force the emigration question. Alarmists viewed the difficulty as a choice of evils. They asked—Was a population of five hundred thousand persons to remain for an indefinite period unemployed, and yet confined to the narrow limits of the cotton district, for the benefit of the manufacturers? They saw nothing in the future but riot and bloodshed, and no remedy but a wholesale removal of the population. Of the two evils, this, in their opinion, was the least. That a panic should follow the outbreak at Staleybridge was to be expected. But the cry raised, that these people were being held in the manufacturing districts for the particular benefit of individuals, was unfair and illogical. Emigration might be encouraged, but it could not be undertaken either by the Government or by the two great committees. It was suggested to all three, and all had unquestionably the means of promoting it. But even the Mansion House Committee, which had certainly not been unwilling to show its independence of all Lancashire influences, refused to sanction the appropriation of a part of its funds to this purpose. One hundred and fifteen working men of Blackburn petitioned this committee, and made, as it was easy to make, a good case for emigration. They submitted that an adequate cotton supply was not, and would not for a long period, be forthcoming; that while no active demand for labour existed in other parts of England, such as would encourage them to migrate to another district, labour was the great want of the Australian colonies, and that they wished to go there. The committee read and believed their memorial, but did not see why they should assist these men in preference to others equally desirous and deserving. They were trustees for all the unemployed of their funds, which were, moreover, subscribed for the purpose of affording local relief. The position of the Central Executive Committee was less independent. A large proportion of their funds was directly derived from a class who had an immediate personal interest in preventing anything like an exodus of the population. But had they been free from this influence, their funds would not have permitted them to carry out any extended scheme of emigration. They had now in hand about thirty shillings per head for the population they had to relieve, and it would have been obviously unjust to have diminished this amount for the special benefit of individuals at the expense of the majority. It was by no means difficult for those who were best acquainted with the district to convince themselves that a large emigration was uncalled for, as well as inexpedient. There was the hope of a revival of the cotton trade, a certainty that the number of unemployed would be lessened by absorption from the labour demand of other districts as well as by the ordinary outflow of emigration. The health of the people was good, and food was not wanting; there was no reason to suppose that the recent infraction of order would be repeated, and there was no doubt but that when the raw material should arrive, there would be a scarcity of hands for its manufacture. And were it permitted to appeal to subsequent facts, it would be conceded that they were right who refused to send the operatives by thousands to distant labour markets, for which they were totally unfit, and where their most valuable productive power would be for ever lost.

Inexhaustible as the wealth and charity of England seem to be, it might have been possible to raise a considerable fund for the special purpose of promoting emigration. But more than 1,500,000*l.* had been already subscribed for the relief of the distressed population, and it would certainly have been straining the benevolent tendency of Englishmen to act upon this assumption. To make any material and visible reduction in the numbers now subsisting on relief, it would have been necessary to provide for the emigration of at least fifty thousand persons, which would have been less than one-eighth of the whole number now dependent upon the guardians and the relief committees. But the cost of the conveyance of this number to Australia cannot be estimated at less than 750,000*l.*, and it is hardly too much to assume that no such sum could have been raised for such a purpose. Granting even that these fifty thousand all became happy and prosperous emigrants, then the condition of the cotton districts would not have been less critical, so far as disturbance and riot were concerned, and the distress would have been precisely the same in degree, though lessened to the extent of one-eighth. The unemployed population would not be less turbulent because their numbers had been thinned; none of the causes of disagreement between masters and operatives—between relief committees and their pensioners—between guardians and paupers, would have been removed;

the rate of relief would not have been raised, for it was already as high as a due regard to the rights of labour would permit. The greater part of the expenditure thus incurred in deporting these fifty thousand persons, must eventually have been paid over again by the county, in a decreased export and an increased price of the home consumption of cotton goods consequent upon a rise of wages, until the demand had replenished the Lancashire labour market. It would have been an improvident and impolitic act on the part of the nation, and one of doubtful humanity on that of its promoters.

Outside the cotton districts, the public had been so worked upon by accounts of the distress, and so impressed by the universal efforts made to mitigate it, that they were not in a position to judge of the precise condition of affairs. The riot at Staleybridge gave strength to the opinion, that there existed a wide-spread antagonism between the recipients and the dispensers of relief. It was thought that there was now unusual animosity between the millowners and the operatives. But this was not the case. Perhaps it might be affirmed that at no time, for a long period, had there existed such good relations between them. When the demand for labour is great, then arise most of the disputes between employers and employed. But now there was generally a friendly feeling between the two classes. The masters—at least many of them—had done much to relieve the sufferings of the operatives. Many had given largely, and many had run their mills with undoubted risk of loss. The operatives knew that the stocks of cotton were not worked up, but they knew also that all the factories could not now be running with immediate profit. Many of the manufacturers were members of boards of guardians and of relief committees, and that in this position they supplemented the nominal wages of their *employés* there can be no doubt. But this was perfectly legitimate. Men, women, and children were refused relief unless they complied with the demand of their employer for their services. They were thus obliged to work for twenty or thirty hours or even fifty-five hours a week, in manufacturing inferior Surat cotton, or cotton 'waste,' at which their earnings would perhaps only amount to three or four shillings. In some few cases, even from this paltry sum, a reduction for rent was made, and then 'the relief' made good the operatives' receipts to the 1*s.* 6*d.* or 2*s.* per head standard. In this way the mill-owner gained a certain advantage by the relief funds. But then it may be said, that but for this practice he could not have moved his machinery, nor could this inferior raw material then have been manufactured at all. The transition from the use of American to that of Surat cotton could not have been made but by slow degrees, and while it is certain that the relief funds have materially assisted the general introduction of the inferior material, it cannot be said that they were directly made available for this purpose; while, so long as the operatives obtained the ordinary standard of relief, they were, which otherwise they would not have been, for the most part quiet and contented.

CHAPTER XII.

MARCH—MAY 1863.

THE close of the financial year 1862-63 afforded legitimate cause of satisfaction. The chief branch of the national trade had been suddenly cut off. Half a million of the population had been reduced to a condition of dependence upon charity, and the country had been deprived of their wealth-making labour. They had lost during the year 7,000,000*l.* in wages, and 65,000,000*l.* of fixed capital had been rendered to a great extent unproductive. The luxuries of a large portion of the population living outside the cotton districts, had been curtailed in order that their value might be given to the charitable funds for the relief of Lancashire distress. The savings-banks had suffered an unusual drain to the extent of 2,000,000*l.*, but yet the victory of the Exchequer was complete and decisive. In the Budget of 1862, the revenue for this year, ending 31st March, 1863, had been estimated at 70,190,000*l.* The calculations upon which this estimate was framed, must have been made at a time when it was impossible to foretell the consequences or the continuance of the Cotton Famine. At the close of a year made memorable by the forced suspension of the cotton trade, inflicting all the penalties of famine upon a district containing one-tenth of the population of Great Britain, it could hardly have been surprising if the estimate had considerably exceeded the actual revenue. But the reverse was the fact. The actual receipts of revenue for 1862-63 exceeded the estimate by 533,561*l.*, while the expenditure for the year showed a more than equally favourable condition. The estimate of expenditure had been 70,040,000*l.*, but the actual payments fell short of this sum by 737,992*l.*, thus giving to Mr. Gladstone a total surplus of 1,301,553*l.* The only item of the revenue which gave certain token of the Cotton Famine was the receipts for excise duties. The consumption of alcoholic liquors had considerably decreased, owing to the loss of wages by the operatives. This reduction was estimated to be as much as half a pint per head for the whole population of the cotton districts; but the gain to their health—the consequence of this compulsory temperance—had been far greater than the loss to the revenue.

This was no illusory triumph—no financial victory won by the questionable aid of *rentes* or greenbacks, but the honest result of individual co-operation. England had not mortgaged her future to produce this revenue, for the National Debt was less this year than last by nearly 1,000,000*l.*, and the balances in the Exchequer exceeded by nearly 2,000,000*l.* their amount in 1862. This had been a time, moreover, pre-eminently distinguished for the remission of taxation. A long list of duties had been swept away by the French treaty, the paper duty had died an uneasy death, and the remission of the hop duty had cut away the time-honoured grievance of the agriculturalists of the home counties. It was this policy, indeed, which had made the revenue of 1862–63 possible of attainment; this victory was, in fact, the triumph of free-trade, the splendid testimonial to the national benefits of unrestricted competition. For the trade of the country, loosed from all fetters, had, without the evidence of effort, compensated for a stoppage in one direction by an increased activity in all others.

While finance is the immediate subject of remark, it will be most fitting to mention the balance-sheet of the Mansion House Committee, whose funds were first audited on the 4th April, 1863. In this, as in the financial statement of the Central Relief Committee, there is observable the same scrupulous regard for the integrity of the fund. The cost of advertisements exceeded 2,700*l.*, but this may be also regarded as the cost of collection, and the remainder of the 'expenses' does not amount to 1,000*l.* This committee had been accused of unduly holding back in its expenditure, but one statement is a sufficient refutation of the charge. The Cotton Famine had not yet passed away, yet this committee had already disbursed four-fifths of their receipts.

Early in April, the Staleybridge rioters were tried at Chester. As the prisoners were but a few of the guilty, there was unwillingness to press the graver charge of housebreaking. Including those from Dukinfield and Hyde, about twenty were convicted of rioting, and sentenced to imprisonment for terms varying from one to six months. The punishment was not severe, but its lenity had the advantage of preventing any sympathy for the foolish lads, who had done what they could to bring into disrepute a class vastly superior to themselves in every respect.

But these disturbances had unsettled the lower ranks of the unemployed, and at several places threatening movements were made, which, but for the influence of their superiors, might have proceeded to serious consequences. At Stockport an attempt was made to foment disorder, by a similar class to that which had been guilty of rioting in the Staleybridge district. A considerable number of men had been employed by the Stockport Board of Guardians in making roads and in other outdoor work. The suggestion of a paltry grievance was sufficient to cause a partial strike and to collect a crowd. A few broken windows were, however, the worst result. The men in the relief schools of Stockport flatly refused to join the rioters, as did the better class of outdoor labourers; and this, together with the resolute attitude of the authorities, quickly succeeded in quelling the disturbance.

At Wigan the same agitation prevailed. A procession, numbering four hundred of the recipients of relief, marched to the workhouse, where the board of guardians was assembled, to lay before them a bill of complaints. 'Their hours of work, from seven to five, were considered too long; the guardians were not sufficiently liberal; and they had been called "savages" by a local paper.' It turned out that the local paper had been stating that the use of the epithet 'savages' by another journal was libellous, and ultimately all the grievances melted into cheers, and the difficulty concluded with a willing resumption of work.

The operatives of Ashton-under-Lyne made a movement, but of a more pacific character. The Working Men's Executive Committee of Ashton-under-Lyne issued an address to their fellow-countrymen, asking for their assistance in obtaining a more liberal scale of relief, and calling for petitions to Parliament in order to obtain a grant from the Consolidated fund. The possible intention of this paper was to support Mr. Ferrand's announced intention of bringing the subject of Lancashire distress before the House of Commons, upon its assembling after the Easter recess. A memorial was also presented by the unemployed operatives of this borough to the Central Executive Committee, praying for greater liberality in the distribution of relief. Cases of individual hardship there might and must have been, but there was certainly no general ground for this complaint, and Ashton had received a lion's share of the relief funds. The rate of relief in most places now exceeded 2*s.* per head, and both the approach of summer and the rising price of manufactures, promised an increase of employment out of doors as well as in the cotton factories. These grievances were oftener hatched by idleness than founded on good reason; indeed, the greatest sufferers, as a class, were now the small shopkeepers and small property-owners, upon whom the continued distress was telling much more severely than upon those who had now been for a long time dependent on the relief funds.

But the wave of discontent which was passing over the district most nearly threatened to submerge order at Preston, where, up to this time, great distress had been borne without audible complaint. For some months past, the Preston Board of Guardians had provided outdoor labour for a large number of their dependents. Upwards of five hundred were engaged in earthwork upon land called the 'Moor,' adjoining the town, and in preparing the site for a cattle market. The labour of these men was in proportion to the relief they received, from three to six days a week; so that a married man receiving ten shillings a week, would work twice as many hours as a single man receiving five shillings a week. But their hours of labour had for some time past been nominal only, and the superintending committee now determined that they should properly fulfil their task. The announcement of this decision was made the occasion of disorderly proceedings. The men kept to their work, but intentionally got through so little, that payment for results was had resort to, and this caused a general strike. A relief school, numbering about six hundred 'scholars,' was 'turned out,' and soon a crowd of four or five thousand persons had gathered round the police office. A deputation was appointed to confer with the mayor and the borough authorities. An hour's interview eventuated in the following characteristic address to the crowd by a member of the complainants' deputation:—

'Them that has worked at the Cattle Market and on the Moor, and has done their work and are booked, Mr. Ascroft will look to see that they are paid; and them that has gone away and has left their work as soon as they was booked, will not be expected to be paid.' (Groans.) 'They will be paid to-morrow, those that has worked.' (Renewed groans and uproar, and cries of 'We hev nought to eyt to-neet.') 'Them as is book'd 'll be paid, but them as isn't book'd 'll not be paid, and them as couldn't work for want of tools 'll be paid.' (Cries of 'There's plenty of tools,' and 'Some on us hevn't bitten sin mornin'.') 'You are to go to work i' th' mornin', and work accordin' to th' papper.' ('We won't go,' and great hooting.) 'The six days' men are to have a day for themselves beside Saturday.' (Voices: 'We are just the same as we wor, if not worse.')

Hungry men are always most unreasoning, and as agitation is not paid by wages, it may be supposed that these poor fellows, who had spent a day or two in defining and exposing their complaints, were very much famished. Empty stomachs cannot digest arguments, and too little food is the law-breaker's best excuse, particularly if his own want is spurred by the destitution of his wife and family. The crowd was hungry and excited, but it was not riotous; it could not appreciate the justice of the conduct of the authorities, yet, for the most part, it was determined to keep the peace. But a crowd of five thousand persons is not all of one mind, as a gentle rain of brickbats on the outside of the Preston police-office now seemed to show. 'Those behind cried "forward," and those before cried "back,"' until the police made a sortie and retreat became general. The military were called out, but were soon afterwards marched back again, and three youths appeared before the magistrates the next morning as the scapegoats for the multitude. The affair was over; it had never been more than a tumult, and the peace of Preston was not again disturbed.

The condition of the cotton manufacturing districts was now such as could not fail to attract the attention of Parliament. Outside, there was a growing disposition to promote a large emigration, regardless of the interests of the cotton trade; while within, there was a conviction that something must be done in order to prove that this removal of the unemployed population was not only inexpedient, but unnecessary. There was abundant evidences of a strong faith in the revival of the manufacture, for new mills were rising in every direction. Many of these had been commenced before the occurrence of the Cotton Famine. But assuming this faith to be well-founded, the time was not unpropitious for such an investment of capital. The erection and furnishing of cotton factories could certainly now be accomplished at a cheaper rate than when the demand for capital and machinery became more active. The price of machinery was considerably reduced, and it was certain that more care would be bestowed in its construction than at a time when the machinists were full of orders. The markets were improving. Cotton had been selling at lower rates in March than in any month since July 1862, while the margin between the price of the raw material and that of manufactures was continually widening, to the advantage of producers. In March and April, 'India shirtings' advanced 4*d.* per piece—a sign that the glutted condition of the Eastern markets was passing away. But no active trade could be done in goods without immediately affecting the cotton market, and the prospect of improvement was soon shut out by the rising price of cotton. The stock of cotton in the English markets was not inconsiderable, for there were now 350,970 bales in stock, besides 150,000 in the manufacturers' hands; and in addition to this quantity, there were at sea 301,380 bales, making a total of 802,350 bales. The present weekly consumption was about 23,500, and the export 8,000 bales. The supply would, therefore, last about six months at the present rate of consumption, which was about half-time for all the factories. But the gleams of improvement were very transient, and did not overcome the political terrors which yet influenced the markets. Timid traders feared that the success with which the Confederate Loan had lately been raised might lead to a rupture between England and the Northern States; but happily this most wayward offspring of the Stock Exchange passed its rickety childhood without inflicting damage beyond the circle of its subscribers. This loan has been altogether a mystery to most persons unacquainted with the cotton trade. The success which attended the subscription induced many to suppose that the English public was backing its faith as to the stability of the Confederate Government in the ordinary mode by which the strength of governments is tested. But this loan was in truth a cotton loan, and owed its success entirely to the facilities for blockade-running, which existed in consequence of the inadequate naval forces of the Northern States. The Richmond Government had bound themselves to redeem this stock with cotton at the rate of 6*d.* per lb. The value of Confederate stock will be best understood by an example. Suppose a merchant or manufacturer bought at 50*l.*—a fall of fifty per cent., which was soon reached—and succeeded in running the blockade with a vessel laden with goods, which would sell in the Southern ports at enormous profits. He then laid in a cargo of cotton at a cost to himself of 3*d.* per lb., which in England would realize eight times as much. The consequence was, that blockade-running became an organised business; and so great were the gains of a successful adventure, that it was estimated that the capture of seven vessels would not bring loss to the adventurers, if the eighth were but successful; while the rate of profits of a fortunate run were set at about five hundred per cent.

In the factories, Egyptian and Surat cottons were now the main staples of manufacture, and perseverance, aided by necessity, was slowly overcoming the difficulty and prejudice which were attached to the manufacture of Indian cotton. Yet there was no great demand for factory labour and no immediate sign of an increase. The winter of 1863 might be little better than that but lately passed, while the disturbances which had taken place throughout the district induced many to believe that the population could no longer be maintained upon eleemosynary funds without danger of their own demoralisation, and of continued and more serious disorder. When such a state of things is arrived at, there is never wanting a discussion in the House of Commons; and thither expectation turned towards the latter end of April, wondering by what device the wisdom of Parliament would relieve the distress of the cotton districts.

The self-appointed mover of the subject—who however had some claim to the position—was Mr. Ferrand, the member for Devonport. He had been a champion of the operatives in the agitation to obtain the passing of the Ten Hours Bill, and a champion of the farmers in opposing the abolition of the Corn Laws. Though there is nothing inconsistent in these services, yet inasmuch as the interests of operatives and farmers are as wide apart as it is possible for those of fellow-countrymen to be, the consequence has been that to a great many persons, Mr. Ferrand's political career seems somewhat confused. He was known to be no more the friend of the 'hands' than he was the enemy of their employers; but the terms of his motion disarmed the suspicion which his reputation might have excited, and upon the 28th of April he moved, amid general cheering, 'That, in the opinion of this House, it is the duty of the Government to take into consideration, without delay, what measures may be necessary to relieve the distress which prevails in the cotton manufacturing districts, so that the people may no longer continue unemployed.' Mr. Ferrand's speech was full of the error that the cotton trade existed only for the benefit of the capitalists of Lancashire; in fact, it was a severe bill of indictment against the manufacturers, terminating in a motion purely unobjectionable, but to which the speech was generally irrelevant. The men who believe in the indissoluble isolation of classes are becoming fewer every day, yet there are times when their influence is beneficial, for they alone can rouse a class to put forth its greatest strength. But certainly this was not one of those occasions, and in debating this question of employment for the operatives, there was no demand for the abuse of their masters. Although Mr. Ferrand did not directly state the form of employment he would recommend, the tone of his speech indicated a comprehensive measure of emigration to be carried on with the patronage of the State. To his resolution the member for Carlisle moved, as an amendment, the appointment of a

Royal Commission to inquire into and report upon the subject.

There were therefore three courses open to the Government: they might decline direct interference in the matter, on the ground that both emigration and the supply of labour were better left to regulate themselves independently of any official assistance; they might directly accept the responsibility laid upon them by Mr. Ferrand's motion, and 'without delay' address themselves to the difficulty; or, thirdly, it was open to them to adopt the neutral policy commended by Mr. Potter, and to appoint a Royal Commission. As the head of the department specially chargeable with a difficulty so unprecedented and anomalous, Mr. Villiers might have experienced some hesitation had the question been first raised by the motion of Mr. Ferrand. But for months previous to this discussion, the subject of employment had been under his consideration. In his speech upon the Continuance Bill, he had said that the time might arrive when this question would have to be considered, and since that debate many valuable suggestions had pointed towards the provision of local employment. To refuse to entertain this motion might have been dangerous to the condition of the cotton districts, while to shelve it, by adopting Mr. Potter's amendment, would have been discreditable; but Mr. Villiers' statement, that he had already anticipated the motion, from a conviction of the duty of the Government with reference to the subject, was certainly the most satisfactory reply which it was possible to make.

Already much information upon the subject of employment had been obtained, and the President of the Poor Law Board spoke confidently of the large numbers for which beneficial work might be provided in draining and improving agricultural land. He concluded by stating, that he had already determined to send into the district a competent person to inquire both as to the character of the work to be done, and by what means the landowners and local authorities could be most successfully induced to employ the cotton workmen upon these undertakings. With this announcement that the Government had thus initiated the inquiry, the debate on Mr. Ferrand's motion as virtually terminated, and there resulted an increased confidence in Mr. Villiers' ability to deal with the difficulty. The trusted and experienced member for North Lancashire hastened to make his acknowledgments, and amid general expressions of satisfaction from both sides of the House, both the motion and the amendment were withdrawn.

Mr. Robert Rawlinson, who was the civil engineer intrusted with this inquiry, was well chosen for the appointment. He was extensively acquainted with the district by professional association. After a successful career, he had taken a high position as a sanitary reformer, preferring the public service to private prospects of much greater emolument. He had served the Government for many years and in very responsible capacities. He had been a sanitary commissioner with the army in the Crimea, and was now Chief Inspector of the Local Government Act Office. Eminently practical in his character, he merited the confidence that in this arduous service he would not be led to recommend the undertaking of expensive follies—the infirmity of not a few noble minds in his profession, and the cause of many a monumental failure.

But the subject of employment had long been uppermost with those who were now locally engaged in dealing with the distress. A week before Mr. Ferrand's motion was made in the House of Commons, the Central Executive Committee had issued a comprehensive minute upon the subject. Acknowledging the inadvisability of raising the rate of relief any higher, lest it should interfere with the ordinary demand for labour, they were anxious to point out the various ways in which the indigent cotton workmen might find independent means of subsistence. Wisely recommending such labour as would invigorate their frames, keep their spirits elastic, and prevent moral enervation, they had pointed to the embarrassing fact that there existed from 75,000 to 80,000 workmen whom this question affected. They indicated works of public and private improvement as the most fitting employment, but despaired of such works being undertaken, unless the Government would grant special facilities to local authorities and landowners for obtaining loans at a low rate of interest, repayable by instalments extending over a long period of years.

The operatives, on their part, had shown no disinclination for outdoor labour, when it brought them a fair return in wages. The spade and pick-axe had been somewhat dishonoured in their estimation by association with the work required of them as paupers; and moreover, the operatives, as a class, do not hold these most ancient tools in the respect to which they are everywhere entitled. For they are not without a feeling of superiority to the agricultural labourer, whose inferior intellect they associate with the cultivation and labour of the soil. But, among the better class of the operatives, a desire for the wages of labour in preference to the support of charitable relief, was more than sufficiently strong to overcome this prejudice, and many of them had already been engaged in earthwork, with great satisfaction to themselves and their employers. Earthwork is of course most productive of employment for unskilled hands. But, with regard to extensive works of agricultural improvement, the position of Lancashire is altogether unlike that of any other district in the kingdom. In the first place, it is not by any means an agricultural county, and it is easier for a man to serve two masters than for a county to be both manufacturing and agricultural. Successful farming demands, as its prime condition, the undisturbed possession of the soil. Upon the steady approach of bricks and mortar, it is sometimes forced to that unnatural activity of production known as market-gardening, before it passes into that dreary building condition, which, once assumed, divides it for ever from the primary uses of the soil. But all the surface of Lancashire is not yet building land; there are yet a few spaces where it is possible to stand out of sight of a tall chimney, though it would be bold to predict that any such panorama will long remain consecrated to natural production. The subsoil of the county is very varied, and in many places consists of impermeable strata, upon which land-drainage has been, and is still, very uncommon, though nowhere more needed. The county which manufactures cotton candle-wicks is also the most famous for its supply of rushes, those certain evidences of the want of land-drainage. But agriculture languishes in such close competition with manufacture. A farmer, who is a capitalist, will hardly be satisfied to turn his money once a year by the agency of the seasons, whilst his neighbours, with no fear of the weather-glass before their eyes, can turn theirs many times in the same period. Yet this is not the only reason why there are no large farmers to be found in Lancashire, and why capital is not more largely employed in farming the land of this county. Even on the most extensive estates, it is not easy to obtain any considerable tract of land upon lease; for, in a district where towns are built in a generation, it is not possible for the landowner to foresee how soon the character and value of his property may be altered. Hence he is not disposed to relinquish his power of dealing with it for a longer period than is absolutely necessary. The field which is good for nothing but poor hay to-day, may be wanted for building upon a not very distant to-morrow, so that agriculture becomes rather a *pis-aller* than the most honoured occupant of the soil. A farm of two hundred acres is an unusually large holding. The tenants are mostly poor men, many of them living from hand to mouth, and giving no small trouble to the landlords' agents, whose rental is by no means secure where most of the soil is grass land, and where the tenant's stock is never very valuable. The hindrance to land improvement of next importance to that of manufacturing competition, is the moisture and low temperature of the climate, which renders the soil of Lancashire unsuited to the production of corn, and especially of heavy wheat crops. To a great extent this evil is increased by the want of drainage, which, by reducing evaporation, would have the immediate effect of raising the temperature of the soil. But though with drainage the high lands of Lancashire might produce excellent grass, yet it is not at all likely that even this improvement would make them equally productive in corn cultivation. Besides these superficial and climatic hindrances to agricultural improvement, there is yet another circumstance which seriously affects the production of food in Lancashire, and this is the mineral wealth of the county. That which is primary in the south is but of tertiary importance in the semi-rural cotton districts. A corn-field may be a fair sight enough, but a coal-field pays better, and factories and cottages are more profitable than either. To keep water out of the mines is an object of immediate concern to the Lancastrian landowner, though he is not equally alive to the necessity of conveying it from off the land. And it is to be said that in some mining districts, if he were with nicest skill to drain the surface, it might sometimes happen that the utility of the work would be seriously damaged by the subterranean operations. For, as the seams of coal are gotten, and the props are removed or become decayed, the super-soil falls in, and if the seam should chance to be thick and near the surface, a very considerable derangement of levels will take place. And last, but not least among the hindrances to agriculture, is the usual high price of labour, consequent upon the manufacturing demand.

Notwithstanding these obstacles to improvement, and it must be admitted that they are very considerable, there can yet be no doubt that very great benefit might be obtained by the general adoption of land-drainage. Throughout the whole county, rush-producing pastures are the rule, and a soddened, cold surface-soil the result of such neglect. The immediate benefits of drainage would be a large increase of production, the greater salubrity of the district for human life, the improved health and more rapid development of the pastured sheep and cattle, while manufacturing industry would be directly benefited by obtaining a more copious and more constant supply of water. Rivers and their tributary streams would flow more evenly, to the great advantage of the manufacturers, and the loss of water by evaporation being so materially reduced, the available quantity would be much increased, while the temperature, relieved of this reducing and unwholesome influence, would be sensibly improved.

But for these obstructing circumstances, it is probable that extensive works of land improvement would now have been projected, with a view to the better cultivation of the neglected soil, and of providing employment for the distressed operatives. Such work would have been best suited to them, and would have engaged a far larger number than could be employed in urban works. And, as Lancashire is as thickly strewn with cotton manufacturing townships as southern counties are with villages, there would have been little difficulty of access to the work. To have added 100,000*l.* a year to the productive value of the soil of their county would have been a very satisfactory investment, both of the landowners' capital and of the operatives' labour. This might have been done, and the doing of it would have brought increased wealth to the landowners, and work and wages to fifty thousand men, of whom at least seventy-five per cent. might have been factory operatives.

But the demand for works of public convenience and sanitary improvement was far greater in the towns of the cotton district. In them was collected the unemployed population, and upon them the burden of their maintenance was heaviest. In most cases they possessed a constituted local authority, empowered to carry out such works. These authorities would be expending moneys of which only a ratepayer's share was furnished by their individual members; and if the pressure of the rates could in this way be lessened, or if by means of loans for public works, their payment could be extended over a period remote from this time of difficulty and of no profits, they would have every reason to congratulate themselves on such a result. The landowners were not now the class which was sustaining the burden of the Cotton Famine, and as a class they are usually somewhat slow to move, and especially tardy in uniting for a common object. Here and there would, of course, be found exceptions; the advantages of drainage, of grubbing and straightening fences, and improving roads and watercourses, have not now to be taught, for they are well known by the owners of every acre of English soil. But experience did not warrant the assumption that any widely conterminous extent of Lancashire would thus be taken in hand for the double object of local improvement and of affording employment to the indigent operatives. Badly as the soil of the county needed such improvement, the towns were still more in want of public works. Yet it is difficult to state the evidence of this want, without conveying a wrong impression with regard to the condition of the towns in the cotton district. The sanitary and superficial defects of these towns were not so much owing to neglect, as they were the almost unavoidable consequences of the previous prosperity of the district. There are many towns in the south, wherein quite as little care had been taken to put away these certain causes of mortality, which it needs a costly and intelligent effort to remove. But then their rivers wind through many a mile of sylvan scenery; their atmosphere is not darkened with factory smoke, and in some cases, the grey beauty of their age induces forgetfulness of their sanitary sins. Where sewers are not established deep cesspools are generally used, and that best of disinfectants, the earth, removes by absorption much that is prejudicial to health. But this is not the case in the north, where the extension of the towns has been so sudden. It would be difficult to name a town in the south which has increased with as much rapidity as the most sluggish of the cotton hives of Lancashire. Then the mode of their increase is peculiarly unfavourable to the most salutary conditions. In the south the extension of a town includes a variety of houses; a large proportion of trim villas with surrounding gardens; of the semi-detached class of habitations; of the long rows with front areas and garden pens, devoted to clerks and shopmen; and then there is a certain proportion of more closely packed habitations for the working classes. But in a Lancashire town where the population is mainly operative, there is not this variety, and a rapid increase means little less than the exclusive erection of small dwellings for the factory-working population. A new mill is built, and immediately there is a demand for one or two hundred cottages. During the two or three years anterior to 1861, when the cotton manufacture was increasing so rapidly, thousands of cottages were hurriedly built, and as hurriedly taken for habitation, without regard to the possession of anything more than a weather-tight home. And it must be said, that the working-classes in the cotton district are better housed than in any other portion of Her Majesty's realm. Wooden houses are very rarely to be seen. Red brick or stone, with slate or stone-shingle roofs, are the common building-materials. Very dilapidated houses are not frequently to be met with; but the dampness of the soil beneath the floor is too often a removable cause of disease, and generally this has but a thin covering of porous, gritty flagstones, which forms the chief internal discomfort of the homes of the operatives. In many cases these cottages belong to their inhabitants, who not unfrequently pay off the purchase-money through the agency of some building society; but the majority of them are owned in twos or other numbers up to a dozen, by men who have built them with borrowed capital, and can but ill afford any expenditure not absolutely requisite to procure tenants. In this way many of the towns of the cotton district have extended with unexampled rapidity, and none more so than the towns and districts of Accrington and Over Darwen. The census returns for 1851 and 1861 show, that at the former period there were 1,957 houses, and a population of 10,374 in the district of Accrington. When this decade was ended, the houses numbered 3,265, and the population 17,688. The increase of Darwen has been equally rapid. In 1851 there were 2,134 houses and a population of 11,702 in the district, while in 1861 these numbers had grown respectively to 2,925 and 16,492. The estimated increase in population of Over Darwen since 1861, is not less than 3,000. To meet the demand for houses consequent upon such extentions, called for great effort, and it is not altogether surprising that the addenda of street formation, paving, and sewering should have lagged far behind.

New streets were set out upon estates designed for building, and the fortunate landowner might, perhaps, during his life tenancy, see his rental grow from shillings to pounds. Every man had built his block of houses after his own design, and upon levels chosen by himself; often upon a hilly street the roof line descended with a parallel gradient, and the floor line would be, in one block of houses high above, in another on a level, and in a third below the surface of the street. These, it may be said, were misfortunes incidental to great activity in building with an urgent demand for cheap construction. The streets were generally wide and straight, but the great extensions in the years immediately preceding the Cotton Famine had called a vast number of new streets into existence, which had not yet been declared public and reparable by the local authorities. The condition of these streets was only such as might be expected. Deep ruts were ploughed into their surface by coal-carts, which supported the water that might, but for them, have flowed into many of the houses. They were strewn with garbage thrown from the front doors of the adjoining houses, and what with coal carts, water, and refuse of every description, their surface had become a compound virtually impassable in wet weather, and always seriously prejudicial to health. The Cotton Famine had been, in some measure, the indirect cause of this neglect, for the owners of this cottage-property were not the least distressed portion of the community. The number of such habitations defied the vigilance of any inspector of nuisauces, while the condition of the roadways almost encouraged the inhabitants in their use of them as dirt-heaps. Some of the larger towns in the district contained as many as a hundred streets, the houses of which were inhabited, but yet with the roadways unformed and unpaved. In every township in Lancashire, there were some streets which urgently needed these improvement works. The local authorities had, in most cases, power to call upon the house-owners to perform such works, and upon their refusal, or by arrangement, to carry them out and charge their cost upon the property-owners, in proportion to their respective lengths of frontage; yet it would have been impossible for all the owners to provide the money for these works, while they were losing so much rent in consequence of the Cotton Famine. But if the local authorities could obtain the means of executing these improvements, and make their cost a charge upon the owners, repayable by instalments extending over a period of years, it was evident that much work might be provided at no cost to the ratepayers; indeed affording relief to them, as well as employment to the operatives, and health and improvement to the locality.

But the plague-spot of the poor homes of Lancashire is to be found at the back of the houses. The deep cesspool system is bad enough, but the middens or cesspits of the cotton districts are a very great deal worse. In the unsewered towns of the south, the solid refuse is generally deposited in a hole dug in the ground, which is cleared at very wide intervals, as occasion demands. In Lancashire this is deposited on the surface, exposed in a brick receptacle to the putrefying influence of the weather, to the eyes and nose, and to every sense of those who are about it. Of course the cesspool system is not comparable, in a sanitary point of view, with the instant removal and dilutation of the refuse by means of water-closets and sewers, but also, in a sanitary point of view, it is incomparably better than the Lancashire plan. In the earth, protected from the sun, the sewage is, to a great extent, deodorized; in the midden it stands above the surface of the soil about it, and putrefies with the united assistance of the sun and the rain. In the first case, it is out of sight; in the latter, it is often the disgustingly attractive object of the back yards. Of the one, it may be said that it pollutes the water drawn from the pumps and wells; but this objection is more formidable in the south than in Lancashire, where the water supply is collected upon the surface of the high lands. In Paris, the refuse is deposited in impermeable cesspools, which are always breeding poisonous gases, and multiplying the death-rate of the French capital. In London, it is, or will soon be, hurried away to a distant point of the river Thames. It is better even that the underlying soil of a city should be impregnated than that this gaseous poison should be, as it were, 'bottled' for the destruction of the inhabitants. In considering this subject, which is one of increasing and irresistible importance, it ought to be remembered that this poison is not the unavoidable product of sewage matter, but only of such refuse when putrefied. But for the cheapness of coal in the cotton district, causing large consumption, and yielding a plentiful supply of ashes, which are generally, though not always, thrown into these cesspits, the evil would be much greater than it is at present. Yet even this circumstance acts as an indirect aggravation of the mischief, by necessitating the frequent disturbance of the contents of the cesspit for the removal of these foul accumulations. This is not an isolated condition, referable only to a house here and there, but is the actual state of thousands upon thousands of the houses in Lancashire. And probably more than any other, this has been the cause of the high death-rate which has prevailed in the cotton district.

At the time of Mr. Rawlinson's inquiry with reference to public works, such was the sanitary condition of the towns in Lancashire. The rate of mortality was nearly one-half per cent. per annum higher in Lancashire and Cheshire than in the rest of England, and among the districts in which a high rate prevailed, this stood the highest.

A fact translated into percentages loses much of its force. But an unnatural mortality of half per cent. in Lancashire, means nothing less than the sacrifice of 12,500 lives—a crop of casualities which would make Death's harvest for a sanguinary campaign. It is absurd to charge this awful mortality to the factory life of the operatives, it would be a good deal more reasonable to ascribe it to over-feeding. Their health improved during the years of the Cotton Famine, under the influence of compulsory temperance, of restricted diet, of outdoor exercise, and of greater leisure among the married women to devote to the duties of home. But a far larger advance will have been made to a healthy condition, when the sewage matter is no longer stored close to the houses. No fair comparison can be made between the towns of the north and those of the south in this respect, because the former are so much more dense in themselves, and lie so much more closely together than the latter. So far as population is concerned, a town of very inferior importance in the north would be one of first-rate magnitude in the south. There is scarcely a county town along the southern coast more populous than Over Darwen, yet Darwen is unknown to fame in the roll of Lancastrian towns, and until lately was not possessed of any local government. The sanitary defects of these Lancashire towns are not due to the fact that they are northern or that they are manufacturing, but rather to the rapidity of their growth, and to the circumstance that their population is mainly composed of one class, and that not the most influential, nor the most appreciative of sanitary improvements.

House drainage of any sort was at the time of this inquiry a great rarity in the manufacturing districts, and often, standing pools by the roadside, or at the backs of the houses, coloured with soap-suds, or steaming from the saucepan, revealed how the housewife managed to dispense with a sink. In some places there were sewers, but too often neglect, or the interference of new buildings, had caused them to become choked, and consequently worse than useless. In some districts, a single drain led away the sewage to an outlet upon a lower level. Probably the work it was at first intended to do was trifling, and the locality of the discharge far from observation. But time rolls on, buildings accumulate, many make use of the old drain, the township extends towards the outlet, and it is suddenly discovered that the inhabitants are living round a fever-giving swamp of their own making. Many such cases did this public-works inquisition reveal. Then, as to the rivers. It is one of the penalties of a district distinguished as wealth-producing, that the natural face of the country, with all its most beautiful features, shall disappear. If the rivers of Lancashire should ever again run pure, clean, and alive with fish and insects, much of this improvement will be owing to the sanitary revolution which was an indirect consequence of the Cotton Famine. But their waters have been debased in a manner which must make them glad to hide their shame in the sea. In the first place, every township in the cotton district—and one is very rarely out of sight of another—considers that its first duty to its own character for cleanliness is to make a main sewer of the adjacent river. Dye-works and print-works tinge its stream with many-coloured hues, jets of hot water lend their assistance in preparing the compound, then the water finds it way by means of goits to many mills, and, when thus used for manufacturing purposes, with a large admixture of sewage matter and factory refuse, the stench resulting from it is abominable and sickening. So does many a Lancashire river pass from bad to worse, storing disease upon its banks; until, lost to all purity, it rolls on turgid and unlovely, a victim to its spoilers—but not unrevenged, for has it not fouled their machinery and their mills, and laid stores of putrefying matter on its path through their great towns? As depositories for sewage matter, the Lancashire rivers do indeed possess one very material advantage over those of districts less elevated and undulating, and where consequently a lighter rainfall prevails. At no very distant intervals of time, they are thoroughly flushed by the very rapid accumulation of storm waters. But this has produced in many of the townships, intersected by or bordering upon streams, an evil which they have been slow to remedy, and perhaps in some instances have failed to observe. These floods are sufficiently strong to bring down the streams considerable quantities of soil, coarse gravel, and broken stone. These 'detrita' are deposited where the force of the flood water is checked by the impediments necessary for the traffic of the town, and so by a gradual and almost invisible process, the bed of the stream is raised, very prejudicially to the health and drainage of the town and neighbourhood.

As the Government Engineer proceeded with his inquiry, there could be no doubt that sewerage would be prominently mentioned among the public works required in the cotton districts. These, with the street-surface works, may be regarded as the most requisite improvements within the towns. But there were other public works, not immediately affecting the dwellings of the population, of which this district stood in peculiar need. The water supply of Lancashire is, as is well known, obtained by the construction of artificial lakes among the hills, for storage, from which the water is served through pipes by gravitation. These reservoirs are among the most important public works of the district, and their construction would afford employment for a great amount of unskilled labour. Public parks and recreation-grounds are nowhere more required than in the large towns of the cotton district, both on account of the indoor employment of their population, and of the uninviting character of their immediate neighbourhood. In some places, these had been already established. In some, public cemeteries were required; and in the laying out of these, as well as of parks and recreation grounds, there would be opportunity for the employment of the indigent operatives. Roads which had been made at a time when the demand for labour was too great to admit of their proper construction, might now be improved, a regular width given to them, hills lowered and valleys made straight. Here and there market-places were much needed, and many other minor works, in which surplus labour might find employment.

It was not the want of legal powers so much as the difficulty of obtaining the requisite funds upon sufficiently advantageous terms, which made the local authorities hold back from undertaking these necessary public works. The Local Government Act, which embodied the Public Health and the Nuisances Removal Acts, had given power to districts adopting its provisions to borrow any sum not exceeding twice the amount of the rateable value of their property assessable to the relief of the poor. Local government was never really so cheap and so thoroughly autonomous as it became in consequence of this statute. Prior to its beneficial enactment, any local authority which found it necessary for the public benefit to carry out works involving the compulsory purchase of property, was forced to undergo the expensive and dilatory process of obtaining a private Act of Parliament. And it very frequently happened that their Bill was lost in committee by opposition which would have been ineffective in Parliament. It is not the least merit of this useful Act that local authorities are now enabled to obtain these powers through the medium of the Home Secretary, who, after satisfactory inspection, obtains the confirmation of Parliament at an average cost of something like five pounds. But, under ordinary circumstances, three months would be required to complete the proceedings necessary for the adoption of this Act; and, as all local authorities have not borrowing powers, a most important item in this inquiry was to determine the manner in which such powers could be most readily conferred, and to what corporate bodies they should be given.

In deciding upon the works to be undertaken, it was indispensably necessary that they should be useful—not devised for the sole purpose for creating a demand for labour; otherwise the local authorities would not willingly borrow money for their execution, and they would be regarded by the operatives as a mere labour test—a Sisyphian employment—in which they would have taken no interest and felt no satisfaction. On the other hand, they must be such works as would not have been undertaken at this immediate season, but for the special circumstances which had suggested the inquiry; otherwise, the engagement of the operatives upon them would involve the injury of those who found their regular employment upon such works.

The jealousy which is felt in wealthy, populous, and influential Lancashire of anything like centralisation dating from London is very strong, and can best be appreciated by a Middlesex man if he will take the trouble to consider what would be his own feelings if the seat of government were established in Manchester. It is not therefore altogether surprising that the Government Engineer should have been received in a few places with some suspicion and distrust. Mr. Villiers, in announcing that he had directed the inquiry to be made, had not disclosed his intentions as to the money by means of which the works were to be executed; nor had he stated how they were to be carried out, whether under the immediate superintendence of Government officials or by the local authorities themselves. Therefore they were somewhat in the dark at the time of the inquiry as to what would be the terms of Mr. Villiers' measure. The difficulties which beset the question were so considerable, that a cautious progress was absolutely requisite. Works might be devised easily enough, as they had been in Ireland in 1846, when large gangs of men dawdled their hours away in a manner which is inevitable when no one cares for the completion of the undertaking. In the case of the Irish famine works, their chief purpose was involved in their execution; the men engaged upon them knew very well that their labour had no immediately useful object; the superintending engineers were conscious of the same thing, and the consequence was that these public works became a labour test of the most demoralising character. And this baleful influence was not confined to the labourers only, but extended far more widely, for the superior classes were also to a certain extent pauperised, from the fact that this expenditure was carried on with State funds and under State superintendence. The object which the Government now desired to accomplish was to provide for the employment of the distressed population by a willing expenditure on the part of the local authorities. If the ratepayers were pleased that the works should be undertaken, and to pay for them, every security would be afforded that they would be works of permanent utility; if their officers were permitted and were able to superintend their execution, the first requisites of all public works would be secured. If the proposed undertakings were of a character such as would provide employment for the unskilled labour which the cotton workers could supply, there could be no possible objection to the advance of Government loans at a low rate of interest, and repayable by instalments extending over a number of years.

As Mr. Rawlinson continued his survey of the district,

it became evident that extensive works of permanent utility and sanitary improvement were really needed, and would be undertaken if the necessary powers were given and the money could be obtained at a sufficiently easy rate. In his conferences with the authorities, he avoided the recommendation of works which were not obviously advisable for local improvement, and those proposed were without exception such as the interests of the property affected would have prompted without consideration of the question of employment. Had it been the intention of the Government to contribute in any way, at the cost of the national exchequer, towards the construction of these works, it would have been the duty of their officers to sanction such only as would afford much employment for the indigent cotton workmen. But this was not the intention of the Government; and, therefore, Mr. Rawlinson pursued the most beneficial course in simply encouraging the local authorities and landowners to suggest the works which their own interests would induce them to undertake. Whether or not the whole of the able-bodied men now in receipt of relief would find employment, depended mainly upon the character of the proposed works, and upon the disposition of the local authorities. If only a portion of these men were employed, there was obvious danger that the relief committees would be tempted—in order to economise their funds—to limit the independence of the labourers by preferring married to single men, and so relieve themselves of the costly responsibilities of families; but such considerations were local concerns easily avoided if the Government did not subsidize these undertakings. Landworks would, of course, employ the largest number of men; but the landowners, with few exceptions, did not come forward very readily with proposals. The success which has attended the humane efforts of Lord Edward Howard, and one or two others, serve to prove how great might have been the employment of unskilled labour, had all landlords been equally zealous in promoting it. Yet it must be said, that extensive agricultural improvements would have been found in some places difficult of accomplishment, on account of the distance which the workmen would have had to travel. These works would have had to be carried on during the winter and spring months;

and the operatives are, as might be expected, extremely sensitive to the effects of cold and wet. Their labouring hours must, in such cases, have been necessarily short, their absences on account of the weather frequent, and the consequence would have been that the cost to the landowner would have far exceeded the usual estimate for such works. Their execution, in the neighbourhood of the large towns, by the labour of the indigent population, would have required the provision of conveyance for the men to and from their labour, besides the means of shelter when they were employed in exposed situations. Although all this might have been provided in a district where every considerable town is the centre of a railway system, yet it would have much enhanced the cost of the works. But the force of these considerations, though applicable to the 50,000 unemployed able-bodied men now collected in the towns, was not so with reference to the additional 20,000, who were dwellers in the smaller townships of the cotton districts. They were under no such disability for agricultural improvement; but in all these townships, with very few exceptions, there existed no form of local government other than the usual parochial organisation. Here, at least, the landowners might have come forward with offers of employment. Assuming that they appreciated the beneficial results of land drainage and were willing to drain their estates, they might naturally object to pay 10*l.* an acre, even by thirty annual instalments, for work which might be accomplished for 7*l.* per acre. The result proved that with an apprenticeship of a few weeks, the operatives made excellent field-labourers; but this was not known when the Bill was under consideration. It is reasonable to suppose that the landowners would have come forward more readily if they had not feared the extra cost of the works. But this objection might have been to a great extent overcome, had the guardians expressed their willingness to enter into contracts, if empowered to do so, for the execution of works at the ordinary price and to charge the surplus upon the parochial rates. The extent of work to be undertaken would, of course, have been limited by the number of unemployed able-bodied men in the parish. It is true that the landowner would thus have been called upon to make an additional payment to the rates in respect of his own works, but this would be a considerable reduction from the amount of poor-rate he or his tenants must otherwise be called upon to pay. The same policy, it might well be thought, would have induced the urban authorities to look around them for works of private improvement, in some of which their first object might have been the reduction of the poor-rates. If they had supplemented the contract price by one-sixth, they would still have been easing the pockets of their ratepayers. nearly to the extent of the remaining payment for unskilled labour, to say nothing of the moral benefit thus conferred on those who had already been too long subsistent upon a charitable allowance. It cannot be doubted that all this would have been done, if the entire cost of the maintenance of this indigent population had been furnished by the poor-rates. But it was not so. The funds of the relief committees which now supported the great bulk of the unemployed were supplied from London and Manchester, and, therefore, the strong inducement to charge the local rates with the supplementary cost of private works did not exist. Had there been no gratuitous relief funds, each one of these small townships would have been eager to provide employment in their neighbourhood for their indigent poor, when borrowing powers had been given to the boards of guardians. But on the other hand, had there been no relief funds, what would have been for a long time past the fate of these men? how would they have been supported while the necessary preliminaries were proceeding, and what would have happened to the 250,000 women, girls, and children who were now in the receipt of relief? These funds were an undoubted hindrance to employment, but how much better this obstacle than its absence and starvation!

In the progress of the inquiry with reference to public works, it became evident that a large number of the indigent poor were very desirous of obtaining outdoor employment. There was no doubt that they were capable of such work. They objected to 'test' labour because they were not allowed to work all day, nor paid wages proportionate to the value of their task, and because they thought their poverty sufficiently patent without a 'test.' These were the results of Mr. Rawlinson's survey so far as the operatives were concerned. The course of the inquisition as relates to the framing of the measure to be proposed to Parliament, showed that useful works would be undertaken if both money and power were provided by the Legislature, —that these improvements would afford a certain amount of employment for the distressed population,—that their cost would be borne locally,—that the best possible security existed for their being of such a beneficial character, and that no merely charitable or wasteful undertaking was to be apprehended. Mr. Rawlinson's estimate for the expenditure of 1,500,000*l.* was as follows :—

	£
Materials, &c.	698,645
Skilled labour	175,490
Unskilled labour	431,756
Plant and superintendence	94,109
Land	100,000
Total	£1,500,000

CHAPTER XIII.

MAY—JUNE 1863.

MANCHESTER was not open to the charge of neglecting the question of Cotton Supply in 1863. There was now no longer any doubt that England must look to other sources than America. The threatening strife between the Democratic and Abolitionist parties in the North, which at one time seemed likely to issue in revolution and an abandonment of the war, now promised to terminate by strengthening the authority of the Washington Government, and increasing the ferocity of the struggle between the Federal and Confederate powers. And there was not wanting convincing evidence that the restoration of peace would not bring down the price of cotton to the level of former times. The American crop of 1862 was not estimated at more than 1,000,000 bales, while good authority did not set that of the current year at more than 800,000 bales. A considerable portion of the produce of 1861 yet remained in store, but it was known that nearly 1,500,000 bales had been damaged or destroyed, and that since that year the consumption of America had not been less that another million and a half of bales. There was probably even now as much as 2,000,000 bales stored in the Southern States, but it was far from the ports of shipment, and had they been open to European vessels, it would have been found that these stores were for the most part owned by speculators—some in the North and some in Europe—who would take care not to bring them forward in such quantities as seriously to depress the markets to their own disadvantage. Southern partisans were bidding for the support of Lancashire against the North, on the ground that if the latter were victorious an export duty of *5d.* per lb. would be charged upon cotton, while it was quite evident that the

South must follow very much the same policy when upon the achievement of independence they found themselves in want of a revenue.

The Cotton Supply Association of Manchester, though but little supported by the mercantile and manufacturing community, had long been making strenuous efforts to promote the growth of cotton in other parts of the world, and their exertions had been attended with a great measure of success. It had been seen that, failing America, India was the country from which the bulk of our supply must be obtained. Ever since the Mutiny and the transference of the government of Hindostan from the East India Company to the Crown, the Government had shown no indisposition to promote the construction of public works, and to improve the means of internal communication. But there were two circumstances, hard to be overcome, which yet fought against the efforts of the Association, and these were the want of energy and desire to improve on the part of the natives, and the land tenure of India. The peninsula is large enough to possess many varieties of temperature, and the climatic difficulties could in a great measure be surmounted by the provision of artificial moisture and by determining from experiments the sort of seed best adapted to particular localities. Nor is it probable that the obstruction presented by the land tenure would still have existed had Lord Canning continued to be Governor-General and Lord Stanley Secretary of State for India. But the Indian land-tax is a very important item of Indian revenue, and Indian revenue has had an exhausting race to keep up with Indian expenditure. It was not perhaps altogether unnatural that Lancashire in her trouble should be somewhat careless of the financial interests of India in the prospect of obtaining a sufficient supply of cotton. Nor was it astonishing that the Minister charged with the affairs of India should give an unhesitating dissent of Mr. Bright's proposal to remit for a term of five years the tax upon all lands devoted to cotton cultivation. Yet it is not unreasonable to think that some amendment in the land tenure was demanded. It could not be necessary to the supremacy of the Government that it should continue to be the landlord of the soil of India. On the contrary, it would seem obvious that any measure likely to attract the settlement of English capitalists would be the surest means of strengthening its hold upon the country. The Indian land-tax is an assessment upon the value of the produce of the soil. Of the three presidencies, the assessment bears the most settled character in Bengal; in Bombay the land is to a large extent leased on assessments made once in a term of years, while in Madras, where the ryotwarry system largely prevails, the assessment is, for the most part, made annually.

It would not perhaps be difficult to demonstrate that this system produces a larger revenue than could be obtained from the proceeds of an immediately equitable redemption, but it must be admitted that it is detrimental to the agricultural progress of India. Where there is no tenant right, there can be no liberal application of capital to production. The Government of India is, with merely nominal exceptions, the freeholder of the whole territory, and, to a large extent, it uses its possessions as though it were a life tenant, taking rack-rent, but without the power of granting leases. Inasmuch as cotton is grown in India in rotation with other crops, and not, as in America, until the soil is exhausted, the remission of the tax upon land devoted to its cultivation would have caused much difficulty, besides the loss to the revenue. But if India is to be a main source of the cotton supply, it would appear to be impossible that a more definite settlement of the land tenure can long be avoided.

The Cotton Supply Association, however, devoted themselves mainly to the encouragement of cultivation, wherever persons could be found willing to engage in it. Great success had attended the introduction of the New Orleans variety of cotton plants into the Indian district of Dharwar; but in Berar, long famous as a cotton-producing country, it had been found that owing to want of sufficient moisture, greater produce could be obtained from the indigenous seed. Experiments have proved, not only that the indigenous cotton of India is capable of great improvement by a more careful selection of seed and a better cultivation, but that the Peruvian and other South American cotton plants, having a longer fibre and superior quality, will thrive under the Indian climate. The growth of New Orleans cotton is said to have failed in the north-western provinces of India, but in the south, the presidency of Madras seems capable of a large production of exotic cotton. Although much may be done, and much has already been accomplished by the stimulus of high prices, yet the surest method of increasing the cotton supply is by the direct infusion of English energy, if not actually in the production, at least in the agency by which the cultivation is improved and the crops brought forward. The success which has been accomplished in Dharwar is mainly owing to the exertions of Mr. Shaw; and if the active agency which Dr. Wight introduced in Coimbatore and Tinnevelly had been supported and extended, there would certainly have been a larger leaven of good cotton in the early supplies which relieved the Famine.

Manchester has been well abused for a short-sighted policy—a too willing dependence upon the Southern States of America. But not all the capital and all the energy of the manufacturing districts could have placed India in the position which she now occupied as a consequence of the American war. To call upon the men of Lancashire to lavish their capital upon India, at a time when there was no prospect of this expenditure being reproductive, was an absurdity which nothing but ignorance could excuse. But now that the conditions are altered—now that the Government has made large expenditure in railways; now that the high price of cotton has infused a healthier commercial spirit throughout the peninsula—they cannot be held blameless if they neglect their share of duty. And it may well be thought that a part of this duty is to encourage, by a well-organised and honest agency, the most expeditious and best conditioned production of the raw material upon which their great manufacture is dependent. The cotton planters of India will probably continue to be natives, but there is great scope for the intervention of the English in improving cultivation and in facilitating export. We cannot wonder that the indigenous plant is scrubby, while the native scratches his soil with what is only a ridiculous excuse for a plough. Deep cultivation is one of the first and cheapest lessons of improved agriculture. Such teaching as this, the Government may do much to disseminate, while an extensive cotton agency would perhaps be the best contribution in aid that Lancashire could offer.

The association did not approve the policy of Sir Charles Wood. They complained that Government might do more to encourage the growth of cotton than filling Blue-books with inquiries, and distributing seed and information. They petitioned the House of Commons, with grave apprehensions for the condition and future prospects of the manufacturing districts, yet with confidence that India was capable of yielding ample supplies of cotton of improved quality and condition. They prayed that the policy of Lord Canning with reference to the sale of waste lands might be adopted; that provision should be made for the permanent tenure of lands; that laws should be established providing for the registration and enforcement of contracts, and that public works of locally recognised utility should be pushed forward with all possible speed.

The policy of Sir Charles Wood differed materially from that of Lord Stanley upon the question of land tenure. There were in fact two questions—the redemption of the tax upon lands already in cultivation, and the sale in fee-simple of waste lands. Both would give permanency to tenure. With reference to the first, Lord Stanley had proposed that redemption should be permitted by the payment of twenty years' purchase, when the assessment had reached something like a permanent standard. In regard to the waste lands, in which definition were included vast tracts of Hindostan, Lord Stanley proposed their sale at a fixed price. Some portions of these lands could never be brought into cultivation, while over the remainder there existed certain native rights, which, upon alienation of the soil, the Government could not justly disregard.

The waste lands of India extend by estimation over 250,000 square miles, which is equivalent to about one-third of the whole country. Lord Canning proposed to sell the forest lands at 5*s.* per acre, and the clear lands at 10*s.* per acre. The purchaser would have received a title from the Government, together with an undertaking that if within the space of twelve months from the time of purchase a prior claim was made good, the Government would reimburse the possessor. Sir Charles Wood condemned this proposal for the redemption of the land-tax as being injurious to the Indian revenue, and substituted a regulated sale by auction with a preliminary survey for the disposal of waste lands. In prohibiting the redemption of the land-tax upon the terms proposed by Lord Canning, it is probable that Sir Charles acted the part of a wise guardian of the immediate resources of India. And it may be said that such a change was not urgently demanded. No one acquainted with India would believe that a new law of this permissive character, which invited the natives to change the immemorial usage of their country, to abandon the feudal system which is perpetuated by the English collectors, would have been adopted by them to any considerable extent. Yet, if the object was to promote, by the most direct means, the settlement of Europeans in India, with their capital and energy, their could be no doubt of the success of such a measure. Many natives who might desire to take advantage of the permission would be unable to raise the sum required for the redemption, and very many would retain their preference for investing in gold, silver, and jewels. But English speculators and English colonists would neither want money nor faith in the security of their title. Those who supported Lord Stanley's proposal, considered that there would be no loss to the revenue if the price paid for the redemption were at once applied to the extinction of the public debt. But this could hardly have been the view of an Indian Minister at the time of the Cotton Famine. He must have foreseen that the assessment upon cultivated lands had as yet attained nothing like permanence, and that if India were destined to become the main source of the cotton supply, even the temporary retention of the land-tax would be most advantageous to the Indian exchequer.

But, though it may be thought that the material interests of the Indian Government were inconsistent with the adoption of Lord Stanley's proposal for the redemption of the land-tax, yet the same objection could hardly be made to his scheme for the sale of waste lands. It is probable that the suggestion of an absolute sale of allotments, such as would be made of the soil of a recently appropriated and unpopulated colony, alarmed many who were to do battle with the complex native rights which extended over the greater portion of these lands. A sale upon application, unregulated by regard to these rights, would undoubtedly have created much dissatisfaction, and might have placed the land in the hands of speculators and jobbers, to the discredit of the English name and government. But the preference given to a sale by auction over a sale at a fixed price, cannot have been demanded by virtue of these rights, and was far less conducive to the development of Indian agriculture. It would surely have been possible to combine the due regard for the native right of pre-emption with the settler's privilege of choosing his own location subject to the adjustment of these claims.

Yet it is to be remembered that India cannot be dealt with as a colony—which it is not. There is a wide difference between a dependency and a colony. The one is held in trust, the other in absolute fee-simple. Mr. Cobden has spoken of the peninsula as 'our immense Indian farm,' but this expression is somewhat too regardless of the heavy encumbrances which are upon it, in the shape of the rights of one hundred and fifty millions of people. A sale of these waste lands is the more important, as being perhaps the only measure which will tend to disperse this vast population, to their own benefit and to the greater prosperity of India. At present, they are huddled in density, extraordinary for agricultural districts, upon the deltas and plains, where an easy cultivation demands but little labour. The population of India is spread at the rate of 200 per square mile. The English rate is about 275 per square mile. But, in some of the districts of India best adapted to the growth of cotton, where there is plenty of land ready for cultivation, the population is only sixty to the square mile, while in others, it falls as low as eight to the same area.

Sir Charles Wood's scheme was thus stated:—'The applicant shall deposit with the collectors the estimated expense of the survey and demarcation, and on completion of the survey, the lot shall be advertised for sale by auction to the highest bidder. If the land is sold to some other purchaser, the applicant will obtain repayment of the money he has advanced for the survey. Should he become the purchaser, he shall receive a deed signed by the collector, putting him in possession of the land, subject nevertheless to all general taxes and local rates, and to any other claim, whether of Government or otherwise, that may have been or may hereafter be established in any court of competent jurisdiction.' This may be necessary, but surely the individual who would be prepared to brave all these contingencies, has either a light love for his capital, or an unaccountable desire to be ranked as a land-owner in Hindostan.

A sale by auction might be advisable as a means of exposing native rights, for their immediate settlement. But such a sale, even without these subsequently impending claims, is open to the objection that it may involve the intending purchaser in fruitless journeys, which in India may perhaps be of a thousand miles each, and that it prolongs the doubt as to whether he is to be the possessor of the land which he has selected as being suitable to his purposes. If the Government cannot equitably forego the native rights over these unproductive lands, if they cannot purchase them, there would seem to be no reason why they should not deal with them as the common rights over Crown lands have been dealt with in several of the English forests. These rights are probably capable of definition, and therefore reducible to a certain value. Would it not be possible to accomplish this reduction by a Commission, and to redeem the rights by the conveyance of allotments? Such a policy would make the Government the absolute owner of the remainder, which might be disposed of at a fixed price in parcels of such size as should prevent the prejudicial operations of land-jobbers. If the natives could have no valid objections to such a settlement, then it would be seen whether English capital would engage in cotton cultivation, when a freehold tenure on sure and simple terms was offered for its security, and whether the Indian population would not then spread itself more equably.

It was unfair to charge Sir Charles Wood with failing to encourage the growth of cotton to the extent of his ability, because he refused to assent to measures which he considered unadvisable from an Indian point of view. He acted consistently. When a subordinate instructed the collectors of a district to remit the land-tax for five years, in the case of a limited number of native planters, whose cultivation did not extend over more than thirty acres, Sir Charles forbade such a departure from the established principle, and deemed the results of such an experiment valueless. But no Indian Minister had ever done more to encourage cotton production by other means than legislation.

The Cotton Supply Association did not, however, confine its attentions to India. They established communications with every part of the globe in which cotton could be cultivated with success. They could boast that they had distributed cotton-seed sufficient to plant 225,000 acres. They found valuable allies in the Foreign Office, the Sultan of Turkey, and the Pasha of Egypt. By Lord Russell's direction the English consuls in all the cotton-producing districts obtained information upon the subject, and rendered material assistance in encouraging its cultivation, while the association, favoured with copies of their despatches, thus became possessed of a most reliable and inexpensive agency. Eastern Europe had been quite alive to the opportunity. The Sultan and his pashas looked with useful approbation on the energy of their cotton growers. In Greece it was anticipated that cotton would soon become by far the most considerable of Hellenic products. The governor of Adrianople so far laid aside Turkish lethargy as to circulate printed instructions upon the cultivation and treatment of the cotton plant, in the Turkish, Bulgarian, and Greek tongues. There was new activity as to the raising of cotton in the empire of Morocco, and, in fact, everywhere except upon the ground which for forty years has been the main source of the European supply. And no small share of this activity was due to the exertions of this association. In all parts, planters were looking to them for supplies of seed, for advice, and for encouragement. In the New World a want of sufficient labour was the chief obstacle to production. The German settlers in South America, who form such numerous communities in that splendid continent, were anxious to engage largely in the cultivation, and Australia also received cotton-seed from the association, but the area of cultivation was trifling, owing to the scarcity and dearness of labour.

One circumstance, which now interfered with the cotton trade in an illegitimate and fictitious manner, inconsistent with the simple laws of supply and demand, was the new rule of the Liverpool Cotton Brokers' Association, that no allowance should be made for false packing after the cotton bales had passed the scales and were delivered to the purchaser. The extent to which adulteration had been practised, in consequence of the rapid rise of prices and the speculative condition of the markets, suggested this as the only means to avoid such numerous contentions as would have seriously impeded the progress of business. But better this, it was said, than the premium upon fraud which the new rule awarded. Better this, than that employment should be wanting for so unhappy a reason as the destruction of confidence in the trade. The only way to press the criminality of the fraud back upon its perpetrators, was for the consumer to refuse to treat the bargain as legitimate. An association of cotton-spinners was formed with the object of enforcing claims for compensation where necessary. It was the interest of all to lessen as far as possible, the large percentage of 'waste,' which made the manufacture of Indian cotton so unprofitable. Pebbles were often found in Surat bales, and it was mentioned, that one of these bales contained a stone of no less than ten pounds weight, for which the purchaser had paid the cotton price of 1s. 6*d.* per pound. But the damage to the manufacturer might not have been ended with this unprofitable purchase of mineral for what should have been cotton. There was great danger of ignition should these stones come in contact, as they were very likely to do, with the flyers of the cleaning-machines. In some large establishments, detached blowing-rooms have been erected, mainly to obviate this danger. But the evil of adulteration, which threatened to become a very serious difficulty, has already been, to some extent, remedied by the establishment in India of a system of inspection.

There was certainly now no Cotton Famine, in a literal sense, for supply had been, for some time past, gaining upon consumption. The weekly average import for the eight months preceding the 1st of May, had been 30,800 bales, while the home consumption, together with upwards of 6,000 bales exported did not amount to 25,000 bales per week, so that the stock of cotton in Liverpool, which before the winter of 1862 had stood at 150,000 bales, was now raised to 369,000 bales. Some of these 'bales' were very small; some were Chinese 'piculs,' three of which would only just make up the weight of an American bale; but though the underweight of these bales made the stock seem larger than it really was, the circumstance does not, in the least degree, derogate from the fact, that during the severest months of the Cotton Famine, the stock of the raw material in England was constantly augmenting.

While these exertions to develop new sources of the cotton supply were being made at home and abroad, and while the inquiry with reference to public works was being prosecuted and the Government measure matured, the condition of the manufacturing population was slowly but surely improving. Migration and emigration had not indeed done much to lessen their numbers, though thousands had passed to east and south, and thousands had gone over the sea westward, provided, in many cases, with passages by colonial grants, supplemented by home charitable funds. The interest of Lancashire was to obtain new and increasing sources of cotton supply, not to export the workpeople—by no means to be exerting herself in every quarter to obtain cotton, and at the same time to be sending off the only agency by which it could be manufactured. As for the operatives, many of them had grown weary of doing nothing, had become irritated for want of a better prospect; but for the most part they were peaceable in their conduct, and their health had certainly not suffered but was materially improved. With reference to the health of the population the Registrar-General reported, 'that the legal provision for the distressed, and the spontaneous liberality of their countrymen, have hitherto sufficed to maintain the people in health.' The average rate of relief a little exceeded 2*s.* per head, but very many managed to obtain in money or kind something more than the regular allowance. It is unnecessary to praise their demeanour, because now that the Famine had endured so long, this was clearly the result of an intelligent exercise of reason, which was not dethroned by the cravings of hunger. Yet it should not be forgotten that this population, many of whom were accustomed to an average of 2*s.*, were now living on 4*d.* a day. Many would have been glad to emigrate, and some thought they had a claim upon the State for the means of doing so, but there was a general feeling of gratitude for the relief funds, a conviction that all legitimate endeavours to procure cotton were being made, and that the Government had not been unmindful of their distressed situation. The prospect of employment and wages resulting from the inquiry as to public works materially relieved the mental pressure of the future; but there had never been the faintest agitation for a war with the United States, and for a raising of the blockade. It would be entirely erroneous to suppose that this arose from political ignorance. It was, and throughout the duration of the Famine has been, the direct consequence of the fact, that the leaders of the operatives have strongly favoured the cause of the North. Nor can there be much doubt as to the motives which thus influenced their political judgment. If the question had been one of cotton alone, they would have been in favour of obtaining it. If the question had been one of slavery and cotton together, they would have acquiesced, as the world had hitherto done, in the human wrong, so that they regained the means of comfortable livelihood. Right or wrong, perhaps both wrong and right, it was because they believed that in this war, the cause of democracy, of individual improvement, of freedom of every kind, and of all that is understood by 'progress,' was contending against slavery, against the institutions of aristocracy and despotism—that they were Northerners. As a rule, the operative leader believes this doctrine as firmly as he does that wages should always maintain a certain standard, irrespective of the demand and supply of labour.

It is much to be regretted that the masters were not at this time a little bolder in their consumption of Indian cotton. Yet there were large numbers of operatives engaged, for some time, at least, during the week in the manufacture. Mr. Maclure's returns dealt with a population considerably exceeding half a million; but though these were all termed 'operatives,' it was never pretended that they were all 'mill-hands.' Many were hand-loom weavers, who it may be hoped will never resume their bygone and profitless occupation, and many more were connected with trades indirectly dependent on the cotton manufacture. His return for April showed that there were 322,268 persons at work in the factories, though many of these earned so little as to be entitled to a supplementary allowance from the relief funds. During the month the numbers working full time, now amounting to 192,527, had increased by 33,816. Relief was given to 294,904 persons, whose income averaged 2*s.* 1¾*d.* per head. By the 'relief' 16,251 men and 6,203 boys were kept at school, and outdoor work was provided for 5,483 men. The means of education were furnished to 52,392 children, and sewing-schools were supported in which 33,836 girls and women were taught to be useful in their homes. The reduction of earnings at factory work, consequent upon the use of inferior cotton, was very considerable. In some of those spinning operations in which payment is made to the workers by weight, this reduction was not less than 25 per cent.; but the advance in wages would be in proportion to the skill acquired in the manufacture of the inferior raw material. By means of diligent application, assisted by invention, and also by the improvement of the cotton itself, the earnings in the manufacture of Surat cotton have since its first use steadily increased. The prejudiced detractors of Indian cotton, when driven out of one excuse have always taken refuge in another. In a letter to the Home Secretary, dated April 22, Mr. Baker, one of the factory inspectors, stated, he had been informed, that goods made of Surat cotton would not bleach as well as those made of American cotton; but that he had since had evidence that in this respect there was scarcely an appreciable difference. Yet only a small proportion of the cotton-workers were receiving wages equal to those they had earned in 1860, although the manufacture of Surat was paying the operatives better than it had done in 1862. There was less complaint of the disagreeables attending its consumption. Upon the first use of Surat cotton, the workers complained of nausea on opening the bales, and it was stated that bronchitis and other chest disorders were induced by the dust and short fibres which it gave off in the cleaning processes. But these evils, though doubtless existing, would have been lightly regarded had not earnings fallen off. And the operatives would certainly have used their powers of combination to obtain a rise of wages had not the presence of unemployed thousands suggested the folly of such a prooeeding; but the difficulties of resuming production were not confined to the operatives, and one which may in some degree account for the tardy reopening of many of the smaller establishments, was the increased manufacturing capital required by the rise of prices. As most of the small factories are engaged in producing coarse materials, with a large consumption of the raw material in proportion to the labour expended in the manufacture, it is evident that a fourfold rise in the price of cotton must in many cases render inadequate the limited capital of their masters.

The relief machinery had now attained a near approach to perfection. The Central Committee distributed their funds through the medium of 170 local committees. All had settled down to their work, which mainly consisted of judiciously and carefully dispensing the funds provided by the two great committees. There was very little effort made to increase the amount of local subscriptions, and week by week Mr. Farnall reported a large decrease of pauperism; until, by the end of May, nearly 100,000 pesons had been struck off from his list, since the maximum had been reached on the 6th December. The petty tradesmen were suffering severely, more perhaps than any other class of persons. They saw in many cases the relief committees entering the market against them, and retailing stores to the operatives. As trustees of the relief funds the committees were more than justified in this course, and it cannot be doubted that the operative was thus better served than he would have been at the shop. A great deal more might be said of the actual working of the local relief committees. But in truth, though their labour was great, it was characterised by much sameness. Yet there is hardly a township in the district in which the devotion of some charitable person does not deserve to be held in honoured memory. Week after week the sacks of flour and meal were measured out; week after week the soup cauldrons boiled, and fed their hungry constituencies; week after week men pondered and pottered over their tasks in the schools; and week after week the sewing-schools turned out heaps of clothing, until it became evident that unless they ceased production they must make for stock, or invade the wages fund of the regular workers in the clothing trade. The material of these school-made garments was generally the grey or unbleached cloth as it comes from the loom. This is the common wear among the operatives, who in many cases showed the force of habit in a very decided preference for these over the soft white articles which had been distributed before the establishment of the sewing-schools. Reduced to its common denominators in the totals of the relieved and of the sums expended, the giant work of these committees passes without due notice. The numberless inquiries which it was necessary for their members to make in order to prevent imposition and starvation; the many, many hours of their time devoted to a duty no longer novel or interesting; the firmness which signally defeated several attempts at intimidation, and—with all allowance for individual defects—the kindly charity that presided over their operations, are well worthy of record.

How had the relief system affected them? They knew that they were not dispensing their own money; they knew also that their expenditure was subject to inspection, and that by common consent an average standard of relief had been fixed. It may be safely said that usually these committees were most anxious that no misapplication of the funds should be made, and that well-kept accounts were generally forthcoming. But it must also be admitted that these ministrants of relief had, as might be expected, grown somewhat more accustomed to the system than could have been thought desirable. The relief came, and was distributed very much like an ordinary wages fund. It was never long wanting. Their ears were rarely shocked with tales of starvation, but they heard much which it is well that the more comfortable classes should know and remember. They learned how sharp a suffering, how destructive of all that raises man above the brutes, is hunger; they discovered how bitter to the proud stomach, even of a working man, is the bread of dependence—how cruel and deathly are cold and nakedness.

But the more important question is, how had this life of dependence affected the recipients of charity? They too had grown used to it. They, the most active population in the world, had to a certain extent settled down to a life of inactivity. Yet it is only just to say that in thus accepting the situation, they displayed less demoralisation than would have been supposed to be possible under circumstances so dangerous. They had grown used to 'th' relief,' and regarded it as their unconditioned right. To this extent the majority were demoralised, regarding the relief as theirs, and the conditions annexed to its receipt as the grievous imposts of those who stood between the donors and themselves. This was the doctrine of many. If regular work was offered, their first task was to consider by how much its wages would exceed the sum of the relief they received for themselves and their families, and their willingness was proportionate to the balance in favour of the work. To this extent their love of independence had suffered. A return to factory labour, with full time and good cotton, would employ all the members of their family, and bring home very different wages from that of their own outdoor labour. But surely this is a fault of which every class that has self-knowledge will confess itself guilty. How many of the higher rank scan the round total which represents the profits of hard work, and then fall back contented with the lean figures which stand for idleness and dependence upon the will of others?

On the 8th of June, Mr. Villiers obtained leave to bring in the Public Works (Manufacturing Districts) Bill. The signal merit of his administration throughout this crisis had been, that in the measures proposed to Parliament there was nothing contrary to the principles which in English legislation have been accepted as salutary to the public interests. Yet such concessions were demanded, and might have been made by a more timid or less experience Minister. It will not be denied that it is bad in principle to make loans of public money for gratuitous distribution and in order to meet temporary emergency. Nor does it remedy the evil, that the security for such advances should be unexceptionable and repayment certain. When the difficulty has passed away, and nothing remains of it but the local debt to the State, an unwholesome feeling is engendered on the part of the debtors. But this is the least part of the evil. There is yet the major objection, which is the increasing difficulty of rejecting similar applications. There have been and there will be commercial crises in this country, when claims for public loans might be made upon arguments almost, if not quite, as substantial as those which could have supported the case of Lancashire. Exactly seventy years since such a measure had been carried by Mr. Pitt, and commercial distress had been relieved by the issue of 5,000,000*l.* of Exchequer Bills, of which sum 2,200,000*l.* was advanced in loans. But of late years sounder financial principles have been disseminated, and the State has not been called upon to make such a provision. The nearest approach to it have been the memorable suspensions of cash payments. The Irish Famine loans proved a very unsatisfactory experiment, but even admitting that, under the circumstances of that peculiar case, nothing better could have been devised, the condition of England must be very much altered before any part of this kingdom could justifiably lay claim to the same consideration; and it may be supposed that reasons such as these induced Mr. Villiers to discourage the suggestions involving loans of public money for the relief of Lancashire distress.

But such objections to advances of public money for local application are at once removed when their object is the construction of works of permanent or progressive improvement. The State is then increasing the value of the freehold which is the foundation of its resources, and when the works are completed the locality is benefited at least to the extent of its debt. No dangerous precedent is created, for if the permanent utility of the work is ensured, there is an absolute security against mischief on either side. Such was the principle of the Public Works Bill. Whether the expenditure of the money to be advanced were made with all possible regard to the collateral object of affording employment to the indigent population, did not affect the real security possessed by the State that the works to be undertaken would be of 'public utility and sanitary improvement.' And such, it may well be thought, should be the abiding rule governing the advance of public loans.

The results of Mr. Rawlinson's inspection and inquiries, in which he had been assisted by a long and varied experience of the working of these Acts of Parliament, having reference to local government and town improvements, were thus embodied in one of his reports to the President of the Poor Law Board:—

'1st. There is plenty of useful work to be done at the several distressed towns and places.

'2nd. The local governing bodies, so far as I have consulted with them, will commence such works if they can obtain legal power and the necessary money at a low rate of interest.

'3rd. A large portion of the able-bodied, distressed operatives can and will do this work if paid fair but reasonable wages.

'4th. There is sufficient local knowledge to design and to superintend any works commenced.

'5th. Any advance of money by Government should be as a loan, on security of the entire rateable property of each district at a remunerative rate of interest, and repayable at stated intervals.

'6th. For each loan a petition, with plans and estimates, to be forwarded to some Government office or officer on the spot, if preferred, and a report and recommendation, or otherwise, to be sent in before such loan is granted.

'7th. Advances to be made, not in a lump sum for the whole amount of the loan contracted for, but upon certificates monthly as the work is done.

'8th. The local authorities to be enabled to stop short at any point in the progress of the works, should trade revive so as to call the hands to regular work.

'9th. The money borrowed should not be appropriated for other works than those scheduled in the report leading to the sanction.

'One or two inspectors, as at the Local Government Act Office, ought to do all the Government work required.

'The action of the local authorities must be unfettered, or there will be mischief. There may be advice when asked for, as under the Local Government Act.

'The several town-clerks may, with advantage, be consulted as to the legal clauses in any short Bill, if one is to be prepared.

'There are mostly some local legal peculiarities in each

place which block local improvements. I feel the delicacy, and in some respects danger, in exceptional legislation, but do not know how it is to be avoided in this case.'

The measure, as proposed by Mr. Villiers, had really very little novelty in its provisions. His chief object was to shorten and facilitate the processes by which local authorities could obtain loans for carrying out public works. The preamble set forth, that 'whereas numbers of the labouring and manufacturing classes still remained out of employment, it was expedient to make provision for better enabling local authorities in the manufacturing districts to give employment for the execution of works of public utility and sanitary improvement.' In the specification of the works to be undertaken it was less inclusive than the provisions of the Local Government Act, inasmuch as it gave no power to erect buildings which were not sanitary improvements. But it was more comprehensive in another direction, encouraging works of private improvement, such as land-drainage and the re-formation of agricultural enclosures and occupation-roads. The object of these provisions was to promote the class of works which would afford employment for the largest amount of unskilled labour. The Public Works Loan Commissioners—by no means a new body—were to be the depositaries of the fund, amounting to 1,500,000*l*., applicable to the purposes of this Bill, who were to advance the loans upon the authority of orders of the Poor Law Board, after the Board had satisfied themselves that the borrowing powers were valid, and, through the inspection and report of their officers, that the plans were correct, the estimates reasonable, and the works such as were sanctioned by the provisions of the Bill.

The proposed measure gave universal satisfaction. The 'Manchester Guardian,' on the day following the introduction of the Bill, said:—'As soon as it has become law, no locality which possesses the power of levying rates will be able to allege its want of means as an excuse for not finding employment for its distressed population.' The Central Executive Committee approved it as being in accordance with their views. The Members for the cotton districts, assembled in conference, also expressed their concurrence, and the second reading was anticipated with a general desire that the measure should become law as quickly as possible. On moving the second reading, Mr. Villiers stated that the Bill had originated in a desire to employ the distressed population near their homes; but that it was not intended to establish a system of works under Government superintendence, nor to relieve the localities from the obligation of supporting their own poor. After showing, from Mr. Rawlinson's reports, the description of works to be undertaken, he referred to the existing obstacles to the immediate execution of such works, as being partly financial and partly legal. Alluding, by way of reminder to the country gentlemen, to the fact that upon the abolition of the Corn Laws, Sir Robert Peel had, with a view to the encouragement of agriculture, introduced a measure by which the sum of 2,000,000*l.* was devoted to the purpose of enabling the proprietors of land to drain their estates, and weighing it, as it were, against his present proposals, Mr. Villiers came to the legal difficulties, which were 'a deficiency of powers in particular places either to borrow the money or to carry out the works.' The Local Government Act had never been very popular in Lancashire, probably because it seemed to have a centralising action very nauseous to the rampant independence of a manufacturing population. The Bill proposed to shorten the time necessary for its adoption from three months to one,—a provision which, together with the legislative economy of the Local Government Act, has in a great measure swept away the prejudice that hitherto opposed its adoption. The mode in which the inquiry as to public works had been conducted, was open to the objection that due encouragement had not been given to landed proprietors to undertake works of undoubted utility, which would have provided an operatives' labour fund, far larger than the class of works now proposed. But as the President of the Poor Law Board truly said, it would have been an unjustifiable invasion of private rights to have pushed inquiry in this direction. All that could be done was to provide facilities for the execution of such works of agricultural improvement, of which landowners could avail themselves if they chose to forward the objects of the measure. There would have been a mischievous danger of 'jobs,' if private works were to have been executed at a less than ordinary cost. But against this liability there was the very sufficient safeguard of the contracting local authority, which, to give undue benefit to a landowner, must burden itself with all the excess of cost. Mr. Villiers never pretended that the measure was a panacea, and confessed that it did not strike at the great root of the evils which were now afflicting the manufacturing districts.

Those members of the Central Relief Committee who were most directly interested in the cotton trade, held a desponding view of the winter prospects of Lancashire. They accepted the Public Works Bill as a wise and beneficial measure, but they wanted something more from the Government. In five months their responsibilities had decreased by 68,389 persons. But now they were approaching Midsummer, when a decrease was naturally to be expected, and before them loomed the winter with its inevitable increase of distress. The May expenditure of the local committees had amounted to 74,900*l*., and the total sum of the central resources was 447,967*l*. Besides these funds, the Mansion House Committee had yet about 100,000*l*. available for purposes of relief. At their present rate of expenditure, even these large resources would barely suffice to carry them into mid-winter, and the cotton supply was not yet in a condition to enable them to hope for an increase of employment. Of the 1,500,000*l*. to be expended in public works, Mr. Rawlinson's estimate for unskilled labour was only 431,756*l*., and the weekly loss of wages by the suspension of the cotton manufacture was even now 149,914*l*. Such was the position taken by the objectors to the Public Works Bill. They asked,—Was it sufficient to meet this state of things? The property-owners were not partial to the rate-in-aid, and saw, in gloomy anticipation, with what heavy incidence it might oppress them when the relief funds were exhausted. Some thought that if the Government was prepared to do so much, it might advance another step, and make loans to the boards of guardians. Mr. Ferrand, while giving his 'hearty support' to the Public Works Bill, pointed to the necessity for a large measure of emigration. After facts have proved the incorrectness of these opinions and misgivings, it is easy to censure them as selfish, timid, unprincipled and extravagant. Yet at the time, they had a force which nothing could resist but the firmest faith in the future, and the strongest determination to abide by approved principles. It was a sad but certain fact that the private resources of the poor were now exhausted—that long-continued distress had not been without its pitiable consequences—that the unproductive capital of the district had been vexed with loss of profits and taxed with unusual burdens—that charity had made its grand effort—and that when the present funds were exhausted, it would be difficult, if not impossible, to revive the more than national sympathy which had supported, and was yet bearing, the weight of the distress. But it was no less true that the support of this burden had now become more than ever a local responsibility. The calamity had been sudden in its approach, and the nation had lent its arm to break the force of the blow. But now its possible extent was well measured and well known. The future revival of the cotton trade was regarded as so certain, that the deportation of the operatives would have been a suicidal folly. Yet another year and the spindles would be humming with their wonted activity, and the great wealth of Lancashire would again be to a large extent productive. Hitherto, it could not be said that the district had borne more than its fair share of the burden, and it was certain that there were yet remaining sufficient relief funds to last until the dawn of the new year. It could hardly, then, be too much to demand of the manufacturing districts that they should trust to their own resources for the future, nor would it be just to forget that in most cases the suggestion of this duty was sufficient. How well and faithfully this responsibility was performed has been witnessed by succeeding facts;—how all classes in the manufacturing districts, animated with one purpose and strengthened with one hope, have lived down these doubts and fears, and conquered these difficulties, has become patent to the world;—how these funds, then thought so slender, have been husbanded almost to an overplus, has reflected credit on their custodians. And if it be permitted to support a policy by proofs of its wisdom, drawn from a not distant future, the rewards of victory may well be first adjudged to the Minister, who, in the hour of weakness and hesitancy, refused to sanction the arguments that pleaded for expediency at the sacrifice of principle.

Whatever might be the success of the Public Works Bill in regard to the employment of the distressed operatives, it could not place them in anything like their customary affluence. The average weekly earnings of a cotton-working family are not less than 30*s.*, while it could not be expected that the wages of outdoor labour would amount to much more than 12*s.* or 14*s.* As was said by Sir George Grey in the course of debate, the Public Works Bill was not a Government measure providing employment for the people, but rather a proposal to assist the local authorities in providing employment out of their own resources. The only specific for the evils of Lancashire was a largely-increased supply of cotton, a great lowering of the stocks of goods at home and abroad, together with an undiminished consumption. Emigration was not a specific, because no one fairly weighing the prospects of the cotton workers, with their probable fate, if carried away by wholesale, could have recommended it in sufficient extent to be a curative; for this was a population unrivalled for their skill in a laboriously acquired and most difficult occupation, and to an equal degree unfitted for a rough encounter with Nature.

The Public Works Bill, which, as an exceptional measure, had involved considerable difficulty in preparation, owed much to the assistance its framers received from local experience, and in no respect more so than in its adaptation to every existing local authority invested with powers of rating. To this experience was largely due the valuable modification which gave to boards of guardians the power of a corporate authority to borrow money and to carry out works in those townships of their unions in which no sufficient independent authority existed. But, as though to demonstrate how useful is the blending of legislative with local wisdom, the same influential and important meeting which matured this valuable suggestion, also expressed the unanimous opinion that the Union Relief Aid Act should be renewed, but without the provisions for levying a rate-in-aid. Yet this resolution was not condemnatory of the principle of a rate-in-aid, but rather an acknowledgment that the necessity for such a measure was not proven, and that its use in future would, if exercised upon the counties, only be vexatious and not extensive, while the loans so borrowed, charged upon the unions, would be equally effective over their area with a less oppressive incidence.

CHAPTER XIV.

JUNE—JULY 1863.

From January to June the distress was lightened with a steadily progressive improvement. All the hopeless estimates of local expenditure made upon the cost of relief in December 1862, had happily proved worthless. At Midsummer, the number of paupers had decreased by as much as 41 per cent.; and though the returns of the relief committees did not exhibit anything like an equal reduction, yet their expenditure had fallen from a maximum of 90,000*l.* to 53,000*l.* per month. Forty-seven local committees were enabled to suspend operations. The number of persons relieved solely by the committees had fallen from the maximum of 26th December, when it was 234,078, to 104,792, showing a decrease of 129,286 persons, while the reduction in the number of those relieved by the guardians was equally reassuring. On the 6th December, 1862, Mr. Farnall had reported that there were 271,983 persons relieved by the boards of guardians. On the 27th June, the number was 159,222, showing a decrease of 112,761. In the winter of 1862, the numbers relieved by the guardians and the committees had amounted to 506,061, they were now reduced to 264,014, having become less by 48 per cent.

The Central Executive Committee estimated that the resumption of employment in the cotton manufacture amounted to half-time; but there can be little doubt that it must have exceeded this estimate. The returns of their honorary secretary always had reference to a larger number of persons than had ever been employed in the manufacturing establishments of this districts; indeed, the numbers given in these returns as now working full time, which were 234,642, very considerably exceeded one-half the cotton-working population of the locality. But, besides this number, there were 125,097 working short time. A return obtained in the previous month by Mr. Maclure, showed the existence of this error in his general classification. The dependents of the relief committees had included joiners, mechanics, shopkeepers, colliers, agricultural labourers, domestic servants, and others unconnected with the cotton manufacture to the extent of about 22 per cent. And as the boards of guardians in the bestowal of their relief were in no way limited to one particular industry, it is probable that during the highest rates of pauperism in the winter of 1862, there were but 70 per cent. of the paupers, who were really factory operatives or their dependent families.

It was but slowly the committee realized that that which had been called a Famine was over, and that a milder stage of the severe local disorder, consequent upon the American war, had now been entered upon. They looked back upon the sums they had spent with so much care, supervision, and economy,—they looked on their balances and then forward upon the coming winter, and expressed a belief that their funds would be absorbed before the spring brought the cotton crop of 1863 to their relief. The opinion was not without foundation, for the relief expenditure during the past twelve months had been prodigious. The committees had spent 1,330,310*l.* during the past year, every shilling of which had been made up by voluntary contributions. In the face of this fact, it seems hardly strange that they feared to meet the winter and the future with balances amounting to less than half this sum. Within the last thirteen months charity had provided nearly 2,000,000*l.* for the relief of distress. No single fact in our national history is more honourable than this. It is true that England voted 20,000,000*l.* to abolish the slave trade, and that Lancashire has since paid 20,000,000*l.* to support it; and it is certain that England spent 100,000,000*l.* to prop the Turkish Empire. But it is one thing for Parliament to vote money, and quite another for individuals to take it voluntarily from their own pockets. It may be safely affirmed that such a practical expression of sympathy was unprecedented, and is a very legitimate subject of proud congratulation. The boast of Englishmen has been, that the sun never sets on the dominions of their Queen. Shall we be less proud of the more modern conquest? shall we be less thankful for this convincing evidence that the world itself is at length crowned with a circlet of international union, and bound with the divine girdle of charity? Surely the latter is the better boast. The relief for Lancashire distress came from everywhere. Altogether it amounted, on the 30th June, to 1,974,203*l.*, which had been contributed to the funds of the following organisations:—

	£	s.	d.
To the Central Relief Fund:—			
Home Subscriptions	685,035	0	0
Colonial and Foreign	88,856	0	0
Sale of Consignments	498	0	0
Interest on Balances	6,791	0	0
Value of Donations in kind	111,099	0	0
	892,279	0	0
To the Mansion House Fund	503,131	0	0
To the Cotton Districts and Liverpool Relief Funds	254,380	0	0
To the Local Relief Funds:—			
Strictly Local Sources	283,979	0	0
General Subscriptions	40,434	0	0
	£1,974,203	0	0

The Central Executive Committee issued a statement, exposing their financial affairs from the commencement of their operations to the end of June—a document every way as well worthy of commendation as its predecessor of December 1862.

Not the least useful portion of the expenditure is that from the employment and school fund; but those items which are most honourable to the management of the committee are included in the list of the general expenses. Revenues exceeding those of many a European ruler, had been administered with a charge for salaries and wages equal to about one-tenth per cent.; nor should it be forgotten that the expenses of the Central Executive Committee were largely increased by the cost of distributing heavy donations in kind.

Of the relief funds, amounting to £1,974,203, the cotton districts had given no less than £626,433, and the sums expended in private unrecorded charity would considerably have increased this large contribution. The balance of £643,893 yet remaining available was thus deposited :—

	£	s.	d.
With the Central Relief Committee	371,246	0	0
" Mansion House Committee	75,066	0	0
" Cotton Districts Relief Committee . } " Liverpool Relief Committee . . }	121,380	0	0
" Local Relief Committees	76,201	0	0
	£643,893	0	0

The funds of the Cotton Districts and Liverpool Relief Committees were administered by the Central Executive Committee, and the balances remaining to the local relief committees were mainly composed of grants from the great committees and of promised, but as yet unpaid, local subscriptions.

The expenses of the Mansion House Committee had continued to be very light. This Committee had received 503,131*l.* They had remitted to the cotton districts 419,342*l.* Five thousand pounds had been voted for an emigration fund; and all this had been accomplished at a cost of only 3,722*l.*, of which a very large portion was for advertisements.

But what had been the expenditure in poor-law relief? That the period had been one of much anxiety to the boards of guardians cannot be doubted; they had endured great labour, and, at times, no little obloquy. Yet through all this tribulation and trial they had been victorious in the matter of expenditure, and the great year of the Famine had been passed with an extraordinary outlay for relief of about 500,000*l.* However, this is no mean sum, and could only be raised by a charge of 1*s.* 8*d.* in the pound on the rateable value of the property within the twenty-seven unions in which the distress was centred. The disbursements of these unions for the relief of the poor, during the year from Lady Day 1860, to Lady Day 1861, had been 305,296*l.*; while the same charges for the corresponding period, ending Lady Day 1863, amounted to 813,444*l.* Of this unusual cost of 500,000*l.*, a sum amounting to not less than 30,000*l.* had been paid by those unions of Lancashire, Chester, and Derbyshire, which were not suffering from the consequences of the Cotton Famine. For the succeeding quarter, ending June 24, the expenditure of these twenty-seven unions in excess of that of 1861, for outdoor relief and maintenance of the poor in their workhouses, was 121,000*l*. So that during the period which had elasped since the commencement of the Cotton Famine—from March 25, 1862, to June 24, 1863—the expenditure of the twenty-seven distressed unions of the cotton districts in excess of that of ordinary times, had been, as nearly as possible, equal to the amount which had been locally subscribed to the relief funds. And, therefore, the total charge upon the cotton manufacturing districts, as represented by the relief funds and the poor-rates, in respect of these fifteen months of Famine, had been about 1,250,000*l*. It must not be forgotten that this statement excludes all consideration of losses incurred owing to the Cotton Famine. In wages alone this had amounted to about 10,000,000*l*., while in the profits of wholesale and retail trade, the loss must have been twice as much.

Probably it will surprise the student of this chapter of our national history in the next or a succeeding century, how it should have happened that England, the little mother of the great New World, should have been in difficulties on account of the compulsory idleness of a quarter of a million of her population. He will look upon the myriads in America, in Australia, and New Zealand, and wonder how, with so wide a field for surplus labour, we were embarrassed with a momentary excess, which would seem an inappreciable addition to the great populations of the New World. Yet it should not astonish any one, contemporary with the events of 1863, to find that the distress of the cotton districts was not relieved by an extensive measure of emigration.

The very considerable increase of employment which had already taken place, proved how readily manufacturing production would be resumed when the cotton supply became larger. And there could be no doubt that already such numbers had left the district as would cause a regretable scarcity of labour whenever the raw material was to be had in sufficient quantity to cause a general reopening of the cotton factories. This number had been estimated on good authority at from forty to sixty thousand persons. It is absurd to argue such a question as this of emigration entirely upon abstract grounds. A cotton-spinner, who was also a guardian of the poor, knowing the probable future of the cotton trade, might without any difficulty convince himself that he was not only serving his own interests, but also consulting those of the dependents upon his board, in refusing to assist operatives to emigrate. A resolution was moved in the House of Commons, and afterwards withdrawn, favourable to the expenditure of the loans to be raised under the provisions of the Union Relief Aid Act, in promoting emigration. But was it likely that the employers of labour, men whose mills might for years remain closed if these hands were sent away—was it likely that they would raise loans for such a purpose? Was it to the interest of the cotton workers themselves that they should be deported by wholesale from their country? Mr. Cobden had reminded the House, how, in the exodus which followed the Irish Famine, more than ten thousand persons had died of want and hardship in the Canadas and the United States. Within the district no prominent steps were taken to promote emigration. The Mansion House Committee had voted 5,000*l.* to establish the nucleus of an emigration fund, of which about one-half had been expended; the greater part, in accordance with the regulations of the committee to assist emigration by capitation grants of 1*l.* per head per statute adult for emigrants to Canada, and 2*l.* for those proceeding to any other British colony. By means of the colonial grants, with supplementary assistance, some two thousand operatives had been forwarded to Australia and New Zealand. The National Colonial Emigration Society, in conjunction with the Manchester Emigrants Aid Society, assisted by the Mansion House funds, had sent out two detachments of fifty each, and were about to send a third. The Victoria Society had nearly expended a grant of 5,000*l.* in promoting emigration, while to Queensland more than a thousand of the Lancashire population had already been sent under the auspices of the emigration agent of that thriving colony. But what was all this in prospect of a pauperism of 300,000 persons, if removal was to be the remedy?

It is a tolerably distinct axiom of our unwritten law that both labour and capital are free to find their best market, totally irrespective of what may be, or may seem to be, the momentary or the permanent interests of the British Islands. But it cannot be said that the liberty of the subject is infringed upon, if those who are unprovided with the means of removal are unable to obtain them at the expense of others. Yet the law does contain provisions for assisting emigration. By the 12th and 13th Victora, chap. 103, boards of guardians are empowered, with the consent of the parish, to borrow, for the emigration of irremovable poor, any sum not exceeding 10*l.* per head. But no one has an inherent right to this provision—indeed, it would be more reasonable to argue that every girl had a right to a dowry from the State.

The energetic and practical promoters of emigration had now laid down as a most important principle, that 'assistance' only should be given to those desirous of changing their home. One-third of the cost of removal was to be borne by the emigrant, one-third by the colonial governments, and one-third to be derived from public sources, either special subscriptions or grants. It was impossible to doubt that by the maintenance of such regulations the colonies would obtain a most valuable contribution to their population; but another consequence of 'assisted' emigration is, that it takes the flower and leaves the weed of population. And it is surely not inhuman to allow such a thought to have weight, at a time when it is proposed to apply emigration as a remedy for an exceptional and temporary disturbance of industry? It may well be deemed unwise at such a time to help only those who have, by thrift or through friends, the means of helping themselves—to take away their good influence from their more helpless and less patient neighbours. Of the thousands who thronged the offices of the emigration agents, there were but very few who could, to any considerable extent, help themselves to a passage across the sea. The results of patronised emigration very rarely represent the population. Under such auspices it will generally be found that either the best are taken, to the undue injury of the older community, or the worst, to the lasting degradation of the rising colony. It is scarcely humane to offer a distressed dependent on charity in England a free passage to a distant colony, without knowing beforehand that he will find the means of subsistence. How can he restrain himself from snatching at the promise of regained independence, which relieves him for the time of the burden of self-maintenance? A man can only eat dirt in a metaphorical sense, and a landowner in a new colony may suffer far greater want than an English pauper. Indeed, many errors with reference to colonisation arise from the contrast which in this respect is presented between the mother-country and her possessions. From the conditions attaching to land in this kingdom, an Englishman is likely to place an entirely fictitious value upon its possession. The emigrant upon arriving in the colonies can claim his grant of land; in some, without purchase-money; in others, by a nominal payment. What a marvellous attraction there is in this announcement for the people of an old country, where every rood of land has its vigilant owner, and is swathed in legal parchments! But it is quite possible that nine-tenths of the operatives of Lancashire would have died a miserable death, if, at the commencement of the Cotton Famine, they had been removed to a country wide enough and free enough to give to each family a hundred acres of land. The Member for Salisbury—himself an Australian of much experience—stated, with reference to Queensland, the favourite colony of the Lancashire emigrants, that the class they did not want there—that the class which was now starving in Queensland, was those who came with a certain amount of education, but without capital. This description applied with great force to the cotton operatives, who—though many have become excellent outdoor labourers—were, as a class, totally unfit to be volunteers for colonial labour. The objection does not apply in any similar degree to the few who were able to emigrate, and indeed these gained an advantage from the smallness of their numbers, of which a larger emigration would have deprived them.

There was, in fact, no legitimate demand for emgration. To offer paupers free maintenance and passage to another land is almost equivalent to forcing them from their country. But such a measure can never be even justifiable, unless there is no prospect of an improvement in their condition by remaining at home, and a certainty that they will be well provided for upon arrival in the colony. But at this time the cotton trade was not defunct; it had received a temporary overthrow from a political earthquake, and there was not room to doubt that even if its old foundations were never restored, it would eventually build itself up again as strong and powerful as ever. The English population have never emigrated more largely than about the year 1852, when the numbers leaving the United Kingdom during the twelve months were 368,000. In 1862 this number had fallen to 121,000. But in the first five months of 1863, 97,000 persons left the kingdom to seek a new home, and of this number 66,946 landed in the United States, of whom many a one has since received unhonoured burial along the extended war-line which still separates the armies of North and South.

It was thought by some that the condition of the cotton districts peculiarly suggested the promotion of female emigration. But upon this special subject there was much opportunity for divided opinion. No doubt, one of the great difficulties incident to the Cotton Famine was in finding suitable employment for the girls and women accustomed to factory labour. Inquiry had shown that of a population of 483,810 persons, 224,010 were men and lads above fifteen, 84,100 were married women, and 175,700 unmarried women and girls. These figures represent a very near approximation to the sexual proportions of employment in factory labour, and therefore on this ground there was nothing to suggest displacement. With reference to the married women, there can be no doubt that the lessened death-rate of the cotton districts during the Famine is much owing to their exemption from factory labour, and consequent freedom to attend to their children. The unmarried women and girls would form too considerable a fact anywhere to escape attention; but from the circumstance that in the manufacturing districts there is a demand for their labour, which does not exist to an equal degree in any other part of the kingdom, their condition upon the stoppage of employment is peculiarly embarrassing. There were now some 20,000 of them deriving great benefit from the sewing-schools. But the better class of these girls would not make willing emigrants. Women of worth are ever the most loath of any persons to leave their homes, unless accompanied by their friends. Supposing it had been possible to better very materially the condition of these girls by emigration, and in a still greater degree to contribute to the welfare of the colony in which they were destined to assume the honours of maternity, it is by no means likely that they, in any considerable numbers, would have been willing to leave their homes. And why indeed should they? It would be difficult to find a home where women have greater advantages than in Lancashire. They can earn independent and sufficient wages if they choose to lead a single life, and the matrimonial market is nowhere more active if they prefer wedlock. Experience of former bad times concurred with their own wish in telling them that all this prosperity would soon return and the mills be reopened; and it is quite certain that until then the great majority of them would have given preference to 'th' relief' over the snuggest emigrant vessel that ever was docked. But had they been eager to leave, would it have been possible to have fostered a wholesale female emigration in the face of facts so sad and shameful as the most recent experience had recorded? No system had yet been devised to obviate the peculiar dangers incidental to female emigration. Miss Rye, whose name is most honourably associated with this question, had recently written with reference to an experiment conducted by herself, pointing out that the worst irregularities resulted from the want of due security against them before embarkation, during the voyage, and after landing. Saddest and most deterent of all was her account of the condition of her emigrants on landing. Of the 'Emigrants' Barracks,' in which they were lodged, she said that the worst 'fears of the worst wishers to female emigration were fully realized;' and of those who were designated for the happy mothers of stalwart colonists, that some had become 'women who were known only to night and to evil deeds—women who have never been, and who never intend to go out into service.'

The female element in the population of England and Wales was, in 1861, in excess of the male by 513,706, of which excess, 82,592 were due to Lancashire. Nature beneficently makes a provision for the casualties incidental to masculine existence by a surplus of male over female births, and in 1861 this amounted to 15,538, which is about the usual yearly average. But Englishmen have reversed this natural order of things, by leaving their girls behind them when they go out of their country to lend their strength in establishing the new world. Yet this disparity of the sexes, though greatest in Lancashire, is less observable in the County Palatine than in any other part of the kingdom. In the colonies the difficulty is reversed, and although it would be very unmotherly of England to push her unmarried daughters off by wholesale, yet she may advertise the fact that she has more of them on hand than there are English husbands for. Among the more important advantages of an increase of the feminine population in the colonies, would be the humanising and refining of a society which deteriorates very much in their absence. But the balance cannot safely be redressed by the exportation of unprotected women.

There was now a certain though as yet an indistinct prospect of the revival of the cotton trade. Although a bad season had seriously damaged the Indian crop, yet there appeared but little doubt that Mr. Edmund Ashworth's estimate for the year would be equalled, if not exceeded by the supply. The estimated import for the twelve months was 1,772,675 bales. From all sources, 743,396 bales had already been received, and the larger portion of the supply was expected in the latter half of the year. India had not sent her allotted quota, but the Mediterranean and China had made up for her deficiency. The imports from America had considerably exceeded those of 1862; a circumstance due perhaps in some measure to the stimulus given to blockade-running by the Confederate cotton loan. It became evident that too high an estimate had been formed of Indian production. Looking to the fact that a population of one hundred and fifty millions were habitually clothed in home-grown cotton, it had been supposed that the yearly produce of India amounted to something like 6,000,000 bales. Had this been the case, the urgent demand of Lancashire, and the offer of rupees which was now being made wherever agents could reach the plantations, would certainly have brought two or three million bales to the ports in order to supply the wants of Europe.

But it is probable that the production of India in 1861 did not exceed 2,000,000 bales.

The weekly consumption of cotton had now risen to 27,200 bales, and although these bales were not so large as those formerly in use, yet, owing to their inferior quality and to the difficulties incident to their manufacture, quite as much labour was employed as if they had been of the average weight of American bales. The sales to the trade were considerably less than the quantity consumed, but for the preceding months they had very much exceeded the rate of consumption, and caused an overplus in the hands of the manufacturers. The export maintained its usual position, between a fourth and a fifth of the total imports. It was now evident that the sufficiency of the cotton supply was only a question of time, and it was no longer regarded as impossible to continue the cotton manufacture in the absence of supplies from America. Surat had become too common to be hated, and with an admixture of Egyptian or American, was the staple food of a vast majority of the spindles and shuttles now in motion. It had not been expected that the cotton supply of 1863 would greatly exceed that of the previous year, and making allowance for the heavy stock which lay in Liverpool at the close of 1861, the increased supply of 1863 over that of 1862 was only estimated at 134,650 bales. Those engaged in the cotton trade had not yet become accustomed to omit America from their calculations; they still kept an anxious eye upon the Southern ports, expecting, fearing, or hoping for that avalanche of cotton which would revolutionise all their speculations. The Confederate victories in Virginia at the close of May, when Hooker was hurled back, crushed and defeated, by the brilliant flank movement of the Southern general at Chancellorsville, had disturbed the cotton markets with rumours of peace. But the price of cotton was not now so easily affected, not so much subject to speculative influences as it had been. Supply and demand had begun to resume their proper position; sales were made for immediate working and less for speculation than they had been; the tone of the markets was healthier, although the stocks of cotton were constantly diminishing. There were in Liverpool, at the end of June, but 363,290 bales, whereas at the close of January there had been 406,160 bales; and though it was to be expected that a still further diminution of stocks would take place, yet it was well known that the cotton crisis was past and that a gradual recovery, slow but sure, had now taken the place of the Famine.

Paradoxical as this may seem, it is no longer so when the present and past condition of the trade in manufactures is examined. The incubus, which for the past two years had kept down production to starvation point, was at last lifted by its own exhaustion. At length the surplus production of 1859–61 had been consumed, and the over-fed markets had digested the glut of goods that had been forced upon them. In the previous year, more than the total amount of home consumption, together with 45,000,000 lb. weight of exports, had been supplied from previous accumulations, and there had remained stocks sufficient to supply more than half the home requirement of manufactures for this year. It was from this difficulty that the manufacturing interest was now delivered. Whatever the demand for goods might be, they were from henceforth to find employment in its supply. Of what use was a cotton supply to them while there was no demand for goods—of what avail were new fields to them while raw cotton was dearer than calico; while in the face of political uncertainties it was hazardous to work largely for stock, and required what many of them had not—a large floating capital? Now they might hope to get orders, the fulfilment of which would yield them certain profits and furnish the 'hands' with employment. The Famine was past; from henceforth as cotton came into our ports it would not, as it had done, accumulate there. Whatever might be the price, it would still find its way to the mills. And there was good reason to hope that the consumption of manufactures would not materially decline in consequence of the high price of cotton, because these increased payments were generally made to those countries which had been, and were still, the largest consumers of cotton goods. Demand might now be slow, but it would be sure; there might yet be sad proof that the manufacturing power of Lancashire was greatly in excess of the immediate requirement, but those who wanted goods must now order them of the manufacturer. Already the quotations of the markets began to evidence that the difficulty which, together with the American war, had caused the privations of the Cotton Famine, was passed away, for the margin between the price of cotton and that of goods was now steadily increasing.

But, as a consequence of this, the question of cotton supply had become of vastly nearer interest to the district. If the price of cotton did not affect consumption, all the spindles of Lancashire, including the tens of thousands added during the past two years, might again be employed when only sufficient raw material could be obtained. If the price did affect consumption, it was doubly important to the manufacturing interest that the cost of cotton should be reduced before their customers acquired a taste for other materials, and covered themselves with the produce of other markets. The bale, which in 1861 sold for 10*l.*, now fetched 25*l.*—an advance of price which nothing but an increased cotton supply could withdraw. But there was little reason to expect any considerable reduction in the price of cotton, although the supply of 1864 should show as great an increase as the most sanguine were inclined to estimate. For the stocks of goods being now to a great extent cleared off, and the demand for cotton manufactures being universal, no very considerable reduction of price could be expected until the supply amounted to from three to four million bales, which was an evident impossibility for the next two years, unless in the improbable event of a termination of the war in America.

Fearful of the risk of loss, the manufacturers still kept their mills closed, unless working to order. The cost of starting a first-class mill, including the necessary supply of cotton, would not be less than 15,000*l.*, which, by the sudden patching of an American peace, might involve an immediate and irretrievable loss of from 4,000*l.* to 6,000*l.* As many of the orders now given were for small parcels of goods, the inferior class of manufacturers, who could supply these with more profit to themselves, derived peculiar advantage, to which their very considerable previous difficulties fully entitled them.

The prejudice against the use of Surat cotton was growing faint by degrees, and less altogether. But this material was by no means free from the dirt, leaves, seeds, and occasionally stones, whch have been the legitimate subject of complaint. It was stated that the reduction of wages, caused by its inferior yield of goods, was not the only disadvantage which the operatives endured from its manufacture. Invention and experience were every day lessening this evil. But it was still said that bronchitis and other chest disorders had become more prevalent, in consequence of the use of Surat cotton, and especially in the blowing-rooms, where the atmosphere was filled with its short, waste fibres. Complaint was still made of nauseous affections on opening the bales, and, above all, of the hindrance to manufacture caused by its brittleness. The high price of cotton had produced adulterations at home as well as abroad. In some cases, this was effected by 'sizing' the manufactured cloth very heavily, in such a manner as to conceal the fraud until the fabric had been washed. Some of those who were loudest in their condemnation of the malpractices of Indian packers, were themselves preparing a dishonest surprise for the Eastern purchasers of their Manchester shirtings. Fortunately for the commercial honour of our country, Asiatics, reversing the British custom, wash their skin more frequently than their clothing. Had it been otherwise, the wearers of this heavily sized cloth would have discovered more often, that by frequent immersion it became transparent. It is said that by this means, fifteen pounds weight of the raw material not unfrequently produced twenty pounds weight of the manufactured article. A more venial adulteration was practised, by the mixture of the bleached waste of flax, or of shredded cotton-goods, or of the 'waste' of Surat itself. 'Cotton waste' has become an important commodity during the reign of high prices. It used to be allowed to blow away anywhere, or it was collected for use in cleaning machinery; and when cotton was *5d.* per pound, and the waste only twelve per cent., it was an unimportant affair. But now that waste was twenty-five per cent., and cotton as many pence per pound, it had become a merchantable article, and was gathered for mixing with the cleaned cotton, to the further annoyance of the working spinners. Yet the difficulties which opposed the use of 'Surats' had now been, to a great extent, overcome. It is easy to say that this cotton only required more care in opening and cleaning, more twist in spinning, and more pressure in finishing. But all this had to be learnt, and, in the majority of cases, some adaptation of machinery was necessary. The most important question involved in its substitution for American was that of wages. In the best-managed factories, where Surat cotton had been used for nearly two years, the earnings of those paid according to the weight of goods produced, had steadily risen, until in some, they had reached the high standard of 1860; and there is good reason to suppose, that by the time the whole factory population is again engaged, no very material reduction of wages will be found to have taken place. Yet a reduction of wages would not have caused any diminution in the comforts of the operatives, unless it exceeded the continuous fall which had taken place in the price of provisions during the last year, and which promised to be still greater in 1863. For there was now a prospect of a most plenteous harvest, the excess of which above the average produce, would, it was expected, enrich the country by twenty millions sterling; while, as a consequence of this plenty, it would follow that 20*s.* would buy as much provisions as 24*s.* had purchased in 1861.

Great efforts were now making to stimulate the cotton supply. The association continued to abuse the Indian Government, and, what was to more purpose, to send out cotton seeds and gins. In five years, they had distributed 6,107 cwt. of seed, 642 cotton-gins, and 62 ploughs, besides numerous agricultural implements. Joint-stock companies had been formed for growing cotton in Asia Minor, in Queensland, in Jamaica, in Natal, in West Africa, and in India, but had not generally prospered, because in most cases they had only assured to themselves one element of production, and had designated the land without providing the labour. It began to be understood that new supplies must be drawn from countries where an available amount of labour existed, and failing America, India and Egypt alone possessed this indispensable condition.

The House of Commons devoted a night to the consideration of the question, upon Mr. Caird's motion for a select committee to inquire whether any further measures could be taken, within the legitimate functions of the Indian Government, for increasing the supply of cotton from that country. The debate which followed was remarkable for the absence of any practical suggestions which might have an immediate influence on the cotton supply. Mr. Caird, who is distinguished for his agricultural knowledge, stated that the Indian field of production was unlimited, and that though the climate of India was warmer by 12° of heat than the Southern States, yet that the deficiency of rain might easily be obviated by works of irrigation. It was contended by Mr. Cobden, as the representative of the manufacturers, that the Government —the 'gigantic absentee landlord' of this 'Indian farm' —was blameable, for refusing to encourage the production of cotton by the remission of the land-tax. Sir Charles Wood had declined to allow the remission even upon small patches of land in Madras. But the Indian Minister was thoroughly justified in asserting that the time had passed for offering prizes for the growth of cotton, and in refusing to make experiments, by giving advantages which could not fairly be accorded in one locality only. He maintained that the distress of the cotton districts ought not to be relieved at the expense of the people of India, and that the taxes necessary to defray any expenditure for the relief of Lancashire should be levied in this country. The principle thus laid down was not denied by his accusers, but they considered that the Government was not doing the best for the 'estate' which England held in trust. They contended that the Indian people lived in ignorance of all the laws of political economy; that the results of neglect, of oppression, of the total violation of all economic laws, had to be surmounted; and that therefore, in the interests both of Lancashire and India, the self-acting force of supply and demand should be quickened by official interference. Yet when the price of Indian cotton had increased fivefold in three years, it would seem absurd, as well as unprincipled, to ask for the abandonment of the land revenue. This rise in price was surely a sufficient bonus. If this magnificent premium failed to rouse the Indian ryot to a sufficient appreciation of his own interests, it was not unreasonable to doubt if he would be persuaded by an advantage proffered in another direction. It was suggested in the course of this debate, by an eminent member of the cotton trade, that the time might not be far distant when India alone would consume as much cotton as the whole world now consumed, and there are not wanting indications that this prediction may be realized. But the moral of the debate was spoken by Mr. Bright, in the words that 'there was no short cut to that which it was now wanted to obtain.' He confessed that, not only in the House, but in Lancashire, it was assumed by many that an increased cotton supply could be accomplished by some administrative miracle. It is universally admitted that one of the immediate functions of Government in an undeveloped country such as India, is the improvement and construction of the means of internal communication. But it was not denied that in this respect the Indian Government was fulfilling its duty. The subject of land-tenure was of course still a disputed question, but there existed a general conviction that the cultivation and supply of Indian cotton must extend with the unprecedented demand now prevailing.

Within the cotton districts, there yet remained a vast amount of poverty and distress strangely inconsistent with the glorious summer weather—the plenteous prospect of the coming harvest, and the prosperity of the country, which was dimmed only by the condition of Lancashire. But it was now known that convalescence had succeeded to disease. The recovery by the patient population of their former affluence might be by slow degrees, and would be expensive to the relief funds, but it was certain. And the Public Works Bill encouraged and interested many. Mr. Farnall and Mr. Rawlinson had been traversing the district in all directions, explaining its provisions, and recommending its adoption. They pointed out its threefold benefits; how that, besides effecting permanent and sanitary improvements, the public works would provide many of the unemployed with labour and wages, and greatly assist the impoverished shopkeepers, by creating a very considerable expenditure within the district. For the most part they had been very well received. The local authorities perceived that the measure was not one which menaced their independence, and, while it gave them the means of doing great good, left them without a painful sense of obligation to the State. Among the poor, the project had already had that good effect which in a period of depression is always the accompaniment of a wholesome diversion. A government, during a time of plague or famine, might make a much worse expenditure than in providing the means of combined instruction and amusement. The Public Works Bill gave the distressed operatives something to think of—to talk and to wonder about; it had the effect of raising their minds from brooding over the unavoidable hardships of their condition. They were gratified in being thus made the indirect objects of legislation—they contemplated with interest the changes which the execution of public works would make in their respective neighbourhoods, and some were rejoiced at the prospects of a revived independence.

In the passage of the Bill through committee, it was suggested, but without success, to substitute the cumbersome and immobile action of the parish for the constituted and ready authority of the guardians. Had the undertaking of works in each parish been subject to the consent of a majority of the inhabitants, there would certainly have been an immense increase in the difficulty and delay attending their execution.

Indeed the difficulties which beset all exceptional legislation were never more clearly shown than in the debates upon this Bill. There would seem to be happy security against any danger of revolution while legislators are so jealous of unusual enactments. But it must not be forgotten that this was a measure having a local application only, and one conveying a large sum of money. It was impossible to dismiss from the mind of Parliament the conviction that something was being done, something conceded, for the special benefit of Lancashire. Yet, in point of fact, the measure involved no cost whatever to the public exchequer. The Government could raise the money at $3\frac{1}{4}$ per cent., and it was proposed that it should be repaid with interest at the rate of $3\frac{1}{2}$ per cent. However, it might have been expected that no Lancashire members would suggest obstacles. And after the Poor Law Board had been so long, and so successfully engaged in dealing with the distress—after this Bill had reached its present stage, the suggestion made by Colonel Wilson

Patten, that it would be better if the measure were not administered by this Board, was inconveniently retrospective, if not ungenerous. Another member wanted to know, upon the moment, whether the security to be given for the loans would be good; whether Lancashire distress was not due to overtrading; and whether Government did not think it would ultimately be necessary to have resort to emigration? Mr. Villiers had to bear his Bill through all these hindrances and jealousies, until at length it reached the calmer atmosphere of the House of Peers, where it was accepted by Lord Derby as 'a Bill which will remove many of the difficulties which we have had in finding employment, in finding occupation for the distressed operatives, and thus guarding against the demoralisation that arises from idleness, which must be acceptable to those who have taken a part in the administration of relief to our suffering fellow-countrymen.'

But before the Royal assent made the Bill an Act of Parliament, the question of continuing the Union Relief Aid Acts again occupied the attention of the House of Commons. Up to this time their provisions had been extensively made use of in respect to area, though for a very inconsiderable amount. Eighty thousand pounds had been raised by loan, and thirty-four thousand contributed by rates-in-aid, levied upon different unions. But the measure had not been popular in the district. Parishes and unions had endeavoured to escape contribution by making questionable additions to their expenditure. The security for the loans being of an unusual character, money was not easily obtainable, and the more so, that it was required in a locality where capital always demands a high rate of interest. Distant unions which had been charged with the rate-in-aid had disputed their liability.* Hitherto the Act had provided that where the union was situated in two or more counties—which is the case with several of the unions in the cotton district—the rate should be levied upon the unions of that county in which the 'greater' part of the distressed union was situated. Whether this term 'greater' applied to area or population, or to rateable

* The issue of the case of 'Regina v. the Guardians of the Macclesfield Union' resolved these difficulties favourably to the operation of the Act, by deciding that 'greater' applied to area.

value, which generally follows population, was a serious matter of dispute. In the new Bill the equitable principle of rateable value was adopted, and the possibility of difference of interpretation thus precluded.

The objection to bear each other's burdens was general among all the unions in the cotton district. But who can doubt that a rate-in-aid will always be met with this obstacle? Legislative power exists mainly for the purpose of compelling individuals to subordinate private considerations to the interests of the commonwealth. The agitation for a reconstruction of the measure, and the complaints of Cheshire and Derbyshire over their forced contributions to the relief of distress, which did not actually exist beneath their eyes, were not unnatural. Nobody wished to pay, upon compulsion, for the loss of wages in the cotton districts. The original principle of the Union Relief Aid Act was, that borrowing should not be had recourse to until a fair pressure had been borne by the ratepayers, and the power of obtaining loans from the public funds had been withheld, because the concession would have been contradictory to the principle that such loans should only be made for expenditure in productive purposes.

In committee upon the new Continuance Bill, Mr. Villiers proposed two amendments; the first being, that six shillings should be substituted for five as the charge to be borne upon the net rateable value of the unions before they were empowered to call for contributions from their counties. Experience of the worst season of distress had shown that this amount would render the county rate-in-aid practically inoperative, as no union would endure rates amounting to six shillings, while possessed of the power of borrowing. This power Mr. Villiers now proposed to facilitate by his second amendment, authorising the Loan Commissioners to make advances to the unions, chargeable upon their common fund, and repayable in twenty years with interest at 3½ per cent.—a concession not quite guiltless of wise indulgence. Lancashire has owed much to the exceptional circumstances which caused her distress—much to their incidence upon the national policy—much to the influence and to the dread of her concentrated population. All this, together with the temporary nature of the crisis, and the desirability of excluding discontent from the district, pleaded for allowance of this easy postponement of local burdens, with a force which it might well be thought could rarely so establish a subsequent claim, and the power was given as one strictly exceptional. On July 21 the Union Relief Aid and the Public Works Acts received the Royal assent, and Lancashire—with their aid, together with that of the local authorities and the relief committees, satisfied that Parliament and the country had done more than justice to her situation—recommenced the successful struggle with her difficulties, content for the future to trust to her own resources.

POSTSCRIPT.

Nearly two years have elapsed since 'the passing of the Public Works Act, and in their course two great names, for ever associated with the Cotton Famine, have passed from public life into hallowed memories. That of Richard Cobden will be held in grateful remembrance with the freedom of trade and the peaceful progress of mankind; while the name of Abraham Lincoln will be cherished so long as human liberty and human right are dear to the hearts of men. Faithful ministers of true ideas, representative men of the two great English-speaking communities, their death placed both hemispheres in mourning, and at the same time consecrated their policy and insured its triumph.

The year 1864 was one of very remarkable characteristics. Nowhere was there calm security and unusual prosperity but in the British Parliament and the British Exchequer, while the foreign disquiet and the monetary difficulties of the home market were most disastrously reflected in Lancashire. Early in the year hopes were formed that the summer would witness a very active revival of the cotton manufacture, and though the state of Europe was critical, yet in America the civil war appeared to grow more obstinate and its end more remote and invisible. Then commenced a long chain of events, the baneful operation of which was favoured by the disorganised condition of the cotton trade. The natural course of prices in 1864, with an increasing supply, would have been downwards, but the early-formed opinion of the trade that competition for the arriving cotton would be very great, induced an ill-advised speculation, to which, with other contemporary occurrences, must be ascribed the distress of employers and capitalists in the autumn of 1864 and the spring of the present year.

In January 1864 the Bank discounted this speculation at 8 per cent. Then followed the war between Germany and Denmark, or, to speak more correctly, the war of Germany upon Denmark; but the fears which this event excited were allayed by the decided adoption on the part of the Government of a non-intervention policy. Then arose the Limited Liability mania. It was high summer, and yet the consumption of cotton but little exceeded 30,000 bales per week. All that could be purchased had been bought 'to arrive' at high prices. May saw the Bank rate of discount raised to 9 per cent. Cotton was arriving, stocks were increasing, and there was every prospect of a growing supply independently of America. But the buyers of goods held back. Deep down in the mind of the cotton trade there lurked a conviction that all was not right; in fact, that all was wrong; that the eager speculation of the preceding months had been unwarranted, and that the ominous and unlooked-for condition of the money market had made it ruinous.

Wavering and uncertain was the course of prices through the summer months, and the bubble burst in September. Prices fell down headlong, mills were closed, hands thrown out of work, and many were the recorded failures and many more the grievous losses. Closely familiar, by almost daily travel, with the condition of Lancashire at this period, the writer could not but greatly admire the fortitude and irrepressible energy with which the employers and capitalists of the cotton trade sustained their losses—losses which amount to many millions sterling. The consequence was that while the stocks of cotton were growing week by week until upon December 30, 1864, they exceeded the stocks of the preceding year by nearly 300,000 bales, yet the average weekly consumption of cotton in 1864 only exceeded that of 1863 by about 3,000 bales.

Slowly the mind of the cotton trade—than which there is none more intelligent and prescient—regained its equilibrium. Sad and unwilling, the holders of cotton gave way again and again, now making a desperate stand at some figure which they trusted was the ultimate measure of their losses, then forced down again by news of the triumphant successes of the Northern armies. In vain for them came the termination of the monetary crisis of 1864,—in vain was that magnificent exhibition of progress in finance, Sherman and Grant were their Nemesis, and the sturdy attitude of buyers their overthrow. The fall of Richmond was discounted ere it was accomplished, and the collapse of the Southern Confederacy had been robbed of its effect by an anti-climax.

If the course of prices is not yet settled, it is scarcely possible for the errors of 1864 to be repeated with any such disastrous results to the staple trade of Lancashire, because the determining considerations cannot be so involved in uncertainty. Nothing short of hostilities between England and the United States can prevent the rapid revival of the cotton manufacture, and it is to doubt the common sense of both Governments and both peoples to anticipate such a murder of social progress.

These, in the briefest statement, have been the outward circumstances affecting the industry of Lancashire, during the time which has elapsed since that recorded in the concluding page of the 'History of the Cotton Famine.' Within the district, Charity has continued her beneficent and necessary labours. It has been very satisfactory to observe on the part of the local committees a willingness to suspend operations at the first practicable opportunity. The Central Executive Committee will probably find themselves before long, like our great Minister of Finance, in possession of a disposable surplus, from which splendid burden it is to be hoped they will relieve themselves with equal credit and satisfaction. It would scarcely be possible to eulogize too highly their honorary labours—their title to the gratitude of those whose bounty they have dispensed, and of those to whom their liberal assistance has been given.

It only remains for me to speak of the operation of the Public Works Acts, and I cannot but think that when, from the comfort of a prosperous future, Lancashire reviews the circumstances of the famous years through which she has passed with so much honour to herself and to the country, it is this which will be regarded as the most satisfactory. Not only because these permanent works will leave their useful mark long after the generation which beheld the Cotton Famine has passed away, but also because no circumstance of these years is more creditable than the exhibition of intelligence and energy with which so large a debt was incurred for the execution of public works during a time of general distress. That within a period of two years, a million sterling should have been expended upon sanitary works within this district, is a circumstance which tells of previous neglect and also of a strong determination towards improvement. Upon the completion of the works, it is my intention to offer the public an account of the operation and results of the Public Works (Manufacturing Districts) Acts, and therefore at present I will only make a brief allusion to the subject.

Under the provisions of these Acts, 1,846,000*l.* has been appropriated in 155 separate loans. The works which are now in course of execution in respect of this sum, and all of which are rapidly progressing towards completion, comprise 304 miles of main sewers, 766 acres of paving, flagging, and street formation works, the aggregate length of these streets and highways being 276 miles. The remaining works include land-drainage, the formation of several parks and cemeteries, and the construction of reservoirs for water supply with an estimated cubical capacity of 1,486,675,000 gallons. And, thanks to the Minister to whom I have taken the liberty of inscribing this edition, and to all who have co-operated, no official hindrances have been allowed to circumlocute the administration of these Acts.

The difficulties and delays incidental to the adoption of their provisions by the local authorities, had been much reduced at the passing of the Public Works Act, by the tour of Mr. Farnall and Mr. Rawlinson, to which allusion has been made in the pages of the 'History.' No man has done more to popularise the Local Government Act than Mr. Rawlinson, and the heavy crop of boards which has sprung up in this district during the past two years may be regarded as the very gratifying result of his labours. While it is certain that no equal measure of success would have attended the administration of the Public Works Act, had a larger authority been given to the officials who were charged with its local administration, yet a Resident

Inspector may surely be forgiven, if, in thought only, he did sometimes wish to cut short the tedious deliberation of local bodies, which talked and resolved while the works would have been doing, if their execution had rested with any one of their individual members. But it must be regarded as a remarkable display of activity on the part of some ninety local authorities, that satisfactory works were designed and in active operation within so short a time after the passing of the measure.

Doubtless all this deliberation and discussion was necessary to secure the co-operation of minute interests, and certainly it served and has throughout served a most beneficial purpose, in relieving many from that state of querulous *ennui* into which they had fallen owing to the depression of trade and the sad condition of the district. When the works were fairly started it was soon found that, under kindly superintendence, the operatives made excellent workmen, and very many of them will hereafter point with honest pride at the works to which they have lent a willing and a useful hand. For proof of the generally high character of this local superintendence, it is sufficient to refer to the rarity of accidents even among so many unskilled labourers, and to the generally satisfactory execution of the works. No one who has watched the operation of these Acts would for a moment think of limiting their benefits even as measures of relief, by the precise number of indigent factory operatives who were engaged upon the works. The first effect of the Public Works Act was to spread a feeling of contentment throughout all classes in the district, and there can be no more significant proof of its successful operation than that from the time of its passing no wholesale schemes of emigration have been mentioned, no riot or disorder has occurred, although these two years have included times of sore distress, made sorer by its unlooked for recurrence. The small shopkeepers and farmers, who were greatly impoverished by the previous pressure of the poor-rates, have been materially assisted by the expenditure upon public works, and there are many townships, where the execution of permanent improvements upon the highways, mainly by the labour of operatives—who but for the Public Works Act would have been chargeable to the poor-rates—will, inclusive of the repayment of the yearly instalments of the loan, have effected a reduction of more than 50 per cent. in the highway rates. And it should be remembered that the numbers employed at any one period do not exhibit the number of those who have passed from the public works to other outdoor employment. For example, in the formation of the Manchester Cemetery, the number of factory operatives employed at any one time has never exceeded 130, but up to the end of last March there had been not less than 453 factory operatives employed upon these works, of whom only 28 had been engaged upon more than one occasion.

The total number of men engaged directly upon the public works in November 1864 was 6,424, of whom more than 4,000 were factory operatives. Besides this number it was estimated that at least another 2,000 men were engaged in quarrying stone and in the preparation and conveyance of all the materials necessary for the construction and execution of the works. Inquiry has proved that these men have, upon an average, three or four persons dependent upon their labour, and, taking three as the lowest average, this would give a total of 33,696 persons deriving sustenance directly from the operation of the Public Works Acts. And there has been but little variation from these numbers. The operatives who have laboured upon these works have every right to be called volunteers, and although it is beyond question that the local authorities have not in all cases used their utmost endeavours to promote employment, and in the selection of works have in all cases made their utility the first consideration, it must certainly be admitted that the unavoidable necessity for such endeavours did not exist, and could not while there were ample relief funds for the maintenance of the indigent. I cannot conceive how the distribution of these funds could have been accomplished with greater skill, or judgment, or discrimination than have been displayed by the Central Relief Committee. They have done all in their power to promote employment upon public works; they have exposed neglect, and, as far as possible, encouraged well-intentioned endeavours; they have provided boots and clothing, and supplemented the too slender wages of beginners, but they could not lock up their magnificent funds, nor leave their vast charge—including the women and children, the aged and the sick—to perish for want of assistance. Nor, indeed, would it have been practicable to find employment on the public works for all who were at one time out of work, though a surplus of applicants over the numbers finding employment upon public works has never at all times existed in more than two or three of the ninety places in which these works have been in operation.

But the number of factory operatives engaged upon the public works has suffered much depreciation in the public mind from a contrast with the large total of operatives reported as being 'entirely out of work.' Those who are very familiar with the difficulty, so much increased during the last four years, of obtaining accurate returns respecting the employment of the entire cotton working population, will be at no loss to understand why the reports of the Central Executive Committee have been somewhat inexact in this particular. Unable to obtain accurate returns of employment, or, what is more probable, unwilling to expend charitable funds in the work of an industrial census, the honorary secretary—whose invaluable services will, I hope, meet with grateful recognition—has attached a foot-note to his reports with reference to the numbers returned as 'entirely out of work.' The note is as follows:—'As stated in previous reports, a large number of these persons are earning considerable though irregular wages from outdoor and various casual occupations.'

Now I have observed that the British public has a curious veneration for arithmetical figures, combined with an awkward habit of overlooking foot-notes, and I have more than once found that leading journals have abstracted the numbers returned as 'out of work' from Mr. Maclure's reports without any reference to his foot-note. I must be allowed to say that I am making an explanation, not a complaint. And in taking Manchester as an example of the injurious operation of this inaccuracy as affecting the Public Works, I am influenced by the circumstance that Manchester is the only place to which attention has been directed in a manner not flattering to the administration of the Public Works Act. It would ill become me to be the apologist of the Manchester Corporation.

Yet I am bound to say that for a long time past they have made provision upon their works for the engagement of all, or very nearly all, the indigent operatives who were unemployed in their vicinity.

I take the month of March last, when the city surveyor reported that there were no unemployed factory operatives either on the books of the guardians of the three unions of Manchester, Chorlton, and Prestwich, which comprise the city and form its neighbourhood, nor any upon those of the relief committees of the city, who were fit for employment upon public works, and the public weekly statement made by the clerks to these unions confirmed the accuracy of his report. This was received at the Public Works Office in the same week in which the report of the Central Committee stated that there were 113,794 persons 'out of work' in the whole district, and 17,756 'entirely out of work' in the three before mentioned unions. This report of the Committee, I believe, appeared in the 'Times,' and I am not overstating the case when I say that it would be impossible—for improbable is not the word—for any man whose acquaintance with the state of employment in this district was not most intimate, to have read that report and to have supposed that it could have been contemporaneous with the report of the city surveyor of Manchester. Of course the reader's inference would be that the Public Works Act was a failure in regard to employment, and that there were thousands of unemployed operatives, somewhere or other, always idle and half-starving. But what are the facts? Let us proceed circumstantially. There were at this period 13,957 persons receiving outdoor poor-law relief, and 978 persons receiving charitable relief in these three unions; there were also 203 men engaged upon public works, who with their dependants, according to the before-used scale, would represent 812 persons. Taking the pauperism of the corresponding week of 1861 as normal, there was an excess of 7,969 persons in the receipt of outdoor poor-law relief whose want may be ascribed to the depression of the cotton trade. The number thus accounted for would be 9,759 (978 + 812 + 7,969 = 9,759). But the number reported as being 'entirely out of work' is 17,756, and deducting 9,759 from this number, there is a residue of 7,997 persons.

Now this exposition presents two leading facts: —7,997 persons 'entirely out of work,' none of whom apply for relief nor become applicants for employment upon public works, and 9,759 persons who can only furnish 203 men fit for such employment. The inevitable inference from the first is, that the 7,997 persons were either in receipt of sufficient wages to place them above the need of relief, or that they were mere arithmetical figures, and that not one of them had a local habitation or a name. And the equally inevitable inference from the second fact, that 9,759 persons could furnish only 203 men fit for employment upon public works, is that the remainder of the able-bodied male operatives in this number, being probably men with large families, were supplementing their relief with short-time employment in cotton mills, which usually means 'short time' every day, or by other engagements which they preferred to employment upon the public works. The result being, that at the time when these 17,756 persons were reported as being 'entirely out of work,' with the qualification of the foot-note I have quoted, the Public Works Act was doing all that it was possible for such a statute to effect in respect of affording employment within the three important unions in which they were supposed to reside.

I will not at present refer to the sanitary benefits of these public works, except in one respect and that exception must be the effect of the outdoor labour upon the health of the men, of whom there are now thousands who have changed the complexion, and to some extent the bodily frame of a cotton-worker for those which usually mark the outdoor labourer. No more satisfactory and suggestive record could close the long story of these times than that which proves so unmistakably the decrease of sickness and crime during these years of disturbance in the cotton trade, nor can it be doubted that the construction of these public works will effect a permanent reduction in the mortality of the district.

And now, what is the lesson of these years? I do not speak as a stranger, nor even as a spectator, but as an 'honorary' Lancashire man, if the continued kindness and regard of the people and my ever-increasing respect for them will sanction the assumption. What, then, is 'Lancashire's Lesson?' 'The need of a settled policy in times of exceptional distress.' I cannot think so. The lesson of modern economy is the old lesson, 'sufficient for the day is the evil thereof.' In the rapid dispersion of the Federal armies and in the dissolution of the Lancashire relief committees is there not written a great political lesson, in fact, the great political and economic lesson of to-day? By all means let our Poor Law be improving; let it temper justice with humanity; be discontented while any starve rather than claim its provisions, and avoid the doctrine that a Poor Law admits of final legislation. And such, I think, has been the policy of Mr. Villiers, the greatest Reformer who has ever presided over the Poor Law Board. But let us have no 'settled policy' for crises so exceptional, so impossible of recurrence, in respect of its gravest features, as the Cotton Famine.

It seems to me, that the lesson of the Cotton Famine, writ so clearly that he who runs may read, is, that the happy result of progress, of liberal legislation, of widely diffused education, and of a consequent unity among all classes—with a self-adjusting equilibrium between all forces, whether commercial, political, or social—is that the English people can now afford to be their own insurers against such contingencies, and may safely commit such accidents of the future to its keeping.

R. A. A.

MANCHESTER: *June* 1, 1865.

CPSIA information can be obtained
at www.ICGtesting.com
Printed in the USA
LVHW040029180422
716440LV00005B/356

9 783752 590203